Jane Lane was born Elaine K Dakers and her first novel was published when she was just seventeen. She adopted the pen-name of Jane Lane to reflect the historical nature of her books, Lane being the maiden name of her grandmother, a descendant of the Herefordshire branch of Lanes who sheltered King Charles II after his defeat at Worcester. A versatile and dynamic author, Jane Lane has written over forty works of fiction, biography and history as well as children's books.

BY THE SAME AUTHOR
ALL PUBLISHED BY HOUSE OF STRATUS

Bridge of Sighs
A Call of Trumpets
Cat Among the Pigeons
Command Performance
Conies in the Hay
Countess at War
The Crown for a Lie
Dark Conspiracy
Ember in the Ashes
Farewell to the White Cockade
Fortress in the Forth
Heirs of Squire Harry
His Fight Is Ours
Prelude to Kingship
Queen of the Castle
The Sealed Knot
A Secret Chronicle
The Severed Crown
Sir Devil-May-Care
Sow the Tempest
A State of Mind
A Summer Storm
Thunder on St Paul's Day
A Wind Through the Heather
The Young and Lonely King

JANE LANE

The Phoenix and the Laurel

HOUSE OF STRATUS

First published 1954

This edition published in 2002 by House of Stratus, an imprint of Stratus Books Ltd., 21 Beeching Park, Kelly Bray, Cornwall, PL17 8QS, UK.

www.houseofstratus.com

Typeset, printed and bound by House of Stratus.

A catalogue record for this book is available from the British Library and the Library of Congress.

ISBN 0-7551-0833-7

To
Nora Rowntree

Contents

Prologue

William, Prince of Orange, stood at a window of the Binnenhof Palace, staring down at the reflection of its turrets and gables in the Vyver, one of the principal waterways of the Hague.

It was mid-morning, and the Hague was busy driving hard bargains and waging its perpetual war against dirt. Maidservants scrubbed the pavements outside front doors which were never opened except for weddings and burials; men, clean-shaven and wigless, dressed in slops which reached to their armpits, prodded melons on the stalls and haggled over the price of bulbs and cheeses; women, their plumpness exaggerated by innumerable petticoats, clattered along on sabots to milk large black and white cows; boys flew their eternal kites, and dogs, busy like their masters, drew handcarts.

But the young man who stood at the window of his palace was not interested in this familiar scene. Behind him on the table lay a neat pile of dispatches from his battle-front in Flanders, nearly all containing bad news; he had read them through in his careful and precise manner, and presently would summon his secretary to take down the answers. But meanwhile there was one dispatch which he retained in his hand as he stood by the window, sometimes tapping it in an abstracted manner against his thin lips. So he had stood for half an hour, and still he could not decide how to deal with the matter.

Yet compared with the others it seemed a trifle. The colonel of one of the Scots regiments in Dutch service had been killed, and as supreme commander of the armies of the Netherlands, it was William's privilege to appoint his successor. In one sense his field of choice was large; war was still a gentleman's profession, and there were any number of young men of quality, English and Scots, seeking glory and promotion in foreign service. But William's own burning ambition, the overriding trait concealed behind his frigid manner, demanded that those he rewarded must be what he termed 'useful'. Already he had decided that, for this particular promotion, his choice lay between two men: Captain Hugh Mackay of the Scots Brigade, and John Grahame of Claverhouse, a ritmeester in the regiment of Cabeljauw. For the past half-hour, the Prince of Orange had been considering them in turn.

Mackay was a Highlander, though he detested being reminded of the fact, and had never visited his home in Sutherland since he had entered the profession of arms seventeen years previously. He was now a man in his late thirties, a plump, homely-faced gentleman, who had married the daughter of a wealthy burgomaster, and was become more Dutch than the Dutch. It was precisely Mackay's dislike of his native land which inclined William to give him the vacant command, for it marked him out as a man without sentimental loyalties, a man who saw his own advantage and did not hesitate to take it, a man who could be bought. It was true that he was not a brilliant soldier, for he was slow-thinking and somewhat pompous, and he was not very popular with his men. But if William bestowed this command upon Mackay, it would not be a reward to the soldier but a bride to the man, who one day might prove useful to William the politician...

Yet all the while, upon these sensible thoughts there intruded the face of that other candidate, the incredibly beautiful face of the young ritmeester, known among his fellow Scots as 'Claverhouse', the name of his ancestral estates. William had a very personal reason for being interested in this young gentleman: Claverhouse had saved his life.

It had happened in the spring of this year 1677, when William, endeavouring to raise the siege of St Omer, had been surprised by the French near Cassel, and in a disorderly retreat had found his horse plunging him into a morass. Helpless, the enemy upon him, he had stared death in the face, when long arms had grasped him, he had been lugged unceremoniously on to the withers of a charger, and galloped off to safety. (He had note with amused contempt how his rescuer, even in such a moment, had found time to put a merciful bullet through the head of the struggling horse.) Such a service merited a high reward, and, when William had come to interview his rescuer, so did such on uncommonly handsome face. It had haunted him ever since, its youthful plumpness still hiding the firmness of the jaw, the fine, high-bridged nose, the curve of the short upper lip, and, above all, the eyes, large, deep-grey, romantic, and slightly sorrowful. William's voice had taken on an unaccustomed tinge of warmth when he had promised the owner of that face the first regiment whose command became vacant.

But promises meant nothing to the Prince of Orange. Brought up among enemies, forced to fight for everything he wanted, ruthlessly ambitious, plagued by asthma which augmented a natural morosity and coldness of temperament, he had learned that the keeping of one's word, if inconvenient, was mere romantic folly. And later, investigating the background and character of John Grahame, he had decided with reluctance that here was not what he termed a useful man.

He was an unimportant Scots laird, though he boasted of having the royal blood in his veins through the marriage of an ancestor with the daughter of King Robert III. His late father had been fined by Cromwell for not contributing money to the 'public good', though he had left to his illustrious kinsman, Montrose, the glory of fighting for a defeated cause. The young man's widowed mother, Lady Magdalene Carnegie, a daughter of the Earl of Northesk, had died two years previously, and Claverhouse, as the elder son, had spent six months in Scotland arranging her affairs. (Mackay would never have missed possible promotion by so prolonged a leave of absence.) The Grahames owned a tumbledown castle called Claypotts, the trifling lands of Claverhouse, and a farmhouse in Glen Ogilvie near Dundee. They were not, then, either rich or important; their only great connection was the young Marquis of Montrose, grandson of the hero; and they had a record of loyalty to the Crown which was, in William's eyes, a distinct liability. As for the young man himself, he was reported to be deeply in love with his profession and keen for promotion, intelligent, proud, intensely nationalistic, fastidious, indifferent to wine and women, devoted to field-sports, utterly unbribeable, and with a quick temper which was most conspicuous when he came up against anything which he considered injustice, let the victim of it be himself or another. He was exceedingly popular with his men, but had made himself several enemies among his equals and superiors, partly because of his hot temper, partly, so William understood, because he had a distressing habit of saying exactly what he thought.

No, mused William, the choice was obvious and ought to have been so from the beginning. Mackay was many years Claverhouse's senior both in years and military service; but above all he was a man who would do what he was told with out asking awkward questions. Claverhouse, on the other hand, was clearly a romantic, and William had no use whatsoever for romantics; the species had infuriated him when they had looked at him askance for rewarding the murderers of the brothers De Witt, who had stood between him and the supreme power in Holland. He did not seem to be able to make such men understand that for the ambitious, life was a battle in which he must trust nobody, must never be deceived or give anything away without hope of return, and must judge all men by their usefulness or otherwise to himself.

His cold, hard eyes grew harder still as he fought the one weakness he recognised in his own character. Unlike the Dutch, his father's people, he had never been under the domination of women, but from boyhood there had been a certain type of male beauty which had threatened his command of himself. He feared such temptations and fought them persistently, not only because they were temptations of the Devil (as he sincerely believed they were), but because the ambitious man must suffer no distractions, must be absolute master of himself. For several moments longer he stared down upon the busy waterway below his window, willing himself to see there, not a beautiful face which haunted him, but the prosaic tjalcks with their brown sails, and the cumbersome praams piled with red and yellow cheeses...

Turning briskly at last, he rang a silver handbell to summon his secretary, and spent a busy half-hour dictating dispatches. When these were dealt with, he signed a commission for Mackay to fill the vacant command, and last of all wrote with his own hand a letter to John Grahame of Claverhouse, enclosing a bill for two hundred guineas, and requesting in return the horse which had saved his life. It was, calculated William, at least four times more than the animal was worth; it would mean much to a poor Scots laird; and it was as pretty a compliment as he was capable of paying.

September had given place to October, and William was on the point of departing on a visit to England. In this he had two objects: to persuade his uncle, King Charles II, to give him aid in his war against France, and to marry his cousin, the Princess Mary, elder daughter of his other uncle, James, Duke of York. For Uncle James, Heir Presumptive of the childless King, seemed himself incapable of siring a son, so that when he died, the Princess Mary would accede to the Throne of Great Britain. Or rather her husband, so it be William, would accede; he had not the slightest intention of becoming a prince consort.

Upon the eve of his departure for a country he detested, but one of which he was determined in due course to be King, he received a messenger from Flanders, who brought him two things: a very fine black charger, and a very short letter. The letter ran thus:

> 'Sir,
> According to the command I have received from your Highness, I send you my horse; I pray have a care of him, for he is the best I ever bestrode. The money your Highness was pleased to send for him, I have distributed among your Highness' grooms and servants here. And I beg leave to resign my commission in your Highness' service; since I cannot serve a Prince who has broke his word.
>
> I have the honour to be your Highness' humble servant,
>
> J Grahame.'

The Prince of Orange read this extraordinary letter several times before deciding whether to be angry or amused. In the end he was neither. Contemptuous of integrity, he was intelligent enough to recognise it when he saw it, and where many men would have judged the letter dictated by pique, he saw it as a manifestation of all he knew of the character of the writer. 'J Grahame' really detested injustice, detested it so much that he was ready to sacrifice a promising military career and future promotion because his commanding officer had broken his word. A stupid man, therefore, but of the kind of stupidity that must be taken into account.

Smiling not very pleasantly, the Prince of Orange sat down straightway and wrote a letter to his uncle, the Duke of York, warmly recommending to his favour John Grahame of Claverhouse, late ritmeester. It should go before him by special messenger. The Duke of York was become extremely unpopular in England because of his conversion to the Catholic faith; because of this also he had placed in the hands of certain great lords, with whom William was in secret correspondence, a chance to clamour for his exclusion from the Succession. It was fitting, therefore, reflected William, signing the letter 'Your Royal Highness' most humble, and most passionately devoted nephew and servant', that this pair of romantics, James Stuart and John Grahame, should become patron and protégé.

Part One

The Man

Chapter One

(i)

The minister of a tiny parish in Dumfriesshire leant against the door of his kirk and sobbed like a child.

It was not the Sabbath when, for one of his calling, tears were *de rigueur,* but a Monday morning; his parishioners stood in groups behind him, sharers in a human as distinct from a goodly grief. The women cried quietly into their kerchiefs, the Elders, gathered aloof from the herd as befitted their superiority, buzzed in agitated argument as to whether this could or could not be a Visitation from the Lord, and even certain parochial sinners, condemned at the last Kirk Session for various venial sins, ventured to pause in their penitential task of repairing the roof of the church to gaze with sympathetic eyes at their minister.

The hollow ring of horse-hooves coming down the street caused every head to turn in that direction, and the bairns began to jig up and down with excitement as three horsemen, one riding a little in advance of his companions, came trotting between the rows of thatched houses, scattering hens and pigs; for in the dull light of January they had seen the gleam of steel and the scarlet coats of his Majesty's soldiers. And when the foremost horseman was recognised, their mothers dried their eyes and began a hasty ordering of their toilet; not only could Captain John

Grahame of Claverhouse, commanding one of the three independent troops of horse recently raised in Scotland, be relied upon to deal with the parochial disaster, but he was the bonniest young gentleman ever seen in the south-west. Braving future rebukes from the pulpit, the women stared in frank delight at the well-known figure, slight but strong, which rode so elegantly a beautiful sorrel mare.

He wore a long-skirted scarlet coat, with an officer's scarf knotted round the waist, and a steel corselet protecting back and breast. His two men had ordinary head-pieces of iron, but he wore a big hat, ornamented with a plume of feathers, upon his long dark locks. His sword, looped up for riding, the spurs on his long jacked boots, the stirrup-irons, the curb-chain, the pistols in their holsters on the saddle, all gleamed and glinted from good polishing. The mare's coat was as smooth as satin, and her rider's was creaseless and free from the slightest stain. There were fringed buff gauntlets on his hands, and over his left shoulder was slung a short cloak, scarlet like his coat, fastened with a cord over the breast. But to the women all this smartness was as nothing in comparison with the beauty of the mouth, the upper lip so attractively short, the lower one slightly outthrust, giving just a hint of pugnacity, the brilliance of the calm, deep-grey eyes, and the exquisite modelling of nose and jaw.

"My, she'll be a gey lucky lass wha wins yon for her man," murmured one stout housewife to another.

Claverhouse lifted his hat politely as the minister came running to his stirrup.

"The good Lord Himsel' must have sent you, Captain Grahame," cried the poor man, his face all blotched with weeping. "Yon limbs of Satan were here in the night-time, and wait till I tell you what hellish mischief they've been at."

It took the minister a long time to come to the heart of his story. He was a young man, full of scruples, and this was his first parish; therefore he deemed it necessary to make Captain Grahame understand that his own conscience was clear, and that therefore what had happened in the night could not be a Visitation of the Lord. Walking beside him towards the Kirk, Claverhouse had perforce to listen to a rehearsal of the Sabbath labours, of how there had been the usual Morning Exercise from eight till twelve, and the Afternoon Exercise from one till four, of the proper rebukes given to the sinners perched in the gallery called the Stool of Repentance, and of the plentiful tears (a sure sign of grace) which the Lord had been pleased to bestow upon His servant. The minister went so far as to give Captain Grahame a sketch of his morning sermon, his 'Ordinary', as it was termed. For the past eighteen months, it seemed, he had preached his Ordinary on one of the twelve wells of water and the three score and ten palm trees of Elim (Exodus xv. 27), and yesterday, having turned the last tree into fruitful evangelical teaching, he had been able to announce, with the full approval of his Elders, that 'Next Lord's Day he would change his Ordinary'.

And then, after so much spiritual labour, so abundantly blessed, there had come the horror. He had been aroused from his bed by a loud knocking on the door of his manse; upon opening it, he had seen a group of men, anonymous in the dark, but when one of them had spoken he had recognised the voice as that of Kenneth McKie, a Galloway man and a hot Covenanter. Denouncing him as Amalek, and asserting that he must be cut off even as the Canaanites were cut off from the land, McKie and his friends had forced the minister to accompany them to his little kirk, and there to witness what they termed its 'purging'.

"They broke the bell which hung upon the tree yonder," wailed the minister, "saying that the Lord is not to be summoned by His Creatures, and the sand-glass on the pulpit they broke likewise, for the Lord's mind, said they, is not to be limited by glasses. (And how am I to ken when the two hours of my sermon is up, Captain Grahame, if I have no glass?) And they tore in rags the gown I wear upon the Sabbath, terming it the black gown o' prelacy, the garment o' Baal's priests, and they committed indecencies with the Book of Common Order, because it contains the Belief and the Conclusion; cursed be they, they cried, wha adds anything to what is written in the Word."

Having wrecked the inside of the kirk, exulting that they had now cast down the walls of Jericho, and warning any that rebuilded to beware of the curse of Hiel the Bethelite, they had concluded by threatening the minister with death if he would not cease to pray for the King (referred to by them as the Bull of Bashan), admitted any to the Lord's Supper who had not subscribed to the Solemn League and Covenant, and in short behaved himself as a minister of the Anti-Popish, Anti-Prelatic, Anti-Erastian, True Presbyterian Remnant of the Kirk of Scotland.

"And they were no' havering, Captain Grahame," cried the minister. "McKie had a muckle great whinger at his belt."

While listening in attentive silence to this tale of woe, Claverhouse had been busy inspecting the scene of the outrage. Like every country kirk in Scotland, it was a wretched little place, with a floor of bare earth, a roof of turf laid over rafters, and tiny windows wired upon the outside for protection, since glass was so precious. Within there was a strong and nauseous stench from the corpses buried but three feet beneath the floor, mingling with the lingering stale odour from yesterday's congregation. But it was not this homely poverty, which made Captain Grahame's mouth thin with disgust.

Upon every hand were signs of wanton and savage destruction. The creepie-stools upon which the congregation sat and which they kept stored in the kirk, were smashed in pieces; the metal basin used for baptisms, and ordinarily fixed in a frame upon the pulpit, had been taken down and used by someone for the relieving of nature; the precious glass of the windows lay in splinters on the floor; and upon the sides of the pulpit, the most conspicuous object in the building, were chalked texts from the Minor Prophets, obscure curses and savage denunciations.

"Your poor wee kirk!" exclaimed Claverhouse suddenly.

The good man flushed with gratitude.

"Ay, my poor wee kirk, sir, and wha's to find the money to mend it? I dinna care for their threats against my life; as the Lord sees me, I dinna care for them. But it's no' right or just that such limbs of Satan should plague the godly so, and all because we pray for his Majesty, as good subjects should, and willna meddle in civil matters, which are no' our business so we be free to worship the Lord in our ain fashion."

"It is neither right nor just, as you say, sir," replied Claverhouse quietly. The note of authority in his voice, no less than his imaginative sympathy, so far cheered the minister that the poor man felt ashamed of his late despair. "Now, I am upon my way to attend a meeting of the Commissioners for Locality at Sanquhar, and there I believe I shall find Sir John Dalrymple of Stair, in whose regality lives this Kenneth McKie. As Heritable Bailie, Sir John's duty is to punish the offender at his Court, and I promise you I will see that it is done. Likewise will I bring the affair to the notice of my Commander-in-Chief, who will lay it before the Privy Council in Edinburgh. Meanwhile, do you take care never to open your door to any who knocks in the night-time, and you must arrange with your parishioners to set a guard around the kirk, that no further mischief befalls it. And of course you will give an account to the Kirk Session to lay before the Synod."

"Ay, I'll mind and do all yon, Captain Grahame," promised the minister eagerly.

Five minutes later, to the tune of many 'God bless you's' from minister and Elders, and warm cries of farewell from the women, Captain Grahame was riding on his way.

(ii)

At the door of the great house of Sanquhar, with the bloody heart of the Douglases carved in plaster above it, Claverhouse was informed by an underfed servant in a ragged livery that his lordship was walking in his policies. Concealing a smile, the visitor left his mare in the charge of his escort, and himself went to seek the lord of Sanquhar in the overgrown gardens and orchards.

It really was extraordinary, he reflected, how any man as rich as William Douglas, third Earl of Queensberry, could be so mean. He hoped that on this occasion he would be spared the embarrassment of an encounter with Queensberry's wife, and of hearing that poor lady confide to him that she had no money for a new gown. Could the story be true, he wondered, glancing up at the chimneys from which, even on so bitter cold a morning, no smoke issued, that my lord's sister, though married to a wealthy baronet, carried on the family tradition of parsimony to the extent of sitting all day on the banks of the Arran, which flowed past her husband's policies, and offering to carry travellers over on her back at a halfpenny a time?

But his amusement vanished abruptly when he found the owner of Sanquhar on the terrace, and saw that his only companion was Sir John Dalrymple of Stair. There were few men Claverhouse actively disliked; among the few, Sir John had the honour of first place.

He was an advocate, with the same crafty legal mind as his father, Sir James, who had been a judge under Cromwell, was now President of the Court of Session, and was considered the greatest institutional jurist of his day. His mother was popularly said to be a witch, though she was hot for the Covenant. Sir John had inherited his mother's capacity for hatred, and his father's smooth tongue, though he could scold like a kail-wife when his temper was up; his ordinary air was one of false and patronising joviality. Portly, well dressed, with a slightly porcine countenance, which set oddly with the cool and wary eyes and the compression of the lips, he walked on the terrace of Sanquhar, pausing now and again to sniff at the game hung up in the fig-trees, where it was maturing and acquiring an added delicacy of flavour.

His companion, the Earl of Queensberry, was a very different person. He was dressed as usual in a very old and delapidated dressing-gown over an assortment of undergarments, so that his figure appeared quite shapeless; his wigless head was encased in a turban which looked as though it had begun life as a sack. (There was a jest among his friends that when my lord had to attend some public function, he walked thither in his old clothes and carried his finery in a cloak-bag.) The little that could be seen of his face at the moment, enswathed as it was, was a pair of close-set eyes, a red nose which did not lack humour and which had an occasional twitch like a hound's, and a mouth perpetually a little wet and which bedewed his auditors when it formed the letter S.

"Well, here you are at the long-last, Clavers," cried my lord, genially patronising. "Dalrymple here and myself were taking a bit walk to keep ourselves warm this seasonable weather. You'll be glad to stretch your legs in our company, after your long ride from Dumfries, while you give us the news."

"I shall be glad of a few words with Sir John here, my lord," said Claverhouse briskly, "before we fall to our business of the locality. When I passed through Dalblaith just now, I found that certain Covenanting rogues had been at their tricks again, threatening the minister and despoiling his kirk, and he tells me that the ringleader was one who was out in the Pentland Rising, and who has never ceased since then to incite to revolt. I'm speaking of Kenneth McKie, Sir John, who dwells within your regality of Glenluce."

"Then you can rely upon me to deal with the man at my Hereditary Courts, Clavers," returned Dalrymple suavely, "and to fine him if I find him guilty."

"I hope I can," replied Claverhouse, looking the other straight in the eyes.

Those eyes narrowed.

"What you would like," said Dalrymple softly, "is a civil commission as well as a military one, if I am not mistaken, whereby you would be able not only to arrest but to fine and imprison as well. Maybe you'll get it from your patron, the Duke of York, though I must say I would be sorry to see the military given leave to meddle with the ancient powers of the Sheriffs and the Heritable Jurisdictions. To my mind, that's an ill thing."

"It would be an ill thing in normal times, Sir John, but I must beg leave to remind you that the times are far from normal. Ever since his Majesty's Restoration, there has been a sort of people here in the south-west who endeavour to fall to rebellion again under the cloak of religion; each indemnity offered them they reject; commissions sent to enquire into their grievances fail to find a reasonable spirit in them; they will have nothing short of leave to force their Solemn League and Covenant down the throat of every man, woman, and child in the three kingdoms, and they declare that it is lawful for them to harry and to slaughter all who will not subscribe to it, from the King downwards. It is not twelve years since – "

"My, my! You'd make a fine preacher yourself, Clavers," sneered Sir John *sotto voce*.

"It is not twelve year since we saw two thousand of these fanatics marching upon Edinburgh," the other went on, ignoring him, "and had they not fallen to their usual dissensions among themselves, they would have captured the town. It is proved that they were promised aid from Holland, with which country we were then at war. What they did once they will do again, unless prevented; I tell you, sir, that it is but a small step from shooting a trooper in the back as they did one of mine last week, despoiling churches and threatening peaceable ministers, to plunging the kingdom into civil war. Moreover I must remind you that England is in a state of most dangerous unrest with the madness of this pretended Popish Plot, a plot which all honest men know is being used by my Lord Shaftesbury and other malcontents to tamper with the Succession. Such lords would like nothing better than to see a rebellion in Scotland."

Sir John had been regarding him in contemptuous appraisement. Now he gave a small laugh.

"Dod, you're quite a knowledgeable young gentleman, it seems, and concern yourself with matters of State."

"I concern myself with the King his service," snapped Claverhouse, his temper rising, "both as a loyal subject and as an officer of his Army. My lord, I do appeal to you; am I not right in what I have been saying?"

All this while the Earl of Queensberry had been listening in a fret of uncertainty and agitation, considering a number of facts, each of which seemed to cancel out the other. My lord had three obsessions: money; an itch for royal favour; and jealousy of anyone who might have the power of stepping in front of him in the King's eye, or whispering ill things of him into the King's ear. He liked Captain Grahame; and he did not like Sir John Dalrymple; on the other hand he was beginning to be jealous of the former because, a mere Angus laird, he had been given, through the influence of the Duke of York, the command of a troop of horse, and Sir John not only was related to him by marriage, but was necessary for his scheme in bringing about the ruin of the Duke of Lauderdale, the ruling Minister of Scotland.

He was aware of the Covenanting menace, and honestly both feared and detested it; he knew that Sir John and his father were guilty of 'resetting' or harbouring rebels who happened to be their tenants, but he preferred to ignore the fact because the Dalrymples would make dangerous enemies. He sympathised with Captain Grahame's determination to protect peaceable ministers and congregations and to keep the south-west quiet, but he was determined that, if he could prevent it, Captain Grahame was not going to get a civil commission which would enable him to interfere in the Heritable Jurisdictions, for as the greatest landowner in the district he resented any sharing of such powers. Lastly, both Dalrymple and Claverhouse were infinitely his inferiors in birth and fortune, and ought to be reminded of the fact; yet it would not be policy to offend either, in particular Claverhouse, who had an extremely persuasive manner, and unimportant though he was, might be useful in putting in a word to his patron, the King's brother, which should further Queensberry's pet ambition – to be made a duke.

Fumbling under his dressing-gown, my lord helped himself to a pinch of snuff, secretly, so that good manners did not compel him to offer the box to his companions, and then exclaimed, spitting his S's right and left: "Ech me!

here's an ill thing that gentlemen should quarrel this fine morning. But you did right to bring the outrage at Dalblaith to our notice, Clavers, and you ken fine you can rely upon Sir John here to punish the offenders. And doubtless you'll be writing of the matter to his Royal Highness. I hear you're thick-and-pack with the Duke, and make your reports to him of all that passes here in Scotland, eh?"

Claverhouse turned away his head to conceal a smile; my lord could be so very childish.

"I make my reports to my Commander-in-Chief, my lord. His Royal Highness has enough to trouble him without my little affairs. And now, if the rest of the Commissioners are arrived, I beg that we may dispatch our business, for I have a world of matters awaiting me at Dumfries."

Queensberry shot him a glance in which embarrassment was mingled with defiance.

"Hech," said he with exaggerated regret, "I fear you've come upon a wasted journey the day, Clavers, so far as the Commission is concerned. For there is not one of them here but Dalrymple, the rest being at Embro' on their affairs, and so, not being a quorum, we cannot proceed to the business of providing hay and corn for your troop-horses. But I'll tell you what I'll do; if you'll name the amount you need (and pray let it be moderate, for you ken it's the lean season of the year), I'll consult with the other Commissioners by letter, and no doubt you'll get what you require."

Claverhouse was standing stock still upon the frozen flagstones of the terrace, his face flushed with a colour, which owed nothing to the sharpness of the morning, and his lower lip thrust out.

"My lord," he said shortly, "it is a week since I notified your lordship that I would be here the day to meet the Commissioners appointed by the Privy Council to provide locality for my troop, of which Commission your lordship is the head. With respect, I must say that it is an extraordinar' thing to me that I should be obliged to ride thirty miles on the King's service only to find those absent whose business it is to provide the necessities for it."

"You canna expect gentlemen of affairs," retorted Queensberry, bridling, "to lay aside the business which takes them to Embro' only for the providing of fodder for troop-horses."

"I expect, my lord," said Claverhouse crisply, "to be provided with the necessities of my service, among which is horse-fodder, and I look to receive it from those appointed by the Council to give it me. I need not remind your lordship that the price fixed by the Council for hay and corn is higher than that paid locally, and yet since the time I received my commission I have met with no willingness among the heritors to sell me this fodder."

"And I'll tell you why," said Queensberry confidentially, laying a hand upon the scarlet sleeve. "It is because you demand three pecks of corn and eight stone of hay for each troop-horse per week, whereas my Lord Airlie and my Lord Ross, your fellow captains, are content with two of the first, and seven of the second. You'll need to climb down a wee, Clavers."

"Horses that must travel sometimes fifty miles in a night are not to be stinted in their food," began Claverhouse, but he was interrupted by the clanging of a bell in one of the turrets of the great house, summoning the household of Sanquhar to their frugal dinner.

"I'm mortified Clavers," said my lord, not sounding it, "that I canna ask you to dine, but I was no just expecting company, and you'll be ettling to get back to your duties. I'll mind and write to the other Commissioners without delay, and enquire of them when it will be convenient to have a meeting on the matter of locality."

"Your lordship must excuse me if I say," said Claverhouse curtly, "that my horses cannot wait upon the gentlemen's leisure. Since my Commission empowers me to do so in case of necessity, I shall make so bold as to take what I require, giving your lordship's heritors the just rates for it, for I will not have my horses either starve or live upon the country."

And with that, bowing low to Queensberry, and briefly to Dalrymple, he walked away with his head in the air.

(iii)

It was mid-afternoon when he arrived back in Dumfries, his headquarters. During the ride he had conquered his irritation with the mean Queensberry, but his anger against Dalrymple still smouldered. It was men like that, he reflected, who were responsible for half the troubles in the south-west; some deliberately encouraged the Covenanters, others fined them and put the money into their own pockets. He was not at all sure that the whole system of Heritable Jurisdictions was not outmoded; such sheriffs and bailies were little kings, having the power of pit and gallows, and if they happened to be secret rebels themselves, the situation, especially in times of emergency like these, could be disastrous. Moreover his sense of justice was outraged by the fact that little rogues suffered, while the great ones who underground encouraged them, got off scot-free. There was nothing he could do about it, however, except bring the attitude of Sir John Dalrymple to the notice of Lord Linlithgow, his Commander-in-Chief (who would take no action); so he thrust it into the background of his mind and prepared to give his whole attention to whatever business awaited him at his headquarters.

As he rode up to the Globe Inn in St Michael Street, and glanced with simple pride at his standard flying from the roof (a flag embroidered with his coat-of-arms and a St Andrew's Cross in the large canton), a corporal ran out to his stirrup.

"Your replacement has arrived from Embro', sir," said the man. "The quartermaster has not arranged a billet for him before you've had a blink o' the fellow."

Claverhouse did not miss the significance of those last words.

In the custom of the day, he had raised his own troop from among his kinsmen, tenants, and friends, so that it resembled a feudal following of old. But if a replacement were needed, it was the habit of Lord Linlithgow to fill the gap in an arbitrary manner with a soldier from one of the few garrisons in Scotland, or by a new recruit, his lordship's object being to get rid of difficult or unsuitable men by palming them off on Captain Grahame. For not only was Captain Grahame a mere Angus laird, whereas the Earl of Airlie and Lord Ross, the captains of the other two independent troops of horse, were important personages, but Grahame appeared to have a knack of turning difficult recruits into fine soldiers, and moreover never once had complained of the replacements he was sent.

As he walked into the narrow passage of the inn, Claverhouse saw this latest replacement and smiled ruefully. There sat sprawling on a bench, with his long legs stuck out before him and his arms folded, a gangling young man with the pale cheeks of a town-dweller and a shallowly handsome face. His scarlet coat was unbuttoned, his carbine was lying on the floor together with his headpiece, and his gorget was nowhere to be seen. His long thigh boots were splashed with mud, and large dirty footmarks on the passage told that he had not troubled to wipe them when he came in; his head was shaven as though ordinarily he wore a periwig. He looked the picture of insolence and sullenness, and he did not rise as Captain Grahame approached him.

Silencing with a gesture the corporal's angry remonstrance, Claverhouse halted in front of the young man and stood there, quite silent, his experienced eye summing him up. A powerful body when it filled out, the figure for a good horseman, no vice in the sullen face, vanity that could be turned to good account, and a very strong smell of stale liquor.

"You've had a long ride from Embro' ", said Claverhouse pleasantly at last. "Have you dined?"

"He was offered meat, sir", the corporal answered for him, "but refused it. He's as dorted as a bear."

"And what is your name?"

"Jock Johnson," mumbled the recruit surily.

Again Claverhouse was silent, this time so long and somehow so significantly, that at length Johnson became uncomfortable. Presently, with deliberate insolence, he made room for his new captain to sit down upon the bench at his side.

"It is customary," said Claverhouse, still mild and pleasant, "for only one to sit during a talk between a captain and a trooper. And since upon this occasion the trooper chooses to sit, the captain must needs stand."

A pause. Then, very reluctantly, Johnson lurched to his feet; and in the background the corporal smiled. It was marvellous how Captain Grahame did it; with the common men there was never an outburst of the famous temper; as hot for discipline as any officer in Scotland, somehow he managed to instil it without a suspicion of harshness.

"Come along, Johnson," said Claverhouse, leading the way up the stair. "You and I must have some private talk."

He took the man to his chamber on the first floor of the inn, a plain, neat room, half bedroom and half office. A very small man, whose appearance was oddly hirsute because hair sprouted luxuriantly from nostrils and ears, though there was none on his lip, glanced up with an affectionate grin from sponging a waistcoat on the table, then darted an inquisitive look at Johnson.

"Away with you, Tam, to the kitchen, and finish your task there," said Claverhouse. "And bid them send me up some cold meat and ale in ten minutes' time; I have not dined the day."

"Hech, Master John!" cried the little man in dismay, "did ye no' dine with the Earl o' Queensberry? I've buzzed it a' roond the toon ye were dining with his lordship in his fine castle – "

"Then you buzzed it wrong," interrupted his master, shooing him out into the passage.

He shut the door, walked to his table, and sat down. Neat piles of papers, some with dangling seals, lay on this table. In one corner of the room was propped a furled colours, smaller than the flag which waved from the roof; a map of south-west Scotland hung upon one wall; on a homemade shelf was a modest array of military books; and near the papers on this table lay a bridle with a broken cheek-strap. Immediately he saw this object, Johnson stepped towards it, putting out a hand to feel the leather.

"Twelve hours at a stretch in rain and mirk," observed Claverhouse, his quick eyes noting the gesture. "No leather in Scotland will thole it. Are you a horseman, Johnson?"

"A harness-marker," mumbled the other, withdrawing his hand and relapsing into his former surliness.

"But now you are a soldier in my troop of horse," said Claverhouse, still without a hint of sharpness, "and must observe the courtesies of the honourable profession of arms, one of which is to address your officers as 'sir.' Come, man, you've a grudge, and had best void it ere it fester. Tell me, were you impressed?"

"Ay," cried Johnson, suddenly giving his bottled-up indignation its head. "Caught by the press-gang and had the King's coat forced upon ma back. And it's a black shame, I'm telling you, that a decent body canna make an excursion to the Capital o' his country without getting himsel' dinged into the army whether he wad or no."

"And what," asked Claverhouse dryly, "did this particular decent body do in the Capital of his country that he fell into the hands of the press-gang?"

So bit by bit the story came out. It was a not uncommon one. Jock Johnson, son of a prosperous harness-maker of Aberdeen, the idol of the lassies of that town, last week had become the fortunate legatee of a deceased uncle. His native place proving too tame for the celebrating of so glorious an acquisition of wealth, he had treated himself to a trip to Edinburgh; from that point onwards, it seemed that everything had become a little vague, but Claverhouse was well able to fill in the gaps in the tale. An obliging caddie offering to conduct the stranger to some tavern where the best society was to be found, Edinburgh strong-ale going to a none-too-steady head, the best society listening to the story of the legacy and making the most of it, the beating of the ten o'clock drum and the pressing invitation of the best society to go finish the entertainment in some lodging, the drunken walk through the streets at that fearsome hour when Edinburgh good wives emptied their slops through their portholes, Johnson too ignorant of Edinburgh ways to know the warning cry of 'Haud yer hand!', an unsavoury stream descending upon his head, tipsy rage overwhelming him, a fight; and the swift descent of the press-gang on the look-out for some victim to send to the Commander-in-Chief of his Majesty's Scots Army.

"Well, if it had not been the press-gang it would have been the Town Guard, or, more likely, since your misfortune happened on a Saturday night, a band of patrolling Elders,

Jock," said Claverhouse, smiling in a way which made it impossible for the other to take offence. "And since a soldier you have become, whether you like it or not, you had best content yourself. Maybe you'll think better of the service after you've made trial of it. It's the best life in the world, Jock, to my way of thinking, and I've followed the profession of arms since I was four and twenty, which is six years by-past. I'll allow it's not over-pleasant service here in the south-west, but you'll be working for your King and country – what did you say?"

"I said, it's a queer way of serving King and country by harrying a parcel o' puir folk only for worshipping God in their ain fashion", burst out Johnson defiantly, his disgruntlement finding vent in defending these people called Covenanters, about whom he knew little and cared less. "Ay, I've heard the doolfu' tales of the persecution here in the south-west, the wee groups o' folk a-praying on the muirs because they willna stomach bishops and Popish haverings fairded-up as Episco-Episco – " finding that he was unable to pronounce the word 'Episcopalianism', Jock left it and went on, more righteously indignant than ever – "and the sodgers a-flinging them into jail, and a-shooting o' them, and only for cleaving to the faith o' their fathers."

He paused, quite astonished by his own eloquence. Leaning back in his chair, Claverhouse regarded him with serious mouth but twinkling eyes.

"Tell me, Jock, are you a Presbyterian?"

"I am that."

"And yet you are not persecuted for cleaving to the faith of your fathers?"

Johnson fidgetted uncomfortably.

"Do you know what the Covenant means? I don't think you do, so I will tell you in a word. It was a pact made between certain of our fellow-countrymen in 1643, and, as they blasphemously claimed, Almighty God, to force Presbyterianism upon all his Majesty's subjects, even those of Ireland who are Papists. The third party to this bargain was the party which rebelled against the late King, and who bartered their religious freedom for Scots military support. But the Covenant is not incompatible only with Monarchy; Cromwell himself, who had signed it, found himself unable to carry out its terms, and he drummed the General Assembly of the Kirk out of Embro'."

Johnson's stare was still sulky, but he was listening.

"At the restoration of our present King," continued Claverhouse, picking up a quill and beginning to fray out the feathers as he talked, "his Majesty gave to all men in Scotland, save Papists, the right to worship as they pleased, whether Presbyterians or Episcopalians, so only they would give obedience to the civil authorities. But the Covenanters will not have this; they will acknowledge no authority save what they term their consciences, and they will not yield obedience to an Uncovenanted King or to his delegates. The majority of Presbyterians reject the Covenant, and are content to have the four bishops appointed by the King, because they are there, not in any way to interfere with the form of worship, but to make sure that the synods and presbyteries and kirk-sessions do not claim that authority over a man's secular life which in the days of the Covenant brought such tyranny on Scotland. Now, a man may pray in the privacy of his home as pleases him, even though it be against the King; but if more than five of such men pray and preach together, that is termed a conventicle, and to attend a conventicle is against the law, to go armed to it, as many do, is treason. And these conventiclers are the poor harried folk you spoke of just now. I'll add one word more: the Covenanting ministers preach openly not only that it is unlawful to give obedience to the King and his delegates, but that it is lawful, and pleasing to Almighty God, to slay them."

There was a long pause. Johnson seemed to have nothing to say, but it was clear to his officer that he was not without intelligence, and that he was busy digesting a point of view he had never heard put before. It was plain also, from the fact that he no longer glowered, that he appreciated the trouble Captain Grahame had taken to explain the situation to him.

"I like the system of impressment as little as you do, Jock," said Claverhouse, with an abrupt change of subject, "but since it is permitted by the Law, and for many centuries has been a method of recruitment in times of emergency, it is not for you or me to girn at it. And I'd have you remember two things from the start; first, that I expect my men, whether volunteers or impressed, to obey orders without question and to do their duty to the uttermost. And next that I never require them to undertake any task, to run any peril, or to suffer any hardship, which they will not see me ready to share with them. You must take my word for this now; later I hope you'll learn it of your own experience. Come," he added, flashing Jock a smile so charming that the other grinned despite himself, "how say you? Will you give soldiering a fair trial?"

"Ay," replied Jock without hesitation. And then, to his own astonishment, he added, quite naturally, " – sir."

"Good lad!" cried Captain Grahame; and called "Enter!" in response to a tap upon the door.

It was the corporal, who after smartly saluting presented a sealed paper. Claverhouse broke the seal, read for a moment, frowned, and stood up.

"Bid the trumpeter sound the *Boot and Saddle*," said he. And when the corporal had gone, he said to Johnson, in that dryly humorous tone which the new recruit was to come to know so well: "You had best eat that dinner you refused sinsyne, Jock, for you have maybe a fifty mile ride ahead of you in search of those suffering saints of yours."

Chapter Two

(i)

Twenty minutes later, Captain Grahame was riding at the head of ten troopers over the old bridge across the Nith which separated Dumfries from Galloway. Except for the sentry left behind at the Globe Inn, he was taking the full complement of men he had at his headquarters, for because of the difficulty of obtaining 'locality', it was impossible to have his troop of sixty quartered all together, a fact he greatly disliked. He had pointed out to his Commander-in-Chief many times in vain that while troops had to be divided in this way, and quartered wherever supplies happened to be available, they were rendered vulnerable to attacks by the Covenanters, and would be useless in an emergency requiring concentration.

They had not ridden a mile out of Dumfries before the whole nature of the countryside changed. Mile after mile there was nothing but whaup-haunted moor, grey granite rock, unfriendly hills lowering in the background, a pervading smell of bog-myrtle, the whinnying bleat of snipe and the swooping wail of the lapwing. Peaty burns snarled beside the track; brown bent and dead heather and an occasional twisted thorn shivered in the icy wind. Here and there a 'murder-hole', a black pool which never froze and from which no beast would drink, winked an evil eye;

and as they progressed into the heart of Galloway, more and more frequent became the death-traps known as quakin' quas, stretches of evilly green herbiage concealing bottomless mud.

Set in the waste of moorland was an occasional cothouse, wretched little hovels without a chimney, the peat-smoke wavering through a hole in the roof, board roughly nailed across glassless windows to keep out the rain, and a midden, larger than the house, standing beside it in a sea of liquid green filth. Far up on the hillside huge yokes of oxen could be seen, ploughing pitiful little rigs, because the ground below was too swampy; black-faced sheep glared inhospitably upon the intruders; and once, passing some children gathering firewood, a stone came whizzing in the direction of the troop, making a horse shy violently, and shrill voices yelled some biblical curse upon the Uncovenanted. Remembering the impact of Galloway upon himself when first he had been given his commission and sent to police this district, Claverhouse cast a sympathetic glance at the new recruit, who was riding just behind him.

"Losh, it's a God-forecasten country," murmured Jock, catching the glance.

"I've grown to love it, for it's my district," said Claverhouse, with simple pride. "I ken every inch of it, and every man and woman who dwells in its bounds. I'll make it peaceable yet, and that without bloodshed. I'll jalouse we've come on a wasted journey, Rob," he added to his quartermaster, Robert Grahame. "My Lord Linlithgow's letter was a week upon its journey, and the conventicle he spoke of will not have had the civility to sit and await the coming of the King's soldiers."

"Ay, they're by-ordinar' quick to get wind of our coming, sir," grumbled the quartermaster, who did not share his captain's love of his district. "I think the Deil himsel' must be the blasties' scout."

Claverhouse glanced round upon the lowering hills.

"Hech! poor bodies," said he. "I'm thinking you and I might have been tempted to turn Covenanter, Rob, if we'd been born as cut off from the rest of Scotland as are these Gallovidians. It's a sour and savage country, and ever has been since it was the home of the cattle-reivers. For us on the east coast there are ports and roads and markets, the traffic of Europe on the sea, the pack-horses and the post-boys on the roads. But in Galloway there is but the tilling of sour ground and the herding of sheep and cattle. Small wonder the folk here-away find entertainment in the ravings of fanatics and in harrying the law-abiding."

The drove-road on which they travelled passed presently the deep lip of a peat-moss from which the fuel had been cut away for a hundred yards. Claverhouse called back an order to his men to make a wide detour, and noticing Johnson's look of surprise, said to him dryly:

"A bonny place for an ambush, Jock, and one your suffering saints relish greatly. It was from such concealment that poor Anderson, whose place you are filling, was shot in the back last week."

The early dusk was falling when at last Claverhouse called a halt.

"There's a bonnet-laird lives yonder," said he, "who's a known resetter. I've a mind to call on him, just in case he's the bad luck to be harbouring a conventicle-leader at present." As the troop dismounted, giving their horses in the charge of one of their number while they went forward on foot, Claverhouse said to Johnson: "You're new to this work, Jock, so I'll give you a word of warning: take care never to stand with your back to any person in the house, either man or woman, if you'd return to Dumfries with a whole skin."

(ii)

As they approached the house, which was a little larger than the hovels they had passed on their ride, it appeared to be deserted, except that they heard, eerie and thin, the wailing of a child. At a word from their captain, the men spread out, some to keep guard, others to search the byre and peat-stack, while Claverhouse himself, taking with him his quartermaster and the new recruit, knocked upon the door. There was a considerable interval before a woman's voice demanded to know who was there.

"It is Captain Grahame," answered Claverhouse crisply, "seeking admittance in the King's name. Come now, open to me, goodwife, for I would like ill to have to break down your door."

Slowly and reluctantly the door was opened a few inches, and there could be seen in the aperture a portion of a female figure swathed in a coarse woollen plaid. She held a crusie-lamp in one hand, and with the other kept a firm hold upon the door.

"Is the goodman within?" enquired Claverhouse, quietly setting his foot in the aperture.

"He's awa' to Glasga'," replied the woman sourly, and she was about to slam the door in his face when he pushed it open and entered, followed by his two men.

The next instant Johnson gave a bleat of dismay, as he saw a brawny female arm upraised and a flail about to descend upon the head of his captain: but it appeared that Captain Grahame was well used to this sort of reception. His hand shot out and caught the woman's wrist, twisting it expertly so that the weapon fell to the floor.

"You foolish taupie," he chided. "You'll get yourself drowned one of these days if you assault the King's soldiers. Now see here, goodwife, you ken fine why I'm come. Your man's a known resetter, and I've reason to suspect that he has harboured Mr King, one of the most mischievous of the field-preachers. Your house must be searched, for such are my orders and I have a warrant for it, so you'd best content yourself."

She had been staring at the intruder with a look of black hate, and now opened her mouth to a stream of abuse, mixing homely oaths with biblical cursers in a manner which amazed and disgusted the uninitiated Johnson. But Claverhouse took no sort of notice, going quietly and methodically about his search. It was not a pleasant task, but since it had to be done he performed it thoroughly, and also with a queer delicacy, for his years of soldiering had never made him callous. He would have every grain of meal out of a kist before he was satisfied that the kist had no false bottom, but then he would make his men replace the meal which he had scooped out on to an old sack. It was with a gesture of apology towards the woman (who was still screaming abuse) that he withdrew from a press the black kelt coat the laird wore on the Sabbath, that he might peer behind it; his hands were gentle but efficient as he examined the wall-beds. In a tiny closet he came upon the child whose thin wailing had been heard from outside the house. It was a boy of five or six, stark naked, his wrists tied so tightly to a hook in the wall that the flesh was swollen. His large eyes ignored the intruders and blinked fearfully at his mother, and his blue-cold body flinched instinctively from a blow.

"What ails the bairn?" enquired Claverhouse sharply.

"He keeked frae a window on the Sabbath," answered the child's mother in a voice of doom, forgetting even Claverhouse in the enormity of her son's crime. "He profaned the Lord's Day, and has brought a curse upon his father's hoose."

Claverhouse hesitated a moment, then shut the closet door.

"I ken fine," said he shortly, "that it's useless to quote from the New Testament in a Covenanting house, but I'll tell you this, goodwife: Galloway would be peaceable enough were it not for seditious preachers and women who know not Christian charity, from whom the good Lord deliver us!"

As he opened the door across the passage, holding up the crusie-lamp which he had taken from the woman, the latter ceased her cursing for a moment to say sharply:

"My weans are abed yonder, and I'll thank you not to rouse them frae their sleep."

He made no reply, but stood for a moment looking at the big heap of straw, which served as a bed, and in which could be seen four little heads motionless in slumber. But he was not looking at the four little heads; there was a strange mound in the centre of the straw, a mound too large to be formed by a child's body; and as he looked there issued from it a muffled groan.

"I'm thinking there's more in the bed than your weans, goodwife," said he, and handing the crusie to his quartermaster, he pulled aside the straw.

The mound disclosed itself as the figure of a man, curled up, his arms clasped about his middle, his haggard eyes staring at the intruder.

"So there you are, Mr Wilson," said Claverhouse dryly. "You'll need to come with me, and pray come quietly that you do not disturb your bairns."

"I meant no harm, no harm in the world, Captain Grahame," moaned the laird, rocking himself to and fro as though in anguish of mind or body. "I ken fine I shouldna have gaed to the conventicle, but the goodwife left me no wale but I maun gae, and it was fine to hear the psalm, and hearken to the strange burning words of the minister, and when he spiered of me would I give him shelter for the night, I couldna deny him, I couldna refuse hospitality to one who asked it. But he's awa' now, and I'll not be harbouring him again, I swear it. I'm a leal subject of the King – "

"The King!" violently interrupted his wife, turning the stream of her abuse upon her husband. "Will ye unthrone Jesus Christ, ye blastie, and set up yon apostate who is excommunicate and given o'er to Satan? The Deil rides and dings Charles Stuart and his Council through moss and muir, and he will keep them in torments for a' eternity. Charles Stuart is a Bull of Bashan, and a' his Council and his sodgers are Kine of Bashan, and it is ilka man's duty to kill them according to that Scripture which is in Exodus, twenty-one. They shall stand at the left hand of Christ in the Day o' Doom, and He shall say to them, Gang awa tae everlasting burning. Ye ken why this Visitation is come upon us – ay, ye ken it fine, ye backslider. Ye used one of the new-fangled fanners to thresh the corn sinsyne; ye raised the Deil's wind and outraged the Word which saith, The Spirit bloweth where it listeth. Ye took the power oot o' the mouth o' the Lord… "

During this harangue, which had been shouted above the wailing of the now awakened children, Claverhouse had been helping the laird to his feet.

"Instead of raving like a kail-wife, mistress," said he curtly to the woman, "you were better to find somewhat to relieve your man. He's a cruel fit of the gravel, and a sup of milk with some fennel in it may ease him while I see what my men have been at. It's no manner of use, Mr Wilson," he added, as the laird began a whining plea for mercy, "I'll have to arrest you and send you to Embro', for those are my orders, and you've confessed to resetting. But neither the King nor his Council desire the ruin of any man, and if you're penitent you'll find mercy, never fear. And I'll plead for you myself, for it sticks in my mind that you'd live peaceable enough were it not for this wife of yours and her ravings."

Leaving the quartermaster and Johnson in charge of the prisoner, he went outside to receive the report of those who had been searching the byre and the peat-stack. In the latter they had found concealed a number of weapons, a bundle of ugly looking implements of local manufacture which had curved knives attached to a pole, obviously for the purpose of cutting horses' bridles, a dozen muskets, and as many cheap swords. Sending an order to his quartermaster to bring the laird down, Claverhouse stood looking at the weapons with his lower lip sucked in, and especially at the swords; he had unearthed others of the same kind in Galloway peat-stacks, with marks upon them which betrayed that they were of Dutch manufacture.

"The States of Holland," said he grimly, "are becoming ever more generous to our home-bred rebels with presents of this nature. I like it not."

The bell in the Midsteeple of Dumfries was tolling the hour of ten when the weary little troop clattered over the bridge once more. The return journey had been made a walking-pace, partly because of the perils of 'murder-holes' and quakin' quas after dark, partly out of consideration for Mr Wilson's sick condition. It was obvious to Claverhouse that the laird's sufferings were genuine; he was doubled up with pain, and had so far forgotten Covenanting principles as to accept a sup of brandy from Claverhouse's flask, though anything which had the duty on it was banned by the Covenant.

On reaching the Globe Inn, Jock Johnson discovered to his disgust that the troopers' day was not yet ended. Each man must attend to his horse; the beasts must be led in turn to the water-trough, taken to their stalls, rubbed down, and fed, and these things must be done very thoroughly indeed. Captain Grahame was there to supervise, running a hand down a sweaty flank, inspecting each manger to make sure that the oats and chaff were properly mixed, with an eagle eye for any skimping of the job. When he came to the stall where Johnson, half asleep upon his feet, was unenthusiastically rubbing down his horse with a wisp of straw, Claverhouse took the wisp from his hand and completed the task himself.

"A long day for your first in the King's service, Jock," said he, with that irresistible smile of his, "but you'll get used to it. We're all weary men and beasts, and we've earned our oats and our straw. You'll find a hot supper awaiting you in the kitchen yonder, and" – with a grin which suddenly made him look very boyish – "mulled ale to wash it down, if your outcast with Sir John Barleycorn is over. You've done fine."

As Johnson stared at him, the last trace of disgruntlement left the new recruit's face. Murmuring his thanks to Captain Grahame, he did not have any difficulty in adding the word 'sir'.

(iii)

Having obtained a hot posset for his prisoner and seen him settled down on a truss of hay in the barn, Claverhouse at last ascended to his own chamber.

As usual at this hour, it presented a very comforting appearance. The curtain before the wall-bed was withdrawn, giving a view of coarse but clean Holland sheets and homespun blankets neatly turned back; a fire of peat glowed upon the hearth, and in front of it reposed Claverhouse's nightgown and slippers. On the fire itself simmered a pot which gave forth a savoury odour, and nearby stood a large tub, covered with boards, with steam creeping through the crevices. Presiding over this scene of comfort (so unusual in a Scottish inn), was the little hirsute man named Tam.

Tam had been born and bred at Glen Ogilvie, the modest Grahame house near Dundee, and ever since the laird's death, when the elder son, John, was five years old, had attached himself to him as watchdog and nurse. When, at the age of ten, Master John had become a student at St Andrew's University, Tam had accompanied him and had shared his studies, returning home with him three years later when Master John had graduated. And when in 1672, Master John had made his great decision, to embrace the profession of arms and learn his trade in foreign service, Tam had taken it for granted that he should go to Flanders also, though he feared foreign parts like the devil and was convinced that every man outside Scotland was a Papist. And since Master John had been pleased to throw up his commission under the Prince of Orange and become a hunter of Covenanting rebels through the moors of the south-west, Tam had continued to be with him, bullying the landlords of small inns for hot water and clean sheets and fresh meat and the best furniture in the house, determined that Master John should have the comfort which was his right, even in this outlandish part of Scotland.

As soon as he heard his master's footsteps on the stair tonight, Tam flung open the door and proceeded to scold in the fond tone of a nannie.

"Come awa' ben with you, Master John. It's not to be told what hours you keep, and in sic weather. Aff with yon wet duddies afore you catch your death."

Well used to his servant's fussings, Claverhouse merely smiled, and suffered himself to be assisted out of his uniform and boots, and encased in his nightgown, before sitting down to a belated supper of broth and cold meat. Tam, meanwhile, after setting the boots aside for cleaning, and clucking over the dampness of the coat, tried the temperature of his master's bath and set a washball beside it. It had taken him years to overcome his conviction that to bath daily, as Master John insisted on doing, was asking for consumption or the falling-sickness; converted at last, this unusual fastidiousness had become his pride and his favourite boast to the landlords of the inns where his master quartered. So also was the fact that Master John changed his shirt once every week, instead of only at Whitsun and Martinmas.

His supper finished, Claverhouse wiped knife and spoon on a napkin and put them away in the little leather case in which they travelled about with him, then stripped for his bath. Carefully scrubbing the long arms and legs, the flat back, and the narrow shoulders, Tam kept up a monologue on the iniquities of the Covenanters. His knowledge of them was hazy in the extreme, but it was sufficient for him that they kept his master up to all hours of the night, and, given the chance, would not scruple to pistol him, as upon more than one occasion they had pistolled his men.

After the bath came the most important ceremony of the toilet. Master John had never adopted the fashionable periwig, ostensibly because he detested the idea of wearing somebody else's hair, actually (as Tam was well aware, being acquainted with all Master John's virtues and weaknesses and loving them equally), because his vanity prevented him from cutting off his own luxuriant dark locks. These locks must be brushed and combed, no matter at what hour their owner finished his day, and their ends must be twisted round thin pieces of lead so that in the morning they would appear in loose waves and curls. Over this uncomfortable coiffure, Tam wound a turban, partly for warmth, partly because Master John might take it into his head to go down in the middle of the night and see if all was well with his troopers or his horses; and as

Claverhouse rose from before the dresser, there was a ritualistic exchange between master and man.

"You'll be awa' to your bed the noo, Master John."

"Not yet a while, Tam; I've letters to write."

"Och, you and your letters! D'ye ken it's past eleven o' the clock?"

"I ken that fine. Redd-up the room, and then away to bed yourself."

Tam took as long as possible over his tidying of the room. Though utterly trustworthy in the sense that he would sooner have cut his throat than betray one of his master's secrets, he possessed that nannie-like conviction that it was his duty to acquaint himself with all his master's concerns. Thus he would listen shamelessly outside the door when Master John had a visitor, and nothing delighted him more than a chance to read some obligingly unsealed letter. (It was often a matter of contemptuous amazement to him that men of his class in England could neither read not write.) Not that there was often anything interesting in the letters which Master John received or wrote, but it was enough for Tam to acquaint himself with what the Commander-in-Chief was writing to Master John, and especially what Master John was writing to the Commander-in-Chief, because here and there among the formal phrases could be found some specimens of that dry wit so characteristic of Master John and so greatly relished by Tam.

Passing to and fro across the little room, emptying the bath out of the window, smooring the fire with damp, turfs, pushing the brass warming-pan (a luxury which, like the knife and spoon, travelled about with its owner) between the sheets, Tam stole quick glances over Master John's shoulder, gleaning a sentence here and there from the busy quill. He'd a fine hand with the quill, had Master John, not like my Lord Linlithgow's, whose curly script was downright unchristian. Particularly did Tam admire the way in which Master John wrote his signature, making the capital J of his initial intertwine with the capital G of his surname. And one of these days, thought Tam exultantly, Master John's merit would be rewarded in a fashion which would enable him to sign himself by some title, as did my Lord Linlithgow. One of these days, instead of plain 'J Grahame', it might be – well, why not the name of his home-town, 'Dundee'?

(iv)

Even since he had become a soldier, Claverhouse had accustomed himself to taking little sleep, and now, refreshed by supper and bath, he set to work with a will upon his correspondence. Letter-writing came easily to him, and he was blissfully unaware that his long, careful, and strictly objective dispatches sent every few days to his Commander-in-Chief were skimmed through impatiently by that gentleman, who was mentally sick of the turbulent south-west and physically sick of a diseased liver.

He began tonight with the affair of the minister of Dalblaith and the outrage perpetrated on his kirk. He described it all with extraordinary economy, yet without sacrificing one important point. He had taken the liberty, he went on, upon several occasions, to suggest the need for small garrisons to be planted in the south-west. A few mobile troops, scattered here and there in so large a district, were useless in protecting the peaceable ministers and their flocks, irritated the people who were in continual fear of having soldiers quartered upon them, and invited the Covenanters to ambush small parties.

Next there was the wasted journey to Sanquhar. He managed this delicate part of his letter without forgetting Queensberry's superior rank or giving rein to his own dislike of Dalrymple, merely reporting what he had said to each, and their replies, and adding that on leaving Sanquhar he had gone to some of my lord's heritors, had paid them the rates laid down by the Council for their hay and straw, and had ordered a consignment to be sent to the various places where his troop was quartered.

There followed an unemotional account of his ride into Galloway, a dryly humorous remark about Galloway goodwives, an exact description of the weapons found hidden in the peat-stack, and the statement that, in the writer's opinion, the storing of such weapons was a proof that the Covenanters meditated armed rebellion such as they had raised in 1666. The one prisoner captured, he added, the bonnet-laird, he was keeping under ward at Dumfries for the present. 'I hope your lordship will pardon me that I send him not to Embro' until he has been tended by a 'pothecary, for he is fair tortured with the gravel.'

Claverhouse added a paragraph about the Covenanters' superior intelligence system. By the time a dispatch arrived with orders to disperse a conventicle, by some mysterious means they had got wind of the approach of the King's soldiers and were away. It was true, as my lord had been pleased to point out, that he himself had a warrant from the Council to employ spies, but the Council had omitted to provide him with money for their payment.

Having reached this point in his dispatch, Claverhouse sat idle for a few minutes, watching Tam who, unable to find an excuse for staying up any longer, was settling on to his straw pallaise, carefully setting a horse-pistol beside him lest any Covenanting rogue came sneaking in during the night to murder his master. There was one other matter which Claverhouse was determined to include in his letter, and he was meditating how best to word it.

The district originally given him to patrol was confined to Dumfriesshire and Annandale, and for some while he had been mortified by the sight of conventicles held right under his nose upon a piece of land which happened to be outside his district. After bringing the matter to the notice of Linlithgow for the dozenth time, he had received an impatient note from my lord, telling him that an order of the Council had extended his authority to cover the land in question, and implying that therefore his complaint was frivolous. It was the kind of snub which Claverhouse simply could not ignore, because it pricked his quick sense of justice. Taking up his quill again, he replied to this rebuke in a fashion very typical of him, respectful but firm:

'My lord, since I have received your lordship's intelligence of this Act of Council, the scruple I had about undertaking anything outside my bounds is indeed frivolous, but was not so before; for if there had been no such Act, it had not been proper for me to have done anything but what my order warranted; and since I knew it not, it was to me the same thing as if it had not been. And for my ignorance of it, I must acknowledge that till now in any service I have been in, I never enquired further into the laws than the orders of my superior officers.'

He signed the letter, sanded and sealed it, and impressed upon the wax his signet-ring which was engraved with his monogram surrounded by a wreath of laurel, the badge of the House of Grahame.

But even now his day was not ended. There was one other letter he must write, and it was only when his professional duties were completed that he could attend to it; for it was a letter which concerned his personal affairs.

A few days previously he had heard from his kinsman, the young Marquis of Montrose. This grandson of the family hero was the sort of man who loves to manage the affairs of others, and he had written Claverhouse to remind him that really it was time he took a wife. He was thirty-one; he made no secret of the fact that he was ambitious of honours and promotion; and this being the case, Montrose had found the very lady for him. Her name was Helen Grahame, and not only had she the family blood in her veins, but also a few drops of the blood-royal. She was the only child of Sir James and Lady Grahame who were resident in Ireland, and through her mother she was co-heiress of Bishop Bramhall, Primate of that country. But what was vastly more important was that she was heiress to the childless old Earl of Menteith; that is to say, she was heiress to his debts but not to his title. Since the Earl's impoverished condition was due to his father's fidelity to the cause of Charles I, it ought not to be difficult to persuade his present Majesty to transfer the Menteith title to Helen's husband when the old man died, if that husband were prepared to take over the Menteith debts.

It was an attractive though a delicate proposition, and Claverhouse had given it much thought. A Grahame earldom, and the fair lands of Menteith, were tempting in the extreme, and although he was by no means rich he had always been careful with money and would be able to raise sufficient for the payment of the old Earl's debts. On the other hand, Helen was the heiress of a very rich mother, and his pride made him hesitate about seeking her hand. As for the emotional side, he scarcely gave it a thought; he had been brought up to believe, in true Scots fashion, that marriage was a business concerned with the disposal of property; had his father not died when he was so young, or had he himself not gone a-soldiering in foreign parts, his own marriage would have been arranged for him long ago. Naturally he would desire his bride to be amiable and well-favoured, and he would make sure that they liked one another before making his proposal; but that was as far as it went.

So he drew a fresh sheet of paper towards him and wrote to Montrose. Was there any likelihood of the young lady and her parents paying a visit to Scotland, so that a personal introduction could be effected? Could Montrose describe her, or, better still, send him her picture? Since he was in London and had the entrée to the Court, could he manage a discreet sounding of his Majesty as to the chances of the Menteith title being transferred at the old Earl's death?

Lastly he wrote to Menteith himself, setting forth the advantages his lordship would obtain from the proposal, and pleading his own cause. It would be a terrible thing if this title, so long in the possession of the House of Grahame, should pass to one who did not hear that name. An heir there must be, and since Almighty God had denied his lordship the blessing of offspring, he must needs have an heir by adoption. 'Nobody,' wrote Claverhouse, in his firm, workmanlike hand, 'your lordship could make choice of, has toiled so much for honour as I have done, though it has been my misfortune to obtain but a small share so far.' Nevertheless, he had a free estate of six hundred pounds sterling yearly; he was captain of a troop of horse and received fourteen shillings a day for his service; he was confident of promotion; he possessed Claypotts Castle near Dundee (a castle quite uninhabitable, but there was no need to mention that since Menteith was well aware of it), the lands of Claverhouse, the moor of Ballargus, and the lands and barony of Glen Ogilvie, with all the townships, biggings, orchards, mills, fishings, woods, and mosses lying within the bounds of the same, etc., etc. He had no debts; he enjoyed excellent health; there were those who would answer for his moral character; and his Royal Highness, the Duke of York, was his patron, though so far he had never had the privilege of a personal meeting with the Duke.

The bell in the Midsteeple was tolling the hour of one in the morning when at last Claverhouse sealed his letter to Menteith. For so important a missive he used a seal which he carried in his pocket; it was engraved with the crest of the House of Grahame, a phoenix rising from the flames. Then he rose, stretched himself, knelt down at the table and said his prayers, put off his night-gown, and, stepping over the now sleeping Tam, climbed into his wall-bed.

It had been a most typical day.

Chapter Three

(i)

It was in all the pride of a new honour that, four months later, Claverhouse took a few days leave of absence, spending them as usual at his home in Glen Ogilvie, the house known among his family as 'Glen'.

It had been recommended to the king and approved by him that in the districts where the Heritable Sheriffs had proved themselves unable or unwilling to deal with the Covenanting menace, the Council should appoint sheriffs-depute, their powers being restricted to the fining and imprisoning of those found guilty of subscribing to the seditious doctrines of the Covenant; and the Sheriff-depute the Council appointed for Dumfries, Annandale, Wigton, and Kirkcudbright was Captain John Grahame. It was a modest honour, but a knighthood could scarcely have pleased him better, for it was not only ambition which made him so keen on his job. He had identified himself with this turbulent district of his in a way which amazed his fellow officers; he really cared about its welfare and he wanted its goodwill. The fact that his new honour had increased the enmity of a Dalrymple and a Queensberry was far outweighed by the fact that he could hold sheriff-courts of his own now and in some measure put into practice a policy which always had appeared to him both just and effective. It was the ringleaders, and the great men who encouraged them underground, who were going to feel his rule.

But as he trotted along the familiar track to Glen, with only Tam for his companion, and saw the chimneys built by his father thrusting their fingers into the clear bright sky, he forgot his new honours in the joy of coming home.

It was a modest mansion, built in two storeys, plain from foundations to corbel-stepped gable roof. With its granaries and byre at right-angles to it on one side, and its stables and mews upon the other, it formed the usual square, the fourth side being closed by a wall in the centre of which was an old tower, the scene of many a game of besieged and besiegers when he was a boy. On the west of the house stood the huge stone dovecot, white with pigeons' droppings; on the east a plantation of beech, chestnut and sycamore, the only trees in this bleak, wind-swept landscape. And dotted around that landscape were the townlands, the clusters of cottages inherited by tenants.

Claverhouse was not an emotional man, but he never rode home to Glen without the suspicion of a lump in his throat. All his childhood and his youth were here; Glen had formed him, and he loved every inch of those bleak acres, every stone of that modest house. As he clattered into the courtyard today, with its midden and its water-trough, and the old dog which turned the spit limping out to welcome him, a bell began to ring in the stable turret, and he smiled because he had timed his coming to arrive for the 'four hours', that little meal universal among rich and poor in Scotland, the humble bear-bannock and ale, or the fine wheaten bread and claret, which was served at four in the afternoon.

Yes, it was good to come home, he thought, as he dismounted, and saw familiar faces and familiar things about him; though he was perfectly aware that he could never have stayed at home. The life which was so restful for brief periods, and which his brother David lived so contentedly, would have been intolerable to his restless, ambitious, and energetic nature. It was enough for him to know that Glen was here, with its never-failing welcome of kinsfolk and tenants whenever in his busy life he could find time to visit it, and that the affairs of the estate were so excellently managed by his brother.

And here came David now, shabby and comfortable in his homespun, with his slow countryman's walk and voice, a grin of affection and his hand outstretched, the very embodiment of Glen. As he went into the house with his brother, Claverhouse glanced up with simple pride, as he always did when he came home, to the coat-of-arms carved in the plaster above the door, that coat with its royal tressure which was the privilege of legitimate descent from King Robert III: Or, three piles wavy sable, on a chief of the second three escallops of the field. And above the coat, the crest of Grahame of Claverhouse, the phoenix rising from the flames.

(ii)

For a while before supper he sat with his sister Anna in the still room, where she was making a potion for Alan the factor who was troubled by a cough. Since their old nurse's death last year, there was no woman at Glen to undertake such tasks, for David was unmarried, so that Anna, who lived in the neighbourhood, was often at home to see that the maids were not idle.

She had always been his favourite sister, though four years his senior the nearest to him in age. Magdalene, married to Sir Robert Grahame of Morphie, was a tall and splendid woman, with masses of dark hair like his own; Anna was fair like her father and her younger brother, and was by nature affectionate, impulsive, and vulnerable. But when he had come home from the University at the age of thirteen, he had noticed a change in Anna, and the reason for this change, when he learned of it, had been not without its effect upon his own character.

He had never heard the details of the little tragedy, only that it had been one of those 'misplaced attachments' about which one did not speak. Anna herself had behaved perfectly, for she was of her age and class and there was nothing of the rebel in her nature; there had been no tears in public, and not a murmur when, a year or two later, her marriage was arranged by her mother with good Robert Young of Auldbar, a prosperous merchant. She had made him a good wife, and her son and daughter adored her; she was as affectionate and as kind as of old; but the brother who loved her more dearly than any other member of his family, and in whose nature imaginative sympathy was already strong at thirteen, had realised that something had died in Anna, and that the term 'a broken heart' was no empty phrase.

As he had grown older, he believed that he had learned the lesson which Anna's little tragedy had taught him. It was that the emotions were dangerous things and must never be allowed to become the master. Thus he had avoided those casual amours universal among his fellow soldiers in Flanders, not only from a natural fastidiousness, but because he loathed the giving of pain. The female heart, it seemed, was all too apt to succumb to this mysterious affliction of 'falling in love.' He did not understand what was meant by that term; affection he possessed in good measure; mere sexual desire he accepted, though absorbed as he was in his profession and in field-sports, it had troubled him little; but this thing which came like a whirlwind, this raging hunger of spirit, mind and body for one particular human being, this torment which had made Anna's face like a mask and her eyes blind with a pain she must not show, this remained a mystery. Yet for some reason which he could not determine, her youthful suffering had drawn them closer together. She had never confided in him, he had never presumed to question her, and his unemotional nature prevented him from giving her even silent understanding; still she was curiously close to him in spirit, closer than comfortable David or worldly-wise Magdalene; and whenever he came home to Glen, Anna was there to welcome him.

"*S'math sin!*" said Anna, trying the temperature of her potion with one finger, and giving her brother an intimate smile.

Whenever they were alone in the stillroom together, they talked in the Gaelic; it was their own private tribute to their old Highland nurse whose domain this room had been for so long. All the family had loved Moir, but Anna best of all, and her elder brother thought he know the reason. In the days of that 'misplaced attachment,' Anna had disappeared into the stillroom for long periods, and sometimes when he passed the door he had heard Moir's frail true voice singing the love-plaints of her own people, soothing with the articulate sorrow of a race who were not ashamed of their emotions this Lowland girl and her broken heart. And he too owed much to Moir. It was she who first had put into his head the glory of war and the nobility of the warrior; as a very little boy he had sat at her knee and had listened enthralled as from out the storehouse of her wonderful memory she had told him the tales which formed the heritage of her people, the tales of old Caledonia, of Fingal and his fellow heroes, who had resisted the aggression of the Scandinavian pirates, who had reverenced fairness in fight, mercy to the defeated, the sanctity of an oath, noble intolerance of oppression. The clang of shield and spear had sounded in his head long before he was old enough to formulate the wish to be a soldier himself. When those days came, he was a serious youth studying military history at St Andrews, and Fingal and Gaul had become half-mythical heroes, and his early devotion to them had been left behind him with his horn-book. He did not know that they had played their part in the formation of his character, whether for good or ill...

Sitting in Moir's old sanctuary, with the sunlight of May gleaming on the jars and bottles of home-made medicines on the shelves, he began to talk to his sister of his hopes of the Menteith marriage. He had received from Montrose a description of the young lady, and even allowing for the Marquis' exaggeration, she sounded a fine lass. She was coming over to England with her parents on a visit to London next month, and if he could only prevail upon my Lord Linlithgow to give him a month's leave, he was resolved to go and present himself to Sir James and Lady Grahame.

"It would be a bonny thing for our family," said he, "if we could get the Menteith lands and title. And it will not be my blame if we don't, for I have written near every week to his lordship, and likewise to Sir James. Both seem to favour my suit, but from what Montrose tells me my lady is out for a richer match. Still and on, I'm thinking that if I could be presented, I could persuade my lady to look favourably upon me – why are you smiling, Anna?"

"I was thinking," said Anna, holding up a jar to examine the state of some pickled wood-lice, known locally as slaters, insects supposed to have wonderful medicinal powers, "that you would have little difficulty in persuading the daughter."

He was genuinely shocked. Though not without vanity, he was quite unaware of the effect of his striking good looks and his charm upon the other sex, so that the point of his sister's remark was lost on him. What shocked him was that she should suggest his personal wooing of this heiress, a thing clean against the rules of conduct, especially in so delicate a situation. A proud and sensitive man, it was intolerable to him even to imagine forcing his attentions upon a lady who would bring him a title and a considerable fortune. He tried to make this clear to Anna, but she remained unimpressed.

"Aiblins," she said, going to the steel-glass to set her curch straight as the bell rang for supper, "there's a lassie somewhere with no fair lands and titles, who'll cause that sensible ambitious head of yours to bow to your warm heart one day."

Rather embarrassed, he told her not to talk nonsense. He was one and thirty, and the head of the family, was he not? Not the man to allow his heart to rule his head in so serious a business as marriage. It was precisely the sort of remark which is apt to tempt Providence.

(iii)

There was quite a little gathering around the hearth in the chief fireroom of Glen after supper that night.

Claverhouse occupied the elbow-chair which had been his father's, with Anna on his right hand, busy as usual with her rock and reel, and her stout, genial husband on his left. David sat on a corner of his bed (for this was his sleeping-chamber as well as the living-room), mending a pair of jesses, and rising now and again to persuade a sick sparrowhawk, perched in the ingle-low, to sup a little hyssop. Anna's only son Robin, a tall, well-favoured boy of fifteen, being the youngest member of the party was perched upon a creepie-stool, speaking only when spoken to, for such was the rule.

In a chair slightly withdrawn from the circle out of respect, sat the Grahame chaplain, Mr Edwards, with Alain's *Sighs from Hell*, a pious book he was reading aloud to the servants every evening, reposing on his knees. He was a youth who was studying for the ministry, very thankful to have five pounds a year with board and lodging, in return for putting the tenants' bairns through the Shorter Catechism, saying grace before and after meat, conducting the morning and evening family devotions, and examining the servants scripturally every Sabbath. Claverhouse had a warm affection for him; he was neither eloquent nor learned, but a sort of simple goodness seemed to radiate from him, a genuine humility sweetened the dour tenets of the Kirk whenever he pronounced them.

Finally there was a young kinsman of the Grahames, James Philip of Amerlieclose, whose mother was second cousin to Claverhouse, and whose father was a small laird near Arbroath. He was in his early twenties, and had not long left St Andrews where for several years after his laureation he had stayed on as a regent. But after taking his class through their three years, he had resigned his regency and retired home to devote himself to those classical studies which were his passion, and which at St Andrews must be combined with the mathematics, natural philosophy, and physics. His father was well able to support him, and was proud to have so brilliant a son at home, who, thus left free to follow his natural bent, was displaying no small skill as a poet. His writings had a single theme: the glories of the great Montrose. No one around the Grahame hearth tonight had any doubt that presently Amerlieclose would honour the company with his latest poem on that hero.

After the homely news had been exchanged, and Claverhouse had heard about the amount of spun wool sent to the village wabster, of the coming of the tailor and his 'prentices from Dundee to make up a new suit of homespun for David, of the necessity to forego so many firlots of the oats and barley which made up two-thirds of the Grahame rents, because the season had been so harsh that not even the grey oats could be sown till May, the talk turned upon public matters, and inevitably upon the outrage which had horrified Scotland at the beginning of the month. Nine of the most notorious Covenanters had waylaid the coach of old Archbishop Sharp as he was returning home to St Andrews, had dragged him out of the vehicle, shot him at such close range that the burning wadding had set fire to the gown of his daughter, his only companion, beaten him to the ground, battered out his brains, wounded his daughter and robbed both the dead body and the coachman before fleeing from the scene of their crime.

"The murder was deliberate and very carefully planned," said Claverhouse grimly. "They had made a previous attempt eleven years since, when one of these same villains, Mitchell, misfired and shot the Bishop of Orkney in the wrist, whereof his lordship has since died. On this present occasion they designed to do it at St Andrews, but getting word of the Archbishop's coach being to cross Magus Muir with but two outriders, they took advantage of his lonely state like the cowards they are. We have discovered that twenty-seven of the rogues were agreed upon the murder, and for weeks by-past have been 'seeking the Lord's mind' upon it, as they blasphemously boast. The old gentleman had sixteen wounds in back, head, and face, three in the left hand, and a bullet in the breast. Nor is there any repentance for the deed; there are reports that the villains are glorying in it, asserting that when they saw his blood run, they wished that all the blood of the Uncovenanted was in his veins – if I could but discover where they are lurking, the beastly murderers!"

His passion had a personal note, for when he had been at St Andrews at his studies, the old Archbishop had been very kind to him.

"And you can't get upon the scent of them?" asked Auldbar, taking a sup from the communal ale-bowl and passing it on to Amerlieclose.

"I've quartered every moss and muir in Galloway," replied Claverhouse bitterly, "and though I cannot find them I have a strong suspicion they are there, and enjoying the protection of the Dalrymples. When I have a little leisure, I intend to teach Sir James and Sir John a lesson they will have cause to remember, but while I see signs of a rebellion in force brewing up in the south-west, I cannot attend to such things."

He waved aside the bowl which Amerlieclose was offering him. His face was flushed, and his large eyes very troubled.

"I spoke to you a while syne of desiring some leave, Anna. I must have been daft. There can be no leave for me or any soldier in Scotland just now. My Lord Linlithgow is pleased to term me an alarmist when I warn him of armed revolt, but I am the man on the spot and see more than he does. The Covenanters are blown up with their success in firing at a few troopers through a window and then running away, with rescuing prisoners and murdering lone sentries; if they muster in force, as I am sure they do intend, they could wipe out our few and scattered troops. The whole Scots Army, including those in garrison, is not two thousand men. As for the Privy Council, they are all too busy endeavouring to bring down the Duke of Lauderdale to attend to the weal of the realm, and I believe that some even would welcome a rebellion so it would compass his fall."

Then, noticing the solemn faces about him, he roused himself and said with a smile: "But this is ill talk for a family gathering. Amerlieclose, you're big with a poem, I can see it. Let us have some of that fine Latin of yours to take the taste of the Covenant out of our mouths."

Nothing loth, the young man jumped to his feet and began to recite his latest masterpiece; its text was the answer of Montrose to his death sentence, with its dreadful accompaniments of quartering and the distribution of head and limbs as public spectacles; 'Lest my loyalty be forgotten, ye have appointed five of the most eminent towns in Scotland to bear witness of it to posterity.' Listening to the elegant Latin, Claverhouse remembered his boyhood when he had seen, nailed above the South Port of Dundee, the right arm of Montrose; to the imaginative, romantic child it had seemed to have some message for him, to be beckoning him to some special service, though he did not know what that could be.

He had been born when the Royalist cause was at its nadir; he was an infant in arms when Charles I had met the headsman's axe, a toddler when Montrose had been jolted through the Edinburgh Streets, with the eyes of Covenanting nobles feasting on the degradation of the enemy who had routed them so many times in battle, to the thirty-foot high gallows and the weeping hangman. From then until Claverhouse was twelve, there had been nothing but poverty, oppression, and bitterness. Scotland lay under the iron heel of Cromwell, worse even than the Kirk because it was alien; no one except the English conquerors and unpatriotic Scots had any money; many old families had been forced to sell their estates. Everywhere there were tales of cruelty, injustice, and rapine, breeding hate or disillusionment. The noble idealism which had actuated men like Charles I and Montrose seemed to have died with them; the war which had begun as a crusade on both sides had degenerated into a sordid squabble, with the defeated nursing hopes of revenge and the victors growing ever more insolent with power.

All through those bitter years, the boy Claverhouse had sought refuge with the ancient poets and historians beloved of Montrose, especially Lucan, the hero's favourite. And he had listened with rapt attention to all the stories of the hero himself, told by those who had fought at his side; from his maternal grandfather, the Earl of Northesk, he had heard the details of that astonishing series of victories in the Highlands, from Tippermuir in September, 1644, to the last glory of Kilsyth in the summer of the following year. As he grew older, and especially when he himself decided to be a soldier, he had studied that campaign more objectively, and had admired afresh from this new angle the lightning movements, the capacity to adapt the material available, the moral courage which had made Montrose content to stand for his King when all the other nobles had deserted him, and the spirit which had shamed the hardiest of his soldiers as he had marched so cheerfully beside them through the waste of mountains in a Highland winter.

This favourite study had done something else for the youthful Claverhouse; it had brought home to him very sharply what the Covenant meant. Its God was Jehovah, wrathful, savage; its followers were His Chosen, immune from any man-made law, claiming an infallibility greater than the Pope's, believing themselves instruments of the Divine vengeance. At Tippermuir they had fought under a banner inscribed with the motto *Jesus and No Quarter;* after Montrose's defeat at Philiphaugh they had butchered in cold blood one hundred Irish prisoners, and had flung over the bridge at Linlithgow eighty camp-followers, women and children, the soldiers thrusting back with their pikes those who tried to crawl out of the water. At the execution of the officers, the Rev. David Dickson had stood beneath the scaffold, rubbing his hands in holy glee and uttering words which had passed into a proverb: 'The wark gangs bonnily on!'

And it was this same savage thing which had arisen again in the south-west, and which only this month had slaughtered a defenceless old priest on a lonely moorland. It was this enemy with which Claverhouse had to deal, and which the great ones of Scotland either treated as negligible or fostered underground as the means of bringing down some political rival. It was this enemy, combined with the lack of an army and of those small garrisons for which he had been pestering ever since he had received his commission, which caused his present keen anxiety of mind. There was a rebellion of savages coming, and only himself seemed to see it.

His obsession with the peril was so great that he had to make an effort to congratulate Amerlieclose when at last that young poet completed his latest epic on a hero who had been so notable a victim of Covenanting malice.

(iv)

He lay that night with the curtains of his bed drawn back, as he always did at Glen, so that he could see the moonlight or the firelight illumining those prized possessions, his family portraits. The majority of them could scarcely be called likenesses, for George Jameson, 'the Scottish Vandyke', had painted them as best he could from traditions and research into archives, yet several among them, Sir John de Grahame, the friend and brother-in-arms of Wallace, and Sir David de Grahame, one of the hostages for the ransom of King David II, were brilliant specimens of the painter's art. Best of all was the portrait for which Jameson had had a living subject, the Lady Magdalene Carnegie, Claverhouse's mother.

His father dying when he was so young, she had been the chief influence of his childhood, and lying here in the bed in which she had died three years ago, he thought gently and gratefully of the mother who had brought him up. It was not until after her death that he had realised what a struggle she had had in the difficult times of his childhood, trying to manage on a jointure which in any case needed a strict economy, continually suffering domiciliary visits of the English soldiers, forced to forego a part of her rents every year because her tenants had not the wherewithal to feed their families, compelled to sell what little plate she had left over from that which her husband had sold to pay his fines, so that she might educate her sons and provide her daughters with marriage tochers.

Yet with it all she had given her children a happy youth. She possessed a trait that she had handed on to her elder son, that of thinking for herself, and while observing the orthodox doctrines of the Kirk, she would have none of that disputatiousness which too often took the place of worship among her fellow-countrymen. The word most often on her lips was 'duty', but while she did not seek to hide from her children the demands and the sacrifice it entailed, she impressed upon them also its comfort.

"In particular are womenkind blessed in this," she would say, "for being so much a prey to their emotions, they would be altogether lost when death or sorrow enters their homes had they not children to rear and wool to spin."

It was after Anna's little tragedy that she had said this; duty had forced her to break Anna's heart, but duty she believed would heal it. Her realism and quiet acceptance of facts had given her children a balance against the softening influence of the old nurse to whom they were devoted; and as he grew to manhood, her elder son had realised that her loyalty to the defeated cause of the King during the Commonwealth had been all the more impressive because so unromantic. She was the subject of the exiled young King over the seas, whom she had never seen and of whose moral character she could not approve; and as a matter of course she paid her fine and endured military invasions of her home and did without the graciousness of life, because to have submitted to a usurper would have been a dereliction of duty. The demands this integrity made upon her had worn her out, yet she had remained to the end extraordinarily serene, and had made a friend of death. She had spoken of it on the last occasion when her elder son had seen her alive, on the eve of his going to Flanders to become a soldier; and although neither of them had known then that they would not meet again, what she had said had remained vivid in her son's mind ever since.

"Of only one thing in life can we be certain, John, and that is that we shall die. To many, death is the worst of ills, but the wise see it as the ultimate comfort, the order of release which shall free us from the night with its feverish dreams and bring us into the daytime of Eternity. That last day, says Cicero, does not bring extinction to us, but change of place, and if we live in this world worthily, we ken what place that will be. Each night ere you sleep, place yourself as you would wish to be in your last moments, and in those thoughts and aspirations, so order your days."

He had obeyed her injunction and had found in it much simple comfort and help. It had given him peaceful sleep after a forty-mile ride over the moors of Galloway, after the endless correspondence and the dreary malice of the Covenant, it had kept him from the callousness of the professional soldier, and had blessed him with a sense of proportion. Because he was a soldier, he hoped that death would come to him upon the field of battle, though in his romantic boyhood he had cherished the hope that he, like his family hero, would have the honour of dying on the scaffold for his rightful King.

He smiled to himself now, on the edge of sleep. A second Montrose: that was how he had seen himself in his boyhood dreams. But there would be no need, thank God, for a second Montrose; the Monarchy was restored, the three kingdoms sick of civil war; and the most likely form of death awaiting John Grahame of Claverhouse was a shot in the back from some lurking Covenanter.

Chapter Four

(i)

He rode through the lonely countryside of Lanarkshire at the head of his full troop of sixty men and the greater part of a company of dragoons.

Three days previously there had been an incident of ugly significance, especially ugly since it had followed so closely on the murder of Archbishop Sharp. On May 29th, the anniversary of the Restoration, two noted Covenanters, Robert Hamilton and Thomas Douglas, had made a demonstration at Rutherglen, extinguishing the bonfire lit in honour of the occasion, tearing down the festive oak-boughs, publicly burning four Acts of Parliament, and affixing to the mercat-cross a paper which amounted to a declaration of war. It asserted that the celebrating of the King's Restoration was 'an intruding upon the Lord's Prerogative, giving the glory to the creature that is due to our Lord Redeemer, and setting up a usurping power to the destroying of the interest of Christ in the land.' Hamilton and Douglas had then declared to the people of Rutherglen that they owed no obedience to an Uncovenanted King, and threatened them that if they did not rise up against this Anti-Christ, the Lord would smite them even as Saul had been smitten for sparing the Amalekites.

On the reception of this disquieting news, the Commander-in-Chief had sent an express to Claverhouse, bidding him go upon the trail of the ringleaders; he had failed to catch either Hamilton or Douglas, but he had captured fifteen of their associates, including the Rev. John King, once chaplain to Lord Cardross and dismissed by him for seducing a maid-servant, and these prisoners he was now escorting to Glasgow, sixteen miles distant, where was quartered Lord Ross and his troop of horse. But since he had one hundred and twenty men at his back, Claverhouse was approaching Glasgow by a roundabout route, hoping that he might have the luck to surprise an armed conventicle. He was more than ever convinced that the Covenanters were on the eve of a rebellion in force, and that the capture of the ringleaders alone could prevent it.

It was a disciplined and smart little body of men who clattered along behind him. His cornet rode with the colours unfurled, surrounded by four trumpeters and a kettle-drummer. The well-polished gorgets and steel caps of the troopers twinkled in the fitful sunlight, and their scarlet coats and cloaks made a bright patch of colour against the drab moorland. Claverhouse was intensely proud of the fact that all his troop was clothed alike, though he had been obliged to meet part of the expense himself, for the sum allowed by the Government was only nominal. But unlike his fellow captains, he could not have endured to have his men clothed in any sort of thing he could come by cheaply, or in the uninforms of some disbanded regiment. Careful though he was with money in his personal affairs, he was generous to the point of extravagance when it came to anything concerning the King's service. But even more proud was he of the knowledge that every man among the sixty was devoted to him, and had learned the strict discipline he had been at such pains to teach them.

Of the dragoons he was not so sure. There was a company of these 'mounted infantry' attached to each of the three independent troops of horse, the captain of the troop being superior to his opposite number in the dragoons; but Claverhouse did not know each man of them personally as he did his troopers. The company quartered in Dumfries Castle several times had caused trouble, for their captain, Inglish, was a man who relished the honour of a commission but not its responsibilities, and more often than not was absent on his own affairs. Only this month his men had been guilty of an act which had brought down upon them Claverhouse's wrath; one of them had shot off his firelock through a window, killing a horse belonging to a poor townsman of Dumfries. Captain Grahame had dealt with the matter promptly and firmly; it was just the kind of thing which was calculated to arouse his wrath. He had paid the owner of the horse compensation out of his own pocket, had clapped the offending dragoon into ward until he could be brought up before a Council of War, and had read his comrades such a lecture on the subject of military discipline that there had been many reddened faces and downcast eyes before he had done with them.

But even when he was angry, Claverhouse had a way with him, and though he would not like to answer for the discipline of the dragoons who now rode behind him on their inferior horses, he was sure of their affection. They were under the immediate command of Lieutenant Stewart, and looked workmanlike enough with their 'dragons' slung over their shoulders, their bandoliers rattling to the horses' movements, and the primitive bayonets which could be screwed into a musket-barrel after a discharge, stuck in their belts. Claverhouse was thinking about these bayonets as he rode along this morning; absorbed in his profession, he spent much time in pondering on possible improvements in weapons of war, and for long it had seemed to him that the present form of bayonet was clumsy in the extreme. Surely it ought to be possible to fix it permanently to the muzzle without having to waste time screwing it in after a discharge?

He brought his sorrel mare to a walk as it began to climb the steep little hill of Drumclog. Leaning forward to pat the sleek neck, he thought that if in the open stretch of moorland over the brae he saw no sign of a conventicle, he would ride straight on to Glasgow; after all, fifteen prisoners was a fair bag, and he was somewhat tired of the continual stream of prophecy with which the Rev. John King was beguiling his ride to prison.

"There is a cloud gathering and a storm coming," the Rev. King bawled above the jingle of steel and the clatter of hooves. "This land shall be turned upside down, and Christ's bride shall be glad of a hole to hide her head in, and the Dragon may so prevail as to chase the woman and her man-child oversea; but there shall be a gleaning, two or three berries left in the top of the olive-tree, of whom the Lord shall say, Destroy them not, for there is a blessing in them. Thereafter there shall be a fair sun-blink on Christ's old spouse, and she shall sing as in the days of her youth. Hear ye, O Israel; ye owe no obedience to the Man of Sin who is called Charles Stuart; all the ceremonies that lie in Anti-Christ's foul womb, the wares of that great mother of fornications, the Kirk of Rome, are his trappings. Sew no clouts upon Christ's robe; take Him in His rags and losses."

"Och, stow yer gab!" cried one of the dragoons, wearied of this eloquence.

Nay," retorted the prophet,"I will fash Christ (if I may speak so, I will importune Him; I will be often at his gate; I will give His door no rest; I will – "

Claverhouse did not hear what else the Rev. King intended to do in the way of pestering his Redeemer. Breasting the hill of Drumclog, he had come in sight of that which drove the Rev. King and possible improvements of the bayonet clean out of his mind. Not a quarter of a mile northwards of him, drawn up in battle-array, horse and foot, were fifteen hundred armed men. In the first shock of that moment, he found himself staring at the banner displayed at their head, and as the wind blew out its folds he could read what was inscribed there in huge, blood red letters:

No quarter to ye active enemies of ye Covenant.

(ii)

A voice inside his mind spoke, very distinctly, two sentences. It is the beginning of the rebellion you have foretold. You have never commanded in battle. Then he was galloping back along his ranks, shouting crisp orders.

"Corporal, see that the prisoners are taken under a strong guard to the farmhouse yonder. Trooper Andrews, you have the fleetest horse; away with you to Glasgow and inform my Lord Ross that I must have all the reinforcements he can spare. Trumpeter Wilson, take a man with you with his napkin tied upon his sword-hilt and go forward to the enemy, offering them the King's pardon if they will lay down their arms. Lieutenant Stewart, send a party of your dragoons to scout round the enemy's flanks and discover how they are armed and the nature of the ground."

Having issued these commands and seen them executed, he cantered back to the head of his men and began steadily to view the foe through his perspective-glass, driving down the fury in his heart; for months he had warned his superiors of this, and had been called an alarmist for his pains. And, always just, he admitted to himself that he had been rash today; he had considered one hundred and twenty soldiers sufficient for the dispersal of any conventicle. But it was no conventicle which was drawn up there; it was a small army, outnumbering his own by something like twelve to one, disciplined men on the one side, but frenzied beasts upon the other. Riding from rank to rank, were ministers, bellowing blood-thirsty exhortations:

"Arise like Phineas and execute judgement! Fall upon the House of Jeroboam with the sword! Our Jesus has set up His Father's standard, and who shall take it down? Blood shall be your sign, and no quarter your word, and the beasts of the field shall make a banquet of the sons of Anti-Christ!"

The soldier in him knew that he ought not to risk a fight against such odds, but he had no alternative. To retreat was to be overtaken and cut to pieces. All the stories of Covenanting cruelty jostled hideously in his mind; there would be no quarter given to prisoners, no mercy to the defeated. He recognised the man commanding the two squadrons of horse as Rackston of Rathilet, one of the murderers of Archbishop Sharp; he saw, swaggering at the head of the foot, Robert Hamilton, he who had burned four Acts of Parliament and urged the people to rebel. Then his mobile mouth set, and his hand tightened on his sword-hilt.

"They want a fight," he muttered, "and by heavens they shall have it." And then to one of the dragoons who came galloping back from a survey of the ground: "What's the position?"

"They are all armed, sir, though some have only pitchforks and cleekies and they've chosen their ground with care, for there's a bog between us and them. We canna attack, but aiblins we could skirmish – "

"What's their answer, Watson?" Claverhouse interrupted, as his trumpeter returned.

"I'm fair shamed to give it you, sir," panted the man. "They say they will lay down their arms if you will do so first. The insolent blasties!"

Claverhouse said nothing, only thrusting out his lower lip. Then he called up his officers, and gave them their orders, cool and unemotional.

"Here is the situation. It is obvious that we cannot retreat, and we cannot attack because of the bog. They, on the other hand, will ken the firm patches of ground across it. There is but one thing we can do, and that is to keep our stand here, where they must charge us uphill. It is possible that they will be divided in their counsels as usual and therefore will delay to attack, in which case our reinforcements may arrive in time. But if they attack at once, we must fight to the last man. I want that understood. Bring the troopers to close-order; place the dragoons on the wings; bid each man hold his fire until the enemy is come to ten paces from us; then, when they have discharged their pieces and are come to shock, let them fall on sturdily with sword and bayonet. The word is 'King Charles and Kirk of Scotland'. Good luck to you all."

Scarcely had he heard these orders shouted down the ranks behind him than that huge mass of men across the bog began to move. There was a bellow which seemed to shake the earth:

"Death to Babel's brats, lads!"

And then, to the lusty chanting of psalms, with the hideously inscribed banner flourished before them, their eyes red as beasts' with holy hate, the Sanctified charged.

(iii)

Not a shot came from the disciplined ranks behind him as that mass of savages came thundering up the brae. There was scarcely a sound from the King's soldiers; only the trumpeters played loudly round the colours in the traditional manner, and the kettle-drummer beat a quick, blood-stirring tattoo. Shoulder to shoulder, grim and calm, utterly confident in their leader, Captain Grahame's men waited to win against overwhelming odds or to die at his side.

They gave their one volley. The enemy who received it was exactly ten paces distant, no more and no less, when the 'trickers' were depressed and the balls let fly. The extraordinary discipline of this little troop, no less than the accuracy of their aim, seemed somewhat to daunt the Covenanters; as dead and wounded fell among them, some were inclined to draw back, becoming mere human beings instead of the Elect who had nothing to do but go in and kill. But the wild charge of so many carried the reluctant along, and as the overwhelming weight fell upon the ranks of scarlet uniforms, mowing them down, the rest took courage, and jostled to get at the figure on a beautiful sorrel mare at the head of the troop. The prongs of a pitchfork were within a few yards of his breast, when the sorrel reared; the pitchfork, missing the rider, plunged into the horse's belly; with a scream the animal bolted, resisting the well-known hand and voice, carving its way through the mass, its guts trailing horribly, a path of blood behind it, foam flying from its lips.

It had carried him half a mile before he could control it. His own will threatened to bolt like his poor sorrel as he was carted thus, helpless, away from the fight. Loss of blood at last brought the animal to a halt, shivering, its knees buckling, sweat pouring down the glossy flanks. He had his pistol cocked, was out of the saddle, and had put an end to the mare's suffering before she had time to fall. Then he was running like a madman, impeded by his boots, had seized the bridle of a riderless horse, and was galloping breakneck to the scene of action.

It was a scene of disaster. He had not known till then what power his presence had over his men. He was an unknown quantity as a commander in battle, to them no less than to himself, yet when he had left them just now they had been standing like heroes, prepared to fight to the last man. Seeing him carried off the field, they had gone to pieces; discipline was forgotten, and in all directions scarlet-clad figures were fleeing; the trumpets were silent, the cornet was dead, and the colours, the precious colours, were flourished in the hands of an exultant Covenanter. Claverhouse galloped straight upon this man, crashed his pistol-butt upon his head, snatched the tattered standard, and, waving it above his head, he yelled at the top of his voice:

"Trumpeters, to the colours! Officers, get your men into rank again! Close-order all and a disciplined retreat!"

At the sound of the well-known voice those flying figures drew together, shame-faced, soldiers once more, trotting in a body before their commander and turning in saddle to fire at the victorious foe. That foe was not pursuing, and Claverhouse, his eyes bitter, a dribble of blood running down his chin, was only too well aware of the reason. Sacrifices of thanksgiving were being offered to a Covenanting God; he heard the screech of the wounded being slaughtered in cold blood, the shots which told of prisoners butchered on the spot, the savage shouts of those who were pillaging and mutilating the dead. And in his ears still rang the mocking voice of the Rev. John King, late a prisoner:

"Hey, Clavers! Will you no' stay for the afternoon's preaching?"

(iv)

Still in his blood-stained uniform and dusty boots, he sat in a Glasgow lodging that night, writing an account of the rout at Drumclog to his Commander-in-Chief. From outside came the noise of men hastily setting up barricades in the streets, the tocsin clanging an alarm, and the voice of Lord Ross frantically issuing orders. But in the little room there was no sound save the dogged scratching of a quill.

He wrote as he always did, objective, unemotional. He had lost ten troopers and thirty dragoons, besides wounded. What the rogues would do next he could not tell, but the country was flocking to them from all sides, and almost certainly they would attempt to enter Glasgow. Lying open on all sides to the fields as it did, it would be almost impossible to defend, but my Lord Ross and he would hold it somehow until further orders. This might be counted the beginning of rebellion, in his opinion. He read the letter over, and added an apology in a postscript:

'My lord, I am so wearied, and so sleepy, that I have written this very confusedly.'

As he sealed the letter with his signet-ring, a momentary bitter amusement was like a taste in his mouth. His badge, the laurel wreath, 'the tree of victory'. Today had witnessed his first command in pitched battle, his first engagement in Scotland, and his most ignominious defeat. But as, having given the letter to a trooper with orders at all costs to get it to my Lord Linlithgow, he sank his weary head down upon his arms on the table, he was not thinking of his own humiliation. He was thinking of the victims of Covenanting hate who lay cold and mutilated on the moor of Drumclog, of the men he had known and trained and loved, and of a sorrel mare which had saved his life at the expense of her own.

Chapter Five

(i)

"My Lord Linlithgow and Captain Grahame, your Majesty", announced Mr Chiffinch, Page of the Back Stairs, as he ushered the two gentlemen into the Closet of King Charles at Whitehall.

The first thing Claverhouse noticed was the enormous number of clocks. Of all shapes and sizes, plain or ornate, they stood on brackets round the walls, busily or ponderously ticking the seconds away in a little orchestra of sound. In front of one of them stood the tall figure of the King, comparing with it his large jewelled watch which he held in his hand. On the entrance of the visitors the voices of the clocks were joined by a shrill yapping from a basket of spaniels near the empty hearth; there was a whiff of perfume in the room, hinting of recent feminine presence; the masterpieces of Raphael, Titian, and Holbein hung between the clocks, with a couple of magnificent Vandykes, the Martyr King above the fireplace, the cold face of his great-nephew, William of Orange, facing him; through the glass doors of cabinets with historical bas-reliefs could be glimpsed crystal vases, velvet-bound books with clasps of gold, and other treasures. The casements were open, admitting a blaze of hot July sunshine and the sound of oars and gulls from the river.

"My Scottish visitors!" exclaimed King Charles, turning with a smile and giving each in turn his capable brown hand to be kissed. "Friends from my fatherland."

Rising from his knees in response to the signal, Claverhouse did not miss the irony beneath the pleasant greeting. King Charles, he had been told, had never forgiven Scotland for the humiliations heaped upon him when the general Assembly of the Kirk had invited him over from exile to become a rallying-point for its army in its quarrel with Cromwell. Motioning his visitors to be seated, the king settled himself in his elbow-chair before the table, an untidy table littered with papers, mathematical instruments, a scatter of quills, a dish of sweetmeats, and a huge book of maps, and began a courteous enquiry as to how my Lord Linlithgow and Captain Grahame were enjoying their visit to London. It was all done with that extraordinary ease and good humour for which his Majesty was famous, he whose ambition in life it was to be easy himself and to make others so.

But Claverhouse observed, during this small-talk, that behind his smiling exterior, King Charles was far from easy at present. The sunlight mercilessly exposed the deep lines on that attractively ugly face, and the network of wrinkles surrounding the large black eyes, the abiding melancholy of which was at such variance with his smile. The large brown hands which lay upon the carved bosses of his chair had the nails bitten to the quick, and one thumb was bandaged as though it had festered. King Charles was riding the storm of this Popish Plot madness which was being used by Shaftesbury and his faction to promote revolution, but it was wearing him out.

"And now, my lord," said the King presently, "to that tedious thing called business. You have an account to give me of the late rebellion in Scotland, and the best thing about it is that we may term it 'late'. For that I have to thank your lordship and the officers and men under your command, not forgetting Captain Grahame here, who presently shall give me the benefit of his personal experience in dealing with the disaffected areas."

As Linlithgow embarked upon his story, his subordinate observed him with sympathy, for my lord could not have missed the politely concealed boredom of his audience. He was a man in his early sixties, often sour and snappish from a chronic complaint of the liver, but a thoroughly loyal person and a good regimental officer, as he had proved since his appointment as Colonel of the Foot Guards raised in 1662. From time to time since that year, he had acted as Commander-in-Chief of the tiny Scots Army, being superseded in this post last month by the Duke of Monmouth, the King's favourite bastard. He had been only too glad to hand over the command, for in such an emergency he was inadequate and knew it; he had no experience of warfare, disliked responsibility, was inclined to panic in a crisis, and desired nothing but to continue to command his beloved Foot Guards of whom he was so proud.

Here he sat now, recounting the story of the late rebellion, tedious and verbose, telling his Majesty a great deal his Majesty knew already, but unable to relate the story except in his own way. Briefly, it was this:

The Covenanters, eight thousand strong, had entered Glasgow on June 6th, Ross and Claverhouse having been ordered to make them a present of it, and for ten days had occupied themselves very happily with despoiling the cathedral and the churches, digging up the bodies of two children of the Bishop and running their swords through them, and quarrelling among themselves upon minute points of doctrine. Meanwhile orders of the Privy Council had called out the Militia and the loyal gentry, and in response to an urgent appeal for help, his Majesty had sent the English Foot Guards north by sea, ordered several bodies of horse quartered in the northern counties to hasten over the Border, and dispatched the Duke of Monmouth with four companies of dragoons and a temporary commission as Commander-in-Chief post haste from London.

On the 16th, the rebels had evacuated Glasgow, and, still arguing, had advanced south-east through Rutherglen; five days later the two forces had come face to face with one another across Bothwell bridge which spanned the Clyde. In the very sharp engagement which followed, the Covenanters had been put to flight, though their losses were comparatively small, and unfortunately, said Linlithgow (a trace of embarrassment in his tone), their leaders, including the murderers of Archbishop Sharp and those responsible for the Rutherglen declaration of war, had escaped. My lord was honest enough to admit that it had been no easy victory, adding with pride that it was chiefly the superior discipline of the Royalist troops which had won the day. The Duke of Monmouth, after receiving the thanks of the Council, had resigned his office of Commander-in-Chief to old General Dalyell; and here was my lord, plain Colonel of the Foot Guards again, to assure his Majesty that the Covenanting menace was over.

There was a pause. Tossing sweetmeats to the spaniels in their basket, King Charles was cocking a shrewd black eye at the young officer who had sat in respectful silence while this tale was being told.

"You look mighty grave, Captain Grahame," remarked his Majesty. "Is it because you do not agree with my lord here that we are finished with rebellion?"

"My humble opinion is, Sir," replied Claverhouse promptly, "that rebellion is like to break out again while it is encouraged underground by certain great ones, and while the ringleaders remain at large."

The King sighed with irritation.

"What are we to do with these fanatics?" he said. "I've given 'em back their General Assembly; they have the right to worship as they please, so they will be obedient to the civil authority; I have offered them pardon and indemnity for past rebellion if they will promise to live peaceable, and they will not. I cannot be teased with trifling rebellions in Scotland every few years; I have too much upon my hands in England. Come, Caption Grahame, tell me how you would deal with the situation."

"Have I your Majesty's leave to speak plain?" asked Claverhouse, disregarding a warning glance from the somewhat nervous Linlithgow (my lord had experience of that frank tongue).

"By all means," said the King, politely stifling a yawn.

"Then, Sir," began Claverhouse with energy, "my humble advice is this: the maximum penalty for the ringleaders, the maximum of mercy for little bodies. The putting of the laws in execution against great and small, while it is just, yet it renders three desperate where it gains one. Likewise from my experience I have learnt that the common folk are inclined to live peaceable if they are let alone; I have had excellent success, since I was granted a civil commission as sheriff-depute, by calling several parishes together and letting the folk know that your Majesty has no desire to meddle with any man's religion, so he will acknowledge your Majesty's just authority, and the result has been that hundreds have begun to frequent their parish kirks who have not done so for seven years by-past. Yet garrisons are an absolute necessity, because as soon as my back is turned the outed ministers will be tempting folk back to the bad old ways again, and in this they are aided by the women, ever the greatest trouble-makers in the south-west."

"They have been known to cause trouble in other quarters of my kingdom," murmured the King. He held up a sweetmeat before a spaniel which sat begging at his feet.

"Then there are the Heritable Sheriffs, Sir," continued Claverhouse, after smiling politely. "It is intolerable that men should continue to have these huge powers if they abuse them. I would have thorough investigation made into how far these gentry have connived at the late rebellion, and such as are proved to have encouraged it should be deprived of their Heritable Jurisdictions."

"Oh fie!" laughed Charles. "Would you have me play the tyrant?"

"Scotland would prefer an absolute King, Sir, to a multitude of absolute sheriffs," retorted Claverhouse, who thought it no laughing matter. "I would propose likewise the raising of a hundred dragoons more than those we have, for special service in the south-west, your Majesty to maintain the men and the country the horses, and if it please your Majesty I would undertake to raise and drill these dragoons without extra pay. By my computation this scheme would cost no more than seven hundred pounds sterling a year, the which may very easily be found by cutting off some idle pensions, by the three independent troops of horse being reduced from sixty to fifty-seven men, and by the withdrawing of the garrison of the Bass and the post of commanding officer there being discontinued, seeing that he has nothing to guard except solan geese and field preachers. The first will not fly away, and the second would be as secure in Blackness or Dumbarton. Indeed, I am not at all sure that it would not be in your Majesty's interests to sell that rock, for I see not what use it is to your Majesty's service."

Linlithgow was regarding his subordinate in open-mouthed dismay; but the King, one black eyebrow raised, stared at him with amusement.

"I perceive," said Charles, "that you have the interests of my service very much at heart, and likewise that you are a brave young gentleman. For I suppose it has occurred to you that at least part of your scheme, if adopted, would make you somewhat unpopular in certain quarters. The Heritable Sheriffs of Scotland have held their powers for centuries and dote upon them; the guard upon the Bass appear perfectly content with their garrisoning of that horrible lump of rock, so long as they receive their pay; and certain officials whose posts I can guess at would thank neither you nor me for cutting them off as 'idle pensions'."

"The King's service," replied Claverhouse promptly, "should be the first consideration of all your Majesty's subjects, whether civil or military."

Charles laughed shortly.

"A counsel of perfection, Captain Grahame, which has passed unheeded by many of my subjects, both English and Scots, as the past forty years have proved." The voices of the innumerable clocks broke into a chorus, chiming the hour of noon, and at the same moment there was a blare of trumpets from somewhere in that great warren of a palace. The King rose in obvious relief. "It is a pity that his Royal Highness, my brother, is not in England, for he has a keen interest in Scottish affairs, and would have valued your report and your advice, Captain Grahame. For myself, it seems to me that the capture of the ringleaders is the first necessity, and I can only wish you a good hunting of them, especially of the murderers of the good Archbishop."

"It is much to be regretted, Sir," observed Claverhouse, a little sharpness in his tone, "that these rogues were not pursued and brought to justice in their flight from Bothwell Bridge."

Linlithgow gave a little yelp of dismay as he saw the King stiffen. Really this was too much! To have presumed to give such revolutionary and detailed advice as Clavers had done, was, in my lord's opinion, bad enough; to hint at any remissness on the part of the Duke of Monmouth, the King's worthless but most beloved bastard, was to risk disgrace. Linlithgow himself had been uneasy over the commission given to the Duke, who was known to be the tool of Shaftesbury and his faction, and who was only too ready to co-operate in their scheme of ousting the rightful Heir, the Duke of York, from the Succession. If Monmouth had chosen to make common cause with the Covenanters, he might well have floated to power upon the surge of the rebellion, but since he had not done so, the fact that he had permitted the ringleaders to escape (acting, so Linlithgow strongly suspected, upon his own responsibility), should be forgotten. My lord glanced nervously at the King. One large brown hand rhythmically stroked the spaniel tucked under his Majesty's arm; his expression was hidden by the great folds of his peruke.

"Captain Grahame," said Charles, very curt, "would it not be better if you rested satisfied that you obeyed the commands of your Commander-in-Chief upon that occasion, and left the reason for his orders to him and to me?"

"I beg your Majesty's pardon," said Claverhouse, absolutely courteous, but as absolutely firm. "Your Majesty was pleased to say that the capture of the ringleaders was the first necessity, and to wish me a good hunting of them, especially of the murderers of Archbishop Sharp. I did nor know whether your Majesty was aware that after we had won the bridge at Bothwell, we were pursuing the rebel horse, commanded by these same murderers, and numbering sixteen hundred men, who were retreating in good order towards Carrick, when orders came from his Grace of Monmouth to give over the pursuit immediately. The reason for these orders I do not know, and as your

Majesty has been pleased to imply, it is not the business of a plain captain of horse to enquire into them; but this I do know, with submission, that those same ringleaders and murderers could all have been caught and brought to justice, whereas now they must be hunted through the bogs of the south-west where they enjoy the protection of certain of the Heritable Sheriffs."

The door was opened a crack, and the anxious face of Mr Chiffinch was seen in the aperture. Then, as suddenly as it had hardened, the King's face creased in laughter.

"Go away, Will! Go away!" he cried, flapping a merry hand towards the face in the doorway. "I am being treated to a Scots sermon, but from an honest man for a change." And then, as the door closed softly again: "Will Chiffinch is infected with this Popish Plot madness; he is Oates-ised, and fears that every man I receive in privy audience has a consecrated dagger hid beneath his coat and a Jesuit's gown tucked up in his breeches. You're not a very ambitious young gentleman, are you, Captain John Grahame of Claverhouse?" added Charles, one eyebrow raised humorously.

"Yes, Sir, I am," replied Claverhouse simply. "I hope for due promotion for faithful service, and due reward for good work done."

"I doubt you'll get either in this wicked world." remarked Charles. "I admire honesty, but during my life I have observer that it seldom gets its just reward. And now I must detain you no longer from the pleasures of the town, though it runs through the Galleries that you care not for wine, women, or cards, the three principal entertainments we have to offer out visitors. Tell me, are you married?"

"No, Sir," answered Claverhouse. "Yet I hope ere I leave London to have gained the hand of a certain young lady."

"Odsfish!" murmured the King, his eyebrows working furiously, "I hope you do your wooing with more finesse then you have used with me this morning. God keep you, my lord, and you likewise, honest Captain Grahame," and he extended his hand to be kissed.

"I'll tell you what you've done Clavers," burst out my lord, as they descended the private stair. "You've said farewell to all your hopes of promotion, and there's a fine morning's work!"

(ii)

"Now mind what I've told you, Clavers," implored the young Marquis of Montrose, taking his kinsman's arm as they alighted from their hackney before the Blue Boar in the Strand. "In discoursing with my lady you must be full of pretty compliments and gossip of the Court. You must not imagine that plain good manners are enough in London; there is a world of modish talk and behaviour a man must master ere he be accepted in polite society. I would to God you would wear a periwig like the rest of the town," he added, glancing with disapproval at the carefully waved and glossy locks which fell over the scarlet-clad shoulders of his kinsman. "Now have you the speech I taught you pat, to rehearse to my lady when you present these gewgaws which I prevailed upon you to buy at the New Exchange just now?"

Trying hard not to be irritated, Claverhouse murmured that he had. He was sincerely grateful to Montrose for the latter's efforts to help him to the hand of Helen Grahame and the fair lands of Menteith, but he could not believe that all this fuss was necessary. Each time he paid a visit to the Grahame family, he must go loaded with what Montrose described as 'gewgaws', expensive gloves and essences, fans with scenes from this ridiculous sham Popish Plot painted upon them; he was not rich, and he had been bred up to be careful with money. As for learning the mincing walk and affected speech of the beaux, he considered it beneath him, and he was convinced that Helen would despise him if he tried to ape them. He had formed an excellent opinion of the young lady since they met; during their polite exchanges, which were all that the delicate situation allowed him, she had appeared to him sensible, intelligent, and warm-hearted.

Montrose whisked him through the common-room of the inn, firmly ignoring the figure of Sir James Grahame, Helen's father, who, in an advanced state of intoxication as usual, sat slumped in a chair.

"You've put a fearful handicap on yourself, Clavers," the marquis observed peevishly, "by getting into his Majesty's disfavour."

"But I have told you, cousin," protested Claverhouse, not without some heat, "that I am not in his disfavour. I said only what I considered it my duty to say, and his Majesty has greeted me very kindly when I have waited upon him in the Galleries, or have encountered him in the Park – "

"Pooh! so he does all the world", interrupted his kinsman contemptuously, preceding Claverhouse up the stairs. "But it is the common cry of the coffee-houses that you ventured to criticise his darling by-blow, and will remain a plain captain of horse in consequence. Your hat in your hand, Clavers; remember to make your congie to my lady so that your periwig – your hair – just touches the floor, and then to toss it back – like this. And if Captain Rawdon is present, you will understand why; it is to make you jealous, and therefore you must please my lady by being mighty stiff with him."

"But I wanted to talk to him about a greyhound he has for sale," objected Claverhouse. "The price is fantastic, but Rawdon has hinted that he might come down – "

"A greyhound!" Montrose again interrupted, this time in a fierce whisper, since they were just outside my lady's door. "You're here to win an earldom, and you prate about greyhounds!"

He produced a comb from his pocket, and scratched with it upon the door. A female voice bidding him enter, he went in with Claverhouse at his heels, and immediately performed the elaborate bow he had indicated to his kinsman.

Presenting his 'gewgaws,' and making his little speech, Claverhouse observed with some distaste the figure of the lady whom he hoped to make his mother-in-law. She was a little plump creature whose feet were placed upon a high footstool to conceal the fact that they did not reach the floor. A wig of an impossible red framed a fat face with greedy eyes; a foolish little dog snuffed and yapped on a cushion at her side; and on her lap reposed a comfit-box, a quizzing-glass, a fan, a pile of news-sheets, and a silver pomander. Her elbow chair was placed near the window, so that she might have a good view of the Strand and its fashionable throng. Opposite her, upon a couch, sat her daughter Helen, working at a piece of embroidery; and hovering behind the couch was a young gentleman in the uniform of his Majesty's Life Guards.

"Well now, my lady," said Montrose, after Lady Grahame had ended an account of whom she had seen in the Park that morning, what a queer mode this was that the Duchess of Portsmouth was setting for ladies padding their gowns to look eight months gone, and the latest bit of scandal she had heard from an acquaintance concerning the Duke of Monmouth making improper advances to his child sister-in-law, the Duchess of Southampton, "here is one can give your ladyship all the news of the Court, since he is bidden almost daily to wait upon his Majesty in privy audience. Is that not a fact, Clavers?" he added, frowning hard at his kinsman.

"I have had but one privy audience," said Claverhouse, who detested that kind of lie. "And since it concerned the affairs of my district in Scotland, I fear it would make but dull hearing."

"But I am in labour to hear of it," cried my lady spitefully. "For it is the common cry of the town that you read his Majesty quite a lecture, you venturesome young man. Were you not afraid of being put into the Plot by Dr Oates? who scruples not, they say, to accuse of treason any man who has the misfortune to be out of favour, more especially those who enjoy the patronage of the Duke of York. 'Ounds, Captain Grahame, it is a fearful city in which we live at present, and I vow you are wishing yourself back in your peaceful Scotland, playing the country squire."

If she had set out to provoke her daughter's suitor who denied her the scandal she adored and who, for all his uncommon good looks, was a mere laird, she succeeded most admirably. Claverhouse explained, indignation not quite concealed by his courtesy, that Scotland had just suffered a most dangerous rebellion, and that far from 'playing the country squire,' he was a soldier and a sheriff-depute, and that his military and civil duties occupied all his time. He was beginning to enlarge upon these duties, when a spool of embroidery-silk came rolling across the floor to his feet.

It was very neatly done. It sent the gentleman of the Life Guards (who was none other than Captain Rawdon, heir of Lord Conway), springing after it, and it absolutely obliged Captain Grahame to break off his discourse, pick up the silk, and return it to its owner. Having got her suitor to her side, Helen proceeded to keep him there. Ignoring his crestfallen rival, she gestured to the couch, smilingly inviting Claverhouse to sit beside her. Montrose, meanwhile, keeping a firm hand upon Rawdon's sleeve, began to entertain Lady Grahame with some choice piece of scandal.

"You were speaking of your duties in Scotland, Captain Grahame," said Helen. "It must be a most strenuous and dangerous life you lead."

She saw the large dark-grey eyes fire with enthusiasm, and knew that her intuition had not misled her. His voice warming as he talked, Claverhouse embarked upon the story of how he had made Galloway peaceable, and what a triumph it had been for him when it had remained so during the late rebellion. For years before he had been sent thither, he said, it had been almost in a state of war, the kirks quite deserted, the peaceable ministers in terror of their lives, and near every man guilty of resetting. The obstinate rebels he had hunted out of the district, the little men he had punished by some trifling fine which he had made them put into the poor-box; and he had made a habit of giving notice to any parish which he heard was particularly unruly, that he would be present at the Morning Exercise upon the Sabbath, and that after sermon he would call the roll and fine all absentees.

"I am fair astonished, madam," said he enthusiastically, "at the success of such measures. I have found few ambitious for the honour of martyrdom, and since these folk have discovered that the king has no desire to ruin any man, nor I to enrich myself by fines, I am become acceptable enough. And what is most extraordinary is that there are now two or three hundred at the kirk every Sabbath, whereas when first I came into Galloway there were not more than half a dozen, so fearful were honest folk of the malice of the rebels, or else so much in love with the ravings of the field preachers. Not only almost all the men come but likewise the women, and it is these who have been the most obstinate in frequenting the conventicles, and – madam!" cried Claverhouse, breaking off in dismay as he noticed the girl's head downbent and her shoulders shaking, "have I said aught amiss? You're not – you're not weeping, are you, Madam Helen?"

She raised her face, and he saw that indeed her eyes were bright with unshed tears; but they were tears of laughter.

"You must excuse me, Captain Grahame," choked Helen, trying to control herself; "I know I appear ill-mannered, but I cannot help but think that – that maybe the field-preachers have no chance when you are their rival. I'll vow there is a rare decorating of caps and mutches among the sisters of the Covenant when you give notice that you will be at the kirk, such a jostling for a good place where they may see and be seen – Lord! Captain Grahame," cried the now hysterical Helen, stuffing her handkerchief against her mouth, "pray, pray don't look at me like that!"

His expression was, indeed, extremely ludicrous. The idea that the women of Galloway, the Sanctified, the grim handmaids of the Covenant, could have been induced to come to church from such a sinful motive, had never occurred to him, and the suggestion of it mortified him to the heart. He had been so proud of taming Galloway without bloodshed or severity; it had taken so many months of unpleasant routine work; and he had just submitted a long and detailed account of his success to the Privy Council. It would be humiliating in the extreme if their lordships had the same fantastic idea as Madam Helen; he could almost hear their sniggers and their bawdy jokes.

But gradually, as he stared at the girl who was trying so hard to stifle her laughter, he forgot his wounded pride. He had thought her intelligent and sensible, and so she was; also, it seemed, she possessed a keen sense of the ridiculous, and she could laugh with the abandonment and infectiousness of a child. It was so refreshing after the artificiality he had found in the bright, shallow world of London society, that he found himself laughing with her; he glanced across at the group around her mother, and seeing Montrose's eyebrows signalling to him in frantic enquiry, the whole situation became suddenly so ridiculous that he was threatened with Helen's hysteria. He rose and stood with his back to the group, shielding the girl form those prying eyes. It was their own private jest, his and Helen's and he wanted to share it with her; more than that, he was filled with a sudden impulse to abandon the tedious wooing of her mother and the Earl of Menteith, and to tell this natural young lady in a perfectly natural manner that, never mind estates or titles, he wanted to marry her; for he realized that he did.

It was a moment which might have changed the whole course of his life.

But the moment passed; for, shoving it roughly aside, came Fate in the guise of a breathless trooper. Hasty feet on the stair, a perfunctory knock upon the door, and a voice informing Captain Grahame that his Majesty was taken desperately ill; he was lying at death's door; and my Lord Linlithgow commanded Captain Grahame's immediate presence at Windsor Castle.

(iii)

It seemed that on the previous day, returning from a sea-voyage round the coasts, his Majesty had played a long, hot game of tennis and afterwards had walked late by the river. In the morning he was shivering with ague and in a high fever, and the doctors shook their heads. During the ensuing week, Claverhouse had no time even to think of Helen Grahame, much less to call upon her, absorbed as he was in the crisis which confronted two kingdoms. For the Heir Presumptive, the Duke of York, was in exile in Brussels; the bastard Monmouth was very much at hand; and what my Lord Shaftesbury intended to do if the King died now was obvious from the broadsheets issued daily from his lordship's headquarters in the City, seditious and hysterical tracts which warned the people that if they would not demand a Protestant Successor, their City would be fired, a Popish army under the Duke of York would invade, and in the immortal words of their City Chamberlain, they would all rise next morning with their throats cut.

For hours every day during this critical week, Claverhouse stood among the crowd in the ante-room to the Royal Bedchamber at Windsor, listening to the whispered talk around him, watching the faces of Ministers of State, of Judges and Bishops and courtiers, and hearing now and again through the half-open door of the Bedchamber a week voice calling for water. Grief for the man who was his King, for the charming, cynical gentleman who had rebuked him so roundly at Whitehall, mingled with the learning of a lesson he was never to forget: only a handful of the great ones present cared about the effect of this crisis upon their country; the majority were concerned solely for their posts and their estates.

It would seem to him after a while, when things became normal again, a harsh judgment; yet he was to carry it at the back of his mind all his life. And in the light of it he examined his own conscience. He was perfectly aware that if the worst happened, if the King died now and Shaftesbury succeeded in foisting Monmouth on the Throne, his career was ruined, for he was a protege of the Duke of York. What then, was his own reaction to that threat?

Well, the blow to his ambition would be bitter; he did not underrate it. But he knew, without conceit, that his ambition would count for nothing if set in the balance with his loyalty. He had been born with a strong sense of justice; he had been reared by a mother whose watchword was duty, and whose personal integrity she had passed on to her children; when, at Whitehall, he had said that the King's service should be the first consideration of all his Majesty's subjects, he had stated, very simply, his own creed. He took no credit for the fact, but that fact was that he was incapable, literally incapable, of participating in or enduring injustice, of betraying his lawful Sovereign, or of deserting his patron, let the consequences of that incapacity be what they would...

Towards the end of that fateful week, Linlithgow confided to his officers an important piece of news. It seemed that the moderates in the Council, alarmed by Shaftesbury's open treason, had sent a secret, urgent message to the exiled Heir Presumptive, inviting him to hasten over to his brother's side. It was news which affected Claverhouse both as subject and as man; with the rightful Successor on the spot, Shaftesbury must find his treasonable intentions thwarted; and Captain Grahame would have the opportunity at last of meeting the patron who had obtained for him his present commission. It was with the keenest interest, then, that he observed the gentleman who, on a certain morning at the end of the week, came fairly running out of the Bedchamber into the crowded anteroom, his face radiant with joy.

"My lords and gentlemen", cried the Duke of York, "the very best of news! By the blessing of God, his Majesty is so far recovered that he is calling for a dish of partridges for his dinner, and swears that he will go to Newmarket next week and win the Twelve Stone Plate".

Amid the hum of compliments, sincere or formal, which rose from all sides, Claverhouse's shrewd eyes observed his patron.

He saw a tall lean man, whose brisk manner was curiously youthful for his forty-seven years, but whose tightly controlled mouth and lined face made him look older. Fair as his brother was dark, more handsome than Charles but less attractive, he had something of the stiff dignity which had distinguished his father. There was more than a hint of defensiveness, an attitude natural enough, reflected Claverhouse, in one who had been the target of an opposition which had grown fiercer with the passing of time, who had preferred the following of his own conscience to every other consideration, had given up every post and office, even that of Admiral of the Navy, the passion of his life, rather than conceal the fact of his conversion to the Catholic Church, and who, at the command of the brother he had served so faithfully, had consented to go into exile while the bastard Monmouth lorded it in London. The simple virtues of a man who could act so, were writ large on that lined face: honesty, courage, absolute sincerity. It was not until the eyes, glancing round the crowded room, encountered for a moment his own, that Claverhouse observed another characteristic: an utter lack of shrewdness.

He could not tell why, but as he noticed that lack, something seemed to happen to him, as real, as unexpected, and as profound as love at first sight. James, Duke of York, was his future King and his patron, to whom he owed loyalty and gratitude; but the man possessed of those eyes claimed something else: his chivalry.

Chapter Six

(i)

The day was so mild that it might have been spring instead of the end of November, when, in the park surrounding Holyrood House, the great ones of Scotland promenaded behind the newly appointed Lord High Commissioner, the Duke of York. It was not an exercise they relished; like his royal brother, the Duke was accustomed to walk very fast, oblivious of the weather, and at an hour when sensible gentlemen were still abed. But the great ones were automatically jealous of one another, and they were not going to miss a chance of getting the royal ear by being absent at these promenades when their rivals were present.

Immediately behind his Royal Highness came that gross mass of flesh, the Duke of Lauderdale, still the ruling Minister despite all the intrigues against him; he lumbered along, breathing coarse stories into the ear of the intensely embarrassed Chancellor, Rothes, who, afraid for his own place, detested being selected as Lauderdale's companion. A few paces behind came members of the Party, the clique pledged to bring Lauderdale down. They were principally of the Douglas tribe, still the most formidable House in Scotland, headed by the Earl of Queensberry. His lordship was in a little lather of anxiety lest it might rain and spoil the finery he grudged having to wear on these occasions; with one ear cocked to catch what Lauderdale was saying, he was carrying on a conversation with another great Douglas, his brother-in-law, William, Duke of Hamilton, a ruffianly person, always in wine when he was not at his prayers (for he was secretly for the Covenant), mutinous when out of power and insolent when in it, a man who knew but one way of reacting when his will was crossed, to bully, bawl, and bluster.

Two by two, like a school crocodile, the lesser lights of the Party followed their leaders; among them were Sir James and Sir John Dalrymple, Lord Drumlanrig, Queensberry's eldest son, and the Hon. James Douglas, the Earl's brother, by profession an advocate, but at the moment angling for Linlithgow's command of the Foot Guards. The Hon. James fancied himself highly, and yearned to put on the scarlet coat; he was a little cock-sparrow of a man, for ever glancing round to compare his ramrod back and out-thrust chest with the unmilitary bearing of others.

Next walked two men by themselves, metaphorically as well as actually. They were the Drummond brothers, the elder, Earl of Perth, the other (to his chagrin) plain John Drummond of Lundin at present. Accomplished dancers, born story-tellers, possessed of great charm and no fortune, these two gentlemen were the darlings of Edinburgh society, and enlivened with their wit the dull debates of the Council. But on the other hand they were looked at askance because, at any rate for the moment, they neglected to come into the Party on the one hand, or to range themselves openly on the side of Lauderdale on the other.

Bringing up the rear, in all the glory of scarlet and gold lace, came a group of Army officers. There was honest Linlithgow, loathing everything and everybody as his liver always caused him to do at this hour of the morning; there was old Drummond of Cromlix, who could boast (and did to the point of tedium) of having fought for his Majesty at Worcester, twenty-eight years before; there were the Earls of Annandale and Airlie, and Lord Ross; and of course there was 'Old Tom'.

That was the nickname given him by the dragoons he had commanded for so long, though the Covenanters had more uncomplimentary titles for him. His real name was Thomas Dalyell, and he was turned eighty years of age. With the crushing of the late rebellion and the lapsing of the temporary commission given to the Duke of Monmouth during that emergency, Old Tom had achieved a life's ambition; he had become Commander-in-Chief of the Scots Army, and he had insisted on being answerable to none but his Majesty (he was not going to have the Council, a parcel of civilians, interfering in matters military). He was what is called a 'character,' and he took great pride in being so. He wore always the tight-fitting jacket with narrow sleeves which had gone out of fashion in the 'thirties, and since the execution of Charles I he had never shaved his beard. Thick and show-white, it flowed down almost to his waist, though his head, never covered by a periwig, was completely bald. His immensely tall lean figure, thus accoutred, was the delight of the street urchins whenever he visited London; it was the bugbear of the Covenanters, who swore that he was a warlock, that his figure cast no shadow, and that bullets had been seen to hop off his buff-coat.

Actually he was a plain, blunt soldier, bred very hardy from his youth, a formidable disciplinarian, proud as a peacock, and intensely relishing the myths which had grown up around him: that when he was in one of his famous rages, men dropped dead with fright, and that when he had fought in the armies of the Tsar Elexis, he had roasted prisoners alive. With age he had grown more and more testy and childishly difficult, and increasingly was there one sure way of arousing his hostility: not to quail before that fierce manner of his which, as an officer, he had found much more effective than actual punishment.

And there was one young officer in his army who had aroused that hostility to the most bitter degree. Captain John Grahame was always respectful to his General, but he was not in the least afraid of him, and never feigned to be so. More, he presumed to offer advice on matters military. Speechless with rage, Old Tom had listened to him talking about the need for small garrisons in the south-west, actually presuming to advise General Dalyell, nearly fifty years his senior in age and thirty in military service, on a matter which concerned the Army. There had been a scene. Old Tom had exhibited those alarming symptoms of an apoplexy which in a few years time was to carry him off; he had bellowed, spluttered, raged about young puppies teaching old dogs, and had beaten the furniture with his cane. Captain Grahame had listened in a calm and respectful silence, and then had said the same thing all over again, this time with sarcastic politeness. Had it been possible, Old Tom would have seen to it that Captain Grahame was relieved of his commission forthwith. But it was not possible, for, by some means or other, Captain Grahame had been able to insinuate himself into the favour of the Duke of York, who regarded the Scots Army as his particular province; and there was Captain Grahame now, walking alone with the Duke at the head of the procession.

Yes, there he was, reflected Lauderdale and Hamilton and Queensberry and the rest. A mere captain of horse, a laird with a modest estate and only one great connection, always chosen by the Lord High Commissioner, the King's brother, to play golf at Leith, to try out a new horse, or to talk on any matter under the sun. "I must ask Clavers about it," the Duke would say. "He'll be sure to give me the plain facts". They were all having to revise their estimations of Clavers, and they detested it. Captain Grahame the nonentity, who never minded doing the most dangerous work or the most thankless job, had been useful; Captain Grahame the favourite companion of the Heir Presumptive was a very different proposition.

"Womanish beauty and an insinuating manner", murmured Sir John Dalrymple (who had heard all about Clavers' advising his Majesty to enquire into the loyalty of the Heritable Sheriffs). "I wonder what favours he's soliciting from his Royal Highness the day. Och, we'll see him a duke yet", he added spitefully to Queensberry, whose pet ambition was the strawberry-leaves.

(ii)

"Make it legal for the Covenanters to go to a conventicle, sir," cried Claverhouse, utterly oblivious of all these jealous gentlemen, "and the whole point of life will be lost to them. They are born aginners, as we say in Scotland. They do not want liberty to worship how they please; they demand the right to make everyone else accept their own narrow creed. And what of the conforming ministers and people, the majority of the Presbyterians, who have suffered the most severely at the hands of these fanatics? Are these to remain unprotected from the violence of a few? Your Royal Highness had an example of what the Covenant means in what fell out at the Mercat Cross but yesterday. According to your orders, I went thither and offered the two rogues condemned to be hanged a free pardon if they would but say 'God save the king.' They refused to say it. They would not admit that Bothwell Bridge was a rebellion, or that the slaying of Archbishop Sharp was a murder. Instead, they gloried in both deeds, and boasted that the Lord had said to them, 'Well done, good and faithful servants'."

"I wonder you have not a Bedlam here in Scotland in which to confine such silly people," retorted the Duke, his face flushed with feeling. "You may as well hang lunatics. But this I do assure you, Captain Grahame: that if ever I come to the Throne, all men shall have liberty of conscience to worship as they please, the Catholic equally with the Church of England-man, the Covenanter with the Presbyterian. And when that justice is done (and I wonder that you should demur at it, being so in love with justice), you will see men of every creed become good subjects."

It was hopeless, reflected Claverhouse, to argue with the Duke on the fantastic idea of religious toleration in the sense in which he meant it; yet Captain Grahame's exasperation was less than his sympathy. His growing friendship with the Duke had taught him that the agony of following his own conscience at such a cost had burned itself deep into the man's character, and had begotten the dangerous belief that men of all creeds could be as he was, loyal to his King as well as to his Faith. Misrepresented by the great ones who desired his ruin that they might foist a puppet on the Throne and rule in his name, James was determined to see sincerity in every man who embraced an unpopular creed. Those who, like the rebels executed yesterday, persisted in refusing to acknowledge the civil authority, he dismissed as mad, and had cried out that if their blood was shed it would lie heavy on the nation.

It was a blind spot; and yet there was something very likeable in it. And that was precisely what the great ones missed in their estimation of Claverhouse's attachment to the Duke: a simple liking. The protective affection born on that day when first he had seen his patron in the flesh, had grown steadily during the remainder of Claverhouse's stay in England, a stay which had terminated in his coming north in the Duke's train when his Royal Highness was permitted to exchange exile in Flanders for politely disguised banishment in Scotland.

In the free and easy atmosphere of Newmarket, whither Claverhouse had accompanied the Duke after the King's recovery, they had got to know one another very well and from patron and protégé had become fast friends. The young captain of horse had spoken frankly of his ambitions and had met with as frank an encouragement. To James, who had fallen in love with the profession of arms when, during the long years of exile before the Restoration, he had served with distinction under the great Turenne, it was right and proper that this other young soldier should expect promotion as the reward of good service, for he shared with Claverhouse the notion, absurd to their contemporaries, that reward should be earned and not intrigued for.

But Claverhouse's growing affection for the Duke remained essentially disinterested; it was the man he loved much more than he valued the patron. James' honesty, loyalty, and absolute sincerity, were refreshing and endearing; his lack of shrewdness, making him so vulnerable, aroused in his protégé a latent protectiveness, even while it sometimes exasperated him. To James, mankind was divided into vast flocks of sheep and very small herds of goats; most men were honest, a few were complete knaves. The former he was prepared to trust, even if he did not like them; indeed, over-scrupulous and conscientious as he was by nature, the more he personally disliked a man, the more he was prepared to give that man the benefit of the doubt.

This trait in him had disclosed itself very sharply to Claverhouse at Newmarket. The Duke had been speaking of the late rebellion in Scotland, and Claverhouse had mentioned a thing which had both angered and troubled him very keenly in his patrolling of the south-west; the discovery of Dutch arms in the possession of the rebels. His indignation, and his confidence of being able to speak as man to man to the Duke, had betrayed him into a criticism of the Prince of Orange, who, as the ruler of Holland, must be aware of this encouragement given to Scots rebels, even if he was not the prime mover in it. Claverhouse had been quite unprepared for the storm of anger which had broken over his head.

"You will have the goodness to remember, Captain Grahame," James had rapped out, "that his Highness, the Prince of Orange, is my nephew and my son-in-law and you will never again venture to suggest that he is guilty of such base treachery as to encourage His Majesty's rebels."

Well, that was the second occasion on which Claverhouse had got himself a royal rebuke, but it was significantly different from the first. The cynical Charles would hear no criticism of the son he knew to be worthless; the unshrewd James resented criticism of his nephew and son-in-law precisely because he had no personal liking for that young man and therefore must accord him the most scrupulous justice. He did not like him, but he trusted him; Orange was of his own blood and was the husband of his best-loved daughter; he wrote long fulsome letters every week assuring his father-in-law of his duty and affection; it was only natural that James should trust him.

But remembering the cold-eyed, ruthlessly ambitious gentleman who once he had rescued from death and who had offered him two hundred guineas and a broken promise in return, Claverhouse feared that that trust might prove very dangerous, not only to his patron, but to the nation generally

(iii)

He stayed another week in Edinburgh before returning to his duties in the south-west, and mildly enjoyed the gay life which, with the coming of the Duke and Duchess of York, had invaded the town.

There were horse-races on Leith sands, and a daily round of golf with a ball stuffed with feathers and a horn-faced club; to the scandal of the godly there were stage-plays in the Queen's Chocolate House by the Water Gate, with the Court ladies taking part and coming down afterwards to mingle with the audience. There were tea-parties in the Duchess' apartments, with all the ladies flocking to admire the beautiful young Italian Duchess, to smile behind their fans at her step-daughter, the Princess Anne, greedily devouring confectionaries, and to pretend they liked this queer foreign beverage that was all the rage in England. There were levees, balls, banquets, and receptions, with every lodging in Edinburgh packed to capacity with great lords and humble lairds, pawky provosts from Dundee and Aberdeen, and picturesque Highland chiefs. It was on the evening before his return to active service that Claverhouse made the acquaintance of one of these chiefs, and both the meeting itself, and an incident which preceded it, were so strangely dramatic that he never afterwards forgot the occasion.

The Duke was holding a levee in the enormous ballroom of Holyrood House, part of the palace built during the present reign; it was hung with portraits of all the Scottish kings from the half mythical Fergus to the Union of the Crowns, each bearing a strong resemblance to the next, as the contemptuous English were swift to point out, for the portraits had been painted in two years under contract for the Scots Privy Council. Upon chairs of estate beneath canopies, placed on a dais at one end of the long room, there sat the Duke and his young Duchess, receiving the various personages who, after giving their names at the door, were escorted by a Gentleman-in-Waiting on duty to the Lord Chamberlain, who presented them.

Claverhouse was standing near the dais, listening to the Lord Advocate, Sir George Mackenzie, whose younger brother, Colin, had been his fellow student at St Andrews. As usual, Sir George was holding forth in a very earnest and erudite manner, and Claverhouse was listening with interest to this gentleman who, besides being the most brilliant lawyer of his day, was an historian, a moral essayist, and an authority upon heraldry. But to Claverhouse he was much more than a personage; he was the only personage in Edinburgh who had given Captain Grahame a frank and unpatronising friendship, and who had congratulated him sincerely upon the favour accorded him by the Duke of York. Sir George detested the Duke's religion, and did not care very much for the Duke as a man; but he did like Claverhouse, and he was glad that the younger man had found a patron.

Mackenzie's intelligent, humorous face, with its upturned nose and very long upper lip, was flushed with his earnestness tonight, as he impressed upon Captain Grahame the vital importance of all pleas being written in Latin; this, he said, was a universal language, and 'repaired the confusion which had punished the adventurous builders of the Tower of Babel'. Claverhouse was just wondering whether he was sufficiently acquainted with Sir George to ask him whether the tale was true that in his youth he had written something called a novel, a thing he had actually made up in his head, when a sudden flutter among the gay company distracted him. The murmur of talk died, and in the hush a man's voice spoke, a voice which rang out with simple pride, yet without a trace of arrogance.

"It is Mhic Dhomhnuill Dhuibh," proclaimed the voice, "come to offer his homage to your Royal Highnesses."

"Cameron of Lochiel," whispered Mackenzie, flashing an angry glance at the English and Lowland lords who were smiling contemptuously at the Gaelic name. "The greatest gentleman benorth Tay."

Claverhouse observed with interest the figure which came, stately and with immense dignity, up the centre of the room, led by the Gentleman-in-Waiting.

It was the figure of a very tall man who, though old, carried himself like a youth. He had a bold aquiline nose, teeth of a dazzling whiteness, small, quick bright eyes, and over his lips a pair of most magnificent moustachios which curled downwards like the handles of a pair of tongs. These, like the hair which fell to his shoulders, were jet black without a thread of grey. He was dressed in all the picturesque glory of the Highland chief; tight-fitting trews of the Cameron tartan encased his muscular legs from waist to toe where they ended in a pair of buckled shoes; a coat of bright green velvet pleasantly set off the red of his tartan, and his *filleadh mor* or great plaid was rolled about his shoulders, fastened upon one of them with a great silver brooch. He carried in his hand the flat blue bonnet of the Highlands, decorated with a spring of cranberry, his clan badge, and with three eagle's feathers, the insignia of a chief.

Presented by the Lord Chamberlain, Lochiel kneeled, and with a grace and dignity which far surpassed the bearing of the greatest of the Lowland nobles, kissed hands.

"I bring your Royal Highnesses loyal greetings from all my people," said the old man, his English perfect and made particularly charming by a slight stiltedness of phrase. "From all the children of Manus Mac Cairbre who dwell on both sides of Loch Linnhe, between Loch Eil and

Loch Arkaig, and from Loch Leven northwards to Ben Nevis, the king of all the bens of Gaeldom. The blessing of the Trinity be upon you; may you, and your son and your son's son after you, reign long upon the Throne which the Great Being has bestowed upon the House of Stuart."

There was a suppressed snigger from someone in the crowd of courtiers, and James sharply turned his head in that direction. Then, giving Lochiel the signal to rise from his knees, he returned a gracious answer. He spoke of the old man's record of loyalty to the Crown, of his father, the friend and ally of Montrose, of his own revolt against the usurping Cromwell, and of how, through all those bitter years, the Highland warrior had stood for his King, justly boasting that he never led his men save to victory.

"His Majesty has thanked you personally, sir," concluded the Duke, "for your many services on his behalf. And now, as his representative, it is my pleasure to show the world in what honour his Majesty holds Cameron of Lochiel. Pray, sir, give me your sword".

Every eye in that great room was fastened jealously upon the old Chief as, frowning in plain bewilderment, he detached the weapon, an ornamental walking-sword, from his belt, and in its sheath presented it to the Duke. Glancing swiftly about the company, Claverhouse noted resentment on some faces, particularly on those of the Earls of Atholl and Huntly, Highlanders who never visited their native lands unless some political reason dictated it, and who left the management of them to factors. The Duke, meanwhile, was struggling to draw the sword from its scabbard; but all his efforts failing to achieve this, he handed it back to its owner, saying with a smile: "Lochiel's sword never used to be so uneasy to draw when the Crown required its services."

Modest for all his pride, and therefore still un-comprehending, the old man took the sword, wrenched the blade from the sheath, and offered the hilt to his Royal Highness. With a graciousness which did not come so easily to him as to his brother, and therefore was the more impressive, James exclaimed:

"See, my lords and gentlemen, Lochiel's sword gives obedience to no hand but his own!" The candlelight glinted on the blade as it touched the old Chief's shoulder. "Rise up, Sir Ewen Cameron."

In the buzz of talk which broke out as the new knight rose from his knees, Sir George Mackenzie, himself pure Highland in blood, stepped forward to congratulate his fellow Gael, and after a moment or two drew him towards Claverhouse.

"I make Captain Grahame known to you, Lochiel," said he. "I am sure you will welcome any man of his name for the sake of the great Montrose."

The old chief towered over Claverhouse for a few moments without speaking. His keen black eyes had a rather strange expression in them, as, extending his hand, he said solemnly at last:

"I salute Captain Grahame, and he and I will meet again, for so it is decreed. Only he will not then be called Captain Grahame."

As he bowed with courtly grace and turned away, Mackenzie answered his friend's puzzled glance.

"Lochiel is said to have the 'two-sights' as it is termed among his people," he whispered. "He sees that which is to come. It is not a gift men relish, since the prognostics are generally of a gloomy nature, yet for once it seems that Lochiel has been given a happy event to foretell. For what can he have meant by saying that you would not be called Captain Grahame when next you meet, unless it were to foretell your promotion?"

Chapter Seven

(i)

If the Lord Advocate had interpreted Lochiel's strange prophecy aright, it was not immediately fulfilled.

Another two years of quartering the moors in search of the murderers who could so easily have been captured after Bothwell Bridge, of arranging billets, fighting wordy battles with obstructive sheriffs and bailies, writing long and detailed dispatches to his Commander-in-Chief (old Tom Dalyell now, who, if he replied at all, did so in a manner which made clear his dislike of young officers who refused to be awed by him), and Claverhouse was still plain Captain Grahame. And still a bachelor. Lady Grahame had captured the heir of Lord Conway for her daughter, so that painstaking courtship was wasted, and Captain Grahame must look elsewhere for a wife. He was disappointed but not heartbroken, and he was too busy to mope. Moreover, there was one particular piece of work he had to do which was become almost an obsession: he had to deal with Sir John Dalrymple.

For in his conviction that examples must be made of great men who abused their powers, he was resolved that this cunning, dangerous, and brilliant lawyer should be held up as a warning to others. In the summer of 1682, he was ready to come to grips with Sir John and to carry the war into the enemy's Heritable Jurisdiction of Glenluce; he sent notices to the district that, by virtue of the power given him by his civil commission, he was about to come thither to hold a Court for the trial of those guilty of absenting themselves from their parish kirks, attending conventicles, and resetting.

He was very nearly prevented from holding that Court or any other; for a band of assassins, numbering one hundred and twenty Covenanting ruffians, laid an ambush for him near the Billie Inn on the Upper Tweed, and it was only by some accident that he was detained two days in Edinburgh and so missed the appointment with death. Afterwards he wondered whether there was not something rather suspicious in the furious astonishment with which Sir John Dalrymple greeted him in Glenluce. At all events, Sir John lost all control of himself; openly flouting the authority given to Claverhouse by the Council, he absolved his heritors from attending the Court, held one of his own in which, to his fury, his heritors disowned the accusations he had made against Claverhouse in their name, and, quite beside himself with rage, offered Captain Grahame a bribe of one hundred and fifty pounds sterling in return for a promise not to meddle with his Heritable Jurisdictions.

Edinburgh was immediately entertained by a law-suit which cause the greatest possible excitement, and which lasted right through the autumn. The result was a triumph for Claverhouse; he had defeated a very sharp lawyer aided by two of the most eminent advocates in Scotland, and he had heard Sir John sentenced to the payment of a five hundred pound fine and the loss of his Heritable Jurisdictions. The Privy Council before whom the case was heard, gravely complimented Captain Grahame, and with pompous patronage asserted that 'John Grahame has done his duty and has acted faithfully and diligently'. Their lordships received a slight shock when, in this same month of December, the long-delayed promotion came at last, and Captain Grahame became Colonel Grahame overnight.

To emphasise the fact that this was a particular mark of royal favour, a regiment was created specially for him, by the economical method of taking from the Foot Guards and the Earl of Mar's Regiment one hundred men apiece, and nine troopers from each of the three independent troops of horse to make up a fourth troop, and, in order to find the new colonel's pay, discharging General Dalyell's aide-major, marshal, and quartermaster – another black spot marked up against Claverhouse by Old Tom. Further than this, the regiment received an honour unique in the history of the Army; it was named the King's Own Regiment of Horse. It was clothed in red and yellow, the royal colours, and its kettledrummers and trumpeters had the King's cipher embroidered on their coats. To fill Claverhouse's cup of happiness to overflowing, he was allowed to retain the personal command of his original troop, the survivors of the faithful and devoted sixty who had shared with him the months and years of labour which had turned a savage district into a peaceable one.

The first thing he did when he had given the order to the manufacturers for the new uniforms and for the standard with its small canton marking his rank, was to ride home to Glen, that he might share with his family the joy of his rising fortunes. It ought to have been a very proud and happy little holiday, but it was ruined for him by a misunderstanding with his sister Anna, the first which had ever blighted their relationship.

Gathered about the hearth in the chief fireroom of Glen, he was pouring out to the admiring circle the news that he was to go to England in the spring, specially selected by the new Lord Chancellor, the Earl of Aberdeen, and my Lord Queensberry who, since Lauderdale had fallen at last, was become Lord High Treasurer and the ruling spirit in the Council, to give the King an account of the state of the Army and of Scotland generally.

"The reason why they have selected me for this honour," he added dryly, "is because they are pleased to say I have a way with me of obtaining favours for my friends, and am high in favour with the Duke of York who, since the total discredit of the Popish Plot and the defeat of Shaftesbury's faction, has the chief influence at Court."

"But since plain Sir George Gordon is become Lord Chancellor and Earl of Aberdeen, and the Earl of Queensberry is now a marquis," said Anna's husband from his corner, "I see not why they are in need of anyone to solicit favours."

"Why the matter is this," replied his brother-in-law. "You will have heard of the affair of the Scottish Mint, of how my Lord Hatton, Lauderdale's brother, is accused of defrauding it to the tune of seventy-two pounds sterling? Well, now that Lauderdale is brought down, the great ones here have a mind to set his brother alongside him, and they are pressing for an enquiry into his defalcations. If he is found guilty he will be fined in some huge sum, and Aberdeen and Queensberry look to have the chief share in the spoil. The first desires the greater part of the Hatton estates, the second the dukedom left vacant by Lauderdale's disgrace, and they are pleased to entertain the belief that through my friendship with his Royal Highness I may get for them what they desire."

"Ay," murmured David, leaning forward to poke the fire with his boot, "so runs the world. These great ones have never shown you any friendship, brother, while his Royal Highness was under a cloud and you a plain captain of horse."

"I should be of an unforgiving nature if I refused their friendship now it is offered," said Claverhouse rather shortly, "and likewise a fool, for I have a favour of my own to solicit from his Majesty through the Duke's influence. I have never asked one before, but now there is somewhat I desire, and most passionately, from the Hatton business; you mind that in 1668 Hatton was granted the Castle of Dudhope at Dundee, which for generations belonged to our kin, the Scrymgeours, and which passed to the Crown on the death of the first Earl of Dundee without issue. Dudhope is too trifling to tempt the great ones, especially since it carries with it the Constabulary of Dundee which would necessitate the owner of Dudhope making his home there, and it's a bit of a grim old stronghold, in bad repair. But it is just what I want. I cannot have the patience to build and plant, and I must have a house befitting my new honour; ay, and a wife to share it with me," he added, glancing with a smile about the circle. "My Lord Balcarres, who is given the command of the fourth troop of horse, has promised to find me some well-tochered lass from among his connections. And would that not be a bonny thing, for me to be Constable of my native town, and to have a castle but half a mile from our lands of Claverhouse?"

There was an enthusiastic chorus of assent, but his quick ears noted that Anna alone remained silent. Glancing at her in hurt reproach, he saw her head downbent over her spinning, so that he could not make out her expression, but the strong bond of affection between them made it horribly plain to him that for the first time in all their lives she was withdrawn from him in spirit. So he too fell silent, the evening ruined for him as painfully he pondered on what could have upset Anna; and when the gathering broke up at last, he caught her hand.

"A wee crack in the stillroom," he said, "before bedtime, and ere I forget it, the quartermaster of my old troop has the jaundice, so I'll need to take one of your potions for him. The Edinburgh 'pothecaries are like to kill the poor body with their town jollopings."

She did not reply, but she went with him to their old nurse's sanctum and, still without a word, began taking down jars and bottles. He sat by the peat-fire and stare into it; often they had sat in this room together in a companionable silence except for Anna's singing; she sang over every task, a habit she had learned from Moir whose people lightened all their toil with songs. But Anna was not singing this evening, and the silence between brother and sister was not at all companionable. It was she who broke it at last, abruptly.

"My son is mad to enroll as a soldier in your regiment," said she, taking burnt earthworms from a jar and beginning to mix them with a decoction of wormwood.

He gave a small sigh of relief. This must be the cause of Anna's odd withdrawal from him; she did not wish Robin to become a soldier, and she feared that her brother would encourage him. For the next five minutes he endeavoured to convince her that the service was the best and most honourable profession in the world, that there was no likelihood of his regiment being sent overseas, and that Robin should be under his personal care. He was going on to assure her that her son would make her proud of him by rising in his profession, when she interrupted with a remark which jolted his whole spirit.

"That is precisely what I fear," she said, in a low, troubled voice. "That he will rise in his profession, and become changed – like you."

He could only stare at her, cut to the heart.

"When I was listening to your talk belowstairs," went on Anna, her hands trembling so much that she could scarcely continue with her task, "I could not believe it was the Iain I knew." (She had lapsed by habit into the Gaelic which they always spoke in this room, and somehow that most expressive language, with all its tender childhood associations, made yet more painful her words.) "I did not realise until tonight whither ambition may lead a man; I deemed it a laudable thing in you that you were ever ettling for honours and promotion. But when I heard you talk as though you were become one of the vultures who fly to the carcase of a fallen Minister, thinking of nought but to share in the feast – "

"That's bitterly unjust!" He had sprung to his feet, his face flushed with angry hurt. "My Lord Hatton is a rogue who has defrauded the King and the realm; it is right that he should suffer for it, and that loyal men should reap the benefit of the estates and honours lying vacant by his fall. I am not a romantic, Anna; if a soldier under my command deserves to be turned out of his place, then I give that place to another, and I would not respect that other if he said he could not accept the gift because it sprang from the disgrace of a fellow man. Och, what is the use of discoursing such matters with a woman!" he cried, sitting down again before the fire, and thrusting out his lower lip.

"You must forgive me," said Anna quietly, "that I presumed upon our strong affection which has caused me to speak so plain. It is that affection which makes me so troubled for you."

"Well, I shall not accept Robin into my regiment," said her brother, refusing to be moved by the appeal in her voice, "if that will ease you."

He saw her wince at the sarcasm in his tone, a sarcasm he had never used with her before, but she said quietly:

"I do not desire Robin to go a-soldiering, because he is very much akin to you in character, and such a profession is apt, from its very nature, to make men hard and ruthless – "

"Even my enemies," he interrupted bitterly, "have never accused me of those faults. Even Sir John Dalrymple, my worst enemy, brought no charge of harshness, much less of cruelty, against me, when he raked the muckheap of falsehood in his accusations before the Council."

"That is not what I meant," she began, but Claverhouse swept on unheeding.

"You think because I have this new honour that I am become a lickspittle to men like my Lord Queensberry, and that there is not a thought in my head but how to make friends with the great and to get me, by obliging them, ever fresh awards. I have never intrigued for reward, Anna, and I never will, please God, either for myself or other men. I will earn them for myself if I can, and I will ask outright for them for men I believe it is in the King's interest to honour. My Lord Queensberry is petty, jealous, and mean; but likewise is he absolutely loyal and honest, and therefore it is of the first importance that he should be of equal rank with Duke Hamilton, his brother-in-law, who has great influence on the Council and who I strongly suspect to have encouraged the Covenanters and who I know to be a Covenanter at heart. Aberdeen likewise is a staunch servant of the Crown, his father was the proto-martyr of loyalty in the reign of the Covenant, and if he is not encouraged at this time, he may fall an easy victim to the intrigue which strives to set up the Earl of Perth in his place. My Lord Perth is my friend; but of all men in Scotland he is the least suited to become Chancellor."

She made no comment on this speech, but came and sat down on the hearthskin as she had used to do when she was young. In that attitude, and with the candle-light soft upon her face and her fair hair, she looked as he remembered her in her girlhood; and his hurt indignation was overwhelmed by the fact that he and she had come near to quarrelling.

"Anna."

"I ken fine I'm a foolish woman," she said, looking steadily into the peat, "and I've not been able to make plain to you what's in my mind at present. But you've been more than a brother to me; you've been a – a hero, an ideal. When we sat on our creepie-stools here beside this hearthplace, and listened to Moir telling us of the Fiann, of Gaul of the blue shield, of Oscar and all that gallant band, I believed they were born again in you, and that you were destined to become as they were, great noble warriors fighting only because they could not endure injustice or the broken word. I was a foolish romantic lass, and should have outgrown it, but there it is, and indeed I did not mean to hurt you, or to make you believe I deemed you hard and worldly. It is only – och, I cannot say what I mean. But I wish to heaven you would fall in love."

He jerked up his head and stared at her, almost open-mouthed, laughter struggling with his distress.

"What in the world has that to do with anything we have been discoursing?"

"A great deal, I think. I have always prayed that you would never suffer the pangs of love, Iain, but now I am not sure that I was right to pray so. For there is nought worthwhile in this world to be got without pain, and I do not like this talk of well-tochered ladies found for you by your noble friends, and I'm thinking that that good cool head of yours needs to be balanced by a heart which could never be aught but affectionate, yet which must needs grow a little thin and diminished if it is denied its proper food."

He laughed at her, embarrassed, then turned the talk to other matters. But when he left Glen a day or two later, he was painfully aware that somehow he had failed Anna in not being able to live up to her impossible ideal of him, and unreasonable though it was of her to expect it, he was just a little sad.

(ii)

He was six and thirty and still unmarried when, in the April of 1684, he rode over the Abbey Bridge at Paisley and turned up the carriage-way leading to the fine house which William Cochrane, first Earl of Dundonald, had bought from the Hamiltons thirty years ago. He had left his troop in the town, and his only companion was young Lord Ross, the major of his regiment, and the son of his old companion-in-arms. His face, in which the romantic beauty of his youth had matured into an austere handsomeness, was preoccupied, for he was come here on a distasteful and possibly a distressing mission.

Generally his star was in the ascendant. He had got Dudhope, though he had not yet lived in it; he was newly made a Privy Councillor; and he had just received a personal letter from King Charles, thanking him for the good work he had done in Galloway, which had remained quiet during the recent desperate attempt of Shaftesbury to attain the revolution my lord had failed to achieve through so many years, by the Rye House Plot, a conspiracy to assassinate his Majesty and his brother on their way home from Newmarket. The Privy Council, now that he was one of them, treated with a new respect this rising man, who was not only high in the royal favour himself, but had such a way with him in obtaining honours for his friends. (He had got the promise of a dukedom for Queensberry, whereat my lord promptly had set about the ruin of the Chancellor, Aberdeen, using as his ally my Lord Perth, whom he hated, but who wanted the Chancellorship for himself.) In the most flattering terms the Council had besought Colonel Grahame to turn his attention to Ayrshire and to see whether he could not make that notoriously disaffected district as law-abiding as he had made Galloway when he was plain captain of horse.

So here he was, and not very pleased to be here, especially at the Place of Paisley. For first, his companion, Lord Ross, was kin to the Cochranes, the owners of the Place, and secondly, though he himself had no personal acquaintance with Lord Dundonald, he knew him by reputation as a thoroughly honest old gentleman, who had never participated in the treason of his family. If he had been guilty of harbouring some of the Scots traitors pledged to make a rebellion in Scotland synchronise with the Rye House Plot in England, it could only have been out of natural kindliness for friends and kinsfolk in distress, or for fear of his masterful daughter-in-law, Lady Catherine, a rabid Covenanter, who, because Lady Dundonald was old and frail, ruled his household. But the fact remained that one of his sons, Lord Cochrane, Lady Catherine's husband, had ordered a minister to pray at his deathbed for the success of the rebels in the year of Bothwell Bridge, and that another, Sir John Cochrane, had been up to the neck in the Rye House Plot, and had fled to Holland when it misfired. All in all, it was going to be a difficult morning, but he was still faithful to his policy of making examples of the great.

As they rode up the carriage-way, Lord Ross enlarged upon the manner in which Dundonald has improved the property, and how devoted he was to the pursuit of horticulture.

"You should seek his advice in the matter of planting at Dudhope, Clavers," said Ross, who, being of higher social station than his colonel, used considerable freedom with him. "You canna bring a wife home to it in its present bare state, and good grief, if the ladies of London and Embro' dinna capture you soon for one of their marriageable daughters, they're less tenacious than I deemed them. Colonel of a regiment specially made for you, a Privy Councillor, and the owner of a bonny castle – ay, you're a fine match, Clavers, and there's a muckle fluttering in noble dove-cots to put the fetters of wedlock on you, I'm telling you that".

"I believe my Lord Balcarres has at last found one of his connections he thinks might suit," said Claverhouse, without any particular interest.

Ross snorted in contempt.

"Balcarres! There's a fine agent you've picked. A man so absent-minded that it's a jest throughout Scotland that he forgot to go to his own wedding, and in the end of it married his wife with a mourning-ring. Likely he'll forget that the lady he's chosen for you is wed already – "

"My lord happens to be a friend of mine," interrupted Claverhouse shortly. Balcarres had earned his particular loyalty and affection because, as captain of the newly raised fourth troop of horse, he had shown his Colonel not only the respect due to superior rank, but a warm friendliness, whereas the other captains, now Lord William Douglas and young Lord Ross, being of superior social rank resented his authority over them and made no scruple about showing it when occasion served.

Ross said no more; there was something about Clavers when he was annoyed that made him more formidable than Old Tom himself and his famous rages. As they approached the gateway of the Place, with the horse passant of the Cochranes carved in the stonework, Ross broke the silence to murmur uneasily:

"I hope in the Lord we can contrive to avoid an encounter with my Lady Catherine. Och, she's a terrible tongue in her, and the sight of the King's uniform is enough to set it beating like a flail. I was dead scared of her when I was a bairn, with the awesome tales she told me about Hell, which she seems to know at the first-hand, and I'm sorry for her younger bairns, the Lady Jean and poor wee Thomas, though they have their guid-parents to sweeten life. Malcolm," he called to a serving-man who had appeared from the stables at the sound of their approach, "where will we find his lordship just now?"

The man told them that the Earl of Dundonald was in his orchards; and thither, after giving their horses into the care of the man, Ross conducted his Colonel.

"I trust we don't find his lordship in company with some wanted kinsman of his," said Claverhouse grimly. "It's ill arresting a man in the presence of his own folk."

But they found his lordship in the harmless company of his gardener, and absorbed in the pursuit of his favourite hobby, which consisted in the growing of various foreign fruits and flowers. He was a stout, heavy-faced old gentlemen, with small humorous eyes, a crooked nose, and several chins; he was in his woollen nightgown, his bald head protected by a tasselled cap, and his hands earthy from the planting of a very small, very miserable-looking tree, which he was now regarding with childish pride.

"It's a good day which brings you here, William", said he to his kinsman, Ross, "though I'll confess that scarlet coat of yours made my wame cold for the moment. Not that my conscience isn't clear, you understand, but it's just that I'm never sure what my daughter-in-law has been up to".

He paused to look enquiringly at Ross' companion, and on being presented, raised his bushy eyebrows in half humorous dismay.

"You're welcome for your ain sake, Colonel Grahame," said he, "for I ken fine you're an honest gentleman, and my kinsman here has sung your praises very aft. But it's a delicate situation till I hear if you've come as Claverhouse the guest or Colonel Grahame on military duty. William will go bond for my ain loyalty, and you ken fine I owe my title to his present Majesty; but all Scotland kens I've a son overseas with a price on his head".

"It is an unpleasant situation for us both, my lord," said Claverhouse, politely brisk, "but we must e'en make the best of it". He drew a paper from his breast and handed it to Dundonald. "Here is a list of rebels I am ordered to seek in Ayrshire, and I will take your lordship's word for it whether or no you ken their present whereabouts".

The old man fumbled for his spectacles in the pocket of his gown, set them on his nose, slowly read through the list of names, and then, with a relief which could not but be genuine, shook his head.

"I'm willing to swear upon the Book, sir", said he solemnly, as he gave the paper back, "that I've no idea where any of these persons are at present, though I'll admit that some among them are dear friends of mine. Yet because I'm an honest man, I'll tell you blunt, Colonel Grahame, that I would not go bond for my daughter-in-law's being able to swear as much".

"Then I must needs questing here ladyship," said Claverhouse, adding with his charming smile: "But first, pray tell me, my lord, what kind of a tree is that you have been planting. I'm no horticulturist myself, but my brother David is a keen one, and is for ever agleg to hear of the latest novelty in the art".

Dundonald's grave look vanished, and he became the enthusiastic gardener.

"It's my new damson," he said, lovingly fingering the infant tree. "My neighbours tell me I shall never rear it in this cold clime, but I'm just thinking I shall give them the lie. See the bonny fat buds upon it; next year you must visit us again and eat damson-tart." A ponderous great bell, which once had summoned the monks of Paisley Abbey to their prayers, began to ring in the half-ruined tower, summoning the Cochranes of the Place of Paisley to their dinner. "You'll dine with us, gentlemen," said the old gentleman, "I'll take no denial. But first I must show you the bonniest sight in my policies. William here kens it fine, but he'll be no the worse for another blink of it".

Waddling along, supported by his stick, Dundonald led his guests towards a little stone garden-house built upon a knoll, from which eminence could be obtained a view of the whole range of orchards. Here in the North it was still winter, yet amid bare boughs could be seen already a little froth of blossom, and the old Earl described how, when spring came in good earnest, a man could sit here and fancy himself upon some rock surrounded by a sea of pink and white foam, waving and rippling there below him.

"Ay, when the spring comes – " he said; and broke off abruptly.

For, without the slightest warning, soundless on bare feet, there had rushed upon the three gentlemen from round the back of the garden-house a figure which might well have been that of Spring herself. Fair hair loose and floating behind her, fair face flushed with sheer animal joy, hands holding high her skirts in a manner which proclaimed that she deemed herself alone in this little realm of orchards, with the unselfconscious grace of a child, the unconstrained high spirits of puppy, she came racing on her aimless journey straight into Claverhouse's arms.

(iii)

For a period which might equally have been two seconds or two hours, so completely divorced was it from time, the girl stayed there petrified, her sweet breath on his cheek, her heart beating loud and fast against his own. He was absorbed in a queer little memory; when he was boy, his sister Anna had delighted to lie in wait for him in the whin-park at Glen, and when he came riding home on his pony from the burgh school, would spring out at him, giving him a delicious fright. He would feel, as he held her, that it was some wild creature of the woods which had come into his arms, something sweet and strange and soft, which would nestle there for an instant before bounding off again into a world which contained no human cares. But that wild creature was tamed long ago; an odd kind of fear stabbed at him, gone before he could identify it, as this girl who might have been the ghost of the youthful Anna stayed there in his arms, too startled to move, her eyes staring at him in bland dismay.

Then everyone came to their senses. The girl drew back with a sharp exclamation, and became a young lady caught behaving like a gipsy's child. In the background, Ross gave a suppressed chuckle; old Dundonald fondly tut-tutted; Claverhouse pulled off his hat and bowed.

"What for do you look as blate as a sheep, Jeannie?" chided the Earl. "Hech! I dinna ken what the gentlemen will think of you, leaping about like a bairn and whittering into the arms of one of his Majesty's colonels. Come awa now, make your hair decent, and let me present you. Colonel Grahame, this is my guid-daughter, jean Cochrane, and a conversible, well-lettered lass she is, though you would not think so by the way you've seen her behaving this morning."

"I am very sorry, guid-sir," murmured the girl, her sunburnt hands fluttering from disordered gown to wildly tangled hair. "I'd no notion you had guests; it was so bonny a morning, and och, I've been listening for hours to my mother's catechising me on my election and grace, and ech me! there is it. I ask your pardon, gentlemen, for my unmannerliness, and am your humble servant," ended Jean, making a formal curtsey.

During the exchange of compliments and polite talk which succeeded, Claverhouse observed the girl. She must be in her early twenties, he calculated, remembering what he knew of the Cochrane family; she was fair, plump, with a pale but healthy complexion, a long neck, a straight nose, and a small and somehow comical chin. She was very faintly marked with the smallpox, but so faintly that the tiny scars seemed to enhance her prettiness, lending it piquancy. It was plain that she had been into polite society, and was, as her grandfather had said, a conversible lass with excellent manners. Recovering from her embarrassment, she made all the proper replies, perfectly at her ease now; and by the time they all went in to dinner in the great house, the incident of her first appearance seemed quite forgotten.

But as he played the guest at a meal which was made cheerful by the absence of the Lady Catherine, Jean's formidable mother, and the presence of her grandmother, a tiny old Fifeshire lady, full of grace and charm, he was absorbed in another and seemingly irrelevant memory, one he had forgotten for years: Helen Grahame's helpless laughter on a certain occasion when he had called upon her family at the Blue Boar in London. Why such a trifle should return so vividly to him at this moment was more than he could tell; the fact remained that several times during the meal he had to rouse himself to listen to what Lady Dundonald was saying to him, and to reply to some questions from her husband.

At the end of it all the guests rode off again, speeded on their way by compliments and pressing invitations to return. Turning to bow once more as he rode down the carriage-way, Claverhouse saw the girl standing with her arm through her grandfather's, a most decorous young lady now, fair hair confined by a ribbon, shoes upon her feet, smooth skirts covering her ankles, the model of a Scots lass of good breeding taking farewell of a stranger who for a brief time had been a guest in her home.

It was not until they were clattering over the Abbey Bridge once more that Claverhouse exclaimed suddenly:

"Dod! I clean forgot to interview my Lady Catherine concerning that list of rebels."

"Well, you canna very well go back now, Clavers," said Lord Ross. "It would look mighty odd, and forbye I'll swear my lady would refuse to see you!"

"But I shall call tomorrow, for it is my duty to see her," said Claverhouse; and then, so suddenly that Ross started, he broke into a shrill cheerful whistling.

(iv)

He was as good as his word, and called at the Place of Paisley on the morrow; but if he went only because he considered it his duty to interview the Lady Catherine, he might have spared himself the pains.

He had had considerable experience in dealing with the sisters of the Covenant in Galloway, but his methods that had met with such success among those fanatical goodwives were singularly unsuccessful here. Lady Catherine received him in a chamber hung with tapestries portaying choice scenes from the Old Testament. Above the hearth, Jael stood before the exhausted Sisera, offering him butter in a lordly dish and concealing with the other hand a tent-pin and a hammer; between the windows two and forty children were being devoured by she-bears, while Elisha regarded with complacence this grisly carnage. A portrait of John Knox, looking not unlike old General Dalyell in one of his rages, glowered upon the visitor from over my lady's head; and open upon her knees she held a copy of the Reformer's *Book of Discipline*, which bore signs of constant use. She answered all Colonel Grahame's questions with biblical quotations, very skilfully walking on the thin ice of treason by this method, entangling him in a maze of words, a twisting of phrase, a wrenching of sentences from their contexts. He knew, and she knew that he knew, that when she pronounced the curse of the Lord upon King Ahab, she was really referring to King Charles; but he could not prove it, and neither could he accuse her of concealing the whereabouts of King Charles' rebels when she boasted of the escape of Lot from the wicked Cities of the Plain.

It appeared to be a wasted interview, and yet he repeated it. During the next few weeks he was constantly at the Place of Paisley, when, for a man so active and so devoted to duty, it would have seemed more profitable to have hunted the game for himself. And after foundering for an hour in a morass of Scripture, it was understandable as well as courteous that he should go and pay his respects to old Dundonald, who was always delighted to receive him and to show him some new specimen of horticulture. Then delicate little Thomas, the baby of the family, would come running with a Greek author he was finding difficult to read, or Lady Dundonald would send a servant to beg Colonel Grahame to visit her in her apartments, where in her sweet frail voice she would entertain him with the folk-lore which was her passion; or (and with increasing frequency) the Lady Jean would invite him to join a hawking-match or a game of bowls.

Best of all were those rare occasions when, for a brief half hour or so, he would find himself alone with the girl, carrying her basket when she went to pick flowers in the portion of the gardens quaintly called the Mustard Yard, or when she conducted him to the garden-house, the scene of their first dramatic encounter, to admire the increasing beauty of the view as tree after tree burst into blossom. He was quite convinced that he contrived for himself these *tête-a-têtes;* he would have been astounded had he known with what care and scheming the Lady Jean contrived them for him.

Though the Jean he came to know during those weeks was not the wild creature who had rushed all unawares into his arms that day of his first visit, she retained something of the carefree joyousness which he associated always with his favourite sister in her youth, and considering the rigid and gloomy Calvinism of both her parents, this joyousness was quite astonishing, nor was it to be accounted for only by the kindly influence of her grandparents. It was, he discovered, a quality inherent in Jean; she was sufficiently intelligent, she was all that was meant by the term 'well-bred', she had most of the accomplishments proper to a young lady of her station; but essentially she remained natural, a creature of warm human loves, devoted to her grim mother even while she suffered severely from that lady's preoccupation with her election and grace, demonstrative, tender, and claiming happiness as her right.

Claverhouse was perfectly aware of what was happening to him, and in moments of clarity he was both bewildered and dismayed. He was thirty-six, and he had believed, and with some excuse for it, that his head would always be able to control his heart; he had been convinced that this conquering by the emotions, this cataclysmal experience termed falling in love, was peculiar to the female sex; certainly he had never dreamed that he could suffer it himself, he so unemotional, so content with an impersonal devotion to the Monarchy and his profession, his warm human affection for kinsfolk and friends. And now he was overwhelmed by an obsessional emotion which made it difficult for him to attend to his duties, robbed him of appetite and sleep, at one instant bore him up on to the peaks of a happiness he had never dreamed existed, the next precipitated him into the dark depths of despair. He who had been at such pains to avoid hurting any female heart, now knew that if he could not have Jean Cochrane for his wife, it was his heart that would break, not hers.

Oh, she liked him; humbly he suspected that she loved him; but it was not only the new humility of the lover which gave him the painful conviction that his love ran deeper than hers. Jean was a spendthrift with her heart; she scattered love at large over kinsfolk, friends, her waiting-woman, favourite animals; he, who liked most people, loved but few. Yet it was this very prodigality of her affection which he found the most endearing thing about her, that and her natural joyousness. It seemed to him little short of miraculous that she had escaped all taint of the dreary Calvinism, the intellectual narrowness, of her parents, and that to this daughter of one of the most bitterly Covenanting families in Scotland, this young plant of grace, the Covenant meant nothing. He was too blinded by love to digest this fact in all its bearings; he did not realise that for Jean Cochrane only human beings were important, and causes and creeds and ideals existed not at all.

Absorbed in his shy yet ardent wooing (so ludicrously different from that of poor Helen Grahame, of which he could not think now without a blush of shame, so sordid did it appear with his obsession with titles and estates and his long, business-like letters to Menreith), it did not occur to him that his love for Jean might affect his career, or that it could be of any interest to outsiders. For the first time in his life he was ruled by impulse, with his head completely conquered by his heart. He attended to his duties punctually and thoroughly, if a little mechanically, but the heart into which Jean Cochrane had rushed as her joyous young figure had rushed into his arms, remained preoccupied with its own business.

When he was in Edinburgh on his Privy Council duties, he would slip off to visit the best tradesmen who had their shops in the tall narrow land called the Luckenbooths near the Parliament House, seeking little gifts which would please a lady, wryly remembering Montrose and his 'gewgaws', wincing with shame at the memory of how he had grudged the expense of such trifles, spending recklessly now, deliberately hunting for the most costly goods. And often after his letters were done, those careful letters connected with the staff-work which, as a full colonel, occupied more and more of his time, he would sit up into the small hours of the morning, his quill drawing little pictures, sketching the horse passant of the Cochranes and encircling it with the laurel wreath of the Grahames, or just writing Her name over and over again for sheer delight in it – 'Jean, Jean, Jean'.

His long-covetted Dudhope, too, he saw from quite a new angle; it must be made to please a young lady who had the refined tastes of her grandmother and who shared her grandfather's interest in horticulture; and on hasty visits to Dundee he would interview glaziers and masons, ordering fair windows to replace the arrow-slots, rooms to be enlarged and panelled, new fireplaces to be put in. He bought a copy of *Reid's Scots Gardner*, newly published, and poured over it for hours, his forehead wrinkled as he tried to master the mysteries of planting and sowing and grafting; he sent lavish orders to nurserymen, for acorns at six shillings the pound, beech-mast at fifteen shillings, so many ounces of the newly imported silver-fir, and a rolling-stone to keep flat and neat the still nonexistent lawns.

It was old Dundonald who broke the spell and brought the lover down to earth again. One day when Claverhouse called at the Place, the Earl drew him into the Little Dining Room, the closet where he transacted with his factor the business of his estates, and kindly but firmly asked Colonel Grahame his intentions.

"You're honouring us with many a visit just now, Clavers", said he dryly, "and I'm just wondering is it only in the service of his Majesty. Mind you, we're gey fond of your company, but tongues are apt to clack, ye ken, ay, even those of the Sanctified, and it's becoming a delicate situation. You're a gentleman of honour, and I ken fine you would not speak to a lassie in the way of a proposal before you had approached her guardian, who in this case is myself."

"My lord", cried Claverhouse, his proud face flushed, "I am fair shamed I have not approached your lordship on a matter which lies so near my heart, by the truth of it is, I – I scarce know myself at present; I'm all mixtie-maxtie, as they say. Forbye, I feared I'd never get your lordship's consent – "

"You'll never get my daughter-in-law's," interrupted Dundonald, with rueful humour. "You ken that fine."

Claverhouse was silent, his lower lip thrust out in obstinacy.

"But you'll just make shift without it, the pair of ye," continued the old man, his smile broadening, "if I ken aught about ye. Och ay, Clavers, the lassie fair dawts upon you; I've seen it these weeks syne; and for myself there's no gentleman in Scotland on whom I'd rather bestow her. Now, you'll be wishful to know what you may look for with her in the way of a tocher – "

"I care not a rush for tochers!" passionately interrupted the lover. "I'm willing to marry her in her smock."

The old man leaned back in his chair and laughed till the tears ran down his face.

"Ech me! Ech me!" he spluttered. "You're as brisk in love as in war, Clavers." Then, wiping his eyes, he became serious again. "Nay, we'll need to debate upon the settlements, and you'll not lack for my blessing or my wife's, but there's a matter which troubles me a wee, and that's the separating of a mother and a daughter and the making divisions in a household, for it's not only my daughter-in-law who's hot for the Covenant in this family, you ken that fine. If the old troubles should stir again in Scotland, Jeannie would have a husband who must take strong hand to crush them, for yon's his duty, and she'd have kinsfolk she loves dearly on the other side. Weel, weel, a woman should forsake her kin and cleave to her husband, so the Book tells us; but ech me, I canna help wondering what fate has in store for the pair of ye."

They were words which were to recur to Claverhouse very often, and very tragically, in after days.

Chapter Eight

(i)

During all these weeks, Claverhouse remained in blissful ignorance of the fact that his love-affair formed the chief topic of conversation round the 'tea-equipage', the camp-fire, and the card-table. He was a rising man, and his vivid personality could not be ignored; his notable victory over Sir John Dalrymple, his enjoyment of the royal favour, the creation of a new regiment for him, his extraordinary success in Galloway, his nomination to the Privy Council, his intimate friendship with the Heir Presumptive, all these had brought him firmly into the public eye, and everything he did was of interest to friends and enemies.

And now he had gone and fallen in love with the most unsuitable girl in Scotland, setting tongues clacking in taverns, garrisons, and the houses of the great. With very few exceptions, his friends disapproved; with no exceptions at all, his enemies rejoiced. For friends and enemies alike saw one inevitable outcome of the match: it would ruin Clavers' career, and it would cost him the title which otherwise would have been bestowed in due time.

There were battles fought over it. Jock Johnson, now a corporal, broke the head of a dragoon who was sniggering at the tale of Colonel Grahame getting himself entangled with a Covenanting lass; the Cornet of Claverhouse's original troop of horse, each member of which regarded him as a god, challenged one of the troopers to meet him at dawn on the Burrough Moor, to answer for his, the trooper's, observation that the Lady Jean was no fit match for Colonel Grahame; Colonel Grahame, insisted the Cornet, was not to be criticised in anything he chose to do. Lord Balcarres, discussing a flagon of wine in Sir George Mackenzie's handsome library, interrupted the Lord Advocate's passionate denunciation of witches being tortured before trial (which was illegal, he cried, and in any case he detested this persecution of poor silly old women), to remark that he had heard talk of Clavers marrying the Cochrane girl, and was disgusted by it; he himself had gone a long way in his negotiations for the hand of some noble connection of his own for Clavers, and there he must go and marry into a rebel house.

The faithful Tam was torn between chagrin and delight. He was in the best position of all to know what was brewing, for not only did he hear his master pacing up and down at night when usually he was at his correspondence, not only did he notice instantly that Master John was off his food, but Tam had caught many a glimpse of those idle sketchings on odd bits of paper, and had stared with round eyes at touching attempts to draw a horse passant or to break into verse, and at the name 'Jean' written over and over again. Och, and the sinful waste of money on something called a Mustard Yard at Dudhope, not to speak of new-fangled fire-places and imported glass for the windows; and the fuss there was if a curl of the famous dark locks was not properly arranged of a morning, and the time spent in deciding which neckcloth set the best, and a pair of lady's gloves, smelling strong of perfume and costing the Lord knew what, wrapped up in silver tissue, all ready to be presented.

It was exquisite for Tam to know, while others could only speculate and gossip; but on the other hand he had looked for a bride of far more exalted station when at last Master John decided to wed. His own choice had been no less a person than the Duke of York's younger daughter, the Princess Anne; and why for no? Master John had the royal blood in his veins, hadn't he?

Old Tom got wind of the story, and chuckled maliciously into his beard. So the young puppy who as a mere captain of horse had presumed to advise a veteran, the upstart colonel whose pay must be found by cutting down part of the General's staff, the turkeycock who failed to quail before the famous rages and who actually had been sent to advise General Thomas Dalyell on a recent tour of the south-west, was infatuated with a daughter of the Covenant, was he? In his heart Old Tom knew that Colonel Grahame was an excellent soldier, and that if he had got his way with the planting of small garrisons, the south-west would have been safe from rebellion long ago; but the General was small enough to harbour private grudges, and he hugged to himself the hope that Claverhouse's lovesickness might provide Old Tom with that opportunity for revenge for which he was waiting.

There were other, even greater, personages, who relished the situation. In the piazza of Holyrood House, bewigged heads were laid together, noble tongues gossiped as busily as those in tavern and camp. The Marquis of Queensberry, his dukedom in sight, his native jealousy wide-awake again, Claverhouse's usefulness to him ended, spat his S's into the cocked ear of his ruffianly brother-in-law, the Duke of Hamilton.

"Have you heard this queer tale they're telling about Clavers, now?" he hissed, his nose twitching like a hound's. "Daft over Dundonald's guid-daughter. Mind you, I'm a great admirer of Clavers, and there's no a man in Scotland will be more sorry than myself if he goes and misses the chance of further promotion by marrying into a rebel house," righteously added the Marquis, who at the moment was striving might and main to get his brother, the Hon. James, made Commander-in-Chief in place of the obviously failing Old Tom, and who had just succeeded in obtaining for the Hon. James the command of the Foot Guards in the place of Linlithgow.

"Uh-huh, uh-huh," murmured Hamilton, furiously using his tooth-pick, "and I'll jalouse he's not fashed himself with seeking his Majesty's consent. For my ain part, I would not permit the lass's brother, the Lord Cochrane, so much as to lay before me his proposals for the hand of my daughter Susan, before I had laid the whole matter before his Majesty and his Royal Highness. But he'll need to gang warily, will Clavers, which I misdoubt he'll do," happily added his Grace, "having such a muckle high opinion of himself and imagining he's answerable to none for his actions, not even to his Majesty."

(ii)

Striding impatiently up and down the little garden at the back of General Dalyell's lodging in Glasgow, Claverhouse paused as at last the General's servant came hurrying towards him.

"It's no manner of use, sir," said the man, his flushed cheeks and air of confusion telling their own tale, "his Excellency willna see you. He's no verra weel, he says, and keeps his bed. The truth o'it is sir," added the servant in an undertone, "he's in one of his huffs, and has been rating me for naething sinsyne he woke this morning."

"Then I must give you a message for him," replied Claverhouse. "Pray tell his Excellency that if I am wanted on his Majesty's service, I am to be found at the Place of Paisley, where I look to be for a week at the last."

Beckoning to his companion, Lord Ross, he walked briskly out into the Gallowgait and mounted the horse which Tam was holding for him. He could afford to be merely amused by Old Tom's huff today, for it was Tuesday, June 10th, his marriage morning. He had called on his Commander-in-Chief just now before riding to Paisley because such was his duty, and not even his wedding-day was going to make him neglect it. Now, that duty done, he was free to give himself up to his private affairs.

The whole world wore for him this morning the golden light which only the happy see. The chapmen trudging by with their creels, the pack-horses, tied nose to tail, with a bell upon the leader, the post-boy with his raucous horn and his bag of mails, even the dirty women and children working the 'ten feet coal' in the shallow, ugly heughs which scarred the landscape, all became beautiful in this magic light. He wanted to gallop the seven miles to Paisley, but presently even a trot became difficult because of the traffic, which streamed along the narrow causeway set in the middle of the soft earth of the road.

They were his wedding guests, these ladies and gentleman, who were jolted in their cumbersome, unsprung coaches, some with running footmen to make the way clear ahead, and with two fellows, armed with their long poles for the freeing of the vechicle if it sunk into a rut, clinging on behind. Others rode a-horseback, with a cloak-bag strapped on the saddle; on the coach doors and on the sleeves of the footmen was the horse passant of the Cochranes, that crest which Claverhouse had sketched so often and so fondly in the small hours of the morning. The Cochrane clan was coming in force to the wedding of its kinswoman who had been tempted by a handsome face to forget the loyalty due to the Covenant; from the stiff greetings they bestowed upon Claverhouse as he passed them on the road, it was plain that their presence at the wedding was dictated solely by their duty to Dundonald, the head of the family.

The bridegroom was prepared for such coldness; already he had had to suffer the utter refusal of Jean's mother to sign the marriage-contract and her ostentatious withdrawal to her dower-house. But, having resolved to do all in his power to overcome this hostility by his conduct, even denying himself and his own kinsfolk the happiness of their witnessing his wedding, he would not permit it to cloud his happiness. Jean loved him enough to defy the mother to whom she remained devoted; old Lord and Lady Dundonald had given him their blessing; and it was Jean he was marrying, not these sour-faced ladies and gentlemen who bowed unsmiling to him upon the road.

The Place of Paisley wore festive air, he saw with gratitude, as he trotted up the familiar carriageway. Dundonald and his gentle lady had done their best to make it a joyous occasion, and among the innumerable guests alighting from coach or saddle in the courtyard there were plenty of young lassies eager to rub shoulders with the bride to catch the coveted 'marriage-infection', plenty of young gentlemen anticipating the feasting and the dancing which would continue for a week after the knot was tied. Dundonald had evaded in the customary manner of the wealthy the Scots law which ordained that all marriages must be celebrated in the kirk; he had paid the fine of twenty shillings into the poor-box and the simple ceremony would be performed in the seclusion of the Place, thus avoiding the giving of offence to the bridegroom on the one hand, to kinsfolk on the other, by a controversial sermon from the 'Chair of Verity', otherwise the pulpit. The old house was decked with tapestries hung from the windows and with flowers and green boughs over the doors; pipers and fiddlers could be heard tuning up, the servants were clothed in new liveries, and a pervading odour of cooking told of the venison and the game and the butcher's meat which presently would be served in a lavish feast.

After making his greetings to Dundonald, Claverhouse was escorted upstairs to a little room set aside for him, and here he changed from his uniform into the sky-blue satin coat and vest embroidered with true-lovers-knots, made for him by an Edinburgh tailor, with a neck cloth of expensive lace, silk stockings, and shoes with stiffened ties. Tam, in his element, fussed and finicked, administering a final polish to the silver buttons, giving a last flick to the shoes, rearranging the dark curls which the ride had ruffled, pulling at the long coat-skirts to see that they set properly. Even the most disapproving of the guests who waited at the stair foot to watch the bridegroom descend, had to acknowledge privately that this persecutor of the Covenant was a very beautiful gentlemen; but then, they added dourly, beauty was ever a mark of the Beast.

In the chief fireroom of the Place, he awaited his bride; and here she came now, walking demurely between the two young kinsmen assigned to her as 'protectors' since the signing of the contract, and followed by girl cousins, bearing the bride-cup, a large silver bowl of wine. She was dressed in a white satin gown which, according to custom, must not be tried on beforehand or altered in any way, and Claverhouse was touched to notice that it did not quite fit her young figure; its simplicity was spoiled, too, by the innumerable ribbons lightly sewn on to it, the bride-favours for which the guests would scramble afterwards. Nothing remained of the wild young creature who had come flying round the garden-house into his arms on that never-to-be-forgotten morning, but her eyes, as she gave him one swift glance, were shining with a happiness akin to his own.

Kneeling side by side on rich cushions, John Grahame of Claverhouse and the Lady Jean Cochrane were made man and wife by a minister in the sober black gown of the Kirk. There was tense silence among the guests while the fateful words were being spoken; and in that silence Claverhouse heard a sound from without. It was the hollow ring of hooves coming at a gallop up the carriageway; and as he heard them, something cold seemed to clutch his heart.

There was a commotion at the door of the apartment, an angry buzz of voices, a ring of steel; ladies drew their skirts aside and gentlemen glared, as a man in a scarlet uniform pushed his way in the direction of Lord Ross. A hasty whispered conversation, and then Ross, red with embarrassment, approached the bridegroom, who had risen to his feet.

"I'll have to leave you, Clavers. A message from the General; there's an armed conventicle at Blackloch, and he orders me to ride thither without delay."

"The message was for you?" asked Claverhouse sharply. My lord merely nodded. "You are mistaken; I know Old Tom better. You must be my proxy at the wedding-feast." He jerked his head to the trooper who was hovering in the background, and bit out: "There are two and twenty of the Life Guards quartered in Paisley; call them out, and bid them be ready to ride with me in a quarter of an hour from now."

He dared not trust himself to speak to Jean; only by a hard desperate pressure of her hand did he silently implore her understanding. Then with set face he hastened from the room and up the stairs. He was unwounded by Old Tom's childish malice which the message to Ross had conveyed, and which said, plainer than words, that on such a day Colonel Grahame would be sure to put his personal affairs before his duty; he felt no anger against the testy, difficult old General; he was absorbed in the knowledge that already, in the first few moments of his married life, he must cause his Jean distress. He must humiliate her, publicly and dramatically, in the presence of her assembled kinsfolk; he must seem to justify all the Cochranes' disapproval of the match.

There was a little pulse beating in his cheek as he flung open the door of the room wherein he had put on his wedding garments so short a time before; his voice was cold and flat as he bade the astonished Tam help him to change back into his uniform; with steady and deliberate hands he put on the scarlet coat, slung the short cloak from his shoulder, belted on his sword, shoved his legs into the stiff black boots with their rowelled spurs. At the sight of that face, even Tam was silenced.

It was not a gesture of defiance he was making; upbringing, character, long habit, made only one decision possible. In heeding the voice which had spoken to him in the pettily spiteful accents of Old Tom, he was but following his strongest instinct: to obey the call of duty. But he would look back upon this day; not so very many years hence he would look back upon Tuesday, June 10th, 1684, and see it as a kind of dress-rehearsal of that which was to come. Today his duty was plain and obvious; he was the senior officer present, an officer in the service of an enthroned and powerful King who gave protection and due reward for duty done. All private interests, even the greatest of them, his young wife's happiness, must be subordinated to so obvious a duty; today it was as simple as that.

Simple, but bitterly hard; and he thought, unconscious of what the future held for him, that life could never be so cruel again. The wedding guests were gathered in the hall once more as he came hurrying down, and they made no scruple of letting him see what they thought of his conduct. Even old Lord and Lady Dundonald stared at him in blank dismay; plainly they were wondering what had possessed them to give their beloved grand-daughter to a man who could forsake her on her wedding-morn.

And she, the bride of a few minutes, ran up to him as he strode purposefully towards the outer door. She said not a word, but her eyes were huge with appeal, brilliant with unshed tears. They met in a square of sunlight, two solitary figures, the one in scarlet, the other in white, the colours of death. His heart was too full for him to bid her farewell in words; but for a moment he cast conventionality aside, and, forgetful of the spectators, caught her in his arms. Into the hair dressed up in formal ringlets he breathed the only complaint his self-command permitted him:

"They might have let Tuesday pass!"

It was a cry from the overcharged heart of John Grahame, the man. But it was John Grahame, the King's soldier, who sprang into the saddle and who, all that day, throughout the night, and all next day again, hunted vainly over moss and moor the enemies of King Charles.

Interlude

December, 1684

The members of the Scots Privy Council sat round the table in an apartment at Holyrood House, each thinking his own thoughts while being treated to an harangue by the Hon. James Douglas, Colonel of the Foot Guards.

Charming, witty Perth, newly made Lord Chancellor, smiled to himself as he remembered the epigram with which he had delighted the company at his sister's, Lady Errol's, late night. He was pleased with all the world at present, for he had made a most timely move when, last May, he had gone over to the Douglas clique. It had been clear to him for some while that Queensberry and his following were going to succeed in bringing down the Earl of Aberdeen, just as they had brought down Lauderdale, and by throwing in his lot with them at the right moment, he had been rewarded with the Chancellorship.

Queensberry, a duke at last, was thinking much the same thing from a different angle. Perth had been useful to him in getting rid of Aberdeen, and he himself, as Lord High Treasurer, had all the power without any of the dangers of the Chancellorship. Perth would do excellently as a puppet, and if it became necessary to ruin him also, that should prove easy because he was throwing out sundry hints about his leanings towards the Catholic Church. The same applied to his brother, Drummond of Lundin, just made Secretary of State for Scotland, and a most useful person to have in London, close to the ear of the Duke of York, who had such a liking for him. Queensberry had been at great pains to make it clear to both the Drummond brothers that they owed their respective offices to him, and he was gratified to find that they were duly grateful. But you never could tell, reflected Queensberry, secretly helping himself to pinch of snuff; gratitude was so apt to be a short-lived virtue.

Old Tom Dalyell dozed peacefully in his chair, his aged head sunk into his beard. Pleasant little dreams visited him; he had got his beloved dragoons regimented at last, and he had not grudged the huge expense of clothing them all alike in stone-grey uniforms. Ay, and next year he'd go one better, and have every man of them mounted on a grey horse. Dalyell's Dragoons! Dalyell's Scots Greys!

The Duke of Hamilton, lovingly fingering the Garter ribbon which he had got at Lauderdale's death, was remembering with satisfaction that he had wept copiously at prayers this morning. It was a sure sign of Grace, and really he had been indulging himself a little too freely with the bottle of late; he had feared that the Lord might see fit to chastise His servant for these excesses, but since the Lord had been pleased to edify His servant's household with the sight of such tears at his devotions, it was plain He was minded to be indulgent. Nevertheless, reflected Hamilton, he would have to be more abstemious; liquor made him careless, and he had had a very bad fright just recently when his underground encouragement of the Covenanters had been discovered. That upstart of a Clavers had actually dared to suggest that his Grace should be made to answer for it, but fortunately his Grace's high rank, and kinship with the all-powerful Queensberry, had saved him.

The Earl of Atholl sat glowering at the Earl of Perth. Atholl had wanted the Chancellorship, had wanted it passionately, and he considered it an insult of the greatest magnitude to lose it to Perth. He was by nature a brooder, and he had brooded ever since; he was busy at it now; the

Hon. James Douglas, noticing his lordship's fixed stare, preened himself on having gained his lordship's serious attention to what he was saying so eloquently.

Sir George Mackenzie, Lord Advocate, fingered his long upper lip and decided that when Douglas stopped havering at last, he, Sir George, would persuade the Council to listen to his arguments against this beastly witch-hunting. Poor wretched old women, the victims, often as not, of their neighbours' malice, and the particular object of Covenanting cruelty, hung up by their heels with lighted candles between their toes to make them confess to carnal intercourse with Satan; he detested it. Of course there were genuine witches, but it was illegal for any subject of the King to be tortured before trial, and he was not all sure that one of these days he would not try to get it made illegal altogether...

"I'm fair shamed," the clipped tones of the Hon. James continued, his little figure stiff as a ramrod as he stood before the table, his hard blue eyes glancing complacently from one Councillor to the next, sure of their close attention, convinced of their admiration of him in his military role, "I'm fair shamed to have had such men in my regiment as the gowks your lordships have been pleased to examine just now. Yet I am glad your lordships have heard for yourselves their complaints, for I feared you'd scarce credit it if I told you of their audacity in protesting against their dismissal. I'm proud of my regiment, my lords, and I'm minded to make Scotland proud of it, and I'll have no man in it that's not amenable to discipline. That's the word, *discipline,*" repeated the advocated-turned-colonel, with a glance at Old Tom, that formidable disciplinarian, whose command of the Scots Army he hoped to gain when the veteran had the good taste to die at last (and damn it, he was eighty-five). "Ay, and I'll have them smart forbye. I'll not thole soldiers that refuse to shave off their beards, for they must look young and brisk, my men, and all of the same height, not one man lanky and the next short. And if their uniforms don't please me, they'll buy new ones out of their pay. As for the beastly custom which prevails in other regiments, of the inferior officers keeping ale-cellars, I'll never away with it. It wastes the soldiers' time when they are off-duty; a soldier should never be off-duty, my lords," cried Douglas, in an ecstasy of self-righteousness. "He's dedicated, soul and body, to the service of his Sacred Majesty, and what free time's permitted him should be employed in taking necessary rest ere he is called to his exercises again."

The Council roused themselves to utter a chorus of compliments. Queensberry beamed upon this younger brother of his, whose career as an advocate had been so distressingly undistinguished but who was proving himself such a model colonel; Perth (thinking privately how exactly like a turkey-cock the little man was), promised to report the Hon. James' zeal to the Secretary of State in London; Hamilton solemnly congratulated the officer who had set his face against common men's drinking; and Old Tom, remembering the vast expense he had been put to in clothing his dragoons in their grey greatcoats, observed that it was a novel idea, this about constraining soldiers to buy new uniforms out of their pay, but that it was worth thinking about.

Then, in the midst of this general adulation, there came a jarring note.

"I'm just thinking," observed Colonel John Grahame, "that your regimental rules are not very good for recruitment, Colonel Douglas. New uniforms out of their pay, and no ale-cellars – good grief! It's enough to make any likely lad think twice before accepting the King's coat-and-conduct money."

There was a pause of outrage. Then Dauglas burst out: "Are you taking the side of these mutineers, Clavers?"

"Mutineers?" repeated Claverhouse, twisting the signet-ring upon his finger. "We have heard no word of mutiny. The fellows examined just now were dismissed, so you have told us, because they objected to certain arbitrary and revolutionary rules made by their new Colonel. They all have excellent records of service; I have taken the trouble to discover that."

"Hech!" spluttered Douglas. "Here's a fine thing when a brother officer, ay, and one famous for discipline himself, should stand up for soldiers dismissed for a breach of discipline."

"It appears to me, Clavers," said Perth, anxious for peace, "that if the men have their uniforms free in the first place, it's reasonable they should pay for replacements."

"And it appears to me," cried Queensberry, his S's making a little shower-bath over his cravat, "that my brother here kens his duty, and is not to be called in question in the discharge of it save by his Excellency the General here."

"I understood," retorted Claverhouse, with a touch of that sarcasm which warned of rising temper, "that the Council was called upon to examine and to debate the complaints made by these dismissed soldiers. As a member of this Council, and not as Colonel Douglas' brother officer, I take leave to voice my opinion."

"Which is clean contrary to that of the majority of this honourable Board," cried Douglas triumphantly.

"So it appears. I think it extremely unjust to dismiss men who have served his Majesty faithfully and well, only because they are of the height which God made them, or because they refuse to shave off their beards and cheat the world they are younger than they are, or to deny them the ale-cellars which, from time immemorial, it has been the custom of the inferior officers to keep, or to constrain them to buy new uniforms out of their pay, especially when, as has been shown in this case, the old are still serviceable. I am, as you have been pleased to remark, as keen as any man for discipline; but I am yet more keen for justice, in particular where it concerns men who cannot defend themselves, and therefore I take leave to say that in my opinion these men ought to be taken back into the service, and compensation made them."

Douglas rose with a harsh scrape of chair-legs.

"I'll thank you, Clavers," he shouted, "to mind your ain business."

"Tch!" murmured Queensberry, his nose twitching, "Clavers was ever the great one for justice, though it's a queer kind of a notion he has of it. I mind in the old days when he was a plain captain of horses, he'd make it so my heritors could not pay me my rents because they must part with their oats to feed his troop-horses; and here he is now, championing offenders against their ain colonel. But aiblins," he added softly, "we should mind that Clavers has gotten him a new softness for all rebels since he took a Covenanting wife."

Claverhouse was on his feet in an instant, shaking off Mackenzie's restraining hand. The sarcasm vanished; the temper, notorious in youth, slipped the leash which the years had fastened to it; ignoring Douglas altogether, he turned the full force of his fury upon the most powerful man in Scotland.

"It is not the first time you have made that insinuation, my Lord Duke of Queensberry. I am not deaf, neither am I a fool, and I ken fine what you've been whispering behind my back and hinting to his Royal Highness. You've misliked me since the days when it was my duty to seek locality in your district, when I was, as you say, a plain captain of horse. Since I got my promotion, you have feigned friendship because you see I have the favour of the Duke of York, but now you have gotten you the strawberry-leaves you were so keen for me to solicit for you, you have no further use for me and would kick me into the gutter where, in your opinion, I belong. My marriage has undermined my loyalty; I am not above pocketing the fines it is my duty to collect from resetters; I employ my time attending to the affairs of my Constabulary when I ought to be attending to my military duties – och, I've heard it all, but always at the second-hand. Today is the first occasion when you have been man enough to say to my face what heretofore you've whispered behind my back. I compliment you, my Lord Duke of Queensberry!"

"Clavers! Clavers!" whispered Mackenzie urgently; but the other swept on unheeding. His hands laid flat upon the table, his large eyes snapping with fury, his slight figure dominated the room.

"I have not the honour to belong to the House of Douglas – that House, by the way, which King James V refused to have mentioned in his presence because of its treacheries and treasons; I am not a major baron of Scotland; my father was a simple laird. I have attained to my military rank and a seat on the Council only because I have a glib tongue and know how to play my personage – hech! you're like any kail-wife gossiping round the Tron. But I will tell you this blunt, my Lord Duke: when it comes to those who cannot defend themselves, ay, even troop-horses, I'll not thole injustice from you or any other. As for myself, I am content to let my conduct speak for me; and if ever the time comes (which God forbid) when knaves shall think to play the game of '41 again and plunge these kingdoms into civil war, I will prove that the laurel of the Grahame takes not second place in loyalty to the highest in the land, even to the bloody heart of the House of Douglas."

Then, without ceremony, he was gone, and his footsteps rang on the flagstones of the passage.

April, 1685

There was silence for several moments after the pretty notes of the virginal faded. Jean Grahame looked wistfully at the figure of her husband as he stood with his back to her in the window embrasure.

That was your favourite air I was playing," she said at last, gently reproachful, *"Through the wood, laddie"*, and you were not listening."

He turned with a sigh and an apologetic smile, and began pacing restlessly up and down, touching her hair in an absent caress as he passed her.

"Master Provost and his lady are coming to drink tea," went on Jean, resolutely cheerful, "and afterwards you will be able to discourse with him about these poor men in the Tolbooth," A pause. "John," she cried suddenly, near to tears, "do you not like being at home with me?"

He was kneeling at her feet in a moment, his lips on her hands. She noticed, looking down at his bent head, a few while hairs shining amid those dark locks of his.

"For months after we were wed," continued Jean, "I scarce saw you; you were for ever on your military duties or else in Embro' on Privy Council business. And now that at last we can be together, you are so restless, you are like a prisoner, you do not seem able to content yourself with this dear Dudhope of ours, or with the reforms you are making in your Constabulary, or – or with me."

"Jeannie." There was something almost frantic in his tone and look. "I cannot make you see that while it is paradise to be with you, I am galled beyond bearing by the wreck of my career, by my unmerited disgrace, and by idling here without employment."

"But you are not idle," protested his wife, stroking his hair. "It is a wonderful thing you are doing in working for this reform of the law, whereby poor petty thieves shall no longer be liable to the penalty of death; and though Master Provost does not approve, I am sure you will win him over,"

He rose abruptly and began to pace up and down again, beating his hands together in a kind of anguish.

"If I could but get leave to go up to London and lay my case before his Majesty!" he raged. "He forbids it until I have begged Queensberry's pardon. I will not beg his pardon; I will not buy back my offices at such a price."

"And it was all because of me you had this outcast with his Grace," said Jean sadly.

He flung round in passionate denial.

"It was not! My dear love, Queensberry used this quarrel only as an excuse to bring me down. He was fearful I would get the command of the Army when the old general died, and he desired it for his brother. When I lost my temper with him at the Council board, he had me. Up must go my Lord Perth, his under-spur-leather, to London, to whisper in his Royal Highness' ear how rude I had been to the Lord High Treasurer, and in London there was the Lord Moray, another Douglas ally, to keep the campaign of misrepresentation going bonnily on. And a fine victory they had. They took my district from me – my district which it had taken me such years of labour to make peaceable and law-abiding – and sent Colonel Douglas there to show me how it should be managed; ay, and from all I hear, he is like to set it by the ears again. And when King Charles died, and Queensberry was made Lord High Commissioner for Scotland, his Grace saw to it that my commission as Sheriff and my Privy Councillorship which lapsed with his Majesty's death, should not be renewed. A man who cannot keep his temper, said they, is not fit to be trusted with administering the King's justice or keeping his secrets."

"His present Majesty should have known better," said Jean indignantly, "seeing that he was your friend and patron when he was Duke of York."

"King James must needs support his Ministers and his Officers of State," her husband replied abruptly, "and he is too just ever to be swayed by personal preferences. Yet if I could but see him, and defend myself against these lying tongues which tattle like so many serving-wenches – "

He broke off at the sound of a knock upon the door. It was Tam who entered, very self-important, very excited, bearing a letter.

"A foot-runner brought it, Master john, from Embro', not from the letter-office at Dundee but straight here to Dudhope, ay, and when I took a wee keek at it, I kent fine the reason. The Royal Seal on it, Master John; likely his Majesty has writ to you with his ain hand," added Tam, making a determined effort to peer over his master's shoulder as Claverhouse broke the seal.

He was so absorbed in his reading that he forgot to dismiss the prying Tam. It was his wife's hand on his sleeve that roused him; as he glanced at her, she saw chagrin oddly mingled with joy in his expression.

"I'll need to leave for Embro' at once," said he. "A personal letter from his Majesty in which he positively commands me to make apology to Queensberry, since he desires to restore me to my offices and cannot do so while I am at feud with his representative in Scotland. His Majesty is pleased to say that my services are essential to him, for there is a warning that the Duke of Monmouth and my Lord Argyll intend an armed invasion."

May, 1685

The L-shaped Castle of Dudhope looked very pleasant and stately in the sunshine. Tall and rosy-grey, it stood upon its eminence, two castles under one roof, the older one, of the late thirteenth century, pricked with arrow-slots, the 'new' buildings, of the mid-fifteenth, homely with glazed windows and prettily rounded turrets. The ivy clothing the drum-towers rustled in the wind which blew off the Tay, and the few flowers in bloom in the newly laid-out gardens bent this way and that, lacking protection as yet from the nursery of oak and silver-fir planted for that purpose. High over the four-storied castle reared the bare head of Dundee Law, and far below it nestled the little burgh, with its two quays and its substantial walls, and the gulls for ever wheeling over it, white flecks against the broad blue river.

Tired as he was, Brigadier Grahame of Claverhouse took the stairs in the south-east tower two at a time, and strode eagerly along the passage towards his wife's apartments. With his hand upon the door-latch, he became aware of a figure hovering in the shadows at his side.

"My lady is no for receiving the day," said the voice of Elspeth, the gentlewoman who had been Jean Cochrane's companion since childhood. "She bade me tell you so."

For a moment he could only stare in utter bewilderment. Then he said sharply:

"Is my lady sick?"

"She's no," replied Elspeth, insinuating her angular figure between him and the door, "but she's no receiving onyone."

He was dead tired, and his anger rose.

"You presume upon your long service with my wife," he snapped. "Have the goodness to stand aside."

Her eyes regarded him with plain hostility for a moment; then, with a shrug of her shoulders, she moved away, saying maliciously:

"Och weel, ye'll find oot for yersel'."

He tried the door, and found it locked. Rattling at the latch, trying to control his irritation and anxiety, he told himself that he ought to have dismissed Elspath in the first days of his marriage, when he had discovered what an influence she had over her young mistress, how hot she was for the Covenant, and what a born trouble-maker. But he had not had the heart to do so, especially when he must be away from home so often. His repeated rattling of the latch and calls to Jean, at last resulted in the door being unlocked. Stepping in, and slamming it behind him, he forgot everything in the joy of seeing her after a month's separation, and made to seize her in his arms. But she drew back instantly; her eyes were swollen with weeping, her face pale, and she stared at him in a kind of horror.

"Don't touch me!" cried Jean. "There is blood upon your hands."

His arms fell to his side, and he stared in his turn, bewildered, desperately hurt, fighting the beginnings of exasperation.

"Jean is this a welcome for your husband returning from active service? I'm tired out, darling – "

"The blood of the innocent," she interrupted, her voice shrill, her manner almost wild. "I've heard the tales they are telling of what you have been at in the south-west. They are calling it the Killing Time, and you they are naming Bloody Clavers, the persecutor in the service of a Popish King."

He clenched his hands tight to retain his self-control.

"Love, will you listen to me? The first thing King James did upon his Accession was to issue an Act of Indemnity, offering pardon to all at that time declared outlawed for the rebellions during the reign of his brother, if within twenty days they would take the Oath of Allegiance to their lawful Sovereign, or, failing that, left the kingdom within the space of two months. But certain among the Covenanters refusing to do either and making plain their intent to bring new rebellions upon us – "

"I care not for any of this – "

"You will please to hear me out." (His tone sharpened a little.) "During the past few years, the south-west has become peaceable, the ordinary folk there growing weary of fanatics who take care of their own skins while inciting others to risk theirs; but since last autumn there have slipped over from Holland trained agitators, in particular one Renwick, whose so-called 'Declaration' was nothing less than the old call to murder and revolt. The first fruits of it were the shooting dead of two Life Guards, and the murder, by four men in the night-time, of the peaceable minister of Carsphairn. Those who thus outrage the law, and refuse to acknowledge that it has authority over them, must expect to be treated as public enemies, and the government of King Charles and his Successor has acted with necessary firmness. It has ordered certain senior officers to seek out these murderers and all who subscribe to their hellish principles, to offer them, in the presence of two witnesses, the disowning of Renwick's Declaration, 'in so far as it declares war against His Sacred Majesty, and asserts that it is lawful to kill such as serve His Majesty in Church, State, Army, or Country', and if they refuse this, then to subject them to military execution."

He paused, but she said nothing, merely standing there in a theatrical attitude of shrinking and horror.

"It was not a pleasant task I was called on to perform," he said grimly, "but please God it has served its purpose and saved the kingdom from a rebellion such as we saw at Bothwell Bridge, a rebellion which would have been far more dangerous than any former one, seeing that Monmouth and Argyll are about to invade us – "

"You may excuse it how you will," she interrupted, sobbing, "but from my friends and kinsfolk I ken fine you have the blood of martyrs on your hands."

"Then you must choose whether to believe your friends and kinsfolk or your husband, who is in the best position to ken the truth."

"Hundreds of martyrs," sobbed Jean, burying her face in her hands, "hundreds of poor persecuted bodies, shot on their ain hearthstones by you and your men."

"You do me too much honour, madam." Nervous exhaustion, combined with the shock of her attitude, made him use with her for the first time that biting sarcasm he reserved for his enemies. "My so-called martyrs are three: John Brown, Mathew McIlwraith, and Andrew Hislop, all old offenders, all caught red-handed with stores of arms, all refusing to disown Renwick's Declaration – a declaration of war against their country. The first two I caused to be shot by a firing-party in the presence of two witnesses, according to my orders; the last, since his case seemed to me to require a legal opinion, I handed over to a magistrate, Sir James Johnson of Westerhall, himself a former Covenanter, who ordered summary execution, though I pleaded for the fellow's youth. For these three I will answer to Almighty God when my time comes; for the present I am satisfied that I have observed the orders of the Privy Council and have rid the kingdom of three dangerous rebels."

She had dropped her hands from before her face and was staring at him; and now there was nothing theatrical about her look of horror.

"How can you speak so to me, John?" she whispered. "You cannot love me if you speak to me like that."

So then of course he forgot everything except his love for her; and soon there was only the bittersweet happiness of 'making it up'.

But next day he must try to reason with her again, to persuade her to understand the situation so that there could be no more of these tormented quarrels between them. Already, deep inside himself, he knew that it was useless; he realised something he ought to have known from the beginning, that her exaggeratedly tender heart was fatal to their mutual happiness. She was feminine through and through, and therefore ruled entirely by her emotions; when he tried to explain to her how grave was the emergency, with Argyll expected at any moment from Holland, equipped with Dutch arms and Dutch money, and depending on the turbulent south-west for the success of his invasion, while Monmouth made a like descent on England, her only reaction was pity for Argyll's lady, a friend of her family. And there was her own uncle, Sir John Cochrane, said to be coming with Argyll; supposing he were caught, she sobbed, supposing he were executed. Steeling himself to a desperate patience, he tried in his turn to appeal to her love for him, reminding her that she had defied her mother and the majority of her kinsfolk for his sake; could she not trust him, then? Had she not known what she was doing when she married the King's soldier whose duty it was to fight and capture and if need be kill the enemies of his country?

But his own heart supplied the sad answer: she had not known what she was doing, and neither had he. A little wild creature had come trustingly into his arms, and there was one enemy from which he could not protect it: life.

August, 1685

Turning into the Lawnmercat of Edinburgh from a visit to the Duke of Gordon in his town house on the Castlehill, Brigadier Grahame paused as he heard someone call his name. He beheld, striding up behind him, a very plump and portly gentleman of middle age, who wore an expression of quite extraordinary complacence. He had something of the air of a merchant who knows all his goods to be of the finest quality, and confers a favour on those he permits to purchase them.

Claverhouse had not seen Hugh Mackay of Scourie for seven years, not since those days when they had been companions-in-arms in Flanders. As they greeted one another, he observed Mackay with those penetrative eyes of his, summing him up as he did all men, but without a trace of hostility. It had not been Mackay's fault that, all those years ago, he had been given a regiment promised to Claverhouse, and as things had turned out, apart from Orange's broken faith, the choice had been all for the best. Mackay, it seemed, had been perfectly content to live permanently in Holland; he was over here now only because King James had borrowed the Scots Brigade, of which Mackay was Colonel, from his son-in-law, Orange, to assist in quelling Monmouth's rebellion. It had arrived too late to be of any use, but, as a compliment to his son-in-law, the King had promoted Mackay to the rank of major-general, making him likewise a Privy Councill or of Scotland. And here he was, come on a brief visit to Edinburgh to take his seat and be wined and dined before returning with the Brigade to Holland.

"I protest I had forgot, sir," remarked Mackay, picking his way round the unsavoury heaps of refuse in the street and holding a fine cambric napkin to his nose, "how exceeding filthy is Scotland. 'The flowers of Edinburgh' is how one of my English friends terms your smells; in no other country in the world would such disgusting streets be permitted. It is particularly unpleasant to me, coming as I do from cleanly Holland; now take the Hague," and he gave Claverhouse the Hague *ad nauseum* all the way down the Lawnmercat.

"Doubtless you'll be visiting your home in Sutherland, sir," was all Claverhouse said at the end of this harangue, "ere you go overseas once more."

"My dear sir," snapped the voice which had hardly a trace of its native accent, "you are pleased to jest. The Lowlands are ill enough to a civilised man; why you should imagine I'd wish to visit a portion of Scotland which is mere savage wilderness is more than I can guess."

"Because you were born there," replied Claverhouse shortly. "When I was serving in Flanders, there were times when I was fair sick for a sight of Glen. A man's pulled back to his native place – "

"A man who has the misfortune to be born in the Highlands of Scotland is despised by every civilised people in the world," interrupted the other violently. Claverhouse glanced at him in wonder; the plump face was red with passion, the voice shook. "I've lived it down, sir, I've lived it down at last, but I suffered torments when I was a young volunteer. Where are you from? my companions-in-arms would ask me. From Scotland? From the *Highlands* of Scotland? Damme, friends, they'd say, have a care how you go near him lest you catch the itch; we'd best warn the folk hereabouts to have a care of their cattle, now there's one from a race of cattle-thieves come among them. And tell me, sir, they'd say, is it true that your people live upon meal mixed with blood from the living cow, and that they eat the bodies of their enemies? Where's your tartan plaid? they'd ask me. Lord! It must irk a Highlandman to wear breeches like a Christian. But I've lived it down, sir, I've lived it down, thank God," Mackay concluded devoutly.

Claverhouse's lips had thinned with distaste during this outburst; he thought he knew most human weaknesses, but never until today had he encountered a man's shame of his native land. As he remained silent, Mackay added, mopping his heated brow with his napkin: "You may fancy you have some experience of barbarians in your chasing of these poor fanatics in the south-west. But you may thank the Lord, sir, that you have never been called upon to chase Highlandmen through their savage mountains."

"Whiles," observed Claverhouse dryly, "it has been the Highlandmen who have done the chasing. Barbarians they may be, though those who were my fellow students at St Andrews were the best-mannered gentlemen I've ever met; but you will remember that they thoroughly routed trained troops when they fought under my great kinsman, Montrose."

Mackay laughed indulgently.

"I know very well," said he, "that your family hero is not to be criticised by an outsider, otherwise I might have somewhat to say about his tactics. But I hope for their own sakes that the Highland barbarians will never have to encounter me and my regulars in battle, for I should make short work of them, I promise you that."

So he strutted along the Highgait, Major General Hugh Mackay of Scourie, blissfully unaware that he had just uttered one of the most dramatically false prophecies of his life.

June, 1688

As Major General Grahame entered the library of Sir George Mackenzie's country house of Shank, near Edinburgh, the figure of his friend, garbed in a shabby old gown, emerged from behind one of the new-fangled stalls built from a design of Wren's in the Bodleian.

"Have you heard the news?" enquired Claverhouse shortly, flinging his hat on to a chair.

"I hear no news at Shank," replied his friend. "I am a private person, Clavers, and not unthankful to be so."

"Renwick is condemned and will be executed next week; he was most ably prosecuted by your successor in the office of Lord Advocate, Sir John Dalrymple."

Tenderly smoothing the vellum of the book he carried, Sir George regarded his friend with some amusement.

"He's a fair bogey with you, Dalrymple of Stair, Clavers."

"You may call him that. One of the greatest enthusiasts for this Religious Toleration, he whose family were so hot for the Covenant, and most zealously undertaking the prosecution of fanatics, while he sends news of all that passes to his outlawed father in Holland. And he's not the only one of his breed to enioy the King's favour. There's Sir James Steuart of Goodtrees, deep in the Rye House Plot and in Argyll's rebellion, now joint Secretary of State with my Lord Melfort in London. There's Duke Hamilton, in London likewise since he was made a Privy Councillor of England: and in Scotland there are hundreds of former Covenanting outlaws come flocking over from Holland and the West Indies, openly forming clubs in Edinburgh, permitted to practise their religion which is nothing less than treason and blasphemy."

"I wonder you still enjoy the royal favour yourself, Clavers," observed Mackenzie, with a sniff, "seeing that you have neither turned Papist nor shown an enthusiasm for Toleration. There are the Drummond brothers now, plain Lundin become Earl of Melfort and so thick-and-plack with the King in London, and my Lord Perth ruling all in Embro'. How many priests has his lordship in his private chapel, and how does Embro' relish having the Mass in her midst?"

"The Drummonds are sincere in their conversion, of that I'm convinced," said Claverhouse, with his old regard for justice, "and as for Toleration, though you ken fine I like it as little as you do, I must needs admit that no religious body has been so persecuted as the Catholics, yet throughout all the troubles of the last fifty years they have remained consistently loyal to the Crown. But his Majesty does not see what this Toleration entails; it has alienated the moderate Presbyterians and the Church of England, and to permit the Covenanters to have their conventicles is to invite them to preach rebellion and murder with impunity."

"Come view my latest treasures, Clavers," said his friend soothingly. He reached for his stick (he had broken his leg some years previously and was permanently lame) and limped to one of the wall-cases newly decorated by a gilder form the Lyon Office. "I've had my *Religious Stoic* bound in velvet, a luxury I can ill afford, yet it will be a bonny thing to hand on to my descendants. Ay, I'm a fair spendthrift since I am become a private gentleman again – "

"You need not have become so," interrupted his friend, refusing this change of subject, "had you not appeared so bitter against Toleration. The king needs every honest man in his service, not knaves like Dalrymple who feign zeal for Toleration only because they believe it will ruin his Majesty."

"And so it will," said Mackenzie, his intelligent face suddenly bitter. "And his Majesty must take the blame. To the ruin of his subjects, including myself, Toleration means just one thing: the return of Popery. I'm a loyal subject of his Majesty, Clavers, but I'll never away with the Pope."

"That is just the kind of thing his Majesty's enemies are saying," cried Claverhouse passionately, "and I wonder to hear it from you. Do you not realise," he went on, beating one fist against the other, "in what peril we stand as a nation? My Lord Perth, honest but a coward, ruling all in Scotland; his brother, honest likewise but hated by all, at the King's ear in London; traitors like Dalrymple and

Goodtrees insinuating themselves into high offices; old rebels flocking into Scotland; and in Holland the Prince of Orange biding his time."

"He'll be your King and mine one day, Clavers," observed the other, unimpressed, "so you'd best content yourself with the idea of paying homage to a man who broke his word to you when you were young."

Claverhouse whirled upon him in sudden fury.

"I thought you knew me better than that, Sir George. You imagine I am small enough to harbour resentment against Orange for that broken word, petty enough to refuse allegiance to him as his Majesty's lawful Successor? I am not. But he is not his Majesty's lawful Successor; the most he can hope to be is Prince Consort to his Majesty's elder daughter. And meanwhile he encourages rebellion, he harbours traitors, he supplies with money and arms the worst rogues in Scotland and in England, he writes fulsome letters to his royal uncle and father-in-law and at the same time permits libels to be printed against him in Holland. Why should he act so unless he is growing tired of waiting to become Prince Consort, weary of waiting for his Majesty to die, and hopes a rebellion here may let him in by the back door? And if I know aught of that ambitious gentleman, there is but one thing would content him if he came to England, the Throne itself – "

There was a dramatic interruption. He had been so obsessed with the voicing of private fears, had Claverhouse, that he had not heard the urgent knock upon the door, and now blinked almost stupidly at the trooper who stood beside him, extending a sealed paper. Then he snatched the paper, broke the seal, and read.

"I am commanded to an Extraordinary Meeting of the Council in Edinburgh," said he to Mackenzie, shoving the paper into his pocket and with a gesture dismissing the trooper. "There is news from England, Sir George. On the

10th of this present month, a son was born to King James."

"So the Prince of Orange will have to wait a long time even to become Prince Consort," murmured Mackenzie with dry humour.

"Yes," said Claverhouse, unsmiling. "I wonder if he will wait."

Part Two

The Hero

Chapter One

(i)

Claverhouse stood upon the battlements of Dudhope Castle, whence he could see the whole length of the carriageway eastwards, and on the north the height of Dundee Law. Upon the summit of that hill was a great heap of brushwood and faggots, with a man stationed beside it day and night, ready to fire the beacon when he caught the gleam of other bale-fires to the south, the warning of invasion. It was late September, 1688.

The last few months has taken their toll of Claverhouse; he was grey on the temples, his mouth, still mobile, had thinned, and his eyes were watchful. It was the face of a man without illusion yet not cynical, self-disciplined yet retaining kindliness and humour, with an air of command and even of hauteur, yet with no trace of arrogance. During the past week, something of the drawn look had receded from it; for not only did the soldier in Claverhouse infinitely prefer an open foe to a secret one, but at long last King James had accepted the fact that his nephew and son-in-law intended armed invasion of his kingdoms, and was taking firm measures to meet the emergency.

That he had for so long refused to believe that fact had been exasperating to Claverhouse the subject, but understandable to Claverhouse the friend, for it sprang from the lack of shrewdness which had aroused his own queerly protective love of the man who had been his patron for so many years. And on this occasion there had been excuse for James' blindness. Not only was Orange his nephew and son-in-law, but he had proclaimed publicly, again and again, that the vast armament he was assembling was intended as a protection against his enemy, Louis of France, and that he had no intention whatsoever of making any hostile act against King James. He had proclaimed it to King James himself, and he had proclaimed it to his Catholic allies in his struggle with France. It was not until the English Ambassador at the Hague wrote urgently that prayers for the Prince of Wales had been discontinued in the chapel of the Prince and Princess of Orange, and that the Dutch Government was now saying openly that the fleet of fifty men-of-war, at least four hundred transports, and fifteen thousand mercenaries, were intended for the rescuing of the people of England from their Popish King; not until certain obscene broadsheets sold in London, informing the citizens that the infant Prince of Wales was the son of a herb-woman and had been smuggled into the Palace in a warming-pan, were found to have been printed in Holland; that King James believed in his nephew's treachery. Convinced at last, he had acted with vigour; he had issued a proclamation warning his subjects to expect invasion, had ordered a general rendezvous of his Army at Salisbury, and had expressed his resolve of leading it in person against the foe.

This was the news which had taken from Claverhouse the intolerable weight which had burdened him for months. With the King squarely facing the situation, with the nation laying aside its anti-Popery mania and uniting against foreign invasion, with a large army in England, and the little Scots force ready to encamp upon the Border and secure Scotland and the North of England from native rebels, Claverhouse did not doubt the overthrow of Orange and his armament. And once that Prince was defeated in open fight, there should be an end to the base underground warfare which he had waged for so long.

So here stood Major General Grahame on the battlements of Dudhope, waiting for a messenger to bring him the order for the Scots Army to march to the Border. All through the past week the Militia had been raised and drilled, the great castles munitioned, the beacons built; precautions, as Claverhouse was wryly aware, which might not have been necessary but for King James' Religious Toleration which had brought hundreds of old rebels home to Scotland, and who, asked how they would behave when Orange landed, had replied ominously that 'They would carry themselves as the Lord should inspire'. But he was confident that the Scots Army, small though it was, could be relied upon to keep the Covenanters quiet during the emergency, though he was not very happy about the man who would command it. After Old Tom's death, Drummond of Cromlix had been appointed Commander-in-Chief; but in March of this year he too had died very suddenly, and the senior officer was now the Hon. James Douglas.

The Hon. James had no commission as Commander-in-Chief, a fact which wounded his vanity to the quick and which he put down to the complete ascendancy of the Drummond brothers, once the protégés of the Douglas tribe, recently their successors in power. The Hon. James was of the same rank as Claverhouse himself, but his kinsman, Duke Hamilton, as a Privy Councillor of England had been able to contrive it so that the commission was dated a few days earlier than Major General Grahame's, thus giving the Hon. James the supreme command without the title. Ambitious as he still remained, Claverhouse remained also a stranger to jealousy, and there was nothing personal in the disquietude with which he contemplated the thought of Major General Douglas commanding in this crisis.

It was a crisis which demanded a cool head, a firm hand, a sense of responsibility, and a gift of leadership, qualities which his Maker had not seen fit to bestow upon the Hon. James Douglas.

(ii)

With a last glance up at the unlit beacon, Claverhouse descended the turnpike stair and went to his wife's apartments.

She was sitting before the first fire of autumn (for the summer had lingered long this year), with her gentlewoman, Elspeth, beside her. They were making a new lining for the cradle which had been Jean's own; low-domed, heavily gilt, painted in bright colours with the armorial bearings of the Cochranes, it had been brought long ago from Sweden by a great-uncle. She looked up from her sewing to greet her husband, smiling at him with that preoccupied contentment which had come upon her of late; her whole being was absorbed in the joy of carrying a child at last, after four years of marriage.

He stood looking fondly down upon her as her gentlewoman served the claret, which, by the physician's orders, Jean took nowadays at the 'four-hours' instead of the fashionable tea, and listened while she chattered happily of a new set of drawn-muslin caps she had completed, and of the quilted bearing-robe, with matching cuffs for the nurse, which was to be her next task. By the time my child is born, he thought, nay, pray God long before, the Dutch princeling will have got the punishment he deserves for all those years of intrigue and treachery, for the cheap swords hidden in Galloway peat-stacks and the

Dutch guilders doled out to any man willing to sell his country and his honour; there will be peace, real peace, and I shall be at Jean's side. I shall hear her dear voice singing lullabies over that cradle, and I will ask Anna to teach her some of the Gaelic airs we learnt from Moir. And when the fair weather comes again, we will walk in our Mustard Yard, our own Mustard Yard, and remind one another of its model in the Place of Paisley, where we fell in love. And we shall never quarrel any more, because, with Orange beaten in open fight, the Covenanting trouble will die down to the ravings of a few harmless fanatics, and no longer will there be Cochrane kinsfolk tempted to rebellion by Dutch gold.

Elspeth scowled at him as she offered the claret, but long ago he had become tolerant of Elspeth's hate. For painfully he had learned the lesson that it was not this mischief-making, jealous woman who stood between him and his wife; it was the clash of their own temperaments. There was passion and there was tenderness, but there was not, and never could be, understanding; he knew that now. There were certain subjects which must be avoided between them if harmony was to be maintained; there were problems he had, connected with public matters or with his work, which he longed to discuss with her, but could not, because she cared nothing for public matters, and she hated his work. So he had learned the loneliness of love without understanding, and no longer offered her a part of himself that she did not want.

He was grateful, deeply, passionately grateful for his blessing, and if his spirit remained lonely, so it was also with the run of mankind. He had married the only woman he had ever loved; soon he would have a child to inherit the modest honours he had obtained by faithful service and devotion to duty; he had risen, without intriguing for it, to the rank of second-in-command of the Scots Army; he was Constable, and lately made Provost, of Dundee; a Privy Councillor and member of half a dozen committees; and, despite all the jealous title-tattle and malicious intrigue of the great ones, he retained the favour and friendship of his King. And to crown all, soon there would be peace and settled government again, and, only forty now, he could look forward to many years of family life, here in his dear Dudhope, and the management of the affairs of his home town, the little familiar burgh he could see from his windows, nestling beside the broad blue estuary of the Tay.

But as he looked down upon Dundee now, his eyes caught sight of that for which he had looked from the battlements: the figure of a single horseman galloping up the carriageway. Suddenly, for no reason at all, he found himself remembering that other horseman, the trooper who had interrupted his wedding, bearing the spiteful message from Old Tom. Well, Old Tom was dead, God rest him, and the message this rider was bringing to Dudhope must be from the Privy Council, calling Major General Grahame back to active service, not, thank God, to quarter the moors for Covenanting rebels, but to guard the Border while the English Army dealt with foreign invasion.

Stooping swiftly to kiss the top of Jean's fair head, he hurried from the room and was in the entrance to the Castle when the rider dismounted from his foam-flecked horse. With some surprise he recognised his friend, Colin Lindsay, Lord Balcarres, still Captain of one of the troops of horse which formed his regiment. Before Claverhouse could greet him, my lord gasped out:

"I insisted on coming myself, Clavers. Orders have just now come to the Council that the entire Scots Army is to march into England to join with the English troops at Salisbury."

(iii)

For a moment Claverhouse could only stand and stare at him. Then he rapped out: "Is Orange landed?"

"Not yet. He is waiting, they say, for a favourable wind; it's thought for certain that he will make for the West of England, and that the most likely place of his landing is Torbay. But these orders, Clavers – they're plain daft."

"From whose hand did they come?"

"They were writ upon the back of a plate – imagine! – by Steuart of Goodtrees, and by the look of them it was done in the midst of a debauch. They're signed by my Lord Melfort."

Claverhouse took the tired horse by the bridle and led it into the courtyard, calling to a groom to take charge of it. Listening to the instructions for its being cooled down before taken to the stable, Balcarres scarcely knew whether to be irritated or amused; even in the midst of such a crisis, Clavers would still find time to care for a dumb beast.

"You'll need to rest yourself, Colin," said the lord of Dudhope shortly, leading the way to his own apartments, "before we ride for Edinburgh, so not another word until you have had meat and wine."

While his friend refreshed himself, Claverhouse stood by the window with his back to the room, watching the wheeling gulls, while his mind digested the situation. The order from Melfort (possibly suggested by the ex-traitor, Steuart of Goodtrees) was, as Balcarres had said, pure madness. King James had a large and excellent English Army, and the little Scots force, amounting to not quite three thousand men, could make no appreciable difference to its efficiency or strength. And to bring the Scots Army south would be to leave Scotland and the whole of the North of England unprotected against the swarms of

Covenanters who Religious Toleration had encouraged to return from exile to their native land.

But that was not the worst of it. The Scots Privy Council, left with only a handful of troops in garrison, and a Militia but roughly trained and of doubtful loyalty, would panic; reviewing in his mind the members of that Council, Claverhouse felt that on only two could he rely: Balcarres here, and Sir George Mackenzie, the latter reinstated as Lord Advocate at the beginning of the year. Queensberry was living in sullen retirement at Sanquhar, the Treasury having been put into Commission; his kinsmen on the Council were all hostile to Lord Chancellor Perth, because the latter, once a most useful tool, had filched the power from them. Perth himself would be useless in an emergency, and had made himself detested by the population of Edinburgh by turning Catholic; the Bishops were alienated by the toleration extended to the Papists and Covenanters; Atholl was brooding harder than ever, cheated a second time of the Chancellorship; the Lord Justice Clerk was none other than Sir John Dalrymple of Stair. Hamilton was in London; but whether his absence in this crisis was a good thing or not, Claverhouse could not make up his mind, only he was sure that in any crisis the sole concern of his Grace would be for his Grace's safety and welfare.

Yet the spirits of the loyal but faint-hearted could be kept up, the Covenanting rebels kept down, and possible traitors like Dalrymple held in check, if the small but efficient Scots Army was not withdrawn from its native soil…

"You must prevent it, Clavers," said a voice behind him, as though answering his thoughts.

He turned sharply, and saw that Balcarres had come up behind him; my lord's amiable face had a queer look of desperation, and with the absentmindedness for which he was notorious, he was picking a piece of wheaten bread to pieces and scattering it upon the floor.

"I prevent it? You mean the taking of our Army south? My dear Colin, you forget that my Lord Melfort, who signed the order, is Secretary of State for Scotland, forbye that Major General Douglas is in command of our Army – Colin, what in heaven's name is in your mind?"

"You have a huge influence over the common men and the inferior officers," gabbled Balcarres, still scattering bread about, apparently under the impression that he was feeding the gulls outside the window. "They would obey you gladly, where they obey Douglas grudgingly. Take command, Clavers, and explain yourself afterwards. In this emergency King James must needs leave the ordering of many matters to the Secretaries, and it many well be that he does not know of this daft message from Melfort."

Claverhouse's mouth had hardened.

"Pray consider what you are suggesting: That I use my influence in the Army to promote mutiny – for that is what it amounts to; that I deliberately disobey an order sent by his Majesty's Secretary of State. I deem that order ill-advised; so much I will admit to you; but it is not for me to question it."

Balcarres took a turn or two about the room, leaving a little trail of breadcrumbs behind him. His agitation was greater than ever; sweat stood out upon his forehead, and his look was almost wild. Suddenly, while he was still at the other end of the room, he stopped dead, wheeled round, and facing the other, cried half defiantly: "Very well, I'll tell you what it is, Clavers. There are some saying that Major General Douglas is a traitor in Orange's pay."

Next moment he would have given much to be able to take back those words. He knew Claverhouse; they had been close friends for years, and he ought to have remembered two of the most conspicuous traits in the

Grahame's character: a burning hatred of injustice, and a detestation of scandal. Balcarres was a tall man, but somehow the slight figure in the window seemed to tower over him, even as its personality dwarfed his own.

"And who are the 'some who are saying', if you please?"

"Och, it's just one of those rumours that go round the town and the camp. But I like it not, Clavers; you ken fine what Douglas is, a wee, strutting martinet, vain as a peacock – "

"And therefore, without question, a traitor to his country."

My lord winced at the biting sarcasm, but his friend had not done with him yet.

"I ken fine that I'm an ambitious man and have a fearful temper; therefore I must needs be a traitor to my country. I ken fine that my Lord Duke of Queensberry is mean and spiteful, that my Lord Atholl is self-important, and my Lord Perth lacking in courage, therefore must they needs be traitors to their country. I ken fine that there is not a man in Scotland but has some faults of character, and therefore must they all be traitors in the pay of a foreign invader. And I ken fine that for daring to repeat filthy rumours about the honour of your commanding officer, who is mine likewise, my duty is to have you up before a Council of War."

Then, all of a sudden, the sarcasm vanished and the dry humour returned.

"Instead of which you will bide in Edinburgh and keep the Council to their duty while I take the Horse to Salisbury and assist in thrashing William of Orange. And a major baron of Scotland though you are, and my dear friend, you will never again venture to suggest to me that I should disobey a royal command, and promote mutiny, because of a rumour which may or may not be true."

"A rumour which may be, Clavers," repeated my lord quickly.

"I intend to investigate it. Let that content you. And now pray excuse me while I make ready to ride."

(iv)

The little Scots Army marched south under drenching rain, Dunmore's Dragoons (once Old Tom's beloved Greys), Buchan's Regiment of fourteen companies, six companies of Foot Guards, one troop of Life Guards, and the King's Own Regiment of Horse; in all two thousand, eight hundred, and thirty-six men. On reaching Penrith, Major General the Hon. James Douglas divided his forces, himself taking the Foot by way of Chester, and sending the Horse under Claverhouse by way of York.

Was it possible, wondered Claverhouse, that the reason for this division was Douglas' determination to avoid a private talk with him? He had endeavoured to obtain one ever since they had begun to march, but always he had failed, and since Douglas was his senior officer it had not been possible to force a *tête-à-tête*. And if this was indeed the explanation, did it lend substance to Balcarres' ugly rumour?

As he rode, mile after mile, through the English countryside (seeing all about him an England getting on with its normal business, the towns busy with buying and selling, the farmers tending livestock and crops), he steeled himself to ponder, unemotionally and coldly, the likelihood of Douglas being in Dutch pay. All his shrewdness and insight into character were called into service; he thrust from him his personal dislike of Douglas, and he held at bay the horror which threatened to overwhelm him at the mere thought of the rumour proving correct. He was judge, jury, and witnesses in the private court of his mind, and the image of the accused must be tried with the most scrupulous fairness.

The verdict he gave at last was 'Not guilty'. The Hon. James had the family avarice and some of his brother Queensberry's pettiness; on the other hand he had never by word or act shown anything approaching disloyalty to King James, he had appeared indifferent to the Religious Toleration which had alienated men like Mackenzie, and he heartily disliked the Covenant. He owed his present rank to James, and though it was true he was piqued by not receiving a commission as Commander-in-Chief, he had the power without the title. His faults were obvious; he was vain, consequential, always on his dignity, and thoroughly disliked by the officers and men under his command; he was, in fact, a silly, tiresome little martinet, and men of that type did not, in Claverhouse's opinion, fit the role of great traitors.

Moreover, he was not partial to taking risks, and if he had been receiving bribes from Orange to betray his King, he was taking a risk with a vengeance. William of Orange was not the man to give money away without expecting return for it, and the only possible return he could expect from Douglas was the latter's attempting to carry the Scots Army over to the invader, or at least to make sure that it did him no hurt. And if Orange were beaten (as Claverhouse was convinced he must be), he would publish abroad Douglas' treachery, in which case the Hon. James would be at the very least a ruined man, even if he managed to escape with his neck.

No, he did not fit the role. And yet, as Claverhouse stared ahead of him through the rain, riding mile after muddy mile through the Midlands of England, some other thought nagged at the back of his mind, for a long while formless. He was eating a belated supper in a wretched little inn at Peterborough, having gone the round of his encampment, when that thought took shape, stark and intolerable.

He remembered suddenly the days when he had stood in the ante-room to the royal Bedchamber at Windsor, and the lesson he had learned as he had waited among the lords and the courtiers for King Charles to die and for Shaftesbury to foist a puppet on the Throne: only a handful of the great ones present cared about the effect of this crisis upon their country; the majority were concerned solely for their posts and their estates. If the Hon. James was in truth a traitor in this other, graver crisis, it could only be because he knew he did not stand alone. For it is never one rat, but a colony, which leaves the sinking ship.

Chapter Two

(i)

It was still pouring with rain when, on a morning towards the end of October, Claverhouse and Douglas had their first private audience with James the King.

As upon the march from Edinburgh, so since his arrival in London, Claverhouse had found no opportunity for a *tête-à-tête* with the Hon. James. The time had been spent in getting the Scots Army into quarters for a brief rest before they joined the English troops at Salisbury; Douglas had fussed and fumed, and found little causes for jealousy; the Horse had been assigned better quarters than the Foot; he ought to have been consulted; scarcely had he got his men into their quarters than he had them out again; they must exercise on the Artillery Ground, and show the London citizens what smart soldiers he had made of them.

Claverhouse, meanwhile, leaving his men and horses to their well-earned rest, had paid several unofficial visits to Whitehall. Everything in the great rambling palace appeared as he remembered it, except for the number of deserted lodgings, some belonging to the principal officers of the Army who were with their regiments at Salisbury, some formerly tenanted by great lords like Shrewsbury, Delamere and Macclesfield, who had been members of Shaftesbury's old faction and who had taken themselves off to their pay-master, William of Orange. But otherwise the stately life of Whitehall progressed upon its normal routine; the two Yeomen of the Almony still fed the poor at a stated time at Holbein's Gate; the trumpets announced that the King was dining in the Great Hall; and the familiar figures of the Gentleman Harbinger, the Supervisor of the Dresser, the Quarter Waiters, the Groom Porters, went smoothly about their respective tasks.

Yet there was an atmosphere about Whitehall which Claverhouse did not like; he tried to tell himself that he was being fanciful, yet it was as real to him as an odour. His mind full of the hateful thought which had formulated itself at Peterborough, he observed the Ministers and the courtiers, and though there was little in their talk or behaviour to lend substance to his fear, he became more and more uneasy. Was it only his imagination which made him think that there was rather too much whispering into the folds of periwigs, that eyes avoided giving a direct glance, that certain remarks conveyed more than their surface meaning? But apart from this, there was, undoubtedly, what he considered a most dangerous dislike of the word 'invasion'.

"His Highness, the Prince of Orange, comes to effect a reconciliation between his Majesty and the Protestant subjects he has offended by his over-riding of the Penal Laws against the Papists," old Lord Clarendon gravely explained to him. "His Highness has stated publicly again and again that he has not the least intention of laying any claim to the Crown, or of doing his Majesty the least hurt."

"Is it not then somewhat surprising, my lord, that his Highness brings with him so large an army?"

"His escort has been grossly exaggerated. It was not to be imagined that he would come without a proper guard for his person, seeing that his nation is at war with France and there may be French ships attempting to intercept him on his voyage; but as for his fifteen thousand mercenaries, they do not exist except in the noddles of alarmists."

Clarendon spoke in good faith, of that Claverhouse was convinced; but he suspected other lips which spoke the same comfortable words, and he mistrusted the eyes which would not meet his while they spoke them. And yet his sense of justice was so strong, his private suspicion so monstrous, that even he, ever the realist, tried to tell himself he was a fool.

(ii)

Time seemed to have swung backwards as he followed the Hon. James Douglas into the King's Closet this morning. He was a young captain of horse again, on his first visit to this holy of holies, given the privilege of a private audience with King Charles because that monarch felt it his duty to listen to a boring tale of disaffection in faraway Scotland. But now he was Major General Grahame, and his companion was not to describe the state of a small portion of Scotland, but to confer upon the imminent invasion of England. In place of King Charles there was King James, and the room was stamped with the impression of a different personality.

The same chorus of clocks ticked away the seconds, but instead of the basket of pretty yapping spaniels there was one lean greyhound stretched before the hearth; the cold eyes and hooked nose of William of Orange were gone from the wall, replaced by a portrait of the Queen; there was not the least trace of a woman's perfume; the great table was piled with orderly stacks of papers; and on brackets round the walls were models of the ships which once upon a time, when King James was Duke of York and a Protestant, he had a sailed to victory against the Dutch.

After the formal kissing of hands, Claverhouse allowed Douglas to open the interview, while he stood in the background and keenly observed his master. He had speculated painfully upon the effect upon King James of his nephew's treachery, and in dark moments had resigned himself to finding a complete collapse, for he guessed what it must mean to so trusting a character to find a near kinsman a traitor. In more optimistic moods he had remembered that the King had been a soldier in his youth, and a fighter all his life; that it had been observed of him by the great Turenne that if any man could be said to be without fear it was the Duke of York; and that he had shown that he possessed that rarer sort of courage which braves unpopularity for the sake of an ideal. Claverhouse's imagination, therefore, had presented him with two pictures, a dark and a light: an old man stricken by shock; an old soldier responding to a challenge. What he saw had little resemblance to either.

King James sat posed at one side of the fireplace, his left arm leaning on a draped support, the fingers splayed in an unnatural position, his right hand holding the Sceptre. The Crown of England, its jewels flashing in the firelight, reposed upon a velvet cushion nearby. He was garbed in robes of state, of purple and ermine, with the blue ribbon of the Garter across his breast and a collar of gold, with an exquisitely chased George depending from it, round his neck. Some six paces from him stood Sir Godfrey Kneller, in a paint-stained gown, an easel and canvas before him, a palette on his thumb, bespectacled eyes moving rapidly from canvas to subject, skilful fingers handling a brush.

"I offer you my apologies, gentlemen," said the King, when Douglas had finished uttering platitudes, "but I have promised poor blind Mr Pepys my picture, and it must be completed ere I go to my Army at Salisbury. Pray be seated."

Douglas began again, describing his march south, sending little glances at Claverhouse which dared him to steal the conversation, but he need not have worried; Claverhouse was content to sit silent and continue his observation of his master. He began to perceive that behind that dignified exterior, the curiously flat tone, the cold graciousness, the expressionless features, a guarded, simple, and isolated mind was struggling to recover itself from shock, was calling upon all the resources of an ageing body and a firm but weary will to forget the personal and to concentrate upon the national. The king was endeavouring to conquer the man.

For it was not just Orange's treachery which must have shaken him; that was bad enough, yet he had never liked Orange personally, though he had trusted him. But there was somebody else involved, there was Orange's wife and James' elder and best-loved daughter, the Princess Mary. Claverhouse had heard the gossip of Whitehall; it was whispered that when his Majesty could doubt no longer that his nephew and son-in-law intended to invade his realm, he had continued to believe in the good faith of Mary. He had remarked to several of the great lords that he felt most deeply for her, whose nature must be outraged by her husband's baseness. He had continued to write affectionately to her, even when, in her letters to her sister Anne and to his wife, she had studiously refrained from mentioning her half-brother, the infant Prince of Wales; he had explained away the discontinuance of the prayers for the baby in her chapel by saying that Mary had always been ruled by her masterful husband; he was sure, he said, that the Princess offered her private devotions for her little half-brother.

But watching the King today, Claverhouse wondered. Just lately he had learned for himself that when once the seed of suspicion takes root in a man, it grows as luxuriantly as a weed. Behind the cold courtesy, the business-like answers to Douglas' fussy reporting, was it not inevitable that James should be thinking: if one of my own blood can write me effusive letters at the selfsame time as he is plotting my ruin, can I trust even my own daughter? Yes, it was inevitable. James was an extremely poor judge of character, but he was by no means a fool; moreover, your too trusting man once he is betrayed, becomes an easy prey to suspicion. The King was resolved to do his duty, but the man must be on the rack. The King was the dignified gentleman whose likeness Kneller was transmitting to canvas as a present for a faithful, humble old servant who had helped to build that navy which had been the passion of the Duke of York, and whose blind eyes would never see it; the man wrestled with horrors, with the memory of a little daughter who had played at this knee, with the image of that child grown to a woman who might at this very movement be playing Goneril to his King Lear...

"If your Majesty pleases to rest for a while," suggested Sir Godfrey Kneller, laying down his brush, "I will retire and finish the portrait when your Majesty is at leisure."

"No, no", said the King, stretching his cramped fingers, "it must be finished today. I am to be a soldier again, Sir Godfrey; I shall have no leisure for a long while." His eyes strayed to Claverhouse, and for the first time he smiled naturally. "It is good to see you again, General Grahame. How does your wife?"

"She doth well, I thank your Majesty. She is expecting a child in the spring."

"I wish you joy." A pause. Each of them was thinking of that other baby, the delicate Prince of Wales, the son who had arrived so late in his father's life, and who had been ushered into the world to the tune of libels hot from Dutch printing-presses. "There will be peace again in the spring, please God, and meanwhile I am thankful to have my excellent Scots Army to fight beside my English one. We shall find work for you and your men at Salisbury, gentlemen."

Claverhouse was wondering how to frame a reply which should convey to King James his own conviction that the little Scots Army would be far better employed in protecting their native land, when there was a scratch on the door, and in came the Earl of Middleton, one of the Secretaries of State, puffing and panting from haste and agitation, his eyes troubled, his periwig awry.

"Your Majesty, an express has just brought the news that Sir Roger Strickland has sighted the Prince of Orange and his fleet in the Downs."

Claverhouse glanced quickly at the King; but James took the news with extraordinary composure. He continued to sit where he was, the Sceptre propped upon his knee; his only reaction was to make a slight movement of squaring his shoulders, a workmanlike and somehow very touching movement, that of a tired old man who has some straining but necessary task to perform.

"Well," he said, "we are prepared. If my Lord Dartmouth and the Navy fail to beat him at sea, we shall do his business for him on land. I must ride to Salisbury tomorrow, and you, gentlemen, must away to your troops and march them thither. Meanwhile, Sir Godfrey, pray complete this picture; Mr Pepys must not be disappointed of his present, and the time is so short."

The last glimpse Claverhouse had of his master this morning was the same as the first, the stiff pose, the fingers of one hand curled as though offering something, weary shoulders braced beneath the heavy robes, unshrewd, honest eyes staring at the model of a ship which, a long time ago when he was Lord High Admiral of England,

James had sailed against England's greatest commercial rival, the Dutch.

(iii)

During his first week at Salisbury, Claverhouse was happier than he had been since leaving Dudhope.

For, riding round the little city of tents and huts which had sprung up on Salisbury Plain, he saw for himself the excellence of the English Army, and in his anticipation of sharing with it the thrashing of a treacherous invader, he was almost reconciled to the folly of leaving Scotland denuded of troops. The men were in very good heart; the King's papistry was clean forgotten in the national crisis, and there could be no doubt that the common soldiers were devoted to their King and hot against Orange. Songs of the Civil War mingled with new ones composed for the occasion, and there was all that camaraderie which had seemed to Claverhouse ominously absent at Whitehall, all that honest facing up to the fact of foreign invasion which the courtiers refused. Including the Scots troops and several regiments brought over from Ireland, King James' army would number forty thousand men, he was told. He noticed an area of vacant tents and huts, and on enquiry found that these had been apportioned to the Royal Regiment of Horse, the Duke of St Alban's Regiment, and Lord Cornbury's Dragoons, all of whom were expected at any moment from Winchester, bringing a train of artillery with them.

On November 5th (a most apposite date, since it was the anniversary of the Gunpowder Plot and always celebrated by an anti-Popery display), William of Orange landed at Torbay. He had evaded Lord Dartmouth and the Navy, and here he was, marching on English soil beneath a banner which proclaimed that he was come to protect the liberties of England and the Protestant Faith, and with an army two-thirds of which were Catholics. He had brought a heavy cargo of traitors with him, whom, reflected Claverhouse, it would be a great pleasure to thrash, including Sir James Dalrymple, father of Sir John, and Major General Hugh Mackay of Scourie. All in all, Claverhouse's spirits were high as he conferred with the other officers, inspected his troops, and lived uncomfortably in a small lodging in a much overcrowded Salisbury. When it came to the question of a private talk with Major General Douglas, the Hon. James was as elusive as ever, but by this time Claverhouse had almost forgotten Balcarres and his rumours. In any case, he reflected grimly, if Douglas had accepted Dutch gold in return for a promise of betrayal, he must be most heartily repenting his folly by this time. No recruits had joined Orange's Standard, and the Mayor of Exeter had just slammed the gates of that city in his face.

Claverhouse was sitting down to dinner one midday, when a message came commanding his immediate presence at the Bishop's House, where the King was lodged. All the messenger could tell him was that a council of senior officers had been summoned; there was nothing unusual in that, thought Claverhouse, as he walked quickly in the direction of the King's lodging, only it seemed rather strange that it should have been summoned at dinner-time. Only a quarter of an hour ago he had heard the trumpets announcing that his Majesty was going to dine. He had scarcely taken his place at the long table in the apartment assigned to this military conference, before the door was flung open by an usher and the King walked in.

Immediately he saw his master, Claverhouse knew that there was something very gravely wrong. The deliberate control which he had noted in James at Whitehall was emphasised to a degree which made the lined face appear masked, and there was something else which Claverhouse did not like at all: that face was a very strange colour.

The King was normally a fresh-complexioned man, and had retained into late middle-age the healthy skin of his youth. But it was not healthy now. It was a queer mauvy-grey, and immediately under each eye there was a little area of red, resembling the flush of fever. The eyes themselves, always mentally short-sighted, were lifeless; every now and then there was that little straightening of the shoulders which had wrung Claverhouse's heart during the audience at Whitehall; and just after taking his seat at the head of the table, his Majesty called for a glass of brandy, a spirit which ordinarily he never touched. He sipped it at intervals, his facial muscles contracting to the fiery taste, while his glance strayed from man to man about the table, from handsome Lieutenant General Churchill, his most intimate friend, to ugly Major General Kirke, from stolid, honest Feversham, Commander-in-Chief of the English Army, to the hard blue eyes and the ramrod-back of Major General Douglas, commanding the Scots – these his principal officers, the men on whom he must rely to defeat foreign invasion, resplendent in their scarlet and gold lace, solemn and respectful of countenance, as they waited for their King to address them.

"My lords and gentlemen, I have very ill news."

The words had come with a rush, but now the King picked others carefully; once or twice there was a slight stammer in his speech, and all the while there was evidence of dreadful, painful effort.

"His Grace, the D-Duke of Berwick, the Governor of P-Ports-mouth, was in that town when orders were sent him from my Secretary for War to ride p-post to Winchester and bring thence to Salisbury his Royal Regiment of Horse. These orders were delayed upon the road – whether by accident or d-design, we cannot tell. His Grace was upon his way to Winchester when he encountered his own regiment, and the royal Dragoons, the one being in the care of Major Littleton and the other of Major Clifford, hotly pursued by some troops of the P-Prince of Orange. His Grace rallied them, beat off the enemy, and then demanded of the two majors what was become of my Lord Cornbury who, besides being Colonel of the Royal Dragoons, was in command of his Grace's Regiment during his absence at Portsmouth. The two majors answered that my Lord Cornbury was – was gone over to the – to the Prince of Orange, and had attempted to carry both regiments with him."

Lifting a hand to silence the exclamations of horror which arose from all sides, the King continued, slow, deliberate, carefully unemotional:

"I pray wait, gentlemen; there is worse even than this. It seems that my Lord Cornbury was in league with Lieutenant Colonel Langton, who, because of the sickness of the Duke of St Albans, was in command of his Grace's Regiment of foot. These two traitors led out their regiments, together with the Royal Dragoons, from Winchester, leaving behind them, on the excuse of forced marches, the train of artillery, and at a certain point upon the march they detached the Horse from the Foot and Colonel Langton marched the Foot to Honiton, where it was received by Talmash, one of the Prince of Orange's commanders, and informed that it was now – it was now in the invader's service. This we know from one of the common soldiers of the foot, who has made shift to join us, and who tells us that most of his fellows are endeavouring to return to our camp."

He paused to take a sip of brandy. The two red spots upon his cheeks were burning now like bale-fires; the grey of his complexion was deepened to the colour of putty.

"Meanwhile, Majors Littleton and Clifford, beginning to suspect somewhat, desired of my Lord Cornbury to see his orders; he refused; and when they pressed him, he told them roundly that he was pledged to bring over the Horse and Dragoons to the Prince of Orange's camp, whither his brother commander was already gone, and he promised the majors immediate promotion if they would concur in his treachery. To their honour they refused, and thereupon my Lord Cornbury went off, taking with him some sixty of the Dragoons and several inferior officers whom he had corrupted beforehand. The two majors marched the rest towards Salisbury, were pursued by a party of the enemy, and this was the state in which his Grace of Berwick found them."

As though the effort it had cost him to tell this dreadful tale, and to tell it without emotion, had exhausted him, he slumped suddenly in his chair; and immediately the chorus of horrified exclamations broke out once more. My Lord Cornbury, son to that worthy old gentleman, the Earl of Clarendon! And Lieutenant Colonel Langton too, so hot in his talk against the invader. It was unthinkable! There must be some mistake! It would kill my Lord Clarendon! Who was to break the news to him? Such base treachery on the very eve of battle...senior officers of the Army betraying their trust...unprecedented...filthy...intolerable... so the voices vied with one another in saying the conventional thing. Only Claverhouse remained silent, his hands gripped together on the table.

"My lords and gentlemen, we are, as you have observed, upon the eve of battle." (The King was sitting upright again, his self-command crumbling, passion breaking through.) "With a loyal army, officered by loyal gentlemen, at my back, I am content to leave the issue to God and to our swords. But no general can fight if he suspects treachery among his officers. I-i-if, then, there is any present in this room who believes the Prince of Orange his cause to be just, in God's name let him surrender his commission and be gone instanter. I shall respect his h-h-honesty; he shall have a safe conduct to go to his new master. Be rebels if your conscience so impels you, but not traitors. Cross swords with me if you must, but do not, as you are men, do not stab me in the back!"

There was one instant of silence. Then a figure sprang to its feet, the handsome figure of John Churchill, a man who owed the King everything, even his life. His voice rang out like a trumpet-note, thrilling and brazen:

"We will stand by your Majesty to the last drop of our blood!"

Then they were all at it, swearing vows of loyalty, protesting against the mere suggestion that they could betray, damning Cornbury and Langton. Only one man of them all sat silent, Major General John Grahame.

He knew the worst now, he knew, as surely as if he had concrete proof of it, that there was corruption in high places, that Cornbury and Langton were but the first of the rats. He cursed himself for not realising before that the little megalomaniac in Holland would never have risked invasion unless he had made sure of finding the support of traitors on the spot. He remembered the Dutch swords hidden in Galloway peat-stacks, the trained agitators slipping over from Holland to stir up trouble when the native ones had failed, the automatic departure for Holland of malcontents certain of finding asylum there.

For years Dutch William had intrigued against his uncle and father-in-law in an endeavour to get him ousted from the Succession; was it likely that having failed in this, and seeing, with the birth of a Prince of Wales, all hope of the Crown passing from him, he would cease to intrigue? He was tenacious, he was insanely ambitious, and he was without scruples; but he would never have risked an invasion of England without the weapon of treachery.

Oh, the men he had corrupted were not all villains; it would have been simpler, Claverhouse reflected bitterly, if they had been. Some honestly feared the return of Catholicism; some were offended by Religious Toleration; with some self-interest would drive them to hope for better officers under William than they had got under James; with them all there would be a preference for a puppet king, who owed his title to their class, to a king by hereditary right, their master. And the plain treachery of a few great ones would be enough to infect the rest, for ever jealous of place and power. He remembered again the Ministers and the Judges and the Bishops waiting for King Charles to die, ready to swim with the tide, feverishly speculating whether their money would be safer on King James or King Monmouth; he remembered his own disgust when, as a mere captain of horse, he had found the great ones of Scotland, even honest men like Queensberry, far more interested in bringing down the Duke of Lauderdale than in taking steps to prevent a dangerous rebellion.

Treachery and self-interest; and Dutch William on the doorstep. And there was nothing in the world he could do about it except watch the noble rats departing, one by one.

(iv)

Though it was very late at night, there was a little crowd collected before the gate of the Bishop's House, as Claverhouse approached it on his way home to his lodging. Links, flaring in their holders, showed him scarlet uniforms mingling with civilian dress, and in the midst of all, the target of anxious questioning, an old and agitated man in the gown of a physician. Beyond the little courtyard the house blazed with light, and figures could be seen passing and repassing behind the unshuttered windows. In the courtyard itself there was straw laid down, deadening the footsteps of the sentries.

Claverhouse paused. He was dog-tired in body, and his mind seemed poisoned by the horror of the past few days. Night after night, always under cover of darkness, the noble rats had slipped away from Salisbury: the Duke of Grafton, one of King Charles' natural sons, Prince George of Denmark, King James' son-in-law, Major General Kirke, the Duke of Ormonde, the officers who, but a few days previously, had exclaimed in such horror at the desertion of Cornbury and Langton, who had refused with such righteous indignation the King's offer of a safe-conduct to Orange if any among them thought his cause to be just, who had sworn to stand by his Majesty to the last drop of their blood. Not one was man enough to go openly; they were drinking the King's health at supper, and next morning were kissing Orange's hand.

Some of them had left odious little notes behind them, dripping with self-justification, full of such phrases as 'the inviolable duties of conscience', 'a high and necessary concern for the Protestant religion', 'the liberties of the people'; others, more honest, made no excuse at all. Some had gone of their own free will, because for years they had been taking Orange's bribes and looked to reap the reward of their treachery; some because they could not bear to think of my Lord So-and-So getting an office they had wanted and had not got under James; others simply because they had not the courage to remain with the sinking ship.

It was, thought Claverhouse, like a hidden disease, this treachery; an apparently healthy body was opened and disclosed, running all though it, the tendrils of a growth. It had infected some of the Scots officers as well, even some in his own regiment; his Lieutenant Colonel, Lord Drumlanrig, and Lord William Douglas, Queensberry's sons, William, Earl of Annandale and young Lord Ross; they were gone with the English rats. The Hon. James Douglas had not yet deserted, but he had thrown out sundry hints which had been enough to tell Claverhouse that he was only waiting for his chance. But all these betrayals palled before the most spectacularly dreadful of all: that of John Churchill, the King's most intimate friend, who had supped with his Majesty in private before sneaking off to Orange...

"Thank God I have found you, sir!" Claverhouse turned to see a young Gentleman Pensioner standing at his elbow. "We have sent several times to your lodgings, but you were not there."

"And you wondered if you must send to the Prince of Orange's camp to find me," said Claverhouse, quietly bitter; and next moment regretted it as he saw the young Pensioner wince.

"My Lord Ailesbury sent me to enquire for you, sir," said he "it being his lordship's turn of duty in the Bedchamber. His Majesty has been asking for you – "

He did not finish the sentence, for Claverhouse was already striding rapidly across the straw-strewn courtyard.

The silence in the King's Bedchamber, once the door was shut upon the whispered instructions of worthy young Ailesbury, was profound. His Majesty was not abed, but seated before a table on which was a mass of papers; he held out a limp hand to be kissed, gave his visitor the signal to rise from his knee, and then seemed to forget him. Etiquette forbidding him to speak before his master opened the conversation, Claverhouse glanced about the room.

It was a sick-room. On the news of Churchill's desertion, the King had been stricken with a violent and most prolonged haemorrhage. Threatened apoplexy (the disease which had killed his brother Charles) had been warded off only by this excessive bleeding from the nose, which had saved the brain from suffusion but had utterly exhausted the sufferer. He had fallen down in a dead swoon, while twin rivers of blood gushed from his nostrils, and with only brief intervals this haemorrhage had continued for three days. The physicians had applied the crude remedy which was the only one they knew; they had opened a vein and drawn away yet more blood, draining the patient white. That they had not killed him was little short of a miracle; observing him with fierce compassion now, Claverhouse wondered whether they had not done something worse.

It was the first time he had seen his master since the shock of Churchill's desertion, and he realised at once that the King's collapse was nervous as well as physical. The bodily weakness was obvious in the shrinking of the tall frame, in the skin which was as colourless as a corpse's, in the flaccid mouth, and in the effort necessary for the slightest movement. And the look in the wandering eyes, indifferent, lifeless, told the friend who loved him that the spirit had collapsed as completely as the body, that the firm, practical, if limited mind was slowed almost to a standstill by shock.

"M-Major G-General Grahame," came the weak stammer at last. The King stopped and peered at him as if trying to get him into focus.

"If I may presume to offer your Majesty my advice at this critical juncture," said Claverhouse, driving down his compassion, "I – "

"T-tomorrow, at a-at a Council meeting. But just now, I have s-somewhat to offer you."

His hand, with a great ring hanging loose upon the index finger, searched slowly through the mass of papers on the table.

"I have never – I say, I have never b-bribed men to serve me, General Grahame," went on the voice which Claverhouse scarcely recognised, "and it is too late to begin now even if I – i-if I would. So you must not think I am insulting you by endeavouring to b-b-buy your service. I desire that you will regard what I am about to give you, as a mark of my gratitude for your constant l-l-loyalty" (Claverhouse gritted his teeth with pain as he observed how difficult it was for the King to enunciate that particular word now) "and firm adherence upon all occasions to the t-true interests of the C-Crown. But as somewhat else besides."

The dull eyes shifted from Claverhouse and looked past him into the shadows of the room, seeming to see something visible only to them. Then, startlingly, the voice spoke without a stammer, dignified, strong, and almost cold. But it was the coldness of the man who feels deeply, and must not show it.

"My daughter, my nephew, my intimate friends, and those who owe me most have broken faith with me. You who have never had any great reward, who owe me little, have kept faith, and I believe will keep it. The integrity of one man cannot save my throne, but it can save my faith in human nature. Because of you, Clavers, and almost I might say because of you alone, I know that all men are not to be bought. That is the message this gift brings to you," he concluded, taking up a sealed parchment and holding it out to Claverhouse, "this gift which may not be worth the paper it is writ upon. It is a token of friendship; pray accept it so. And now, sir, you must excuse me; I am not very well."

It was not until he reached his own lodging that Claverhouse opened the parchment. It had the Royal Seal attached to it by a band of silver tissue, and it was a patent of nobility creating him Viscount of Dundee.

Chapter Three

(i)

London presented the most extraordinary appearance when Claverhouse rode into it from Watford on a clear, frosty morning in December. The smoke from burning Catholic chapels mingled with that of festive bonfires; 'No Popery' slogans chalked on the walls were half concealed by gay tapestries hung from the windows; and the crowds milling about the streets were still cheerfully tipsy from welcoming King James back to Whitehall after his attempted flight to France, the very same crowds which, during his absence, had beaten up his fellow Catholics, broken their windows, and given all those signs of mass hysteria which had made London a nightmare during the 'Popish Plot' of 1678.

Accompanied by Lord Balcarres, who had ridden with him from Watford, Claverhouse walked briskly across Whitehall Yard at the back of the Banqueting House, past Grinling Gibbons' beautiful statue of King James, and so to the entrance of the Shield Gallery which his Majesty, on his Accession, had turned into a small Catholic chapel, leaving the Chapel Royal to the Protestants. Slovenly Lord Middleton, one of the few great Officers of State who had remained faithful, stood in the entrance porch with a couple of Pensioners, waiting to escort the King to his apartments when his Majesty had finished his prayers.

"It is impossible to tell you, my lords," said Middleton, "whether his Majesty will receive you. He has refused all privy audiences today."

Claverhouse bowed without speaking, and taking Balcarres by the arm, began to walk his friend up and down the courtyard, doffing his hat to two elderly gentlemen, whose lawn sleeves proclaimed them to be bishops, who emerged, whispering agitatedly together, from the Chapel Royal on the other side of the court.

"Archbishop Sancroft and Turner of Ely," murmured Claverhouse, when they had passed. "Shepherds who, it seems, are wondering whether the Dutch sheep-dog they were so keen to welcome may not prove a wolf after all."

Balcarres only sighed heavily in reply; he simply could not understand the situation.

He had come up from Edinburgh some days previously, bringing letters from the Scots Privy Council (or what remained of it, for Chancellor Perth had fled and most of the others stayed in their country seats, awaiting the turn of events), only to discover that the King, having already sent away his wife and infant son, had disappeared from Whitehall with intent, it was supposed, to follow them to France. His army, which had fallen back on Watford and Reading, was disbanded by his order, but Balcarres had found Claverhouse at the former place, and his men under arms.

"I know no more than you, Colin," Claverhouse had replied to his bewildered questioning, "where his Majesty is or what will happen. I concurred in the decision to retreat from Salisbury because the corruption of so many of the officers made it impossible for us to risk meeting Orange in battle. But mean while I intend to stay here and keep my regiment together; we are but three and a half hundred, but there is not one officer or man for whose fidelity I would not go bond. The rats are gone."

"But they say that Orange lies at Andover," Balcarres had cried in dismay. "What if he sends forces to attack you?"

Claverhouse had smiled grimly, and had handed him a letter. It read:

'My Lord Dundee, I understand you are now at Watford and that you keep your men together. I desire you will stay there until further orders, and upon my honour none in my army shall touch you.'

It bore the seal and signature of William, Prince of Orange.

Claverhouse would say no more then; but when news had come that King James had been stopped on his flight to the coast and escorted back to London by loyal lords, he had told Balcarres shortly that it was vital he had speech with his Majesty, and that his friend must accompany him. And here they were.

(ii)

The two Pensioners sprang suddenly to attention, and a greyhound, which had lain concealed in a corner of the porch, came out and stood before the door with wagging tail and little whining barks. The King emerged alone, putting on his hat, murmured something to Lord Middleton, and, without noticing Claverhouse and Balcarres, walked away towards the gate which gave on to the Privy Garden, the greyhound at his heels. As the two visitors made to follow, Middleton stepped forward in agitation.

"My lords," he said, "his Majesty desires to be private. He will not have even his Pensioners with him – "

"I must take leave to intrude upon him, my lord," interrupted Claverhouse firmly. "What I have to say to his Majesty is of the utmost urgency."

Before the other could make any further protests, he bowed and walked quickly after the King, motioning Balcarres to accompany him.

The Privy Garden was deserted this morning by the courtiers and the ladies who usually promenaded here, a vast and desolate expanse of lawns and walks and empty flowerbeds, concealed from the street by a lofty wall, from the river by the Stone Gallery and the Royal Apartments, and divided from the Bowling Green into which it led by a row of lime-trees. Hoar-frost glistened prettily on grass and bare boughs, and the feet of the two men cracked ice in little puddles in the walks which led to the famous horologe in the centre of the garden. Up one of these walks there went ahead of them, unconscious of their presence, the solitary figure of the King, his greyhound following close at his heels; he walked slowly, his hands clasped behind him under his cloak, his formerly upright shoulders stooping a little. From the street and from the river came the noise of excited crowds; from the palace a trumpet-note and the ring of steel; but here in this great garden was only a private gentleman walking with his dog.

It was the dog's growl as it turned its head to stare at the intruders which made the King pause at last; stooping to lay his hand upon the lean head, he looked at the two lords in a queer dazed fashion, as they uncovered and bowed low. Then, in a low hoarse voice, he asked:

"How comes it that you, my lords, are with me still when all the world is gone to the Prince of Orange?"

The tone of naïve wonder, entirely devoid of self-pity or of bitterness, was so moving that Balcarres choked with tears.

"My fidelity to so good a master," he murmured brokenly, "must ever remain the same."

James looked from him to Claverhouse; but the latter remained silent.

"Will you two, as gentleman," asked the King, glancing from one to the other with a piteous, searching look, "say you still have attachment to me?"

"Sir, we do say it," Claverhouse answered promptly, his voice firm and strong.

"Will you," persisted the King, "give me your hands upon it, as men of honour?"

In that wintry garden, so significantly empty of its usual throng of courtiers, there was enacted then a strange little scene: three men, no longer for the moment king and subjects, grasped hands in the simplest of all gestures of good faith.

"It was kind of you to visit me at this troublesome time," said James with touching simplicity, though they had been his neighbours.

He walked on again, his step a little brisker; on reaching the great horologe, he ascended the two curving shallow steps on which it stood, and leant against it.

"Sir", said Claverhouse, standing a little below his master, his hat under his arm, "my lord here and I are come humbly to offer your Majesty our advice in this crisis. Is it your Majesty's pleasure that I speak freely?"

"Yes, yes, by all means," said the King, but without enthusiasm. He began to draw a pattern in the frost on one of the dials.

"The question is, Sir, whether you should stay in England or go to France. My humble opinion is that your Majesty should stay here, and summon all your subjects to their allegiance."

"Allegiance," repeated James; and now there was a trace of bitterness in his tone.

"It is true," continued Claverhouse, "that your army is disbanded, and that by your Majesty's own order, yet not so dispersed but that if the drums be beaten twenty thousand men may be assembled again."

"An army of traitors," said the King, writing his wife's initial in the frost.

"Under favour, that is not so. The common men are loyal and have been from the beginning. As for the officers, I have held conference with those who have stuck by your Majesty, and they are all willing and eager to fight. Moreover, now that the Prince of Orange is compelled to show himself in his true colours at last, now that he can pretend no longer that he has come with any intent but to usurp the Crown, many of the honest but mistaken lords who were minded to welcome him, see how they have been deceived and are ready to return to their allegiance. The Church of England, of late so hot against your Majesty's toleration of Catholics and Dissenters, is turning rightabout since she has realised that she has been only the Prince's stalking-horse in his invasion; and as for the common people, your Majesty has seen for yourself how huge a welcome they accorded you when you returned to London yesterday."

"I have seen for myself," said James, his voice flat and cold, "fresh evidence of the fickleness of the common people. They cheer me to the echo when I am brought back from a flight which they themselves forced upon me because they believed the vile slanders my enemies published against me; they burn Catholic chapels one day, and light bonfires for me the next. And my own children, my daughter – "

He broke off and bit his lip. It was not Mary, Orange's wife, of whom he was speaking; it was her sister Anne who, pretending she was pregnant, had used this excuse to sneak out of Whitehall to join her husband, George of Denmark in the invader's camp.

"As for the common soldiers," the King continued after a moment, "I believe them to be honest, but of what use are they without officers, and from my experience at

Salisbury I expect nothing from the officers save treachery."

There was a moment's silence. Then, suddenly, Claverhouse started forward, one foot on the lower step of the horologe, his face, uplifted towards his master, flushed from forehead to chin.

"Then give me your commission to take sole command, Sir," he cried passionately, "and I will undertake to get an army together, to march through all England with your Standard at their head, and drive these Dutch into the sea!"

Balcarres stood amazed at this outburst; it was unlike anything he knew of his friend. An excellent officer, experienced and efficient in policing a disaffected district, but without any experience whatsoever of battle since he had risen to high rank. A man of forty, neither impulsive nor quixotic, essentially the realist, even materialistic, careful always, throughout his service, to observe the commands of his superior officers, a stickler for discipline: that was Claverhouse, not the man who had just made this fantastic offer to King James. His Majesty seemed to be thinking much the same thing, for he only smiled as a father smiles at a child who cries out that he will protect him against all his enemies, and said quietly:

"My Lord Dundee, I am resolved to go overseas, since it is plain what are my nephew's intentions concerning me. You know it is but a short distance between the prison and the grave of kings" – his eyes strayed for an instant to the great stone Banqueting House before which, nearly forty years ago, his father had met the headsman's axe – "and that the Prince of Orange is resolved to deprive me of my liberty is proved by his straightway clapping up my Lord Faversham whom I sent to him as my ambassador. While I had an army I would fight, but what sort of an army is that which is infected with treachery? While I had loyal

Ministers I would remain and take my hazard; what loyalty can a man look for whose own children have deserted him?"

Again his glance strayed, this time towards the many deserted lodgings.

"In France, when I have recovered somewhat of my health and strength, I shall bethink me what I must do to deliver my kingdoms from a foreign usurper. Your lordships shall have my instructions; to you, my Lord Dundee, I will send a commission to command my Scots Army, and to you, my Lord Balcarres, authority to manage the civil affairs of your country. And while God gives me strength, you shall never find me failing in my duty to restore just and lawful government."

Claverhouse opened his lips to speak, for a torrent of words fought for utterance. He longed to tell the King that his leaving England was fatal, that while he remained his nephew could not lay any claim to the Crown, but that by going he would make it possible for Orange to pretend that he had abdicated and that the Throne was vacant. But Claverhouse remained silent, for he saw that nothing he could say would move his master now; James Stuart was a broken man.

(iii)

Not many mornings later, Claverhouse stood at a window in the lodging of the Page of the Backstairs in Whitehall, looking out at the Dutch Guards in their blue uniforms pacing on sentry duty, at little groups of personages whispering together in a silly flutter of agitation, and at shuttered lodgings, the lodgings of the few faithful lords who either had retired to their country seats or had followed their master into exile. King James was gone to France; the Prince of Orange had moved into St James'. His

Highness came over to Whitehall every day, however, on inspections of the palace which soon would be his own (for he had made it quite plain to the traitors that if they were minded to offer him anything less than the Crown, he would return to Holland and leave them to the mercy of the Sovereign they had betrayed), and to hold audiences. And this morning his Highness had summoned to a private audience the Lords Dundee and Balcarres.

"I was at the Chapel Royal yesterday," the latter said suddenly, coming to stand beside his friend in the window, "and it was the strangest thing to hear that fiery Whig, Burnet, praying for King James and the Prince of Wales; he had to do it, for such is the law, but I'll wager the words stuck in his throat. Clavers, why the devil has his Highness summoned us this morning?"

"To offer us a bribe to come over to him," replied Claverhouse, in a flat, unemotional voice.

His friend glanced at him with a frown; he could not understand what was going on in that handsome head of late. Claverhouse had become very reserved and almost taciturn since the King's going; he made no comments on the national situation, listened in silence to the rumours which daily excited the town, took no part in the burning question as to whether Orange would venture to call a parliament and thus outrage the Law, and told his friend nothing of his own intentions.

"Since we have neither retired to our homes nor followed King James overseas," he continued after a moment, "Orange, who was ever of the opinion that all men have their price, takes our presence in London as a sign that we are still in the market."

"Then what in heaven's name are we going to say to him?" burst out Balcarres, snatching off his periwig and waving it about in the air. "Outright defiance will but give him the excuse for flinging us into jail along with my Lord

Faversham and others, where we would be of no manner of use to our master or anyone else."

"Colin," said his friend, turning from the window and speaking with energy, "what you have just said is very true. At all costs, save that of sacrificing our honour, we must remain free men. You had best leave me to do the talking–"

He broke off as the Page of the Backstairs entered to inform their lordships that his Highness was ready to receive.

Claverhouse had visited the King's Closet when it was noisy with yapping spaniels, and when it was guarded by one lean greyhound; today there were no dogs in the room, for the Prince of Orange did not care for animals except in so far as they were useful. (In Holland, dogs drew handcarts or were chained up to protect their masters' property.) The models of ships were gone too; the Prince of Orange could not be expected to cherish replicas of the men-of-war which had trounced the Dutch fleet under James, Duke of York. All King Charles' beloved clocks had been removed, except one, a solid, utilitarian Dutch timepiece. Instead of a whiff of feminine perfume there was an aromatic odour from some herbs burning in a dish; the Prince of Orange suffered form asthma, and already it was whispered that when he got the Crown, he intended to remove from Whitehall, so often flooded in the winter, and buy himself a palace on some higher ground.

He sat with his hat upon his head, the light from the window falling full upon his face with its hooked nose, its cold, intelligent eyes, and its compressed lips. Inclining his head slightly in response to the formal bows of his visitors, he did not invite them to be seated but began at once to speak, rapidly and precisely, addressing himself to Balcarres.

"It cannot be unknown to you, my lord, that the writs are going out for the summoning of a Convention Parliament here in England, to debate upon the form of government which must be set up in consequence of the late King James' endeavour to subvert the Constitution and his leaving the Throne vacant. It is necessary that the like convention be summoned in Scotland, the which shall be done as soon as the multitude of my affairs permits, and I desired to see you this morning to tell you that in this Scottish Convention I am confident of your lordship's support. You are aware that your native land is in a state of the most dismal chaos, and as a lover of your country you must desire to see settled government return. I have spoke with the Duke of Hamilton and several others of the Privy Council here in London, and find I have their good-will; as a loyal Scotsman, therefore, you will, I am sure, be willing to join with the principal of the nobility of Scotland in supporting my claim."

With his habitual absent-mindedness, Balcarres had been standing with his periwig in his hand, unconsciously combing it with his fingers; his amiable face was a picture of agitation and embarrassment.

"Sir", he blurted out, "I can have no hand in doing anything against King James, to whom I have sworn allegiance (as we all have who hold any office), and who has been a kind master to me, though imprudent in many things. I could not have it on my conscience to assist in turning out my lawful King – "

"I must remind your lordship," Orange interrupted with deliberate patience, "that it is not a question of your assisting to turn out King James. He chose to leave the realm, and therefore the Throne is vacant."

"But the Throne is never vacant," cried Balcarres, sending an imploring glance at the silent Claverhouse.

"The Prince of Wales is the Heir Apparent, and forbye King James has not abdicated. I must beg leave to remind your Highness that the word abdicate comes from the Latin, *abdicatio*, which means disowning or renouncing– "

"I am addressing you, my lord," again interrupted the Prince (changing two very delicate subject), "neither as an adherent of the late King nor as a friend to me, but as a patriot who cannot wish to see his country left in confusion, having no government at all."

"But – but, sir," stammered the intensely embarrassed Balcarres, "under your favour, no summons for a parliament can be issued save by the King, and at present the King is overseas. It is against the Law that this Convention is summoned, and it being so, I see not how in conscience I may meddle with it."

The Prince's habitual coldness fired suddenly.

"I bid you have a care how you behave yourself, my lord," he cried, bringing the flat of his hand down upon the table, "for if you are so set upon sticking to the letter of the Law, you shall be left to it, and it may be you will find that a parliament is a better and more powerful interpreter of it than that you call your conscience."

His anger had brought on a fit of coughing, and for several moments he gasped and choked, his hand groping for the dish of herbs. When the steam from these had eased him a little, he said, with a return of his former coldness:

"You have my leave to return to Scotland, my Lord Balcarres; and this I promise you, that if you will abide there peaceably, you shall not be troubled either in person or estates. And now pray leave us; I desire some privy speech with my Lord Dundee."

(iv)

"My Lord Dundee." Orange made a deliberate pause, as though pondering upon the title. "I address you, as you hear, in accordance with the honour so recently bestowed upon you by the late King, and I assure you at once that I have no intention of depriving you of it unless you compel me to do so."

He paused, but Claverhouse merely inclined his head in reply.

"My lord, I will be frank with you, for I have heard that you are a man who loves plain speech. You have never, I believe, made any secret of the fact that you are hugely ambitious; and I admire ambition. You are a soldier; so am I. You have risen in the profession of arms through the excellence of your service, though perchance you have not forgot that you obtained your first commission in Scotland by my recommending you to the favour of the late King, then Duke of York. You have expected, and justly so, to be rewarded in return for your ability and your strict attention to duty; I compliment you upon this, for it shows me you are no romantic. Well, my lord, the master you served so faithfully can pay you no longer; I can, and am ready to do so. You have, at this juncture, three alternatives: to throw in your lot with me, to retire to your estates in Angus and become a private gentleman, or to follow your old master into exile."

Again he paused, and again Claverhouse remained silent.

"For the last," continued Orange, picking up a paper-weight and turning it in his hand, "it seems you have not chosen it, though you might have got you a command in foreign service. For the second, it would appear that the life of a country gentleman is not to your taste. Therefore you must excuse me if I point out to you the advantages of the first. I am at war with France: I need good officers. I am willing, here and now, to give you a commission as Commander-in-Chief of the Scots Army, since in my opinion General Douglas (who already has sworn allegiance to me) is not fitted for that post; or to make you Lieutenant General to my Lord Churchill who is to command the English Army; or, if you prefer it, to give you high rank in my forces which are serving overseas. The late King bestowed upon you a civil honour; I will do better; I will give you supreme recognition of your merit as a member of the profession of arms which you have followed from your youth."

This time the pause was so prolonged that at last Orange said sharply:

"Well, my lord?"

"I was waiting," said Claverhouse, coldly courteous, "until your Highness had finished all you had to say."

"I have said enough, surely, to show you my intentions towards you."

"I beg leave to think otherwise, sir. Without wishing to be offensive, it is my experience that a bribe, when there is the probability of its being refused, is followed ever by somewhat else. I was waiting for the threat."

There was a sudden tension in the atmosphere.

"I may not be your King – yet," said Orange thinly. "I am, however, the nephew and the son-in-law of your late King, and as such I expect to be treated with due deference."

"I beg your Highness' pardon," replied Claverhouse, not troubling to conceal his irony. "Your Highness was good enough a while ago to observe that I am a man who loves plain speech, and your Highness has shown this morning that you likewise upon occasion will make use of it. You have told me that you are prepared to reward me for making a change of masters. I do not think I have transgressed the code of good manners in terming that a bribe."

Orange let the paper-weight fall with a thud upon the table.

"Very well, here is the threat you desire. If you have it in mind to be so mad, my Lord Dundee, as to defy me openly, by word or act, I shall treat you as a rebel deserves to be treated. I would remind you that if I so desired I could summon the serjeants-at-arms and have you warded without more ado."

"That is for your Highness to decide," answered Claverhouse, meeting and holding the other's glance.

The Prince rose abruptly and took a turn or two about the room, a physically insignificant figure with his round shoulders and narrow chest, yet, at the same time, oddly formidable. Then he said with a certain bitterness:

"I know perfectly well what you are thinking, my lord: that it is unwise for me, in so delicate a situation, to throw public men into jail. That is true. Nor have I any wish to deprive you of your liberty unless by open defiance you compel me to do so, in which case I warn you I would show you no mercy. Meanwhile, since you are foolish enough to refuse the handsome offers I have made you (as I take it you do), I have a right to demand an answer to this question: What are your intentions, my Lord Dundee?"

"To return to Scotland, sir," replied Claverhouse without any hesitation, "after I have settled certain personal affairs here in London, and to take my seat in this Convention, albeit it is an illegal body. Its main business must be to decide upon the future government of my native land, and in so weighty a matter it is my duty to give my vote."

"Its main business," said Orange flatly, "will be to decide whether or no to offer me the Crown. And if your fellow Members decide in the affirmative, what will you do then, my lord?"

"I do not know, sir," replied Claverhouse, once more looking directly into the cold eyes.

For the first time during the audience, Orange smiled, not very pleasantly. It was a smile which said plainer than words: Your pride forbids you to accept, without a great show of reluctance, the tempting offers I have made you, as your simple honesty will not permit you, without real struggle, to forsake your old master. But your famous ambition, John Grahame of Claverhouse, will triumph eventually over both pride and honesty; and I make no doubt that you will come to heel at last.

(v)

The Prince of Orange was mistaken in not taking at its face value that simple reply, "I do not know," for it was the truth. Claverhouse had no idea what he would do if the Scottish Convention offered the Crown to the invader.

All through January he stayed in London, busying himself with establishing a secret means of communication with King James in France, and in using all his powers of persuasion to induce the Scots Councillors who were not yet gone north, to stick to their loyalty. He had no longer any military rank; Orange had set about straightway the reorganization of the Army, depriving of their commissions all officers who would not forswear themselves in the Oath they had taken to King James, and crossing off from the Establishment the King's Own Regiment of Horse. But there was one troop in that regiment which quietly disappeared before it could be pressed into alien service, the original troop which had shared with Captain Grahame the night rides and the conventicle-hunting in Galloway; its inferior officers were summoned to a conference in Claverhouse's modest lodging in Drury Lane, and there he gave them their instructions.

"I want ten troopers left with me here in London," he told them, "and for these I will arrange lodgings. The remainder of you will escort my Lord Balcarres to Edinburgh, but you must not wear your uniforms lest you be intercepted on the road. I look to you to find stabling for the horses and quarters for the men in Embro'; and there I desire you all to remain till you hear further from me."

And he had given them money from his private purse for their maintenance.

Meanwhile he remained in London; and Jock Johnson, now his quarter-master but at present masquerading as his servant, shared his lodging. Jock, like the faithful Tam, was very worried. For night after night Claverhouse went out, never returning till the small hours, and never giving any hint of where he had been. The two men would sit up for him, Tam keeping broth hot and every few minutes running out into the dark street to look for his master's return; this was worse than Galloway, this London, full of footpads and bullies after dark. What could Master John be at? cried Tam, and he a viscount too, just as Tam had always known he would be, and so little relishing the honour that he had neglected to have a new seal made with the coronet replacing the helmet of the esquire. Likely he's in conference with the great ones, replied Jock, loyally driving down the suspicion that Major General Grahame (for so he remained to his men) was finding comfort in some amorous affaire.

Both men would have been equally puzzled could they have known that that which drove their idol into the dark and dangerous streets of London was interior conflict. Until that conflict was decided, one way or the other, he could not go home, he could not face his wife.

He was forty, and he thought he knew himself through and through; but now, suddenly and horribly, he did not know himself at all. He was faced with an unprecedented situation in the outer world, and this had precipitated a crisis within himself; it was not so much that he did not know what he was going to do, but what he was going to be. He had thought of himself as a realist, accustomed to face facts; so he was, but there were, it seemed, other aspects of his character, ordinarily dormant, called up by the national crisis, and these aspects warred with the everyday self he knew, so that his whole being was in a torment of conflict. And he core of that conflict was this: for the first time in his life he was being called upon to act solely on his own responsibility.

Throughout his military career he had been most scrupulous in observing the orders of his superiors, even when he deemed them mistaken; he had been outraged when, at Dudhope, Balcarres had urged him to disregard the order from Melfort and usurp the supreme command, even though he had feared that the obeying of that order might ruin the King's interests in Scotland. Certainly he had desired high rank, and therefore, he realised, must have been confident of his ability of acting on his own, but even had he achieved the supreme command of the Army, still he would have been responsible to the civil authority, to the King and to his delegates, the Privy Council. But now, suddenly, he was alone; he had no status except as a Privy Councillor of Scotland; there was no one to whom he could appeal for help or orders; to all intents and purposes he was a private gentleman; the whole outward world was in the melting-pot; and so, he had discovered, was the inner one. What he would do must depend very largely on material events; what he would be must be decided now and for ever.

The realist in him presented a clear cold picture of the situation. King James had left the kingdom and thus had forsaken his trust; never mind the treachery which had impelled him to this, never mind his nervous collapse, he had deserted his post. He had gone to France against the advice of his best friends, including Claverhouse himself. The Prince of Orange was an invader, but he had been invited over by the principal of the nobility of England; never mind the bribes he had doled out, never mind the oaths they had broken; he was here, and he would get the offer of the Crown from the English Convention. He would get it because the majority of the great lords wanted a puppet king who would do what he was told, because the rest would prefer some sort of government to none at all, and because the common people could always be pacified by a façade of monarchy, whereas they detested a republic. The Scottish Convention might not concur in this offer of the Crown; it was Claverhouse's duty to use his best endeavours to dissuade them from concurring; but if he succeeded, what then? Civil war was the only answer; and if it came to a clash of arms between England and Scotland, the issue could not be in any doubt. Orange had a huge army of mercenaries, vast resources of wealth; Scotland was denuded of troops, and was the poorest country in Europe.

That was the realistic side, and he faced it squarely, walking up and down through the dark hours of the night, oblivious of everything but this interior conflict. Whenever he thought of London afterwards, it would be never of busy, colourful Whitehall or the fashionable coffee-houses, but always of lonely Lincolns Inn Fields, a spot shunned by the citizens of Westminster after the regulation lanthorns were extinguished at eleven o'clock, the haunt of footpads, lurking under the wall in the hope of robbing some belated pedestrian. But for some reason or other the footpads left this solitary wanderer alone; almost they seemed to shun the slight figure, pacing restlessly up and down the walks, as though he were a ghost which must vanish at cockcrow. He for his part was unaware of his lawless companions, locked as he was in the battle which must decide not only his own future life but the fate of those dear to him.

The fate of Jean and his unborn child.

She was up there at Dudhope, waiting for him, and waiting for the birth of the baby so long desired, the baby who might in due time become the second Viscount of Dundee. But he could not face her, yet. He could not, with his burning sense of justice, risk the reinforcement of the realistic side of him by the emotional; the other, nameless, unsuspected side must have its chance. He could not bear to hear her voice, to note again the way she had of putting her head on one side when she was considering something, to feel the texture of her hair as it lay all childishly ruffled on the pillow of a morning; he dared not look upon the home they had made together, on the grey castle which was the only favour he had ever asked of King Charles, on the newly sown lawns and the little nursery of trees, the planting and improvements he had made for the delight of Jean. The battle within must be decided here in alien London, here in the dark and solitary Lincoln's Inn Fields.

Often it threatened to become a battle of the emotions, the King's touching expressions of trust in him when forsaken by children and Ministers, set against his own passionate love for Jean and her coming child, two rival ghostly voices appealing to him, claiming his allegiance. But he shut his ears to them, for he knew that this conflict was in a realm which lay deeper far than the emotions; it was a struggle of immortal things. Something had to be decided which was vital to John Grahame, now and in Eternity; only to God and to himself did it signify which side won.

He was tempted, but the point was that he knew it as temptation. He had 'toiled for honour' as long ago he had written to Menteith, and here it was offered him in its most tempting guise: Commander-in-Chief of the Scots Army. And he could have it and yet retain what the world called his honour. He would do his duty as a loyal subject by taking his seat in the Scottish Convention and giving his vote against offering the Crown to Orange; he would not be alone in this; and if the majority of his fellow Members voted on the other side, he would have done all that could be done. Orange would not blame him for it; Orange, who recognized his qualities as a soldier, would renew the tempting offer; he was confident of that. Yet 'tempting' remained the operative word, and something in his soul insisted on giving it its ugly significance.

Then, the attack of the emotions and his ambition alike repulsed, he would be taken in flank by the purely practical. This assault took the form of a voice speaking, sweetly reasonable, and so clear that it was almost as though some wise friend walked beside him, urging him to face the facts.

It is all very well, said the voice, to insist that what you are fighting to attain to is an attitude of mind, but the fact remains that you have got to decide what you are going to do. The Prince of Orange was perfectly right when he said that you had but three alternatives, but if you will reject all of them, you must think of something else. You know perfectly well that if Orange gets the Crown, you will be called upon to take the Oath of Allegiance to him; if you refuse it, you will be debarred from all offices, civil and military; you will not even be Constable and Provost of Dundee. He may not deprive you of your title, but what will it be worth? You will sit in Dudhope, avoided by most men, deemed a romantic by some, a fool by all, and for all the good you will be to anybody (yes, even to Jean, for your restless nature makes you no fit companion when you are idle), you might as well be dead.

Or do you, added the voice, his own voice now, his voice at its most astringent, do you seriously propose to play the dashing hero which made you make that fantastic offer to King James in the Privy Garden? Are you counting on his sending you a commission to command his Scots Army – an army which does not exist? And if he does, what then? Have you a magic wand which can create an army, and pay it, out of nothing? If you are not very careful, John Grahame, you are going to make a fool of yourself, besides breaking your wife's heart, depriving your child of all inheritance, and plunging your country into blood. You are forty, you know; you are not the romantic youth who saw himself as a second Montrose...

So the battle tore his soul in pieces, until his face lost its beauty and became haggard, and his eyes, so alert and penetrative, had that queer inward look of one obsessed.

Yet when, after these tormented walks of his, he went to bed at last, and from long habit tried to imagine that this was his last night on earth, he began to perceive that while in one sense he had a choice and must come to a decision, in another and a deeper, he had no choice at all. He began to see his life as a pattern, worked out thread by thread.

When he was a boy, he had watched his mother working at a piece of tapestry; the stitches were on the wrong side, and seemed to have no coherence, but smilingly she would turn the work, and there was a picture slowly being drawn. Lying here sleepless in his London lodging, he seemed to see the tapestry of his own life, and though he could not tell as yet what sort of picture it was making, he was aware that one was forming and that it was too late to change it now, that everything he had done and said and thought was a stitch in that picture. His childhood adoration of Fingal and his heroes, his boyhood obsession with Montrose, his maturer studies of that great soldier's campaigns, his resigning his commission when Orange broke his word, his hazarding his prospects when he had criticised the Duke of Monmouth to doting King Charles, his forsaking of his wife upon their wedding-day at the call of duty, his championing of common soldiers against the powerful Douglas clique, his continual determination to expose and punish the treason of great men and to be indulgent to the ignorant and poor, his spontaneous offer to King James to take command against the invader – all these had been the stitches in the pattern of his life.

What he had been, he was; and what he was would decide how he must act in the unknown future. In this sense, he realised, he had no free-will. He remembered how he had stood in the antechamber at Windsor so long ago, and had searched his conscience in the light of his judgment of others. He had known, without conceit, that he was literally incapable of betraying his lawful Sovereign, let the consequences be what they would. That was nine years ago, but that essential part of him remained the same. He possessed, whether he would or no, the mysterious thing called integrity, just as he possessed a flat back and dark hair; he could no more root it out of him than he could add a cubit to his stature.

Yet while that core of his character remained unmoved by the waves of emotion and the attacks of reason and the assaults of ambition which broke over it, he found no comfort in it, rather the reverse; whatever it might come to mean to him in the future, in this tormented solitude it was a rock on which he himself and all those dear to him might be dashed to pieces.

(vi)

In February he received an urgent and agitated letter, signed by his two best friends, Lord Balcarres and Sir George Mackenzie.

They wrote him that the Duke of Hamilton had brought into Edinburgh bodies of his armed retainers, and also vast numbers of fanatics from the south-west, the wild-cats of the Covenant, whom he had hidden in cellars and garrets against the time when they would 'protect' the sittings of the Convention. For Hamilton, it seemed, had thrown off all disguise and boasted openly that he was going to rule the Convention and gain a majority vote for offering the Crown to Orange; his right-hand man was Sir John Dalrymple, Lord Justice Clerk, and between them they were cowing the loyal party. Already the Duke of Gordon had agreed to render up the Castle, intimidated by the mobs which Hamilton had brought into the town.

'It is absolutely necessary' the letter continued, 'that you come down to Embro' without delay, for none has more ability than yourself to persuade, and therefore are you the man to win over the waverers and to strengthen the faint-hearted. We will not enter into particulars in a letter, but there are many who have not got what they expected from the Dutch gentleman, others who are jealous of the Douglas influence, besides honest but timid men like Q., who sit at home, and all these must be persuaded to come to the Parliament House and give their vote upon the honest side. You alone have the skill to bring men of different temperaments and interests together, and if you can but carry them to the Parliament House, we believe we shall defeat Duke H.'

A few hours after receiving this letter, Claverhouse left London and took the road to the North. He wore civilian dress, as did the ten ex-troopers who rode behind him. To a London full of merchants fearful lest the influx of Dutchmen should ruin their trade, of soldiers in foreign uniforms lording it about the streets, of courtiers scrambling for places, of traitors, great and small, beginning to complain that the reward of their treachery was less than they had looked for, the little cavalcade appeared merely as a gentleman and his servants riding into the country.

As he rode back, mile after mile, along the road by which he had come to London four months since, a major general then, in command of all the Scottish Horse, Claverhouse still did not know whether the interior conflict was decided. His mind, exhausted by the struggle, seemed to mark time, while one part of it was preoccupied with a strange little dream which had visited him on his last night in London, the most vivid dream he had ever experienced.

He was a boy again, riding his pony to the burgh school at Dundee, and there upon the South Port of the town he saw a grim relic, a black and withered arm. And in his dream the fingers moved, beckoning, beckoning, persistently and inexorably, the dead fingers of Montrose.

Chapter Four

(i)

On Saturday, March 16th, the crowds which filled the space between the Parliament House of Edinburgh and the fifteen-storied lands which had grown up around it, gave it the appearance of a besieged castle, inadequately defended by members of the Town Guard, who, armed with Lochaber-axes, were drawn up before the entrance.

It was a savage mob which milled and bellowed and waved an assortment of weapons there; flourished in its midst were banners, inscribed with old Covenanting mottoes; little groups gathered round ministers who were bawling out impromptu sermons; the figure of Mercy, one of the supporters of the royal Arms over the entrance, lay in fragments on the pavement; and the entire concourse kept up a clamour, bellowing threats, roaring out texts from the Minor Prophets, and shouting the names of those they intended to 'Rathillet' as they called it, in other words slaughter, as that hero of the Covenant had slaughtered old Archbishop Sharp.

Within, in the great chamber where the Estates of the Realm sat together, there was as meagre an assembly as ever had been seen in that place; some Members had absented themselves from fear of the mob, others because they were afraid to attend a parliament which had no existence in law; if King James came back after all, their attendance would make them liable to a charge of high treason. The pale March sunlight glinted in the jewels of the Honours which lay upon the table presided over by the Earl Marshal, and picked out the colours in the Royal Arms emblazoned on the canopy of the Throne. Upon this elevated chair, with the Officers of State seated on its wide, curving steps, sat William, Duke of Hamilton, elected by a very narrow majority as Lord President of the Convention, sober for once, his eyes glancing arrogantly from the Judges of the Court of Session round their table in the centre of the chamber, to the raised and decorated benches of the higher barons, and from them to the plain ones lower down. His voice half-drowned in the uproar from without, a Covenanting minister was preaching from the wall-pulpit, once occupied by John Knox; and high overhead, from the hammer-beams of the roof, hung ancient banners, mute testimonies of many a hard-fought fight.

The sermon ended, Lyon King at Arms stepped from his place, bowed to the throne, and began to speak. The noise of the crowd outside made it impossible for any except those near him to hear what he said, but he had scarcely ended before Duke Hamilton, in a voice of thunder, informed the assembly of his message.

"The Duke of Gordon has broke his word!" he bellowed. "He consented to surrender the Castle on the condition of an indemnity for himself and his associated adherents, and now he seeks to extricate himself from his promise by including in a written list of his adherents every clan in the Highlands. Such insolence is not to be tholed. He shall be put to the horn, and proclamation shall be made discharging his garrison from obedience to him."

"With respect," said Sir John Dalrymple, rising from his seat before the centre table, "I would beg leave to enquire what has caused his Grace to qualify his conditions in this manner. For there is a story going about the good town that a certain person went privately to the Castle yesterday, and met his Grace's furniture coming out. And it is a fact that the furniture was taken back again within the hour; therefore we must conclude that this certain person it was who persuaded the Duke to change his mind about surrendering,"

A slight figure in one of the upper tiers of benches rose to its feet.

"The certain person," said Claverhouse, speaking so incisively that, despite the uproar without, he was heard by all, "is present to spare your Grace the fatigue of answering that question, and to inform Sir John Dalrymple that his story is true. I went yesterday to the Castle; I went alone; and I went for the purpose of persuading the Duke of Gordon that it was his duty to hold the Castle of Edinburgh for his lawful King.'

"You went alone, my Lord Dundee," repeated Dalrymple, falsely jovial. "Now I think you are a very brave man, for the good town is full of those who remember you as a persecutor in the south-west, and who already have begun blockading the Castle.'

"I am very glad Sir John Dalrymple has raised that point," said Claverhouse, addressing the Throne, "for it is one extremely material to the debates of this assembly. First, it is impossible for the Estates to give their votes freely in a matter which so nearly concerns the welfare of the realm, while bodies of armed men are assembled in the town – illegally assembled – and are even now bawling out yonder to the disturbance of our conference. And secondly, it is my duty to make known to the Estates that I have information, and a witness ready to testify to the truth of it, that there is a plot hatched to murder me and likewise Sir George Mackenzie. There is one Binnie, a litster, who heard two men, lodged in his house – "

Hamilton interrupted with his usual bluster.

"My Lord Dundee, you should know better than to fash the Estates with your privy concerns when so great a matter of public business lies before them.'

"But this is monstrous!" cried Mackenzie, reaching for his cane to help him to his feet. "With respect, your Grace, I must speak to the constitutional necessity for this witness to be heard and the matter sifted to the bottom."

There was immediate uproar. Some voices cried "Let him speak," others "Sit down," while the mob outside, catching the clamour, bawled and bellowed more savagely than ever. When at last some sort of order was restored, Hamilton blustered;

"If my Lord Dundee and Sir George Mackenzie have made themselves enemies during the time they have been in the late King's service, that is their blame, and it is the greatest impertinence ever I heard that they should expect the Estates to lay aside their business to debate upon the protection of privy persons."

"I beg leave," Mackenzie began indignantly, but again the Duke interrupted.

"I will have you remember, Sir George," he cried, "that as Lord President of this Convention I have the right to determine who shall speak, and I warn you, and likewise my Lord Dundee, that if you will not sit down I will have you dismissed from this House."

"Your Grace may be spared that trouble," said Claverhouse, before his friend could speak. "I will not take part in an assembly which, since it cannot protect its own members, and seeks to enforce its rule by armed rabble, is but the mockery of a parliament. And I now beg leave to inform your Grace that this very morning there is arrived from King James, who has landed in Ireland, a Royal Commission, empowering the Archbishop of St Andrews, the Earl of Balcarres, and myself, to adjourn the Convention to Stirling, if we think fit. I go thither; and I call upon all here present who love law and liberty to follow me to a town where we may hold our debates without intimidation."

There was a sudden silence, as, bowing formally to the throne, the slight figure walked down the tiers of benches towards the door. There was something so strangely impressive about that figure, which walked briskly yet without haste, and which, resolute and dignified, did not glance round to see if friends were following but seemed content to go alone into that raging mob outside, that even Hamilton was silenced.

Then Sir George Mackenzie rose, bowed to the Throne, and limped after his friend; and one by one, some reluctantly, some defiantly, the members of the loyal party left the chamber.

(ii)

Throughout the remainder of that day, and all the next, Claverhouse was occupied in the task he had set himself. By his powers of persuasion he had got a fair percentage of the loyal party into the Parliament House; he had got them out again; it remained for him to get them to Stirling.

Since his return to Edinburgh from London, two facts had been driven home to him. The first was that for some reason all these lords and gentlemen, though the majority were far greater in rank and importance than he, looked to him to make decisions for them. The second was the extreme difficulty of keeping them to a decision once he had made it.

For though they were ready enough to refrain from doing anything against their lawful Sovereign, they were not ready to accept the consequences of active loyalty. Nearly all of them were related, by blood or by marriage, to the party which was openly for Orange. Hamilton's own son, Lord Arran, was of their number; Queensberry's two sons and his brother were in Hamilton's camp, and so was Lord Murray, Atholl's heir. Sir George Mackenzie himself was kin to his namesake, the Lord Register, a violent Orangeite; Balcarres' connections were similar. They were, then, a clique, and a clique which, in any crisis, tended to prefer loyalty to its members to that due to its King. It was horribly plain to Claverhouse that while they deferred to him in this crisis as the only practical and active man among them, and professed their firm intention of sticking by their lawful Sovereign, they resented him as an outsider, and, for all his new title, a mere laird by birth, and that some of them, notably Queensberry, had not forgotten old quarrels.

They could not, even at such a time, forget their own interests; in the midst of protestations of loyalty and denunciations of the invader, they let fall remarks which showed plainly the nature of their private thoughts. One must remember, said Queensberry, wandering about the fine house he had built for himself on the south side of the Canongait when he was Lord High Treasurer, that King James no longer could protect them; he would be obliged to let his town house, he said, and he did not think he ought to go to Stirling until he had found a tenant. He dared not leave it empty, because of these mobs. Yes, indeed, said Atholl, he was ready to go to Stirling and call out his powerful clan for the protection of the Convention there if that were necessary; but it must be understood that he would be elected President; and his son, Lord Dunmore, ought to be Commander-in-Chief of the Army, he added, darting a jealous glance at Claverhouse.

Sir George Mackenzie, so genuinely indignant when it came to a question of a flouting of law and justice as had happened in the Parliament House; was now obsessed with the opening of the Advocates' Library, which it had been his dearest ambition to found, and with the elegant Latin address he was composing for the occasion.

"The Bar will now be enriched," he cried, limping up and down a room in his house in Blackfriars Street, "with the statues of all the learned in their books, more permanent than bronze. Let them remember Cicero, whose triumph, as Caesar admitted, was greater than his own."

Nevertheless, by Sunday evening, Claverhouse believed that he had accomplished his task. He had appealed to each member of the loyal party according to his knowledge of his character, to the self-interest of one, to the pride of another, to the honour of a third; deliberately he had played upon the sordid nature of men like Annandale, who had turned his coat again because he had not got the reward he had looked for from Orange; he had let loose the full force of his charm upon the sullen, of his vigour on the timid; and by that Sunday evening there was not one man among them but had consented to ride with him the next day for Stirling. The rendezvous was made for their leaving Edinburgh in a body; he had promised them the protection of an armed escort; he had sent an express to Lord Mar, the Governor of Stirling Castle (honest, but at present very sick) to expect them by nightfall on Monday.

He did not go to bed on Sunday night; he had had but a few hours of sleep the night before. He was in the full flood of his correspondence again; he wrote to King James, newly landed in Ireland with a small French force and the promise of twenty thousand native recruits, begging his Majesty to hasten the promised commission for himself as Commander-in-Chief, since without it he lacked authority, and also for the sending of reinforcements to the help of the Duke of Gordon, who shortly would have to face a regular besiegement and whose garrison was pitifully inadequate. He wrote to Lord Melfort, still the King's principal adviser, telling him with friendly frankness that the greatest service he could render his master would be the resignation of his office, since he had the misfortune to be unpopular with nearly all the King's friends. He wrote to various personages whose timidity had kept them absent from the Edinburgh Convention; and lastly he wrote to Sir Ewen Cameron of Lochiel.

In a recent interview he had had with the Duke of Gordon, he wrote, his Grace had told him that Lochiel was forming a Confederacy of the Clans with the purpose of preserving the Highlands for King James. He, Claverhouse, rejoiced to hear this news, and he begged leave to say how much it had heartened him to know that the claymores of the North would be united in their loyalty by so great a gentleman and so valiant a soldier as Mhic Dhomhnuill Dhuibh. As he sealed this letter, he smiled to himself, remembering his only meeting with Lochiel and the Chief's strange prophecy. Part of it was already fulfilled, and in a manner which was both gratifying and humiliating. He was no longer plain Grahame of Claverhouse, he was Viscount of Dundee; but he was no longer Captain Grahame because he had no military rank save that given by a verbal promise. Would the other part of Lochiel's prophecy be fulfilled? he wondered. Would they meet again?

So he sat there writing, in his lodging in Leith Wynd, with Tam, a self-appointed watchdog, standing outside the door, armed with a loaded blunderbuss and ready to deal with any wild-cat of the Covenant who might come creeping up the scale-stair. It was no idle fear which kept Tam at his post. The silence which ordinarily enveloped Edinburgh from the beating of the ten o'clock drum to the early round of the scavengers with their wheelbarrows, was broken by a continual tramping of feet about the streets, by the uproar of the rabble which Hamilton had brought into the town and which had overawed the bailies and the feeble Town Guard. Even the Elders of the Kirk, those pious policemen, whose right it was to take the names of all found loitering after the beating of the drum and debar them from the Lord's Supper the next Sacrament Sabbath, even these dared not interfere with loiterers who enjoyed the protection of Duke Hamilton.

But Claverhouse did not fear assassination, though his reason told him that while he remained in Edinburgh he was in constant danger of it. Something other than reason gave him a queer feeling of being protected; it was as though he had work to do which, until it was accomplished, lent him a charmed life. The will to kill him had been present among the rabble through which he had walked alone up the Lawnmercat and the Castle hill for his interview with the Duke of Gordon; but though they had cursed and threatened him, for some reason or other not even a stone had been hurled.

Late on Sunday night, disregarding all Tam's frantic protests, he went out; for he was free at last to attend to the final preparation for tomorrow's journey. The lords and gentlemen who were pledged to accompany him to Stirling must have protection on the road, and only he could provide it.

When, in London, his regiment had been crossed off the Establishment and he had kept his old original troop of horse together, sending them to Edinburgh to await his further instructions, he had had no definite plan in mind, but had acted by instinct. In a disintegrating world he had desired the comfort of knowing that this body of humble friends kept together, ready for whatever employment he might find for them. Well, he had found a job for them now, though it was not much of a job; they would perform it willingly, efficiently, and without question. With great men he must appeal to self-interest, to principle, even to greed; these simple troopers who had shared his fortunes from the beginning would do as he told them because they loved and trusted him. If he had informed them that they were bound for the Indies, they would have acquiesced so long as he was going with them.

The horses of the troop were stabled in the long row of vaulted apartments which formed the ground floor of the White Horse Inn near his own lodging, a hostelry which, in common with most of its kind in Edinburgh, catered more for horses than for human guests, and which extended from the Canongait to the suburbs in the North Back. He moved from one stall to the next, inspecting the contents of the mangers, making sure each animal had been properly tended, just as he had done after a forty mile ride over the Galloway moors.

"Will there be a fight, sir?" asked Jock Johnson, wistfully. "We're a' ettling for a bit fight, ye ken; we've had none since Bothwell Brig, and yon's a weary while syne."

"I don't know," said Claverhouse, stroking the neck of a sorrel mare, and thinking suddenly of that other sorrel, of Drumclog, of his first engagement and defeat, and of how he had never commanded in battle since that day. "Have you met any of the 'best society' in Embro' lately, Jock?" Johnson grinned his appreciation of an old jest which never failed to delight him.

And when Claverhouse reached his lodging again, at four o'clock in the morning, the old exchange, with a new variation, passed between him and Tam.

"Ye'll be awa' to your bed the noo, Master John."

"No, Tam, it's not worth it. We ride at dawn."

So he sat up at his window in the tall land, looking out into a darkness which was broken here and there by the flare of a torch, and thinking with pain, with desperate longing, of Jean at Dudhope, and turning idly on his finger the ring which bore a simple device: the laurel of the House of Grahame, the 'tree of victory'.

(iii)

The darkness was beginning to lighten into the grey of dawn when he heard the sound he had been waiting for, the hollow ring of hooves coming up the wynd. He was down the stairs, with Tam at his heels, almost before the order to halt rang out from the leading horseman, and he smiled as he felt all about him the presence of humble friends. He was in his old uniform again, and so were they, sixty scarlet-clad figures, with their short cloaks wrapped about their shoulders to protect them from the drizzle, each spur and bit and sword-hilt polished, each horse as disciplined as its rider. Then he was mounted, silent because suddenly he was very moved, and was riding at the head of his troop down the wynd, and out by the Leith Wynd Port. He halted his men immediately outside the gate, for this was the appointed place of rendezvous with the lords and gentlemen pledged to accompany him to Stirling.

Mental and physical fatigue gave him for a while a pleasant lethargy, almost as if he were drugged. Letting the reins fall on his horse's neck, he sat watching the sullen dawn break, with Edinburgh Castle black against it, the cannon sticking through their loops on the great Half Moon Battery, the steel cap of a sentry passing along the battlements, the Royal Standard hanging limp on its pole. He must contrive some way of communicating with the Duke of Gordon on his way to Stirling; he had promised his Grace that he would let him know what he intended to do if the Edinburgh Convention proved itself set upon offering the Crown to Orange. He had not a great deal of confidence in Gordon as a commander, but the man had a keen sense of honour under his foppish and affected exterior, and Claverhouse's appeal to his chivalry had resulted in his promising to hold the Castle for as long as he could. His courage would soon be put to the test; undoubtedly the Duke of Hamilton would order a regular besiegement with such Covenanting rabble as he had at his command.

As the clatter of the scavengers with their wheelbarrows was heard from the town, he roused himself and looked eagerly up the narrow wynd. It was time for his friends to join him, and surely not even the absent-minded Balcarres would be late for such a tryst. He had impressed upon them all the necessity to be away from the town before the rabble thronged the streets again. As the moments passed and still there was no sound of hoof-beats from beyond the gate, he became first a little irritable, then conscious of the first faint stirrings of an intolerable dread. His mood seemed to communicate itself to his faithful troopers, even to the horses; there was a creak of leather as men shifted uneasily, a hoof began to paw the ground, his own horse gave one long snorting sigh. He was about to ride back into the town to discover for himself the cause of this delay when he saw the figure of Balcarres, on foot, and wrapped in his woollen nightgown, come hurrying down the wynd towards him. And as he watched that solitary figure, suddenly he knew the nature of his dread.

"I'm come from Atholl and the rest, Clavers," panted his friend, his fair face flushed with embarrassment. "My lord is set upon biding another day in Embro' and attending Duke Hamilton's Convention in an endeavour to persuade his Grace to send this rabble packing from the town."

Claverhouse sat looking down at him, his own face expressionless.

"What you are trying to tell me, Colin, is that Atholl's heart has failed him at the eleventh hour, and I suppose the rest will follow him like sheep. Very well, you and I will ride without them. I'll find you a horse from somewhere."

But Balcarres' embarrassment only grew.

"You ken fine, Clavers, that so powerful a man as Atholl must be humoured, and it's only twenty-four hours' delay he's seeking. He swears that if he is not able to move Hamilton at the debate this morning, he'll ride to Stirling tomorrow. And there's Mackenzie, too; he says he must attend this opening of the Advocates' Library; he canna disappoint his friends. Och, be reasonable, Clavers; you were ever a hasty kind of a man – "

"I depart even now," interrupted Claverhouse quietly, gathering up the reins. "You and the rest must do as you please, but I have pledged my word to the Earl of Mar to be with him tonight, and I will not break it."

"And we shall follow you, rest assured of that," earnestly promised his friend, "if we fail in our endeavours with Duke Hamilton. What difference can twenty-four hours make –?"

"They will cost your liberty." The voice was quiet and bitter. "Do you remember what you said to me in London when we were summoned to an audience with Orange? In jail we would be of no use to our master or to anyone else. It is not assassination I have feared in Edinburgh, Colin; it is arrest. That you will desire to follow me to Stirling, I have no doubt; that you will be at liberty to do so, I doubt greatly." He gave one quick sigh, laid his gauntleted hand for an instant on his friend's, and with sad affection added the one word: "Farewell."

Then he turned abruptly, called a crisp order to his men, and trotted his horse to the head of the little troop. His mind was filled with one single realization, stark, challenging, final; I am alone.

(iv)

Out into the north eastern suburbs, up the brae to the base of Calton Hill, and so to the Lang Gait, the road which led westwards, with fields and rough stone dykes upon the right hand, and on the left the Nor' Loch; beyond it, towering up there on its rock, the vast black bulk of the Castle was silhouetted against the dawn. His glance was fixed upon that fortress as he rode at the head of his men; a queer mood was come upon him, so that he felt light-headed, almost fey. Already his heart had responded to that challenge: I am alone; already he had felt it act upon him like a stimulant; he was a boy again, capable of great deeds and desperate enterprise.

The little troop was conspicuous on that deserted road, their scarlet coats colourful in the grey landscape, the jingle of steel and the hollow ring of hooves loud in the early silence. They were observed; for as they came level with the head of the Nor' Loch, their leader saw a colours being waved as a signal from the Postern in the outer defences of the Castle, the wall built halfway up the rock. Halting his men at the Kirkhead-brae, near St Cuthbert's Kirk, he dismounted, and flinging his rein to a trooper, he set off on foot.

His men watched, bewildered and dismayed, as, booted and spurred as he was, he began to scramble up the slope below the wall, his boots slipping on the wet rock, his hands grasping at the bleached grass and stunted thorns which grew in crevices. Exhausting and perilous though that climb must be, he seemed to mount as nimbly as a goat, his long dark hair blown about his face, his solitary figure conspicuous in its scarlet, every movement purposeful and somehow dedicated. Intent upon his climb, he heard with indifference the sounds which told him that enemies as well as friends had observed his departure from

Edinburgh; there was a gnat-like buzzing from the rabble swarming upon the Castle hill, and the bells of the town rang backwards, the ancient signal of alarm.

Gordon was waiting for him at the Postern, his elegant figure incongruously armoured, his well-bred voice, the delight of Edinburgh's polite society, uttering compliments and apologies.

"Such inconvenience as I have put you to, my lord; I protest, I know not to excuse it. But it was necessary I had speech with you; another day, and the blockade will be complete. Already a message is sent me from his Grace of Hamilton proclaiming me outlawed, and therefore I fear that by conferring with me you place yourself in considerable danger. Your lordship is riding to Stirling, I suppose, as your lordship intimated you might be constrained to do when you did me the honour of calling upon me last week. But I cannot see," added his Grace, levelling a perspective-glass at the little troop halted far below, "any of your lordship's friends who should be giving you their company."

"Your Grace sees all my friends there below," replied Claverhouse, leaning against the Postern and looking down upon the cluster of scarlet. "Yet I believe I have others in the North. Come with me, my Lord Duke, to your own country; come with me, while there is time."

Gordon was staring at him in amazement; there was something queer about Clavers today.

"But I am pledged, and that on your lordship's own persuasion, to hold Edinburgh Castle for King James."

"Resign the command to your Lieutenant Governor, Colonel Winram, a man of sterling loyalty; your Grace will be of more service to his Majesty in calling out your powerful clan."

"My clan? But why? I protest, I cannot imagine what your lordship has in mind. I understood that your lordship was adjourning the Convention to Stirling, and for my part I have given my word that I will hold this castle so long as I am able, though indeed that will not be long unless I have relief. And you, my lord," added Gordon curiously, "what will you do and whither will you go, now that your hopes of a rival Convention seem cross-bited?"

Claverhouse did not answer for a moment. He stood holding to a bar of the postern, his eyes looking steadily towards the north, as though they could see, beyond the veil of rain, the foothills of the Highlands. Far, far below him was the disturbed ant-hill of Edinburgh, the malice of Hamilton and Dalrymple, the fickleness of Atholl, the indifference of Mackenzie, the futility and infirmity of purpose of Arran, Dunmore, Balcarres. And here beside him stood almost the last of the loyal and powerful, the gentleman famous for his refinement, made for the company of ladies and the elegance of salons, a Catholic because he was bred so, a loyalist because his chivalry prevented him from yielding, without a fight for it, a trust originally valuable to him for the addition it brought to his income.

Suddenly Claverhouse's voice rang out in answer to the Duke's question, an answer uncharacteristic in its drama:

"I go wherever the spirit of Montrose shall direct me!"

Chapter Five

(i)

It was noon on March 30th when a blare of trumpets brought the townsfolk of Edinburgh hurrying to the Mercat Cross near the Parliament House.

And there, colourful in their tabards, picturesque in the livery of the monarch whom some called the 'late King James', and others still plain 'King James', Lyon King at Arms and his brother heralds stood upon the steps of the Cross, ready to read a proclamation. The brazen music of their trumpeters still echoed through wynds and closes, drowning the chatter of the women about the common well, the shouts of the lokman chasing a stray hog, the haggling of merchants and goodwives in the piazzas, the gossip of shop-keepers going to take their 'meridian' in the taverns, the raucous voice of the bellman proclaiming the arrival of the first fresh meat of the season, the soft Gaelic of the chairmen touting for custom, the tirling of the pin on the doors of lodgings. When the trumpets ceased, Lyon King at Arms read out, his voice solemn as befitted the dreadful words, a sentence of outlawry against John Grahame of Claverhouse, Viscount of Dundee; and Edinburgh listened in relishful horror to this, the most terrible of all official proclamations.

First came the verbal stripping of goods and honours, 'all his lands, heritage, offices, titles, possessions, tacks, corn, steadings, cattle, mills, muirs and mosses, goods movable and immovable.' Then the ancient phrases pronouncing him 'intercommuned'; his Grace, the Duke of Hamilton, by authority from the High and Mighty Prince William, Lyon proclaimed (his voice faltering a little, since he was well aware that such authority had no existence in law), "doth hereby prohibit any person or persons to harbour, abbet, assist, or supply the aforesaid rebel and his associates, or to keep correspondence with them, under pain of concurring in their treason and all its penalties." He added the formula (more embarrassed then ever): "God save King James VII and II!"

Edinburgh gave a token cheer, its attention concentrated upon the symbolic acts which followed. While the sentence was being read out, the other heralds had held in reverse a cardboard shield painted with a coat-of-arms and a crest; above the crest was viscount's coronet. Craning and jostling to get a better view, the crowd stared at the devices held thus in the positon of disgrace, and when the ritual was complete, and the shield torn in pieces, there was a rush to seize on the bits of cardboard. One lad was lucky enough to get a fragment with a complete picture on it, some sort of a bird it was, sitting in a nest which seemed to be made of flames. Old folk in the crowd reminded one another how, nearly forty years ago, they had watched a very similar coat-of-arms being subjected to the same indignity, when, alone among the great ones of Scotland, James Grahame, Marquis of Montrose, had stood for a failing cause.

But the crowd around the Mercat Cross missed the heart of the drama. For they did not know what was happening, at this very hour, far away in Dudhope Castle above Dundee.

For a week and more that castle had been in a bustle of preparation for some great event. The women of the household had taken charge, and all day long there was a swishing of skirts in the passages, a subdued twitter of female voices, mysterious activities in stillroom and kitchen. A huge rich cheese called the kenno had been made in the dairy; a woman's shift and a man's shirt, both new, were laid out ready in the chamber where a Dundee midwife was holding a sort of court; a new batch of candles had been prepared for the ancient ceremony of the saining or protecting from fairies, and plentiful supplies of claret were brought up from the cellars for the gossips-wake. All this activity centred round the bedchamber in which the lady of Dudhope lay awaiting the birth of her first child.

And now, at noon on March 30th, the bustle within Dudhope had reached its climax. The bedchamber was crowded with the matrons of the household, ceremoniously carrying lighted candles three time round the bed; the kenno was cut in portions and distributed among these same dames; the infant was plunged by the midwife into a vessel of cold water with a live coal in it, and then, being a male, was wrapped in a woman's shift. A servant wearing the Grahame badge on his sleeve galloped breakneck into Dundee, and ten minutes later the bells of the town broke into a joyous peal, housewives left their baking to shout the news to one another from their forestairs, merchants and apprentices forsook their booths to drink in free wine a health to the Constable's heir, a procession of bailies marched solemnly up the hill towards the Castle, bearing gifts and rehearsing speeches, and youths piled yet more faggots upon the bonfire which would blaze tonight in front of the Mercat Cross.

And round that other cross, many miles to the south in Edinburgh, boys fought one another for bits of torn cardboard, and the wind blew the picture of a coronet into the gutter, and a lad ran proudly home to his mother to show her the trophy he had captured, the painting of a phoenix rising from the flames.

(ii)

The trees about Dudhope had a faint mist of green upon their bareness when, in the middle of April, a long procession wound its way down the carriage-drive, and took the track over the Sidlaw Hills. Riding beside the horse-litter which carried his wife and infant son, Claverhouse cast one quick glance back at Dudhope, at the ivy-clad towers and the grey stone flushed to rose colour in the spring sunshine and the gulls wheeling and crying above the battlements. Then he set his face towards that other home of his, the modest little house called Glen.

There was pain in leaving Dudhope, yet it did not disturb the peace which had come upon him of late; life had become very simple, and at heart he had always been a simple man. Ever since leaving Edinburgh, he had a queer feeling of being guided and directed, a sense of inevitability which had comfort in it, armouring him against every disappointment. He would do what he must do, one step at a time; he had chosen a certain line of conduct, or rather his own nature had forced it upon him; he had started out on a path on which he had no companions, and no guide except the star of duty. The end of that path was not his concern; his business was to follow it, step by step.

He had ridden from Edinburgh to Stirling because he had a tryst with the Earl of Mar; he had found that Mar, sick and despairing, already had rendered the Castle to an officer of the Duke of Hamilton. He had turned homewards; there was nothing more he could do as the King's servant until the Edinburgh Convention decided one way or the other about offering the Crown to Orange, and his own commission arrived from Ireland. Meanwhile, there was one at Dudhope who needed him; his wife was near her time. But on his way home he had had an unexpected and very significant encounter which had confirmed the feeling, amounting almost to a superstition, that he was being led and guided on his path. Pausing for a hasty meal at Dunblane, he had found in the change-house there a gentleman who had introduced himself as Alexander Drummond of Balhaldy, the son-in-law of Cameron of Lochiel; he had been sent with a message from Lochiel to Claverhouse, and was even then on his way to Dudhope. And the message was this: Lochiel had summoned a conference of his fellow chiefs for May 18th in Lochaber, for the purpose of debating on the raising of the clans for King James, and he begged that Claverhouse would come to this conference, and, if his Majesty gave consent, would command the claymores of the North.

"But you have a leader of your own blood," Claverhouse had cried. "The reverence in which Lochiel is held is famous."

Balhaldy had become a little evasive and embarrassed, murmuring that Lochiel was an old man, and that in so weighty a business it was better to have a commander who stood aloof from clan feuds. This remark had been lost upon Claverhouse, who was preoccupied with the memory of how Montrose, when pledged to raise an army for King Charles I and finding none of the Lowland nobles ready to join with him, had found his army in the Highlands. So Claverhouse had sent Balhaldy back to Lochaber to tell the old Chief of the Camerons that he would come to the rendezvous on May 18th; and then, at long last, he had come home to Dudhope, and to Jean.

Through the months of their separation, he had thought of her with pain and longing, tormented by the impossibility of explaining to her his seeming neglect. The crisis in the outer world, and the conflict in his mind, alike would mean nothing to her; he was the husband who had forsaken her on their wedding-day and now put what he called his duty before the love which demanded his presence with her on the eve of her confinement. But in the first few minutes of their reunion, he found that he might have spared himself the anguish; Jean was changed.

It was not that she had any greater interest in public affairs, or deeper understanding of her husband; it was that the treasury of love she had scattered at large was concentrated now upon one single object; her unborn child. She was isolated in her own little tender world, and the revolution, which had deprived the king of his throne and her husband of military rank, was but a faint, unimportant murmur from far away. Even her husband's precarious new honour, and the question as to whether her baby might or might not become in time the second viscount of Dundee, meant little to her in comparison with the fact that that baby, her long-awaited, precious first-born, would soon be held in her arms.

So little James was born, coming into the world and being deprived of his rightful inheritance in the self-same hour; his father was outlawed; and on April 11th the Prince of Orange and Mary, his wife, were proclaimed King and Queen by the Edinburgh Convention. Claverhouse's answer was a declaration of war.

Yesterday, April 12th, in the presence of a few friends and kinsfolk and of his ever faithful troop of horse, he had unfurled upon Dundee Law the Standard of King James, acting entirely on his own responsibility. His commission had not arrived, and he suspected that it had been intercepted; any who joined with him incurred the penalties of treason; he had no written authority, no arms, no allies, no money; his only hope of an army was in the Highlands, the country of men regarded by the world in general and by Hugh Mackay, of Scourie, their fellow Gael, in particular, as savage barbarians.

And now he was leaving Dudhope, perhaps for ever, certainly until King James was restored. He was taking Jean and little James to Glen, to the house which was too humble to interest the lords and gentlemen who already were jostling for his honours and estates. They would be safe at Glen, at least for a while; and in this home of his boyhood he would spend his last night before riding out to win Scotland for King James.

(iii)

It was not until evening that Claverhouse had the chance of a private talk with his brother David, for the day had been taken up with arranging for the accommodation of his troopers in the cothouses of tenants, and with other practical matters. With the vastly increased household in bed at last, he sat down before the fire in David's room, and, business-like and unemotional, explained the position.

"The loyal party has ceased to exist," said he, "I mean as a party. My Lord Atholl has been afflicted with a most timeous attack of the gout and is gone to Bath; Sir George Mackenzie is on his way to Oxford, intending to apply for admission as a student there (at the age of fifty-four!) Queensberry has retired in dignified dudgeon to Sanquhar; Balcarres is in the Tolbooth and Dunmore is warded in his lodging. As for the Bishops, I know not where they are; they are become the Kirk Invisible."

David grunted, and kicked at a log on the hearth.

"I have a month," continued his brother, "before I must be in Lochaber for the tryst with Lochiel, and I intend to spend it recruiting the Gordon gentry in Aberdeenshire and Moray. As a clan they have a record of loyalty, and his Grace, who is their head, is holding Edinburgh Castle for King James. It may be hard for you to get letters to me, Davie, for I look not to be in any place for long, though I hope to make Gordon Castle my headquarters. By the end of the month I must be at Inverness, whither Lochiel has promised to send Macdonald of Keppoch to escort me to Lochaber for the rendezvous."

"Hech! it's wild country up-by," observed David mildly, puffing at his pipe.

"I have two advantages in my endeavour to raise the North. First that I can speak Gaelic, and next that young Amerlieclose has volunteered to come with me, and as you know it has been a pastime of his to study the customs and genealogy of the Highlands. They're proud folk benorth Tay, and it is, he tells me, of the first importance to be acquainted with the history of each clan and with the deeds of their ancestors." He paused a moment, then went on a little hesitantly: "Davie, I must tell you about our chaplain, Mr Edwards. He came to me as soon as I arrived at Glen this morning, and astonished me by begging to accompany me upon this venture. I need not say that I would value his company, yet it seems hard to deprive you of him."

"I hope you'll not be taking Alan the factor," replied David, leaning over to knock out his pipe on the hearthstone. "I've no doubt at all he's as keen as Mr Edwards to be off with you, but there must be someone to have the ordering of Glen while we're away."

"We?" echoed Claverhouse sharply.

"Och ay," said his brother, placid as ever, "I'll be riding with you the morn."

For a moment Claverhouse could only stare at him. Then:

"Davie, do you understand what venture I'm embarked upon?"

"Ay, I ken that fine."

"This is some mad whim." (He spoke almost harshly to cover his emotion.) "You have never concerned yourself with public matters; you are a farmer, wedded to your land. What has got into you that you would exchange the flail for the sword?"

"Not a concern for what you term public matters," replied David, reaching for the tobacco-box to fill his pipe again.

After a moment, finding that he was not going to say any more, his brother leaned forward and spoke almost brutally.

"Likely you have not considered what I and those with me will be called upon to face. You have said that it is wild country in the Highlands; I do not know it at the first-hand, but I know the bogs and the trackless wastes of Galloway, which you do not. I spared neither myself nor any man under my command in those old days when we rode sometimes forty miles in a night, always with the chance of a shot in the back or a horse foundering in a quakin' qua; still less shall I spare any man who joins with me now, when our enemy is not a parcel of ignorant fanatics but a prince who can command the regulars of two kingdoms. I will do my best to alleviate the hardships of man and beast, but beyond that they must take what comes, let it be a march over frozen mountains, an empty belly, or a battle against overwhelming odds."

"I'll make shift," said David, in his slow, countryman's voice.

"And what of your estates, Davie? Do you not understand that if you join with me you will be intercommuned? – you know what that means. You will partake in my sentence of outlawry; everything you have will be forfeit – even Glen."

David puffed comfortably at his pipe for several moments in silence. Then he said, mild and matter-of-fact:

"I've had a wee crack with Auldbar, and we've come to an arrangement. Glen belongs to him now – on paper, you understand. We got a notary to draw up the deed, and it's all signed and sealed, so there can be no argy-bargying about it. Malcolm the notary's a canny man and kens fine how to order such matters so as to keep within the letter of the law. If Auldbar bides peaceable, they canna touch him on account of his son, seeing the callant is still a minor."

"Robin? What has Robin to do with this?"

"He's coming with us the morn," replied David, blandly surprised at the question. "The lad's been ettling for years to go a-soldiering, and now he has his mother's blessing, it's not to be expected he'd bide at home." He shot a humorous glance at his brother. "It's a kind of conspiracy we've been having at Glen, Anna, and Mr Edwards, and Auldbar, and the rest, so you'd best content yourself."

There was a long silence. Then Claverhouse rose, rather abruptly, and laying his hand on his brother's shoulder as he passed, he left the room.

(iv)

He was at his most brisk and practical next morning when he marshalled his little body of volunteers in the courtyard of Glen. The agony of leaving wife and child for a venture which the world must regard as romantic folly, had been glimpsed only by Jean when they had made their private farewells, and he had bent to kiss his sleeping son, the baby named after the great Montrose. But while the pain of parting had been sharp indeed, it had not been complicated by doubts as to whether he was indeed a romantic fool.

The two sides of his nature had fused; he was more than ever the realist, but with all the selfishness and materialism purged away. In what he had done since leaving Edinburgh, and what he would do in the future, he was not quixotic; he was following the strongest instinct in his nature, and he had every hope and intention of succeeding in his lonely task of raising Scotland for his master.

Yes essentially he was human, and therefore it was extraordinarily comforting to find his kinsfolk loyally rallying round him in this crisis of his life. From far and near the Grahames had come, some, like, David, who had never drawn a sword, simple lairds to whom an occasional trip to Edinburgh was a great adventure, rooted in their ancestral acres. Now, cheerfully and without hesitation, they had left those acres to look after themselves, even to be confiscated, had bought themselves weapons of one sort or another, said goodbye to wife and children, and were prepared to follow their outlawed kinsman whithersoever he chose to lead them.

He looked round upon them mounted in the courtyard, that familiar, homely courtyard with its barn-cocks scratching on the middens, and the squawk of a falcon from the open door of the mews. David was having a last word with his factor; Anna was stowing home-made salves for wounds into a pouch; her son, young Robin, unnaturally casual, was looping up his sword for riding; good Mr Edwards, his bible and various little pious books under his arm, was hurrying to the mounting-block; Tam, uttering nannie-like clucks of annoyance, was endeavouring to balance two cloak-bags, crammed with heaven knew what in the shape of toilet-articles and other luxuries, on a led-horse.

Proudest of all was James Phillip of Amerlieclose, for not only was he appointed standard-bearer, but he had bestowed upon himself another office. Packed carefully into his saddle-bags was a store of fine paper, quills, and inkhorn, paper to be inscribed with an epic poem, a narrative in elegant Latin verse of a new hero and his gallant deeds. He saw himself as another Ennius, celebrating the fame of the elder Scipio.

When all were mounted at last, Claverhouse issued brief orders. The volunteers would ride in the centre of the troop of horse; speed was necessary in case the raising of the Royal Standard at Dudhope two days previously should bring some of Hamilton's men in pursuit, and in order to avoid Forfar and Brechin, where there was the risk of interception, they would take the road by Kirriemuir and the North Water Bridge. Then, his eyes firing suddenly, he made a signal to the trumpeters gathered about the Standard, and immediately a brazen call rang out, echoing over hill and dale, setting dogs barking, thrilling the hearts of this handful of men on the eve of their desperate enterprise. Glancing up at the crest carved above the doorway of Glen, Amerlieclose murmured in ecstasy:

"The phoenix himself is rising from the ashes of Montrose."

Chapter Six

(i)

On the day of the raising of King James' Standard upon Dundee Law, there had landed at Leith King William's newly appointed Commander-in-Chief for Scotland. His name was Hugh Mackay.

He was in an admirably resigned mood as he attended to the disembarking of his troops: his own Scoto-Dutch Brigade, reduced to eleven thousand men by the tactful withdrawing of all the Dutchmen in it, and to be made up to its full complement again by Scots recruits; the regiment of mounted infantry which once had been Dalyell's Dragoons, still wearing the grey uniform in which Old Tom had clothed them so proudly, but now, their late Colonel, Lord Dunmore, having refused to serve King William, commanded by Sir Thomas Livingstone; and Colchester's Horse. Most of the men and horses had been sea-sick on the voyage from England, and Mackay, while getting them into quarters, reflected that it was just as well that they had no enemy worth the name to encounter in battle just at present.

Mackay appreciated the honour of his new command, but he could not help regretting that it had not taken some other form. Here he was in Scotland again, he who had striven so hard, through so many years, to make the world and himself forget that he was a Scotsman. And here was the crude and vulgar dialect he detested, the appalling dirt, the gloomy-looking hills so different from flat Holland, the lively bustle of a people who did not know the Dutch maxim that nothing should ever be done in a hurry.

But he was genuinely resigned. He was, according to his lights, a worthy person, and a sincere Calvinist; since it had pleased the Lord to punish him for his sins, and Dutch William to give him this particular mark of favour, by sending him to a country he had visited only once, and then very briefly, in the twenty years since he had left it as a young soldier, it was not for him to complain. And since there was really nobody in Scotland to oppose him except the futile Duke of Gordon and his inadequate garrison, and a rabble of Highland savages who were reported to be stirring up there in the North, he was most thankfully confident that he would perform his duty in a very short time. Then, leaving garrisons to overawe any would-be malcontents, and sending a few troops into the Highlands to teach those barbarians a lesson by laying waste their lands, he would be free to return to England, to a grateful King William, to some pleasant house within easy reach of London and the Court, to the arms of his stout Dutch wife, and to the staff-work which, at forty-nine, was beginning to seem very congenial.

When this plump, complacent gentleman, leaning ever a little backward as he walked, his short legs taking deliberate steps, his simple, somewhat pompous face encircled with the latest mode in wigs, neat little sausage curls climbing in rows without a parting over his head and shoulders, when this gentleman came to Holyrood House to announce his arrival to the Duke of Hamilton, now Lord High Commissioner, he found his Grace in the most extraordinary state of panic.

For some while he could make no sense out of Hamilton's ravings, for the Duke, smelling strong of brandy, merely roared out an incoherent spate of speech, the while he ramped up and down his apartment. When the noble rage had so far exhausted his Grace as to cause him to sink down in a chair and bury his face in his hands, Mackay began in the manner of a merchant dealing with some favourite but difficult customer. It must be, he said, the overawing of the town by the Castle which was causing his Grace such disquiet; but his Grace should recollect that the Duke of Gordon's garrison consisted of only eighty-six men, that he was very ill-provisioned, and that, so far as he, Mackay, had been able to observe, his cannon had done no damage to the town. He cared not a straw for that fop of a Gordon, snapped his Grace; the rat would be starved out in a few weeks, and as for his cannon, he had sent a drummer with the message that he did not intend to bombard the town because of his tenderness for the civilian population. Hamilton added, in a few choice words, what he thought of so womanish a gesture.

Then, patiently pursued Mackay, doubtless it was the fear of troops landing from Ireland. If this were so, he had pleasure in assuring his Grace that his Majesty had exact information of how little there was to be feared from that quarter. The late King James had been entirely misled in regard to the forces available in Ireland; it was an army on paper only; scarce one in twenty of every stand of arms was fit for service; and there was no artillery. Moreover, several Dutch regiments were being shipped over to wipe out what little opposition was to be found in that country; there was absolutely no fear whatsoever of Irish troops landing in Scotland.

He had never even thought of Irish troops landing in Scotland, snapped his Grace, pouring himself another glass of brandy. Mackay sighed. He was beginning to think that the cause of the Duke of Hamilton's panic was the Duke of Hamilton's fundamental cowardice. However, he made a last attempt to bring the thing on to the plane of reason.

"Then," said he, standing with his baton of command propped upon the table, and looking (though he was blissfully unaware of it) very like some portly butcher with his knife propped on the block, "it must be the Highland barbarians who are breeding such unease in your Grace. Now, sir, consider: history has proved that these savages can never be made to fight outside their own wild country, and if their chiefs are mad enough to bring them south, I and my regulars will make short work of them, I can promise your Grace that. But I do not think I shall be put to the trouble of it, for his Majesty has accepted the advice of the Lord Register that a sum of money should be granted by the Treasury (no less than ten thousand pounds sterling) for distribution among the greater chiefs in return for their keeping their clans at home. Meanwhile it is my intention to garrison Stirling and Perth, the two gateways of the Highlands, to call out the Militia of the neighbouring counties, and to – "

Hamilton interrupted, rudely and violently. He consigned the Highland clans to perdition, gulped down a glass of brandy, and burst out:

"It's Clavers I'm feared of, that deil of a Grahame. He's the man will do us all a mischief."

Mackay stared at him, first in sheer bewilderment, then in only half concealed contempt.

My dear Lord Duke, I confess I find this puzzling. We have it upon excellent authority that Claverhouse has but a parcel of ex-troopers and kinsfolk with him, and for himself he's just a silly romantic, thinking to ape his late kinsman Montrose by setting up standards and defying two kingdoms. There is no considerable person will venture to join with him, in particular since he has been put to the horn."

"You don't know Clavers," muttered the Duke of Hamilton darkly. "But I'll tell you this: I'll not rest easy in my bed until that womanish head of his is stuck up on the prick of the Tolbooth yonder."

There was no arguing with that sort of a man, reflected Mackay; and he turned him to practical measures. He went about them in his customary manner, steady, slow, but sure; he was Dutch by adoption, and he had spent twenty years in the professional, strictly-according-to-the-rules atmosphere of foreign military service. He consulted maps, he reviewed his troops, he had long technical conversations with his staff-officers, he set about a regular besiegement of Edinburgh Castle, and he wrote letters to the great chiefs of the Highlands, reminding them of their Eternal welfare, of the need to fight Popery, and of how blessed they were by Almighty God Who had sent them the Protestant Deliverer, King William III, and rather spoiling the effect of this sermon by adding that if they would behave themselves they would be the richer by a considerable sum of English gold.

Then, and not till then, Mackay condescended to deal with the outlaw, John Grahame. He sent Sir Thomas Livingstone to take possession of Dudhope Castle, to capture the person of Claverhouse (who, he was confident, was sitting there ready to be taken) to confiscate all arms and ammunition found in Dudhope, and, with two companies of the Dragoons, to garrison Dundee.

He was pardonably annoyed to be interrupted, in the middle of a staff conference, by the arrival of an express from Livingstone informing him in agitated sentences that Claverhouse was not at Dudhope, nor was he at his ancestral home in Glen Ogilvie. Information of his whereabouts was impossible to come by, but there was a strong rumour that he was making for the Highlands with the intention of raising the clans. Mackay gently tut-tutted. He remembered that in the old days, when they were companions-in-arms in Flanders, Claverhouse had had a certain sort of charm which made him popular with simple and ignorant persons; he knew how to 'play his personage', as Mackay had remarked to his friends. Well, he must not be permitted to play his personage among the sentimental chiefs of the Highlands; and Mackay took firm and comprehensive measures to ensure that he should never reach the Highlands. He sent an express to the sick Earl of Mar, begging his lordship to keep a strict look-out in the neighbourhood of Stirling, and another to Lord Murray, Atholl's heir, warning him to guard his braes. Then, having again applied himself to the maps of his native country, he marshalled into his service two Highland personages – reluctantly, because he did not trust any of his own race, but these two had been loud in their protestations of loyalty to King William, and their respective territories must be crossed by any traveller making for the North. As he had formed, long ago, the worst possible opinion of his fellow Gaels, he was not unduly disappointed in the two specimens he now interviewed.

The Master of Forbes was what Mackay quaintly described as 'a young youth', and he was without any experience of war, but, since his father was old and infirm, he was the virtual Chief of a clan whose territory lay between the Dee and the Don. If the rumour of Claverhouse's going north was true, there was only one route by which he could travel, the road which ran along the north-east and thence, rounding the high shoulder of Scotland, by Elgin to Inverness. If he got as far along this road as to reach the Forbes country, then the Master of Forbes must intercept him. The Master of Forbes said modestly that he would do his best, and was rewarded by a nice little patronising compliment from General Mackay.

Grant of Grant was a much greater personage, and was at pains to impress the fact upon the irritated Mackay. He was quite willing, he said, to order his people to guard the fords of Spey and to spy upon the Grahame, but Mackay must understand that this was not the sort of task he was accustomed to undertake. He was descended, he said solemnly, from the god Wodin, and he then treated Mackay to a long list of his ancestors, real and mythical. He added that if his people captured the Grahame, he would expect to be given in the way of reward Letters of Fire and Sword against his neighbours, the Gordons, with whom he was at feud. He was going on to explain the origin of this quarrel, which was at least three hundred years old, when Mackay, without ceremony, cut him short.

"It will be high time to speak of rewards, sir, when you have earned them."

It was not the way to handle a Highlander, and Mackay was to have cause to regret it.

(ii)

On the last day of April, King William's Commander-in-Chief for Scotland sat in an inn at Fettercairn, writing a dispatch to his master.

Both his conscience and his self-interest had made it plan to him that it was his duty to go in pursuit of Claverhouse along the road to the North; his conscience, because he did not trust either the efficiency or the good-will of Murray, Mar, Forbes, or Grant, and his self-interest because, since this outlaw was held in such strange dread by personages like the Duke of Hamilton, it would be a feather in his cap if he himself effected the capture. So leaving a formidable besieging force about Edinburgh

Castle, and the two companies of Dragoons to garrison a disaffected Dundee, he had come leisurely, reluctantly, but dutifully northwards, his reluctance growing with every mile.

He had set out with two hundred of his own Brigade, four companies of the Dragoons, the whole of Colchester's Horse, and a quantity of arms for the recruits he was confident of enrolling en route. By the time of his reaching Fettercairn, he had been obliged to leave Colchester's Horse at Brechin because the horses were sore-backed, and he had enrolled not a single recruit. To add to his annoyance, the road, now that he had made a personal acquaintance with it, was not a road at all. It was a track obstructed by large boulders, in places flooded, in others a sheet of ice, and on two or three horrible occasions his order to march on the firm looking moorland at its side had resulted in his men sinking into a bog. It was utterly impossible on such a road for his men to keep their ranks, much less to march in step. It was only with a really heroic effort that he kept his temper when Sir Thomas Livingstone observed to him that this was still Lowland country, and that it would be infinitely worse farther on.

Mackay was as much a lover of smartness in his troops as was the Hon. James Douglas, and he had served for twenty years in a theatre of war in which marching troops progressed in formation, vanguard, centre, and rear, with drums beating, colours flying, sergeants on the flanks to see that the men kept step, proper communication arranged with his base, and a large baggage-train. He was not unused to hardship, and during his long service had spent almost as many nighs under canvas as under a roof; but he had never encountered such conditions as those he found north of the Tay.

For apart from the abominable road, there was the difficulty of quartering. The further north he marched, the more wintry grew the scene; it was difficult to believe that it was the end of April. The countryfolk, huddled in their cothouses, had no accommodation for strangers; the soldiers began to grumble dangerously when told that they must bivouack in the open; what remained of their rations was mildewed as a result of the continual icy rain, and food in the little market-towns was scarce and sold grudgingly. Mackay himself was obliged to lodge in the infrequent and wretched little inns, or change-houses as they called them here; and it was in such a hovel, with a peat fire in the centre of the room and its smoke wavering about and choking him before finding its way to the vent-hole that poor General Mackay was writing his letter to King William, snug and safe in Whitehall.

'I am now,' he wrote, 'halted at the foot of those hills which separate the southern from the northern provinces of Scotland, called in history the Grampian Hills.' (He cast a look of extreme distaste out of the window, through which he could see, white and forbidding against the sky, that mountain wall which guarded the Highlands.) 'May it please your Majesty, my intention is to stay here until I have certain notice where Dundee is, and for that end have engaged several poor countrymen, with money in hand and promise of more on their return with sure intelligence, to go in search of him. I confidently expect, within the next few days, to hear where he is skulking.'

He paused, and bit the end of his quill. It was not his habit to complain, but King William could have no idea of the difficulties his devoted servant was encountering, and in justice to himself Mackay felt that some of these should be indicated.

'May it please your Majesty, I fear that the chiefs have no true sense of the deliverance which God has sent them, for I have received no reply to the letters I dispatched to them, save from the laird of Glengarry, the which sent me so insolent an answer that I will not take upon me to rehearse it to your Majesty. Likewise, I find the common people in Scotland very disaffected, and I have had no offer of recruits save from the Master of Forbes, a worthy youth, but as yet bashful before the enemy (having never seen any), who brought me a hundred of his tribe; they were so undisciplined and ill-armed, and looked so little like their work, that with a compliment I declined their services. As for the state of the road – '

And Mackay waxed eloquent for another whole page on the quite intolerable condition of the only road running along the north-east of Scotland.

Half an hour later he was chewing his way through a dinner of salted beef, when an orderly entered to say that one of Grant's men had come in with an urgent message. Mackay brightened. It seemed to him unlikely that his quarry could have got as far as the Spey, but if he had, then Grant's men should have captured him. Pushing his half-finished dinner from him, he ordered the messenger to be admitted.

His inward distaste at the sight of a figure clothed only in a tartan plaid was increased when from its mouth proceeded a spate of Gaelic. He had hoped never to hear that hated native tongue of his again. Having taken great pains to forget it through twenty years, he was obliged to send for an interpreter; and when the message was translated to him his disgust turned to utter bewilderment.

It seemed that during the past two weeks, Claverhouse had been careering all over Aberdeenshire and Moray on a personal recruiting campaign. At Gordon Castle he had been welcomed by the Earl of Dunfermline, brother-in-law of the Duke of Gordon, and though his recruits were not numerous they included all the principal gentry of the Gordon clan. He then had gone towards Inverness-shire, and he had been seen as far north as Forres; his name, added the messenger, with undisguised relish, was inspiring such awe in the North that a minister, observing him at the Morning Exercise on the Sabbath, had omitted the prayer for King William and Queen Mary.

"I have never heard such nonsense in my life," cried Mackay, whose bewilderment was turning rapidly to indignation. "How can he have made a tour of these countries when there are no roads, or have got as far as Forres in so short a space of time?"

"The Grahame," translated the interpreter, "uses the hill-paths, employing a local man as guide."

Mackay's indignation rose by several degrees. Why, he demanded, was it only now that Grant of Grant had sent him this information, seeing that the Chief was on the spot, and must have known of these goings on for a considerable time? The Chief was not on the spot, explained the man; he was still in Edinburgh, having some little sickness upon him (by the way he said this it was plain to the infuriated Mackay that the descendant of the god Wodin was in perfect health but had taken umbrage at the General's brusque manner of addressing him), but he had ordered his people to spy upon the Grahame, and this was the result of their activity.

"Then will you have the goodness to tell me why," demanded the General, "the Grahame has not been captured?"

The messenger replied, with exasperating simplicity, that Grant's people had no orders to capture him, only to spy upon him. At that, Mackay rose in dignified wrath, flapping a hand at the Highlander who was continuing to speak rapidly and excitedly in his native tongue.

"Send my officers to me instanter," he said to his orderly. "It seems that we must march north with what haste we can."

"May it please your Excellency," said the orderly, "this man says that my Lord Dundee is here in Angus."

Mackay stood petrified in the act of buckling his belt.

"Just now he said he was at Forres."

"He says he was there the day before yesterday, sir, but it seems that word reached him there that the Dragoons quartered in Dundee are ready to go over to him if he can return and collect them, and so he is making with all speed to that town."

Mackay's jaw fell, and he stared open-mouthed from the embarrassed orderly to the cunning-eyed messenger. Treachery among the Dragoons! It could not be; and yet, on second thoughts, it might well be, since his own advice of replacing all the old inferior officers had not been followed. Their Colonel, Sir Thomas Livingstone, was William's man, and so was their new Major, Balfour, but the rest had served under Dunmore, some of them under old Dalyell, and they were the same men who had ridden over the Border last autumn under the command of Major-General Grahame to fight for King James.

Then he shook such horrid thoughts from him. Unbelievable though it appeared, he must follow up this fantastic report that the quarry he was pursuing was coming straight down the road to meet him, not knowing he was here. If it were true, not only would Mackay be spared the duty of carrying the hunt into the yet wilder country around Inverness, but with no trouble at all he would have the satisfaction of capturing the outlaw with his own troops. Jubilation altogether conquered dismay and incredulity, when a scout came running in to inform the General that Claverhouse was actually at Cairn o' Mount, only eight miles north upon the road.

Reluctant though he now was to employ the Dragoons, he had no other horsemen with him, and therefore was compelled to send a party of these possible traitors galloping breakneck upon the unconscious foe. He sent them under the command of Livingstone; and it was Livingstone himself who reported to him, a few hours later, that they had pounced upon thin air.

"He must have got wind of our coming, sir," said the breathless and mortified Sir Thomas, "and have taken to the hills."

"Pray talk sense," tartly retorted his superior. "Either you did not search far enough along the road, or else the tale of his being at Cairn o' Mount was false. Taken to the hills indeed!" snorted Mackay, waving an expressive hand towards the snow-clad monsters on his left.

Privately pondering upon the intolerable idea that Livingstone himself might be 'disaffected', the General applied himself once more to the local folk, bidding them search every inch of the country within a radius of ten miles. They took his money gladly, and appeared most enthusiastic for their task; but they did not find any trace of Claverhouse. At least, they said they did not. But during the ensuing days, Mackay began to realise that his care to dissociate himself from the language, customs, and topography of his native land might be playing him false at this juncture. He caught the local folk looking askance at a Highlander who could not speak or understand his own tongue, and all his careful consulting of maps was useless in the immense desolation through which ran this apology for a road.

He sat down and wrote an urgent appeal to King William for reinforcements; and then, heavy-footed, but still dutiful, set out to brave the bleak heights of the Dee and the Don. The only possibility which made sense to him was that his quarry was somewhere ahead along that north-east road; the tales about his cavorting over hill-paths, and dashing up as far as Forres and back in a few days, were just plain nonsense (and possibly malicious nonsense at that, and when he returned to Edinburgh he would have something to say to Grant of Grant). For after all, Claverhouse was a Lowlander, and if this horrible country and its barbarous language were baffling to the Highland-born Mackay, what must they be to an Angus laird?

Chapter Seven

(i)

While General Mackay was comforting himself with these reflections, Claverhouse was rapidly approaching Inverness.

He had done just precisely what Mackay had decided it was impossible for him to do; he had spent three days recruiting in the Gordon country; he had forded the Spey and the Lossie, reaching Forres on April 25th; here by the luckiest chance a messenger from his wife had found him, bringing news which Jean dared not commit to paper. It seemed that the officers and men of the Dragoons quartered in Dundee had sent one of their number, William Livingstone, to Glen, to inform her that if her husband could come to Dundee and collect them, the two companies were ready and willing to fight under his command. Two companies of regulars, of the men of the King's Own Regiment of Horse! He wasted not a moment, but turned in his tracks and went back at full speed, in two days covering more than eighty miles of the road which was daunting Mackay.

But at Cairn o' Mount the local folk had warned him of Mackay's presence at Fettercairn; he was too good a soldier to risk an encounter with a large force of regulars when he himself had but a hundred and twenty men, many of them untrained volunteers. Nor would he risk being overtaken by Mackay by going back along the road; he took to the hills on the west, and by nightfall had put three ranges of them between him and his pursuer. And here he was now, on the first day of May, riding through a country still white with snow for his tryst with Macdonald of Keppoch.

Despite his disappointment in not being able to collect the Dragoons, he was in high spirits. The simple, forthright loyalty of the Gordon gentry had delighted him, and so had the friendliness of the common folk. He was a soldier again; he was in sole command of a tiny but devoted troop; he could adapt himself to this wild, unknown country as though he had been born here, and he was about to meet a powerful ally. He imagined that he would find in Keppoch a gentleman resembling Lochiel, the only great Highland chief he had met since his student days at St Andrews, for he understood that the Gordons were not regarded as being pure Highlanders, either in blood or culture. Moreover, if, as seemed likely, Keppoch had brought a number of his clan to the tryst, it might be possible to make a surprise attack on Mackay, who was plodding along the road behind him.

As he came in sight of Inverness, he was astonished and puzzled to observe that it appeared to be in a state of siege. It was not, he knew, a Highland town; it was a little island of merchants, a wealthy, smug and law-abiding place, its inhabitants detesting their Highland neighbours and holding no communication with them save that connected with trade. But clearly it was not trading that was in progress between Inverness and the untidy mass of men swarming about its wooden walls today. Small, ancient cannon were mounted on the Castle; there was a guard of what looked like civilians hastily armed with swords and muskets, on the handsome stone bridge which led from the south to the north side of the Great Glen, and from the

Tolbooth there came the sound of a bell clanging a continuous tocsin of alarm.

"What's the stir, I wonder?" he said to Amerlieclose who, with the Standard proudly unfurled, was riding beside him.

"I mislike it, my lord," replied the scholar in an agitated voice. "Look at yon cattle-beasts herded there. I very much fear that Coll na Ceapaich has been up to his old tricks again. He's a terrible man for cattle-lifting, though your lordship must take care never to call it by the name of thieving. Yon's word will make any Highlander draw his dirk on you. They regard the lifting of an enemy's cattle as a lawful act, though they look upon the taking of a sheep or a goat as a crime."

Claverhouse put his perspective-glass back into his pocket, and rode down towards the motley encampment, his little troop riding in perfect order at his heels. As he approached, men came racing from the swarming mass to meet him, shouting out in the Gaelic to enquire who he was, their murderous sharp dirks in their hands, barbaric figures, clothed only in the belted plaid, and with the Macdonald badge, a sprig of heather, in their flat blue bonnets. When he replied in their own tongue that he was a friend come to seek Keppoch, they put their dirks away, politely lifted their bonnets to him, and offered to conduct him to their Chief. Trotting along beside his horse, their bright fierce eyes stared at him with childish curiosity, weather-burnt hands feeling the cloth of his uniform, the smooth coat of his horse, the steel of his stirrup-iron. He heard one ask the other:

"Is it the King?"

But as he was conducted through the multitude of their fellows towards the hamlet of houses on the west of the town, where, it seemed, Keppoch was lodged, he was too preoccupied to be amused by the inquisitiveness of his guides. It seemed that Coll na Ceapaich had 'lifted' from somewhere other spoil besides cattle. His men were guarding great heaps of household stuff, the skins of marten, wild-cat, and fox, silver-rimmed drinking bowls and weapons of all kinds, brooches, rings, wearing apparel. His face hardened, and he thrust out his lower lip. Coll was going to have to answer a few questions when they met.

Halting his troop, he dismounted, and taking only Amerlieclose with him, followed his guides to a little round house built of sods with a heather-thatched roof, before the door of which there stalked up and down a very proud looking personage who, whispered his companion, must be the Chief's piper. He was not playing at present, and his pipes were held for him by a gillie. Squatting on the threshold of the house was a group of clansmen, evidently Keppoch's personal bodyguard, for they sprang to their feet and drew their dirks at the strangers' approach, shouting out a challenge in Gaelic. Satisfied by their comrades who were conducting the strangers, they too became all politeness, offering to shake hands as was the manner of their race between all classes, and ushering the visitors into the one apartment the little house contained.

Lying at his ease upon a bed of heather, with a coverlet of rich furs drawn up to his breast, and his long, naked, ape-like arms clasped comfortably behind his head, was a person who could be no other than Keppoch himself, though he was as different from Claverhouse's idea of a Highland chief as it was possible to imagine. (He had one sharp mental vision of Lochiel, the velvet coat, the buckled shoes, the courtly grace.) Very little of Keppoch's countenance could be seen because it was covered with a bush of untrimmed black whisker and beard; out of this bush, like some fierce creature peeping from its lair, his eyes observed his visitors, bright, cunning, wary as a fox's. On the floor beside him, convenient to his hand, stood a *cuoch* with silver handles, the kind of drinking-vessel which in the Highlands was handed down as a family heirloom. Claverhouse's keen eyes noted that upon this particular *cuoch* there was engraved a spring of holly, and his recent painstaking study of clan badges informed him that the holly was the badge of the Mackintoshs.

The only other occupants of the room were three men in Lowland dress, who stood together in a little group facing the bed; indignation and distraction mingled in their expressions, and as Claverhouse entered with Amerlieclose and one of Keppoch's gillies behind him, they broke off what was clearly an angry argument to stare at the newcomers, plainly wondering whether they were friends or foes.

The Chief's own reaction at the sight of his visitors was very different. He leaped from the bed, stark naked expect for a saffron-dyed shirt, a state which appeared to cause him not the least embarrassment and which somehow did not detract from the dignity of the bow he made; then, after ceremoniously shaking hands and uttering a short speech of welcome in the charming, sing-song English of the Gael, he begged his honoured guests to be seated while he dressed himself. Giving them no time to reply, he flapped his hand to the gillie who had ushered them into his presence; the gillie ran on bare feet to the hole in the wall which served as window, and made some signal; and immediately, after a few unseemly whinings, there was a screech of bagpipes

"We must endure this music, my lord," whispered Amerliclose. "It is the custom for every chief to have his piper play him a sprig while he makes his toilet for the day."

Fortunately this toilet proved a simple matter. The gillie spread upon the floor an enormous piece of plaiding in the Macdonald tartan, skilfully pleating it until its length was reduced to some five feet. Keppoch then solemnly laid himself down upon the plaid, so that the lower edge was level with his knees. The unpleated ends he folded across him, and before standing up again fastened the plaid about his waist with a leather belt. A tunic of bullshide, tartan short-hose cross-gathered about his hairy claves, deerskin brogues with the red hair worn upon the outside, and his toilet was complete. The gravity with which this extraordinary dressing was accomplished, combined with the ludicrous distaste with which the three strangers regarded it, caused Claverhouse some difficulty in concealing a smile; but when, the scream of the pipes outside the window mercifully whining into silence again, conversation could be resumed, his amusement vanished abruptly.

"Now ye may take yourselves out of my presence, ye sons of swine," said Keppoch, haughtily addressing the three strangers. "I have the honour to receive a visit from the Lord Dundee; and as for the matter upon which you came hither, I have said my last word. Away to your town, and be sending me what I have demanded ere the sun is sunk into the western wave, or you will be having no town; by the Son of Cursing, I will give it to the flame."

"My lord," cried one of the three, taking a step towards Claverhouse, "I know not what brings your lordship to our country, but I have heard that you are a gentleman of honour, and therefore I beseech you to persuade Keppoch to lay-by the wicked demands and threats he has been making. I am the Provost of Inverness, and these gentlemen are my bailies. Keppoch has sworn that if we will not pay him four thousand merks, he will burn Inverness to the cellars and put all the inhabitants to the sword."

There was a warning flush on Claverhouse's cheeks as he turned to Keppoch and asked curtly:

"Is this true?"

"It is true right enough," replied the Chief in high glee, "and wait you till you see what bonny spoil I have taken on my way hither through the country of the Mackintosh. Ach, that son of little men, who has gotten him bits of sheepskin which he terms Crown Charters for the possession of Glen Roy and Glen Spean, which have been Macdonald country since the days of the great Somerled, he will be mewing, that mountain-cat, when he sees his lands laid waste and his cattle lifted, but he will not venture to unsheath his sharp claws, for the knowledge is at him of how, at the Battle of Mulroy – "

"Inverness is not a Mackintosh town," interrupted Claverhouse, still more abruptly.

"It has been guilty," replied Keppoch, dignified and faintly reproachful, "of unneighbourly practices. I have not forgot how, when I was coming from St Andrews to my father's funeral (may his share of Paradise be his), the Mackintosh seized me and flung me into the Tolbooth yonder, nor was I able to come forth until there was an order made by the Privy Council for it. Your lordship must take the understanding upon you that the Mackintosh and my people have been at feud since the days of – "

He stopped in mid-sentence and in utter amazement; for Claverhouse had turned his back upon him and was addressing the three visitors.

"Sirs, I have the honour to represent King James, our lawful Sovereign, in Scotland, and this I promise you in his name: that I will go bond for the repayment of the ransom demanded of you by Keppoch here, when his Majesty returns to his rightful throne, and in the meantime I give you my word as a soldier and a gentleman that no hostile act shall be done against your town, and that the people thereof shall enjoy my protection."

In their relief at finding this Lowland lord, and one who spoke with such an air of authority, ready to protect them from Highland savages, the Provost and his bailies forgot the injustice of being forced to pay a 'ransom' of four thousand merks (which Inverness could well afford and was used to paying as the price of living in such wild country). They bowed themselves out with many expressions of gratitude, promising to send the money before sunset. As soon as the door was shut behind them, Keppoch began leaping up and down in an ecstasy of childish glee.

"That's the bonny thing that's in it whatever!" he cried. "Creator! I wish now that I had demanded double the amount. They have great wealth, these fat merchants, with their ships upon the river carrying our hides and our salmon and our plaiding to foreign parts – "

For the first time this morning he had been speaking in Gaelic; and now he was astounded to hear his Lowland visitor interrupt him in his own tongue, and in such a tone as no one had ever used with him before.

"I will tell you what you are," barked Claverhouse, facing him across the table. "You are nothing but a common thief and robber, and an enemy of King James his cause!"

(ii)

As Keppoch's hand leaped for his dirk, Amerlieclose stepped quickly between the two men, but Claverhouse, motioning him back with a sharp gesture, continued in the Gaelic, fluently and incisively, his glance never leaving Keppoch's face.

"I am commissioned by his Majesty to command his Scots Army; Lochiel has pledged his word to raise the clans which must form that army; you he has sent hither to conduct me to the conference of the chiefs. And what do I find at our meeting? I find that upon your road hither you have indulged a personal grudge by laying waste the lands of one who might have brought out his clan for King James, and that you are threatening a town which might have been held as a base for your master and mine. But you have alienated it so that it will welcome the troops of the usurper, the strong troops which are even now at Elgin. Therefore I tell you that you are a public enemy, and have gone far to destroy the cause of your King."

Crouched as though making ready to spring at the other's throat, his dirk grasped in one hairy hand, Keppoch had listened to this denunciation with growls of rage, and now he muttered, deep in his throat:

"By the hand of my ancestors, no man speaks to Coll na Ceapaich – "

But once again Claverhouse interrupted, stepping round the table and confronting Keppoch face to face.

"How do you venture," he cried passionately, "to mention your ancestors, those great heroes of the race of Somerled, son of Giollabride! How dare you take upon your tongue the names of those who, for their valour under Bruce, for more than three hundred years have claimed the place of honour on the right hand of battle! Are not your forebears famed for their chivalry in fight, their keeping of an oath, their mercy to the defeated? Must I call your bard and bid him rehearse to you the valiant deeds of Fearghus, or is it not enough to make you take the shame upon you when you reflect upon these noble forebears as they look down from the clouds of the morning, from their hunting and their feasting in the kingdom of the High Chief of the World, and see you betraying the cause of the High Chief of Albin?"

Keppoch's expression had been changing rapidly from rage to astonishment, and mow he stood open-mouthed.

"God be here!" he murmured, letting his dirk fall with a clatter on the table. "This is a very marvellous thing whatever. You have the knowledge at you of my language, of my ancestors, and of the poetry of our bards. By the Crosier of St Fillan, I never met a Lowlander like your lordship." Then, with an abrupt change from awe to the manner of a child who has been caught out in some prank and hopes, by exaggerated penitence, to escape punishment: "By your leave, King Sheumas has no better servant than myself in all Albin, and the spoil I have taken, is it not for his service? Grief is upon me that I have offended your lordship by taking a few cows and by seeking to recover from this town a sum of money long owed to me, but I will not offend again. And now I beg that your lordship will do me the honour of inspecting my clansmen whose fingers itch to draw the broadsword under your lordship's command."

It was clever move of Keppoch's, as Claverhouse realised as soon as he began an inspection of these warriors. His imagination which, in the old Galloway days, had shown him the making of good soldiers in slovenly, disgruntled recruits, saw in these half-naked savages heaven-sent material for the hill-fighting to which he now must adapt himself. Their weapons were primitive, the double-edged broadsword, the ancestral claymore, the needle-pointed dirk, and the nail-studded targe for defence, but was it not with these same weapons that Montrose had won his victories? Keppoch's men lacked anything resembling discipline as Claverhouse understood that term, yet he noted the child-like affection and reverence with which they greeted their Chief, and his entire authority over them. And they were the hardiest men he had ever seen, small, wiry, muscular, their bodies hardened by temperate living, their bare limbs burnt black from exposure to all weathers, their loose and scanty clothing giving them the maximum freedom of movement, their hillmen's eyes as keen as an eagle's. There were seven hundred of them; more than enough, cried Claverhouse, turning eagerly to their Chief, to swoop down upon the unsuspecting Mackay who was resting his troops in Elgin.

But to his bewilderment and dismay, Keppoch at once became evasive.

It would be, he admitted, a bonny thing whatever to fall upon that son of mischief, Hugh Mackay, and if he had only his own clansmen with him, he would be ready to march forthwith. But he had many of Lochiel's Camerons, and they had no permission from their Chief to engage in battle. They were, it seemed, of a conscience so tender that to fight without the orders of Mhic Dhomhnuill Dhuibh was a thing they could not do.

"Then we will make shift with your Macdonalds," said the impatient Claverhouse.

But Keppoch's evasiveness only increased.

"Ach, understanding must be upon you, my lord, that I swore upon the holy iron that I would bring your lordship to Lochiel, and that is why I am come to Inverness. It is a great pity that is in it, for dearly would I have loved to give the eagle his feast of the flesh of little men. I believe," he added, glancing up into the sky and affecting to study it in some anxiety, "that snow will be upon us before the sun is set, and therefore it behoves us to haste on our journey, for there is wild country between here and Lochaber."

A furious retort rose to Claverhouse's lips, but he bit it back. He was not in the least deceived; he saw perfectly well that the only thought in Keppoch's mind at present was to get his booty home. But his knowledge of human character warned him that a second rebuke of a proud man often cancels out the effects of the first; at the outset of his enterprise it had been necessary to show Keppoch who was master, but he dared not crack the whip again just yet.

Moreover, he had as yet no official standing, nothing in writing to enforce his authority; and the army he hoped to raise in the Highlands must be an army of irregulars, of volunteers, largely unpaid, who could be persuaded to accept military discipline only if he succeeded in gaining their devotion to him as a man.

But meanwhile he was not going to Lochaber in the company of a chief whose followers were loaded with spoil. There were still nearly three weeks before the rendezvous, and in the meantime there was much to be done. The hope of surprising Mackay had vanished; there remained the possibility of winning over the indignant Invernessians and persuading them to hold their town for King James. And there was the pressing need to obtain money and horses from somewhere; his private purse was empty; no one would give credit to an outlaw; and his horses were jaded by the speed at which he had travelled and the conditions of this wild country.

Bidding Keppoch a ceremonious farewell, he watched the Chief set off towards his own country, the 'ransom' of four thousand merks safely tucked away in his sporran, his men bowed down beneath the weight of their plunder and driving herds of Mackintosh cattle before them. Then, squaring his slight shoulders, he turned to the task of trying all his charm and powers of persuasion on the rich merchants of Inverness.

Chapter Eight

(i)

'Advancing to Dunkeld' wrote Amerlieclose, in his elegant Latin, 'the Grahame dashes at the open door of the western gate, and there, unexpectedly, comes upon the captain of a hostile troop who has been gathering the revenues of the district. Without bloodshed the hero prostrates him utterly, depriving him of the money and his arms. There he rests to refresh man and horse. But as soon as the sun has hidden his glowing head in ocean, the horses are bridled, and by hidden fords he makes forced march on Perth.'

He paused, wrestling to find words in which fittingly to describe one of the most brilliant and impudent raids in history, his adoring eyes glancing at his hero, still busy with his correspondence though it was one o'clock in the morning.

"What is the Gaelic patronymic of the Fraser Chief?" asked Claverhouse, without looking up.

"It is Mac Shimei Bal-dubh, my lord. But I must inform your lordship that the Frasers are at feud with Clan Donald which nearly exterminated them in 1544 at the Battle of Blar Leine, which means the Battle of the Shirts."

Claverhouse flashed him a brief smile.

"What should I do without you, Jamie, and your knowledge of such matters?"

The young man's face flushed crimson with pleasure.

"Would you not permit me to write some of these letters for you, my lord" he cried, "while you take some rest. Consider how fatiguing these past few weeks have been. A circular letter to all the chiefs and gentleman – "

"No, no," interrupted his leader quietly. "I must make a different appeal to each, according to what I can learn of his history and character. It is you who should be resting, for you are not accustomed to so hard a life."

"This account I am writing of your lordship's noble enterprise," said Amerlieclose earnestly, "is sweeter to me than sleep, and I must note down each exploit while it is fresh in my memory. One day I hope to present this *Grameid* of mine to our young Prince of Wales, whom I have invoked as the patron of my muse."

He paused and looked hopefully at his hero. Sometimes Claverhouse would delight him by asking him to read aloud some of the *Grameid*, and he was burning to do so now. But the busy quill opposite him was scratching on again, so, with only the faintest of sighs, he returned to his authorship:

'Having advanced to the second milestone from Perth, the Grahame halts, and, selecting twenty men from his troop, he steals through the lofty gates of the city before the lark has sung her wonted song, or Aurora gilded the sea with her yellow tresses. At once he occupies the marketplace and the watch-houses; meanwhile the troopers, drawn up outside under their officers, rush to the walls, and there make entrance for themselves; they fill all the streets where the soldiers lie; here and there strong bands storm the houses, some seize the cess-money, others collect arms, others, horses. Now a band of youthful Cavaliers rouse up the commander, Blair, snoring in deep sleep, not having yet shaken off the effects of last night's debauch. From every side they gather the captives together, and having possessed themselves of the booty, with great laughter they raise aloft the ensigns of the enemy, and pluck the orange balls from the standards. And now all the victors, mounted on fresh horses, proud in arms, return in order to their own ensigns...'

Poor Jamie, Claverhouse was thinking, as he sealed his letter to the Fraser Chief, he is longing for me to ask him to read aloud that tedious stuff of his. He found Amerlieclose's hero-worship embarrassing, even irritating; but sometimes the contrast between the elegant Latin description of his adventures and the harsh reality gave him a great deal of secret amusement. Tonight, however, he simply could not spare the time. Drawing another sheet of paper towards him, he began a dispatch to King James.

He wrote in his old manner, concise, unemotional. Finding it impossible to persuade the Invernessians to declare for his Majesty, he had made Mackay a present of that town, and in three days had come by way of Strathnairn, Stratherrick, by the Pass of Corryarrick, and over the Grampians to Dunkeld, his object being to obtain money and fresh horses. In Dunkeld he had found an armed band collecting taxes, of which he had deprived them in ten bloodless minutes, and hearing that the Whig lairds, Blair and Pollock, were in Perth, arming the Perthshire Militia, he had made a surprise raid on the place at two o'clock in the morning.

Blair and Pollock he had captured in their beds; he had seized upon a large sum of cess-money, refraining from taking five hundred pounds of private money which he had found in the same house ('I told them I would rob no man, but what was the Crown's I thought I might make bold with, seeing that what I did was solely to serve your Majesty'), had collected forty good horse and many arms, and with Blair and Pollock in custody had ridden out of Perth nine hours later, the townsfolk cheering him as he went. To the protests of the two lairds he had answered, 'You take prisoners for the Prince of Orange, and I take prisoners for King James, and there's an end of it.'

He was resting his men here at Stobhalla a seat of the Earl of Perth (now in prison) and tomorrow he intended to ride to Dundee, whence he hoped to tempt the timid Dragoons to come out to him. He implored his Majesty to hasten over the Irish reinforcements promised, and he humbly besought another commission, since the first must have fallen into the enemy's hands, and while he had no written authority he was at a disadvantage in persuading men to join him. Meanwhile he remained his Majesty's most humble and obedient servant, Dundee. He sealed the letter with his crest, which still bore the simple helmet of the esquire.

So they sat on through the small hours of the morning, the hero engaged in his campaign of letters, the disciple composing his Latin epic. It was the morning of Saturday, May 11th.

(ii)

During the next five days, Amerlieclose had neither heart nor strength for his literary labours.

First there was the bitter disappointment at Dundee. Drawing up his little troop upon the high ground above the town, Claverhouse rode solitary all round the walls, examining for weak spots and hoping, by this exposure of himself, to tempt the timid but loyal officers and men to make a dash out to him. But their new Major, Balfour, had barricaded the streets, and the new Provost owed his office to King William. In vain did Claverhouse shout to the watchmen on the walls of this home town of his that he intended not the least hurt to Dundee; Balfour and the Provost spoke louder, warning the burgesses that if they dared admit that devil of a Grahame within their gates their heads should answer for it. At nightfall Claverhouse turned sadly away; over eighty miles of the most desolate country lay between him and the trysting-place with Lochiel, and he had but a few days in which to cover them. As the bells of Dundee clanged backwards in alarm, he remembered bitterly those same bells pealing for the birth of his son, and in his mind lay a picture of those streets and houses and kirks, as familiar to him as Glen itself, the landmarks of boyhood, the little domain he had ruled as Constable and Provost, its gates closed against him.

But he had no time, mercifully he had no time to brood in this hectic period of his life. Over the hills and far away was Lochiel who trusted him, and other, touchy Highland Chiefs who must not be kept waiting. The Queen's Dragoons were on their way to Scotland, to reinforce Mackay; Mackay himself was sitting quietly and comfortably in Inverness, waiting for six hundred men he had ordered to be sent him from Edinburgh under a Colonel Ramsay; all this Claverhouse knew from unpaid and most willing spies, the country folk, and not only haste but an avoidance of the road was vital.

So, with a Highlander as guide, he proceeded to cut straight across Scotland. From Dundee through Dunkeld and Comrie to Garth, the going was comparatively simple, but from that point onwards it was a waste of forest and mountain, and the journey became a nightmare.

He had imagined that his dash back from Cairn o' Mount over the foothills of the Grampians to Inverness had prepared him for the facing of any Highland country; now he was undeceived. They went by the *lairigs* or hillpaths, tracks only just passable for the hunter after the long winter months. The gullies were white with snow-water up to their edges, running fast, deep, and incalculable; some of the horses foundered and had to be shot, among them the mount belonging to Amerlieclose, so that thereafter the scholar was fain to walk, with his saddle over his shoulders. The wasteland was without habitation, and the cold on the heights was so intense that their breath froze on their unshaven chins. The Lowlanders in the company were daunted by the physical hardships; the Highlanders whispered fearfully of the spectres which haunted these hill-paths, of Bodach Lamb-dhearg whose custom it was to appear in the guise of a soldier and challenge travellers to fight with him, of Fear Liath Mór, whose giant footsteps could be seen in the snow.

It was one man's personality which alone kept them from panic and from mutiny, one man's spirit which made possible the hideous trek. It was not only to the adoring and romantic Amerlieclose that he seemed a hero now; his own brother looked at him in wonder, the troop which had been with him from the Galloway days regarded him in something approaching awe – this little gentleman who, though the greying locks had lost their famous curl and the beautiful face was haggard and sunken, still contrived to look picturesque in his tattered uniform, this leader who was also a comrade, who, gritting his teeth with the pain of snow-blindness, still would take out his pistol to shoot a horse which had broken its leg.

"It's cleaner than Embro' here, Jock," he would say, suddenly appearing at his quartermaster's side. "No risk of goodwives emptying their slops on to your head."

And:

"Fie, Jamie, have you no more of that fine poem of yours with which to cheer us? What of Hannibal crossing the Alps? Will you not compare us with him? Come, Mr Edwards, let us have a rousing psalm while Amerlieclose is wrestling with that muse of his."

One of the Gordon gentry began grumbling about the weight of his musket and saying that he would leave it in the snow; next moment he was red with shame, because there was Claverhouse offering to carry it for him. Sometimes they passed a little clachan, a village of round black houses, and the folk would come running out to stare at these strange travellers, and then, in true Highland fashion, offer them hospitality in the shape of a bowl of ewe's milk or pieces of salted deer-meat. But the leader of the band would neither eat nor drink until he had divided the best portions among the sick and the very young and the least hardy of his followers. To the romantic he made the journey seem a crusade, to the unromantic a jest. He talked in Gaelic to the Highlanders, and extolled the famous hardihood and courage of their race; he set his troopers singing old songs of the camp; to all he promised rest and refreshment at their journey's end, and anon a battle which should win back Scotland for King James.

On May 15th they made a last bivouac on the shores of Loch Treig; and at noon next day, climbing an outlying spur of Ben Nevis, they saw below them the green hollow where the waters of the Roy met those of the Spean, and felt upon their frozen faces a brearth of soft west country air. Then, as they dragged their exhausted limbs over this last stretch of their journey, a skirl of pipes informed them that Lochiel's scouts had been on the watch, and that they were being welcomed into the country of the Camerons.

And here came Lochiel himself, with his piper stalking before him, his bard and his twelve lads-of-the-belt marching behind, and in his hands a bowl of milk and cream, the traditional offering to honoured guests. Sweeping off his bonnet with the eagle feathers, he bowed with an exquisite compounding of deference and pride.

"My Lord Dundee, I bid you welcome to Lochaber, you and your gallant band. Everything I have is yours to command."

"Your prophecy has been fulfilled, Lochiel," said

Claverhouse, as, after ceremoniously drinking from the bowl, he fell into step beside the Chief. "We meet again, and I am no longer 'Captain' Grahame."

Lochiel bowed without speaking. Glancing at him, Claverhouse thought he caught some odd expression in the bright black eyes which was gone again before he could determine its nature.

(iii)

Lochiel's house was very like its owner, plainly handsome, unpretentious, with a strict regard for tradition combined with an acceptance of modern comforts. Built in the form of a square, with stables, byre, and barns forming the other three sides, it reminded Claverhouse most poignantly of Glen.

During the few days which remained before the conference, he got to know his host and to learn something of the Highland way of life. Lochiel was well read, had travelled widely, and had been often to London and received at Court, but at the same time he was steeped in the peculiar culture of his race, and remained essentially the Highland chief. And all his life he had been a fighter. He loved to tell how he had forced General Monck to a truce with him during the Commonwealth, and of how, before that, he had attacked three hundred English regulars at Achadelew, with only thirty-five of his clansmen, and had slain a hundred and thirty-eight of the enemy, with the loss of but five of his own men. In a personal struggle with the officer, Lochiel had bitten out his throat.

"Act," said he with relish, "God put the villain's throat into my mouth, and it was the sweetest bite ever I had in my life."

Listening to him conferring with his tacksmen, and giving his advice to the humbler among his people who came to seek it upon every matter, Claverhouse was impressed by his plain common sense. There was a curious combination of realism and romanticism in his character; thus he would listen entranced while his bard, drawing his long nails over the harp-strings, recited the deeds of half-mythical ancestors and of those heroes of old Caledonia, Fingal and his companions, of whom Claverhouse himself had learned from his Highlalnd nurse; but while stressing the loyalty of the Gaels to their rightful King, Lochiel would say dryly:

"Your lordship must not be at thinking that we are better than we are. The usurpation of the Prince of Orange outrages our sense of honour and justice, but likewise does it mean the return of the supremacy of feudal lords like Argyll. Always have the Royal Stuarts striven to give us protection from such tyranny, and always have they been ready to lend an ear to our grievances, in particular that of the feudal jurisdictions which are alien to our way of life."

It was a patriarchal way of life; so much was increasingly plain to Claverhouse, as he rode with Lochiel round the Chief's domain. Everywhere the old man went he was saluted with the affectionate reverence due to a father; all claimed descent with him from one common ancestor, even to the humblest of his people, and while his word was law, there was no servility; each man unbonneted to him, but each claimed the right to shake him by the hand. And there was another lesson driven home to Claverhouse during these few days: while the Gaels were a race of warriors, they were also a race of peasants. They maintained themselves by their hunting and their agriculture; thus they could not be expected to remain under arms when there was no actual fighting to be done. Circumstances had forced him to seek their aid at a season of the year when food was short, and when the busy season was about to begin, when the young folk were preparing to drive the lean black cattle up to the corries to find pasture, the young men were at the start of their hunting, the older beginning to plough.

All these lessons were sharp in Claverhouse's mind when, on the evening of May 18th, he sat at Lochiel's right hand in the large hall of his house, and observed the chiefs who had come to the conference. He was observed by them in his turn; he knew it; their quick dark eyes, with more than a hint of savagery in them, were fixed upon him, summing him up. He had been recommended to them by Lochiel as their future commander; it remained for him to convince them that he was fit to be so. His success or failure with this group of touchy, primitive, hard-headed and yet at the same time intensely romantic men might decide the issue of his desperate enterprise, for only at their word would their clansmen fight. With the great ones of the Lowlands he had failed; he must not, he dared not fail with the great ones of the Highlands. And to make this first test the sharper, the chiefs present at the conference represented the various branches of Clan Donald, the most powerful in the Highlands, the most vain, and the most in love with old clan feuds.

There was ancient, frail Glengarry; Glencoe, still hale and vigorous in his seventieth year, who could command no more than fifty fighting-men but whose personal prowess and wisdom made him respected by all; young Sir Donald Macdonald of Sleat; the Captain of Clanranald, a youth of sixteen, who had his Tutor with him; and Coll of Keppoch, his long arms folded, his manner courteous, even effusive, but his eyes wary, watchful, and appraising. At Inverness he had reacted with uncharacteristic meekness to the rebukes of a Lowlander, but Claverhouse was aware that it had been only the first round in the battle for mastery. On the one hand he must wring discipline and obedience from these little kings, on the other he must win their trust and their devotion; and meeting the glances of the fierce bright eyes around the table, he remembered that in the former task even the great Montrose had failed.

Glengarry opened the discussion. He drew from his sporran a paper and smoothed it out upon the table before him, his manner a mixture of indignation and complacence.

"It is a letter I was after receiving from him of Scourie," said he, meaning Mackay, "and it says to me that the Prince of Orange is offering me one thousand English pounds if I will come over to his side. I wrote to him of Scourie, and I gave him the advice that he should follow the example of General Monck and restore his rightful King. Ach!" added the old man with a chuckle, "the wish is on me that I could have been at the rascal's side when he read my letter."

"I too have had a letter from Mackay," said Lochiel, "and I believe there will be something of the same sort in it, but I have not put the trouble upon me to read it, and I beg that your lordship will do so on my behalf if you think fit," and he handed Claverhouse a sealed paper.

Claverhouse's lips twitched with amusement as he read the pompous phrases; it was so exactly the sort of letter he would have expected from Mackay. The gist of two pages of patronising verbosity was the offering of a title and the sum of one thousand pounds sterling in return for Lochiel's declaring for King William. And as he laid the letter down, and looked at the men about the table, suddenly he knew how he was gong to appeal to them. He rose and began to speak, feeling the words form themselves inside his mind, feeling like a man who draws his fingers across the strings of a harp and knows in that moment that he has the gift of music.

"Gentlemen, Mackay has offered you gold; I offer

nothing; I am come to call you to the fight."

At the last word, he saw a hand go instinctively to a sword hilt; he saw old Glencoe put down his snuff-mull and stare at him.

"The Prince of Orange, like Manos, has given his oath to the winds; but let him beware of the fate of Manos; let him remember the words of Fingal after the unprovoked attack on Isitore: 'Are not the thousand ills which grow on every heath, and which the son of the hunter is heir to, a sufficient toil? Why shouldst thou scatter more evils in his way and strew his path with swords? May not the deer of thine own hills suffice thee?' "

The lips of the men about the table silently repeated the ancient tale told at so many *ceilidhs* by their bards.

"Ye warlike Gaels of ancient race, ye martial sons of the mountains, I am come here to seek your aid against a new Manos of the broken word, against the Prince of Orange who has insulted Highland gentlemen by offering them gold in return for their honour. Mackay of Scourie, a man of your own race, attacks his country, and the father of it, who gave him his first commission and bestowed upon him high military rank. The great Saxon lords who swore fealty to their Sovereign, swore it upon their knees in most solemn fashion, calling God as their witness, have wrested the Sceptre from their master and have compelled him to pass in exile to foreign shores. Our land blazes by the hand of her own children, and Britain perishes by a fate she has brought upon herself."

As he paused again, a sound like an angry growl ran from lip to lip around the table.

"Now the slave insults the master, the common soldier his officer and, horrible to see! the son the father. Oh, who is not moved by the miserable fate of his country, and roused to anger? Is there a man of spirit so abject, who has a drop of blood in his veins, that can look upon the mockeries of our times and not prefer death to enduring them? Rather than that the illustrious James, the descendant of Fergus, should become the prey of his unnatural kinsman, who would not meet the clash of arms and present his breast to the dart of death?"

The mutter was louder now. The boy, Clanranald, stared with wide eyes upon the speaker; old Glencoe was crouched as though about to spring to his feet; Glengarry had a hand behind his ear, straining to take in every word; Keppoch sat running a thumb along the edge of his dirk.

"But the Saxons and the men of the Lowlands are bought with Dutch gold, or are too cowed by the might of the usurper to behave themselves like men unless others shame them by valiant example. And this is why I am come to the Highlands. It has been told me that your noble forebears considered it disgraceful for a warrior to retire from the fight upon any pretext whatsoever, and that when Gaul of the blue shield found himself alone in the midst of a multitude of foes upon Ifrona, he engaged them single-handed until they slew him. Wherefore I know that you will not be daunted by the hordes of foreign mercenaries the usurper will send against you, for you are the heirs of your fathers' valour, who rejoiced in gallant deeds. How say you, descendants of heroes? Will you join your right hands in eternal bond with mine, and increase the glory of your name and race?"

With a movement so violent that he knocked over his chair, old Glencoe was on his feet.

"Where is there one," he cried, his voice suddenly youthful, "that is like to the Grahame, since Fionn and Ossian are no more? Oh glory of your country, noblest of the Scots, never came to Lochaber since time began, a stranger more pleasing to our race. While you have the life in you, I fear not for King James, nor will I admit Albin's sceptre has fallen beneath the Dutch yoke. I bless the Great

Being who has preserved me to see this day, and though my clan is but small, there is not one able-bodied man within it but shall draw the claymore for the Grahame, the hope and guardian of the Royal Stuart."

The were all on their feet now; they were like men intoxicated, hugging each other, the young Captain of Clanranald jigging up and down in boyish glee. Then ancient Glengarry lifted his hand to silence them.

"From every region of the Grampians," said he, "we shall gather our clansmen; this very night the fiery-cross shall go forth to the uttermost parts of Gaeldom, and shame shall be upon the chief who heeds it not. My age and my infirmities forbid me to come in person to the field upon this great occasion, but my son shall bring my three hundred fighting-men to the muster; not one shall stay at home." Slowly and ceremoniously he drew his dirk and laid his lips upon it. "I pledge my faith to you, oh Grahame, upon the holy iron, and I must tell you that this is the most solemn form of oath among our people."

Watching the other chiefs follow his example, Claverhouse remembered another pledging. He heard the voices of Atholl and of Annandale, of Mackenzie and Balcarres, of powerful, wealthy lords and gentlemen, his friends, promising to ride with him to Stirling, swearing to stand firm in their allegiance to King James. And not one had kept that promise save in the form of negative and futile loyalty.

But he knew that the loyalty of the Gael could never be negative; he knew that he, a Lowlander and a stranger, had won the chiefs of the Highlands to his side. Like Montrose before him, he had found him an army among those whom the world termed barbarians; and in deep humility he prayed that he would make the same glorious use of it.

Chapter Nine

(i)

Eleven days later he marched into Strathspey at the head of an army of more than eleven hundred men, the largest force he had ever commanded.

On a lofty plateau near the south end of Loch Lochy, he had watched the clans come in to the muster. Chiefs great and small had responded to the summons of the fiery-cross, which was called also the Cross of Shame because all who refused to obey its message were considered disgraced; the clansmen were come at the word of their chiefs, knowing and caring little for what cause they were asked to fight. But instinct had told Claverhouse that no general could command irregular troops unless he made himself acquainted with every man among them, and during the days of the muster he had set out to win the devotion of the clansmen as already he had won that of the chiefs.

Refusing Lochiel's offer of a house the old man had prepared for him, he had encamped with his troops in Glenroy; nothing, he guessed, was more calculated to arouse the Highlander's admiration than an indifference to comfort. He would watch a game of shinty, showing keen interest, applauding the players, asking to be shown how to handle a stick. He would sit down at a camp-fire and listen to the proverbs and the stories, accept a pinch of snuff and watch men dancing while one of their number accompanied them with the "mouth-tune." He would tell them stories of his service in foreign parts and in Galloway; wide-eyed they listened, easily thrilled, easily amused, inquisitive as children. Lochiel was astonished at this Lowlander's success with them; ordinarily they were reserved with strangers, they distrusted all Lowlanders; but this Angus laird who could speak fluent Gaelic, and knew their genealogies and their ancient poems, was almost like one of themselves. They paid him the highest compliment of which they were capable; they gave him a nickname and addressed him by it – Iain Dubh nan Cath, Dark John of the Battles. (He smiled wryly to himself; Dark John had commanded in only one battle, the disastrous Drumclog.)

"Look you now," said Lochiel solemnly, "when my people give their hearts, they do not take them back again. We know not here the fickle friendship of the Saxon."

He was proud of his success with them, and very grateful for it, but he was too much the realist and the soldier not to be aware that an army of loving children has its disadvantages. They must never be allowed to remain idle or they would get into some mischief; they must never be asked to fight away from their native hills; they claimed the right to return to their homes after a battle, for this was not only necessary among a race of agriculturalists, but immemorial custom; and they could never be taught discipline in fight. They were terrified of cavalry; Claverhouse was half amused, half dismayed, to observe how they scattered when he exercised his veteran troop. There was a legend among them that the war-horse was trained to kick and bite, and that this was the reason why, unlike their native garrons, he was shod. Though many of them were trained to the use of the musket, they had no faith in its efficiency, looked upon it as a dishonourable weapon, and persisted in throwing it aside after firing one round.

"Understanding must be upon you, my lord," Lochiel told him, "that in their own country my people's very irregularity in fighting is their strength. Wait you till you see them charge with the claymore; wait you and then you will understand whatever."

But Claverhouse was anxious. He knew the strength of Mackay; he remembered Bothwell Bridge where only the superior discipline of the King's troops had won the day; and he knew from his scouts that Mackay was even now marching out from Inverness to meet Colonel Ramsay and his reinforcements. On the other hand, Mackay, it appeared, had not the vaguest idea of the whereabouts of his enemy, and was in a country largely hostile to him; of the clans, only some of the Grants and Forbeses had joined him, and he had no garrison anywhere in the Highlands except one which consisted of sixty men commanded by a Captain Forbes in Ruthven castle. It was on purpose to deprive him of Ruthven that Claverhouse was come into Strathspey.

But before calling upon them to undertake this task, he was going to give the clans a treat. His instinct told him that the inauguration of his campaign must be marked by some ceremony; his men must be got into the proper mood. And as luck would have it, there was an obvious occasion for such ceremony; today was May 29th, the anniversary of King Charles II's Restoration.

So here he stood on a little hillock in Strathspey, rather like a benevolent schoolmaster surrounded by boys on a half-holiday. It was broad, heathery country, comparatively level, with woods of pine and weeping birch, and the Spey racing between its boulders. The rounded summits of the Cairngorms, still snow-covered, loomed up in the west, but in Strathspey it was summer, with golden plovers piping mournfully, the aggressive blackcock fighting their eternal battles, the white cotton-grass blowing in marshy places, and the new vivid green of the bracken clothing the hill-slopes.

He watched with affectionate amusement the scene below. From early morning there had been a felling of pines and a gathering of brushwood for the great bonfire which he himself would light upon the summit of the hillock. The men sang at their work, as they sang at every task; the neighbourhood was filled with their voices and with the pipes, some playing a gathering-rant, others practising a pibroch, the pipers stalking up and down with the traditional stately step of their kind, the tartan ribbons fluttering from the drones. Clans friendly to one another were encamped side by side, with a great deal of solemn handshaking and exchanging of news; those at feud were grouped apart, glowering at one another even while they joined in the preparations for mutual rejoicing, now and again shouting token insults.

The ramifications of these feuds appalled him; they went through every degree from a refusal to fight side by side to a mere frigidity of manner. Thus Cluny had failed to bring in his Macphersons because, by rescuing the Mackintosh when the latter's life had been in danger at the Battle of Mulroy, he had offended Keppoch, the victor in that fight, and Cluny had written to Claverhouse that if he came, the whole of Clan Donald would stay at home. Grant of Glenmoriston had brought a handful of his clan, and Lochiel had had difficulty in preventing his Camerons, who had a century-old quarrel with the Grants, from driving them off again. Young Robert Stewart of Appin, a boy who had left college to bring out his clan, had a personal and brand new feud with William Fraser of Foyers, so that Stewarts and Frasers, hitherto friendly, were now growling at one another like angry dogs.

Yet Claverhouse loved them all. Four days' acquaintance with these clansmen had won his heart; he loved their simplicity and their eagerness for war, their courtesy and their pride, their self-respect and their utter lack of affectation. His experiences in the South during the past six months seemed the more hateful by comparison with the sincerity he found among these Gaels; in the company of great lords and wealthy gentlemen he had listened to false promises and meaningless compliments, had been fain to test every vow of loyalty, wondering whether it rang true, had been forced to appeal to self-interest, to greed, to vanity, finding nowhere the single-hearted forthright courage which the times required. He had found it now, among Mackay's "Highland barbarians"; and he was going to show Mackay what those barbarians could do when they followed a leader they trusted.

"To the due honour of the late King," he cried, standing bareheaded on the mound before the unlit bonfire. The pipe-music and the singing had ceased and the clans stood below him in a great circle. "To his natal day, and the day of the happy Restoration of the Monarchy; to the success of our present Sovereign, James son of Charles, and to a second Restoration, with glad lips I drink this cup. *Deoch slainte Righ*!"

He lifted the *couch* which had been handled to him with due solemnity by Lochiel, and drained the wine at a draught. Then, taking a burning brand from Young Glengarry, he put it to the huge heap of brushwood and logs; there was a crackle, a puff of smoke, here and there a bright little flame darted up, and at the same instant the pipes broke again into their wild music. With whoops of delight the clansmen responded; the strong-ale which was their favourite drink had been served out among them; they drank on their knees to King James and a second Restoration, then fell to the dancing and the games and the drinking with which they celebrated all joyful occasions.

But Claverhouse was the schoolmaster, though an indulgent one; he gave them half an hour to enjoy themselves, and then he bade his trumpeters sound, the brazen music overtopping even the pipes. Feet paused in the steps of a reel, hands held the ale-can suspended, dark eyes stared at him in wonder and reproach. Conspicuous in his uniform he stood on the hillock, with the fire blazing and crackling behind him, the great cloud of smoke ascending straight in the still air. When, save for the roar of the fire, there was silence, he lifted his hand and cried:

"We have ha our bonfire, friends, and now – to battle!"

He heard as it were an echo of that magic word go rippling through the throng. Then with a yell which made the hills resound, broadswords were snatched from their sheaths, and war-cries merged in the screaming challenge of the pipes.

(ii)

He lay tossing restlessly on a bed of skins, seeing the anxious face of Tam appearing and disappearing through the haze of fever. For days he had fought off this sickness, but it had beaten him at last; his splendid constitution had succumbed to a long, long period of too little sleep, forced marches over mountain wastes, food eaten only when he could find the time for it; his mind was sick with disappointment and with the childish evil of Macdonald of Keppoch.

His knowledge of men, which so seldom failed him, had caused him to give Keppoch the command in the reducing of Ruthven Castle; if the Highlanders in general were like children who must never be allowed to become bored, Keppoch was a boy who, lacking lawful employment, turned to crime. He had undertaken the task with great enthusiasm, making scaling-ladders and filling the ditch about the castle with faggots and brushwood; but his enthusiasm had turned to disgust when Captain Forbes had sent a message to Claverhouse offering to surrender in three days if by that time he was not relieved. Claverhouse had accepted the terms because he was convinced that relief was not coming; from his scouts he had heard that Colonel Ramsay, marching to join Mackay, had lost his nerve when he had come into the braes of Atholl and found every Murray there itching to fight for King James, had blown up his ammunition, and had scuttled back to the safety of Perth. And on receipt of this news, Mackay himself had hurried down the Spey to the shelter of Castle Grant.

At the end of the three days, Captain Forbes had been obliged to make good his own terms; he had surrendered Ruthven; and to the indescribable disgust of Keppoch had been allowed by Claverhouse to march away with his sixty men.

"Have you been taken out of yourself, my lord?" Coll had cried to his commander. "Those sons of swine will be away to Mackay, and they will let him know where we are and of what strength – "

"I gave my word to Forbes that he and his garrison should go free if they surrendered," interrupted Claverhouse shortly, adding with a dry smile: "But now that they are gone, you may fire the castle, lest Mackay should seek to garrison it again."

He had intended this as a consolation prize to Keppoch, hoping that it would satisfy Coll's lust for destruction; then, having heard from his scouts that Mackay had left Castle Grant and was encamped upon the shores of Loch Alvie, he had set out with his whole force to surprise that General – or rather he had imagined that he had all the clans with him until he had noticed the absence of the Macdonalds of Keppoch. He did not need to enquire what had happened to them; looking back, he had seen the whole sky reddened with the reflection of flames.

"It is Mackintosh country yonder, my lord," Amerlieclose had sighed. "And the great pile that is burning to the west is the Mackintosh's castle of Dunachton."

There had been no time then for dealing with Keppoch, no time for anything except hounding Mackay. For King William's Commander-in-Chief had got warning of his danger and had not waited to meet the foe; standing not upon the order of his going, he had fled, with Claverhouse hot-foot after him, chasing him through the woods of Rothiemurchus, through Abernethy to Cromdale, across the Avon at Ballindalloch, and on past Craigellachie, war-pipes screaming *The King shall enjoy his own again,* the van of the hunters pouring shot into the quarry's rear, no rest for pursued or pursuer, a chase across Scotland, with the chance of a battle always about to materialise, always refused by a Mackay who had once prophesied that he and his regulars would make short work of Highland barbarians if ever he met them in battle, who now was forced by those same barbarians to strike camp three times in one day, and who never stopped running until he came to Edinglassie on the Deveron, with wide flat country and reinforcements ahead. Claverhouse dared pursue no further; the clans would have no chance against regulars in country such as this.

He had not told them that, of course; he had not mentioned the fatal word 'retreat'. They were going back to Lochaber to await reinforcements from Ireland and to join with other clans pledged to come in to him; that was what he said. But meanwhile he had no food for them; hardy as they were, so gruelling a chase had exhausted them; and worst of all, he, the leader whose personality had been vital for the maintaining of morale, was stricken with fever. And behind them now, getting his breath and itching for revenge for that ignominious flight, was General Mackay and his reinforcements...

It was yesterday when he had felt the sickness master him, an enemy of whose presence he had been aware for some time, waiting for its chance to strike. Stabs of pain in his head, an exhausting dysentry, and a faintness which had made him reel and almost fall from his horse. He had kept up somehow and had ridden the five miles to the unfurnished castle of Auchindoune; he did not remember arriving, and all last night he had tossed and muttered in fever, plagued by a recurring dream. He was at Drumclog again, and he was being carried off the field by his maddened sorrel; it was his frst command in battle, and he had not struck a blow. His troop had gone to pieces without him, Captain Grahame's disciplined troop of horse. They were fleeing in disorder; they were being butchered; and he was helpless, carted off the battlefield by a bolting mare. He had awakened then to see faces looking anxiously at him, to feel sweat pouring off him, and some queer-tasting drink being forced between his lips.

He must have slept deeper after that, for now, lying here in the light of morning, he felt that the heat of the fever had receded, leaving in its place enormous weakness. He had never been seriously ill in his life before, and the term 'a sick man's fancies' had been meaningless; now he was discovering for himself what it meant. He was no longer delirious, but he found that the peculiar kind of weakness which follows delirium was more daunting an enemy, because it threatened his faith in himself. It showed him his own figure pacing up and down Lincolns Inn Fields in the night-time, stalking out of the Parliament House, climbing the Castle rock at Edinburgh, setting up the Standard at Dudhope, riding out with a handful of volunteers to win back a kingdom; and it was the figure of a fool. He heard his own voice making passionate speeches, appealing to mythical heroes, haranguing in a foreign tongue; and it was the voice of a romantic playing the hero.

He was filled with self-shame and self-hate, so that he winced with it, felt it poisoning his veins. Because his vanity had tempted him to imagine himself a second Montrose, he had forsaken his wife and infant son, he had thrown away everything precious and worthwhile, he had enticed friends and kinsfolk to follow his mad footsteps, he had raised the clans to their inevitable destruction. He hated himself, and he hated Amerlieclose and his pretentious Latin epic, his hero-worship and his adoring eyes; he shivered at the laughter he seemed to hear echoing up from the South, the laughter of the sane and the worldly wise, of honest Sir George Mackenzie who, like a sensible man, had done what he could for a fallen master and then had accepted the inevitable, of Balcarres and Dunmore, who were content to suffer a spell of imprisonment rather than outrage their consciences, but were not stupid enough to think that they would be doing anything noble or praiseworthy in ruining their families by flinging pebbles at a giant, who remembered that there were other loyalties besides that due to a King who had deserted his post...

"I give thanks to the Three Holy Ones," said a familiar voice, "that your lordship is somewhat recovered, for I see you are. There is health in the herbs of the mountains, and these I was giving you to drink during the night. Ach, the strength will come back to you if you will be patient."

"It is strength of spirit that I need, Lochiel," said Claverhouse, managing a smile, and taking the old man's hand. "What herbs of the mountain can give me this?"

For some moments Lochiel said nothing, looking down upon the sick man with an expression which was both solemn and tender.

"There has never lived a man so valiant," said he at last, "but sickness may overcome his heart which is stout against every human foe. But now I will tell you somewhat which may ease this sickness of the spirit. I am gifted, as you may have heard, with the 'two-sights'; when there was the first meeting between us, I told you that which has come to pass, and now I tell you that the future holds for you a great victory which will give your name to the song for evermore. I have seen the vision of it in the evening, by which I understand that it is near, yet not immediate; I have seen the fairy washerwoman washing the winding-sheets of those who will fall in this battle; and I have heard the voices of my ancestors rejoicing for the victors in this glorious fight. Wait you, wait you, my Lord Dundee," added the old man, grave and mysterious, "you are destined for greatness, you are marked out for victory in battle."

Then, as Claverhouse lay looking up at him, half comforted, half sceptical, yet feeling the old man's personality, much more than his words, drive away the fog of bitterness in his mind, Lochiel said with a complete change of tone:

"It were well that your lordship had your health again, for our people need you sorely. They are foraging far and wide, and this is dangerous when Mackay is so near, and now there is Coll na Ceapaich come in to us, and he is boasting of the booty that he has gotten him in the lands of the Mackintosh; it is very pleased with himself that he is, the rascal."

Beckoning Tam to help him, Claverhouse struggled to his feet. His will, which had seemed powerless to fight his own sick fancies, had roused instantly in response to this challenge; there was something practical to do, something unpleasant but vitally important, a battle for mastery to be fought, not with the sword, but with his wits, his knowledge of human character, and the force of his own personality.

"It is time to deal with Coll na Ceapaich," said he grimly. "I have left it over-long."

(iii)

He said nothing to Tam while his servant helped him to dress; he was hideously weak, and he must save all his strength for what he had to do. It was an effort which brought him into a sweat again to struggle into the scarlet coat (sadly stained and tattered now, for all Tam's care of it); he had to bite back his irritation when the little man nagged at him for leaving his bed. But he must have his greying hair brushed as carefully as ever, his neckcloth properly tied, his sword belted round his waist. He was going to be, not the familiar, comradely Iain Dubn nan Cath, but my Lord Dundee, King James' Commander-in-Chief (without a commission), and he was dressing for the part. He had taken many a risk in his life, had Claverhouse, but perhaps never such a risk as he was going to take this morning. It had not needed Lochiel's agitated murmurs to remind him that to offend Keppoch entailed offending the whole of Clan Donald; and Clan Donald accounted for nearly half his army.

When he was dressed, he took up in a position in the window embrasure, supporting himself against the mullion but in such a way that he appeared to be merely leaning at his ease; then he sent Tam to summon all the chiefs and officers of his army to his presence. They entered, with Keppoach at their head.

To say that Coll was pleased with himself had been an understatement. The bush of whisker which covered his face was gashed by his grinning mouth; his savage little eyes positively danced with glee; and his figure presented the most ludicrous appearance, decked out in samples of his plunder. Like some silly child he waved his hands about, displaying the rings he had forced upon his fingers; on his shaggy head there sat a helmet with a broken plume; in his belt was stuck a pair of very handsome silver pistols; and instead of his plaid he wore a steel back-and-breast and a long rich cloak of marten which, in the heat of the day, was causing him to perspire freely. As soon as he entered the room, he burst out, with just a hint of defiance in his tone:

"By the son of Luno, I have the good news for your lordship. That rascal of a Mackintosh is well punished for his refusal to join the Standard of his King; there is not a roof in all his country but is given to the flame, scarce a tacksman but now dangles from a tree, and as for that brave castle of his which he stole from my forebears, it is but a nest for the buzzard and the crow. Ach, and the bonny herds of cattle I have driven off from him; well did he think he had hidden them in his corries, but Coll na Ceapaich can find a cattle-beast as the cunning hunter finds the deer in their mountain homes. And when your lordship comes into Badenoch, into my country, your men may fill their empty bellies, for all this spoil is at your lordship's service. I will claim nothing as a reward for my labour," added Coll, magnificently generous, "save a sheltie which is of the breed of Luath the horse of Fingal and which bore me swiftly to your lordship's side."

Claverhouse looked at him for a few moments in silence; there was something about that silence which made Keppoch a little uncomfortable, and there was a look in the dark-grey eyes which caused him to lower his own.

"The horse may bear you back to your own country, Keppoch." (The tone was quite, cold, and utterly decisive.) "For you are dismissed the King's service."

There was a rustle and a muttering among the chiefs, those of Clan Donald instinctively drawing round the figure of their kinsman. Keppoch began to bluster:

"Now the burning of your heart towards you, no man living speaks in that fashion to a son of Somerled. I bid you beware, my lord."

"I do not like threats," said Claverhouse, still cold and quiet, "and I am speaking to one whose presence in the army I have the honour to command will work its ruin. I would much rather serve as a common soldier among disciplined troops than command such men as you, who seem to make it your business to draw the odium of the country upon me. I beg, therefore, that you will be gone immediately, with your men, that you may not hereafter have an opportunity of affronting me, as his Majesty's representative, at your pleasure, or of making the well disposed persons who serve under me a cover for your robberies."

"The place of the dead be yours!" shouted Keppoch. "I will go, and these my kinsmen shall come with me. All of the Clan Donald shall leave you – "

"It is a matter which the other branches of Clan Donald must decide for themselves," interrupted Claverhouse, not raising his voice. "I will say to them but this: that if they go they share in your disgrace. They shall have no part in the great battle which is coming, which one who has the two-sights has told me is near and which shall be a glorious victory. When they hear the tale of it, your children shall ask, what glorious deeds did our fathers do in this fight? And they shall be answered, your fathers were not permitted to draw their swords because disgrace was on them; they were absent from their ancient place of honour upon the right hand of the battle; the song does not record their names."

Again there was silence. He had turned, and was looking out of the window, affecting indifference while he was acutely aware of the shuffling of feet and the agitated whispering among the group of chiefs. After a pause, he said, not turning from the window:

"I am waiting, Keppoch. You heard my command."

There was an audible swallow from Coll; then a voice, soft, hesitant, ingratiating:

"Why now, let not you take the haste upon you, my lord, in sending away one who loves you, and is a sworn servant of his Majesty. Great sadness is upon me that I have offended your lordship, but by the Cross of Christ I swear that I thought only to serve you. I said to my men, my Lord Dundee is away to beat the chicken-hearted Mackay (a bad meeting to him!), and when he has sent that coward to the Isle of the Cold Land, my lord and his brave men will be after needing food. Therefore, said I, we will lift a spoil from the Mackintosh that we may feed his armies, and I must tell your lordship," concluded Keppoch earnestly, "that we took cattle-beasts and shelties only, save for a few goats, but not one sheep did we take, for that is against our law."

Claverhouse felt that threat of hysteria which comes with physical weakness, and had to bite his lip to prevent himself from laughing. Yet beneath his amusement was enormous relief; he was perfectly aware of the risk he had taken and of how near he had been to losing the whole of Clan Donald. Instead, he had gained a victory much more effective than that he had won against Keppoch at Inverness.

"I am aware," he said gravely, "that cattle-lifting is a practice justified by tradition among your people; yet the wise chiefs are striving to wean their clansmen from it, because it breeds feuds and bloody revenge, and these are ill things."

He turned and looked round the group of chiefs. Lochiel nodded his head in grave agreement, and even old Glencoe, the most notorious cattle-thief among them, made no protest.

"We are now upon an enterprise," continued Claverhouse, "which must decide the future of our King and of our country, and it is necessary that we lay-by all private quarrels, that all the people of the Highlands may join together; for our enemy is strong. The Mackintosh could have brought many men to the Standard, but now he will stay at home, or it may be even that he will join Mackay. And there is Cluny likewise; I need his Macphersons; but he will not bring them to me because the Macdonalds will not fight by their side. Yet Macdonalds and Macphersons and Mackintoshs all will suffer equally if King James does not return to us, for the usurper cares not for the welfare of Gaeldom, and he will put you all under the dominion of great feudal lords like Argyll."

He paused to let the lesson sink home.

"There is a great battle coming; a seer has foretold it, and indeed it is why I am come into the Highlands, that I may meet Mackay in pitched battle, and best him, for then shall the great men of the Lowlands, those who are loyal but lack courage, take heart and declare for their lawful King. We return to Lochaber that we may join with Irish reinforcements which are being sent to us, and that we may bring in other clans from the Isles; then shall we be strong and we shall gain that decisive victory which alone can benefit our royal master." Suddenly his gravity vanished, and looking directly at Keppoch, he smiled. "Meanwhile, you say truly, Coll na Ceapaich, that my men have empty bellies, and since you are so skilful in finding out the corries where the cattle-beasts are hidden, you shall seek them here in the Grant country where, since Grant of

Grant is a declared rebel, they are lawful prizes of war. And if you succeed in this task, I shall reward you with promotion, Keppoch; I shall make you Colonel of the Cows."

Then he too was rewarded. His understanding of the Gaelic character, so painfully learnt, had not misled him. The 'promotion' which would have insulted a Lowlander was received by this Highland chief as though it had been a knighthood.

(iv)

He had over a hundred miles to travel before he was safely back in Lochaber, and every one of them was a strain to mind and body. On that gruelling march in the other direction he had been the pursuer; now he was the pursued; only a day's march behind him came Mackay, with strong reinforcements and a temper which displayed itself by the hanging up of stragglers from the clans in search of food. And there was an enemy more formidable than Mackay; hitherto Claverhouse had walked with his men, now with one clan, now beside another, delighting them with his intimate knowledge of their history, amusing them with his jokes, inspiring them with the hope of a battle. Now he was so weak that he had to be lifted on to his horse, and the clansmen, lacking the inspiration of his personality, began to slip away to their homes. Ill news brought by his scouts added to the weight on his spirits; there was a rumour of some disaster in Ireland, and a report that Mackay had arrested some of the Dragoon officers suspected of 'disaffection', and that he had advised that they should be 'put to the question', in other words tortured, in Edinburgh.

Yet even such a nightmare journey had its lighter moments. At Cromdale a sentry mistook a flock of sheep for a surprise attack by Mackay in the night-time, and the whole encampment rushed to arms. Claverhouse, while enjoying the jest, sent for both sentry and officers, praising the first for his alertness and the second for their quick response to the alarm.

A day or two later, encamped in the Abernethy woods, he was roused from sleep by the sounds of battle in the distance; in an instant he was struggling into his armour; but when dawn broke there came in sight a band of hilarious Highlanders, mounted on English cavalry horses, bare feet ignoring the stirrups, bundles of muskets and swords tied on the saddles. It was Hector Maclean of Lochbuie who, with two hundred of his clan, had been marching to join Claverhouse, and who, on his march, had been attacked by three hundred English Dragoons. Terrified as usual of soldiers on horseback, the Macleans had made for the nearest hill; unwisely the dragoons had dismounted and had ascended to destroy this apparently craven foe. In the very act of dismounting they had dispelled the Highlanders' fear of them; their captain and six men had been killed, the rest put to ignominious flight, and Lochbuie and his two hundred had ridden off in triumph with the spoil.

Lochaber was reached on June 12th; and his scouts having reported that Mackay, after laying waste the lands of the loyal Farquharsons, had retired to Inverness, Claverhouse resigned himself to a period of rest and recuperation for his men, his horses, and himself. It was impossible to keep the clans together while there was no fighting, and when food was short in Lochaber; he temporarily disbanded them, therefore, with instructions to be ready to muster again as soon as he sent them word.

In Lochaber there were letters waiting for him. Still weak from his sickness, exhausted by the long march, and lethargic with the soft west country air which tempted him to idleness of mind and body, he read those letters which seemed to come from another world. Jean had written, filling several pages with her dear, untidy hand. She was staying with her sister and brother-in-law, the latter a staunch Williamite, and she hoped her husband would not take it amiss, but indeed it had been so difficult at Glen, with constant vists from Duke Hamilton's men, pestering her with questions, and besides the air there did not seem to agree very well with her baby; he was not thriving as he should. She enclosed a little wisp of his hair, silky-fine, dark as his father's; she was trying hard to get some money to send her husband; she missed him sorely, dreadfully, and she wanted to know when he would be coming back to her. It was the most loving and tender letter she had ever written him.

There was one from his sister Anna, enclosing a money-bill for five hundred pounds sterling. Her husband, she wrote, begged his brother-in-law to accept his trifle for his necessities; he would have written himself, but he was never a great hand with the quill. She gave him news of kinsfolk and friends, and, without actually stating it, contrived to tell him how proud they all were of him. She hoped her son Robin was well, and it was a great joy to her to know that he was with his uncle. He loved Anna all over again for that letter.

Sir George Mackenzie wrote from Oxford, all about the glories of the Bodleian. He wished he knew where his friend was at present (there were the wildest rumours, it seemed), but meanwhile he was sending this to Glen. He regretted extremely that King James had been so ill-advised as to contemplate an invasion of England by way of Ireland or Scotland, for he, Mackenzie, detested civil wars and disorders. However, he comforted himself with Virgil's reassurance in his Georgic on the Bees:

'That stir of spirits and these great conflicts must

Be still'd and silenc'd 'neath a toss of dust.'

Smiling wryly to cover his hurt, Claverhouse opened another letter which proved to be from Lord Dunmore, Atholl's younger son, a letter smuggled out from my lord's Edinburgh lodging where he was living under ward. It too contained an enclosure, but not, alas, a money-bill. It was a copy of a proclamation recently published offering one thousand pounds sterling for the capture of the person of John Grahame of Claverhouse, dead or alive. He smiled absently, put the letters into his pocket, and turned to a practical task.

In bidding a temporary farewell to the clans, he had kept Lochbuie and his two hundred Macleans with him, for despite Lochiel's assertion that the Highlanders' irregularity in fighting was their strength, he was too much the professional soldier himself not to try to instil discipline. The fact that the Macleans had run away from the dragoons before the latter dismounted gave him the excuse he wanted to try to cure them of their fear of cavalry. So every day he began his task of training the Macleans by mock charges of his little troop of horse in the carse land by the river, patient but inexorable, so that men like Jock Johnson remembered the days when they were raw recruits in Galloway, and had succumbed to the charm and patience of a young captain of horse. Claverhouse had need of both these qualities at present, for no sooner had he begun to persuade the Macleans to meet the charges without running away, than he had to prevent a mock fight from becoming a real one.

For if there were hereditary feuds between clan and clan, there was a most ancient and ineradicable feud between Lowlanders and Highlanders. Each had consented to fight side by side under my Lord Dundee; to ask them to pretend to fight each other was, he found, asking for trouble. The Macleans taunted the Lowland troopers with the tame submission of their race to Roman, Saxon, and Dane; the troopers retorted by jeering at savages who lived by stealing cattle and wore petticoats. Both sides lost their tempers, and but for the presence of their commander undoubtedly would have shed blood. He called the officers of his troop of horse to him that evening, and gave them a lecture which left them somewhat chastened if unrepentant.

"I was but fleaching them about the lugs for idle fellows, sir," protested Jock Johnson, one of the worst offenders. "Och, ye'll never make sodgers o' sic hobbleshaws. Awa' to their hames, the rest o' them, just because there is no a battle the noo. I'd be black-shamed," added Jock righteously, "to hae so much as dreamed of visiting Aberdeen when we passed it on our march north, and me on active service."

The activity of the day was equalled by that of the night when there arrived at long last his commission as Commander-in-Chief. (Another had been sent by King James long ago, it seemed, but must have been intercepted.) Now that he had official standing, he could make at least a show of commanding where before he had been obliged to coax, and night after night he poured his energy and enthusiasm into letters, sitting up into the small hours, his head nodding now and again with weariness, then jerking upright, the dark eyes closing for a few seconds, and then the scratching of the quill again. He was burning himself out, but he neither knew nor cared; he was the one solitary beacon-fire of loyalty, and while he could light others, he must blaze.

On July 18th there arrived in Lochaber the long-awaited Irish reinforcements: seventy-five officers, three hundred newly raised half-naked, and totally undisciplined soldiers, and thirty-five barrels of powder. Ships loaded with biscuit, meal, and beef had been captured on the voyage. This was due, he realised at once, to the futility of the officer in command, a Colonel Cannon, a tubby little man with a perpetual smile which disclosed a few rotting stumps of teeth. Claverhouse summed him up in the first five minutes: worthy, utterly honest, and utterly uninspiring, and so thankful to leave all the responsibility in other hands that he ended almost every sentence with the phrase, "it is for your lordship to decide."

Immediately there was further trouble. Neither Highlanders nor Lowlanders liked the Irish as a race, and it was vain to remind them of how gallantly they had behaved under Montrose.

"The Irishers and these Hielandmen speak the same heathen tongue, sir, and yet they canna understand ane word the ither says," Jock Johnson told him in high glee.

His chaplain, Mr Edwards, who had borne most patiently with the queer mixture of Christianity and nature-worship which he had encountered among the clans, was profoundly shocked by the brazen Papistry of the Irish. They were praying to the Virgin Mary, he said; he had heard them; and they would not come to his sermons. Yes, he knew that some of the clans were Papist, but if his lordship could understand what he meant, it was not such a virulent kind of Popery. Claverhouse comforted him as well as he could, preoccupied as he was himself with the bitter disappointment of the look and number of his reinforcements. His old anger threatened to fire as he realised that Melfort had utterly misled him as to the help he might expect from Ireland; but the iron self-discipline of the last few months enabled him, with scarcely an effort, to forbear a sharp letter of protest. Instead he turned to the task of turning yet more raw recruits into good soldiers.

He would need every man of them soon, for a crisis was coming. Edinburgh Castle had surrendered, thus setting free Sir John Lanier and his blockading force; Mackay was in Edinburgh, collecting yet more reinforcements before marching north again to deal with the solitary menace to his master's power in Scotland. The battle foretold by Lochiel was imminent, and upon its issue everything depended.

On July 22nd, Claverhouse sent messengers with the fiery-cross to summon the clans to meet him at Blair Castle on the 29th; he wrote to Cluny, who at last had consented to bring out his Macphersons, to meet him at Garva-on-Spey with all the arms and provisions he could get; and he wrote one last long letter of appeal to Lord Murray, Atholl's heir, who consistently had refused to answer his others, reminding his lordship of the fact that his clansmen were manifestly on the side of their lawful Sovereign, informing him frankly that by virtue of his commission he had ordered his lordship's factor, old Patrick Steuart of Ballechin, to hold Blair Castle in the name of King James, since there was a rumour that Mackay intended to garrison it ('a thing I am sure your lordship would deplore'), and ending, his pen crawling with fatigue along the paper:

'As I write to your lordship, so I have done all others I can reach with letters. I am sure whatever evil befalls the country, the King is innocent, and I have done my duty.'

Tam, fussing in for the twentieth time that night to implore Master John to go to bed, was dismayed to see the dark head lying on the table, the arms hanging limp, and the slight figure slouched motionless in the chair. For one dreadful moment Tam thought that his master was dead, but then as he stared, dry-mouthed and stricken, he saw the head on which the grey hairs had multiplied so rapidly of late, shift a little on the hard board. As Tam went to rouse him, he looked from habit at a letter lying open on the table. It was not a particularly interesting letter to Tam, and ten minutes later he could not have told anyone what it was about. Yet long afterwards he was to discover that one sentence from it had fixed itself into the recesses of his memory, a very simple sentence:

'I have done my duty'.

Chapter Ten

(i)

Looking out through a window in Blair Castle at Schiehallion, raising its prodigious white shoulders to the south-west, Claverhouse wondered dryly what Atholl would have said could he have known, when he had ruined the chance of resisting the usurper without bloodshed by holding a Convention at Stirling, that the friend he had deserted was going to make one of my lord's castles his headquarters, welcomed to it by my lord's own factor, in defiance of my lord's own heir.

Claverhouse had arrived at Blair yesterday, Friday, July 26th, ready for the general rendezvous of the clans on Monday. At Grava-on-Spey he had received a meagre supply of provisions and arms from Cluny, a promise by that chief to bring his Macphersons to the muster, and definite news of Mackay. This news had been brought by young Gilbert Ramsay, an advocate who had just thrown up a promising career at the Bar to fight for King James, and who had been sent by Claverhouse with his last appeal to Lord Murray. The latter, reported Ramsay, had refused even to see him, let alone read Claverhouse's letter; he had been about to besiege his own castle of Blair, held against him by Ballechin, the factor, when instructions from Mackay had reached him, ordering him to join the General with all the men at his command. Mackay, it seemed, had reached Stirling on the 24th, and was marching slowly northwards; he had with him three regiments of infantry, Balfour's, Ramsay's, and Kenmure's, his own Scots Brigade, Leven's west country volunteer Foot, Hasting's Regiment of Horse, Belhaven's Troop of Horse, twelve hundred baggage-beasts, and some small pieces of artillery for the bombarding of Blair, little leather guns called 'Sandy-stoups' after their inventor, two of which could be carried on a horse. The greater part of his army, which amounted to nearly five thousand men, were seasoned troops.

"All this I learned from the Murrays," Gilbert Ramsay had added, "who were dipping their bonnets in a burn and drinking a health to King James, under the very nose of their lord's heir. And the jest of it is that Mackay seems to have no idea what he will do with so formidable a force as he has brought from Edinburgh, for the Murrays told me he believes that your lordship is skulking somewhere in the hills, having but two hundred men with you, and they in great want of all things."

"We must teach him better," Claverhouse had replied, refraining from adding that Mackay's information was correct in one particular: the clans were in great want of food. He had marched on from Garva, over the Pass of Druimuchdar, and down the road he had ridden on his brilliant raid on Perth. On his arrival at Blair, he had caused Mr Edwards to hold a simple religious service in the haughs around the Castle, Lowlanders, Highlanders, Irish, chiefs and clansmen, gentlemen and common soldiers, kneeling in the heather with himself at their head, while the mountains faded gently into that twilight which is a Highland night in summer, and the burble of a stream making a soft accompaniment to the prayers. Afterwards, to Tam's unutterable astonishment, Master John had gone to bed at a Christian hour, He could not have said why, but somehow he had a feeling that on this particular night he needed sleep and had earned it, that he had done everything that could be done, and that the future was out of his hands.

"Ye'll be awa' to your bed the noo, Master John," Tam had said to him ritualistically.

And Tam, had stood open-mouthed at the unexpected reply:

"Yes Tam, I'll be away to my bed."

This morning, watching the chiefs and officers filing in to his apartment for a council of war which he knew must be a very fateful one, he still had that queer impression that the issue of all his efforts already was decided. He was visited again by that fey mood which had fallen upon him when, forsaken by his friends, he had ridden out from Edinburgh, and had cried to Gordon that he was going wherever the spirit of Montrose should direct him. Yet no man present around the council table this morning guessed that he was anything but the realistic, practical Lord Dundee, as he began abruptly:

"The question we have to consider is this: Shall we remain here and wait for the clan muster on Monday, or shall we, this very day, with the little army we have at our command, attempt to force Mackay to a battle when he does not know of our presence in the neighbourhood, and when we may be able to choose our ground? From the reports of our scouts it seems certain that Mackay is advancing by way of Dunkeld and the Pass of Killie-crankie, with intent to take this castle and to garrison it. I beg that each of you, gentlemen, will let me have his opinion freely."

James Seton, Lord Dunfermline, jumped instantly to his feet. He was the most important of the volunteers, for he was the Duke of Gordon's brother-in-law; he had joined Claverhouse on the latter's tour of Aberdeenshire, had shared all the hardships and privations of his leader, and was the chosen spokesman of the gentlemen volunteers on every important occasion.

"My lord," he cried, "my opinion is that nothing but over-whelming numbers can make it possible for us to beat Mackay. If we wait until Monday we shall have those numbers; as it is, we have less than two thousand against Mackay's five."

The other Lowlanders emphatically agreed. What possible advantage, they demanded, could there be in risking a pitched battle at such odds, when their purpose in coming to Blair was, first to gain possession of that strategic fortress, and secondly to await their reinforcements? Why should they change their whole plans just because Mackay happened to be in the neighbourhood and was unaware of their presence?

"It is next to madness," concluded Dunfermline emphatically, "to imagine that a few half-starved Highlanders could be the superiors of numerous, seasoned, and well-fed troops commanded by a veteran."

There was a pause. The argument seemed unanswerable, but, sensitive to atmosphere, Claverhouse knew that this was not what caused the silence. The chiefs were offended by the slightly contemptuous way in which the officers had referred to their clansmen; there was a mutter or two in the Gaelic; and then Young Glengarry, his glance travelling slowly and challengingly along the row of faces opposite him, said with a haughty air:

"You have been pleased to say, sirs, that our clansmen are half-starved and wearied with forced marches. But by your leave, I will ask you this: what do lack of food and hard marching mean to our people, who never have lived soft like the Saxons and the men of the Lowlands, and who come of a race of warriors? It is my wound to think what may happen if we do not fight, for then it may be that him of Scourie will be up with us before the rest of the clans come in on Monday, and then we shall be losing the advantage of attack."

"He will be coming through the Pass of Killiecrankie," chimed in old Glencoe, "and Creator! What better place could there be for an ambush of him? We will pounce upon him as he marches along that narrow defile; we will throw him into confusion and have him altogether at our mercy, he and his men weighed down with so much armour and equipment."

"It might throw him into confusion," observed David Grahame, glancing at his silent brother, "but it would not achieve the decisive victory which is what is required to bring over to us the great men of the Lowlands."

"Right you are there, sir," cried young Stewart of Appin. "We must have the fair combat of Fingal's heroes; we must meet out foes face to face."

One of the officers made an indignant retort, and for a while the argument raged backwards and forwards, everyone speaking at once and growing more and more heated. Claverhouse, meanwhile, sat silent at the head of the table, his glance fixed upon Lochiel, who alone among the chiefs was taking no part in the fierce debate, but sat fingering his long moustachios, his look preoccupied. At last Haliburton of Pictur, a jovial giant of a man who had joined Claverhouse after the raid on Perth, sprang to his feet and cried in tones which overtopped the buzz of voices:

"We may debate it till doomsday and come to no decision. Sirs, there is one here on whose word all else rests. My Lord Dundee, we await that word from you."

As the noise died down and all looked at him expectantly, Claverhouse said, his glance still fixed upon the Chief of the Camerons:

"I have observed that all this while Lochiel has kept silent, but whatever he chooses to say shall decide the matter. For not only has he done great martial deeds himself, but more than any of us here present he has had experience of battle against regular troops, and therefore his judgement shall determine mine."

It was a compliment which ordinarily would have made the old man's face flush with pleasure; but though, in true Gaelic fashion, he deprecated such high praise, and said that his lordship was too good, and that he did not require any man to advise him, beneath this show of modesty there was no gratification. Lochiel's eyes remained preoccupied, and his voice was strangely solemn as he added:

"Yet since, my lord, I am commanded by your lordship to give my opinion on this matter, I will give it in one word: fight."

There was not a man present but noticed how Claverhouse's dark eyes brightened at that word.

"Our men are few," continued the old Chief, "but not one will fail your lordship. If we delay, they will discover that we deem them unequal to battle, and that will take the heart out of their breasts. As long as they are the attackers, hunger and weariness will mean little to them; so it has always been. Employ them in hasty and desperate enterprises, and I have found that with the greatest disadvantages in numbers they have won their most famous victories. Was not Montrose outnumbered by three to one at Tippermuir? Let us attack Mackay when he is not expecting it, and where there is hill country for our irresistible charge; here in the haughs about Blair our men, however numerous, would lose the advantage."

There was a rumble of assent from his fellow chiefs, while the Lowlanders, though by their looks it was clear that they remained unconvinced, refrained from further argument; it was plain to them all that Lochiel had expressed the desire of their common commander.

"My Lord Dunfermline," added Lochiel softly, after a pause, "I believe it is your care for my people which makes you dislike to hazard them in so unequal a battle at this time, yet by your leave I must remind you of the slogan of your noble House. Will a Seton deny to 'Set on'?"

"No, by God!" cried Dunfermline, won over by the friendly challenge. "And the war-cry of your race, Lochiel, shall echo mine. When the Seton has set on, let the sons of the hounds come and get flesh! I am content to be o'erthrown in debate be the gallant Cameron; together we will overthrow the base Mackay."

His enthusiasm turned the scale. Even the most cautious of the officers became infected with it; and as the decision to fight ran like wildfire from the sentry outside the door to the guards standing on the stairs, and from them to the clansmen encamped about the Castle, wild shouts of acclamation came echoing into the council chamber, the bellow of war-cries, and the rising scream of the pipes. But as the chiefs and officers prepared to leave the apartment, Lochiel stayed them. His expression was solemn again, and his bright dark eyes held a hint of something resembling dread.

"My Lord Dundee, I have just now declared in the presence of this honourable company that I am resolved to give implicit obedience to all your lordship's commands, but I humbly beg leave, in the name of these gentlemen, to give the word of command for this one time. It is voice of your Council, and their orders are that you do not engage in person in this battle. Your lordship's business is to have an eye on all parts, and to issue your orders as you think proper. It is ours to execute them with promptitude and courage. On your lordship depends the fate not only of this little brave army, but likewise of our King and our land. If your lordship denies this reasonable demand, for my own part I declare that neither I, nor any man I am concerned in, shall draw a sword on this important occasion, whatever construction shall be put upon the matter."

While the old man had been speaking, Claverhouse had stood motionless at the head of the table, his eyes downcast. Lochiel had spoken in English, so that the Lowlanders present might understand every word he said; the deep solemnity of his tone, and the nobility of his look, robbed his words of any hint of arrogance, and the appeal in his eyes was desperate. The others, both chiefs and officers, seeming to catch something of his anxiety, murmured unanimous agreement; then all stood waiting anxiously for Claverhouse's reply. He said, very quietly, picking his words:

"Gentlemen, as I am absolutely convinced, and have had repeated proofs of your zeal for the King's service, and of your affection for me as his General and your friend, so I am fully sensible that my engaging personally this day may be of some loss if I shall chance to be killed."

As he paused for a moment, it was as if the fatal word cast a coldness in the room, so that one man actually shivered.

"But I beg leave of you," he continued, his voice rising on a note of passion, "to allow me to give one *shear-darg*, one harvest-day's work to the King, my master, that I may have an opportunity of convincing the brave clans that I can hazard my life in that service as freely as the humblest of them. You know their temper, gentlemen, and if they do not think I have personal courage enough they will not esteem me hereafter nor obey my commands with cheerfulness." He looked from face to face, and seeing upon each the same denial, he flung out his hands in sudden emotion. "I am a soldier; you cannot deny me the use of my sword. I have worked so hard for this moment; I have schooled myself to patience all these bitter months, I have made do with the pen when my fingers itched for the sword; the hope of fighting for my master has been the goal which has sustained me. Allow me this single favour, and here I promise, upon my honour, never again to risk my person while I have the honour of commanding you."

He knew, as he watched them, that he had won. He was deeply moved by the reluctance of their submission to his appeal; never until now had he realised how much they loved him. In a low, resigned voice Lochiel, still their spokesman, begged that at least his lordship would consent to lay-by for this occasion his scarlet uniform and wear instead a buff-coat under his corselet, that he might be the less conspicuous to the foe. He made the concession readily enough; though when, a few minutes later, Tam was helping him into his armour, he could not help glancing wistfully at the uniform laid over a chair, the old beloved uniform he had worn since he was a captain of horse.

"I have not fought a pitched battle, Tam," said he, "since Bothwell Bridge. I'd have liked to have worn the King's coat today. For I am going to win this fight," he added, low and exultant. "The very air is charged with victory."

(ii)

By the time General Mackay reached the entrance to the Pass of Killiecrankie (about noon that same day), he had recovered from the temper into which he had flown on meeting Lord Murray yesterday at Pitlochry. There had been ample excuse for his wrath. Here was one of the few Highland magnates who had declared for King William, actually allowing his own factor to shut him out of his own castle.

"If Dundee," Mackay had raged, "has seized Blair through your lordship's gross negligence, I shall burn it to the ground when I have taken it, and I shall hang your factor over the wall. As for these eighty Murrays of yours whom you have left, you tell me, to guard the northern end of the Pass, I trust not one of them; on your own confession, the most of your tribe have presumed to drink the late King James' health and now have returned to their homes. For the eighty, your lordship may do with them as you will, but I am sending two hundred fusiliers to keep us informed whether it is safe for us to venture through this horrid Pass."

And now, having received word from his reconnaissance party that no enemy was in the neighbourhood, he gave the order to march; he was complacent again, secure in the knowledge that he had veterans under him, comforted by the slow, orderly, somewhat cumberous progress of Horse and Foot, by the sight of the long, smooth-bored flintlocks of the fusiliers, by the little leather cannon, by the new cartridge-cases of the Foot who still used the old matchlock musket with bayonets to screw into the muzzle after a discharge, by the whole paraphernalia of a professional army. The solemn beating of the drums was music in his ears; the brisk words of command, the feet marching in step, the dull ring of hooves, the sunlight glinting on well-polished corselets and firearms, the look of his men, disciplined, well-fed, all these cheered his soldier's heart as the long train began disappearing, file by file, into the Pass of Killiecrankie. Though he still hated his native land as heartily as ever, Perthshire was at least tolerable, especially now in the summertime; there were drove-roads and level ground, and the horrible grim mountains which daunted him stood away in the background and could be ignored.

But as soon as he himself entered the Pass, riding at the head of his Scots Brigade, he was conscious of a faint yet growing discomfort of mind. He seemed to have stepped immediately into just the sort of country he feared. The Garry, swollen by rain, roared down beside the track in a succession of cataracts, so that the shouted orders and the drum-beats and the booted footsteps were drowned, and the track itself, so narrow that not more than three men could march abreast, was uncomfortably near the gorge of the river on the one side, the mountain wall upon the other. A while ago he had been wishing he could meet the elusive Claverhouse, skulking he knew not where at present, and punish that outlaw for the ignominious chase across Scotland last month. Now it occurred to him that this was just the place such an outlaw, with his band of barbarians, might choose for an ambush.

Towering crags, clothed with pine and birch, rose up, enclosing him; in places the ground was covered in bracken, waist-high, in others strewn with huge boulders; it was the kind of ground which could conceal any number of sharp-shooters. His men, thrown into confusion, would be precipitated into that hideously turbulent river before they had a chance to fight. When the wind blew the leaf-laden boughs, he felt his hand go instinctively to his carbine; the throbbing of the drums, so comforting just now, sounded eerie and ominous, a deep under-current to the roar of the river; the sunlight had disappeared, shut out by the enclosing hills; he observed how officers and men glanced uneasily from side to side, and that even the horses seemed nervous, tossing their heads and curvetting dangerously upon the narrow track.

But Mackay was not easily moved by fancies. His scouts had reported no sign of Claverhouse; he had it on excellent authority that the clans had been disbanded; he and his army had but a few miles to march before they reached Blair, which could be captured in half an hour, and then there would be the congenial task of turning it into a garrison. (He had not the slightest intention of burning it down, of course, as he had threatened Lord Murray; his object in coming north, apart from dealing with

Claverhouse, was to plant garrisons throughout the Highlands.) So he shouted to his officers to pass the word along that there was nothing to fear ('nothing to fear!' mockingly echoed the hills); he even attempted a little jest about wondering where my Lord Dundee and his few ragged savages could be hiding just now; but he was never very successful as a humorist, and moreover the fact that he himself had not the least idea of the whereabouts of Claverhouse continued to be less amusing than uncomfortable. Deliberately ignoring the temptation to glare at every thicket of alders lest it conceal an ambush, he plodded on with courage.

Nevertheless, it was an enormous relief when at last the long procession began to emerge into the sunlight again, and to his annoyance Mackay found that he was sweating. He blamed it on the warmth of the day, said a prayer of thanksgiving to his God, and pricking his horse with the spur rode forward to a little eminence whence he could form up his men as they came, company by company, and troop by troop, out of Killiecrankie's dangerous defile. In the relief of the moment he was almost prepared to admire the countryside, the wide plain of Rinn Ruarigh, with the slopes of Ben-y-Gloe all empurpled with the heather, and the haughs beside the Garry green with unripened corn. But he could never really admire his native country, and therefore showed his appreciation of his escape from a possible ambush in a manner more practical. He gave permission to his men to rest in the cornfields before marching the three miles which now separated them from Blair. Meanwhile, like the conscientious commander that he was, he galloped forward, a heavy man upon a heavy charger, to inspect the advance-guard and the road.

He had not yet come up with the fusiliers who formed this advance-guard, when he met their officer coming back at the gallop.

"Dundee" panted the officer, drawing his horse upon its haunches, and pointing wildly backwards. "He is – coming – along the road. He is – making for the ridge yonder – whence he may – threaten us with flanking fire!"

Mackay, admirably concealing his dismay at this news, and his fury with his scouts, acted briskly. He sent a vidette galloping back with orders that his men be got into their ranks again; then he wheeled his whole line upon Hasting's Regiment, which formed the rear-guard, as upon a pivot, and marched straight up the ridge in question in order to gain it first. His voice rang out confidently as he enunciated the technical term: "A *quart de conversion* to the right!"; his plump face was smiling as, squinting through his perspective-glass, he saw the enemy which had so frightened the fusilier officers, not more than sixty Highlanders. Really it was pitiful! They could have done him some mischief if he had allowed them to reach the brae, because they could have poured shot upon him from above; but he was not going to allow them to reach the brae; he was going to get there first, and then he was going to eat them up.

He got there first. But he had time only to observe that the summit of the brae was incapable of accommodating more than a three-deep line, before he received the shock of his life.

In the manner of Highland country (of which he was so deeply and deliberately ignorant) there was, beyond this little hill, another, higher than the first, but concealed from his while he had been ascending. And upon this further eminence there was drawn up in battle-array what appeared to his aghast eyes to be the entire clans of the Highlands.

(iii)

"Creator!" bawled Glengarry, flinging his bonnet into the air and catching it again. "The rascal has done just what your lordship intended him to do. Well, look at that now!"

Claverhouse smiled, but said nothing. He too was looking through a perspective-glass, and he too was the professional soldier, quiet, businesslike, watchful, counting the odds against him, viewing (not without dry humour) Mackay's frantic manoeuvres down there.

They had been trained in the same military school, and he knew precisely the difficulties he had forced upon Mackay. And he knew the man himself, worthy, stolid, unimaginative, unadaptable, above all betrayed by his own ignorance of his native land and its language. The 'barbarians' he despised had retaliated by giving him false information of his enemy's strength and whereabouts; the very land itself was hostile to him, surprising him with its peculiar formation. And he had made the fatal mistake of underrating his enemy; he had been tricked into taking up an impossible position because he had believed the sixty Camerons whom Claverhouse had sent as a decoy to be the latter's whole force. He could not attack upon the one hand, for he could not charge up-hill; and if he attempted to retire upon the other, he would be driven into the Garry. But to give him his due, he was making the best of it; fearful of having his flanks turned by so mobile an enemy, he was drawing out his men into a long thin line, breaking his infantry into half-battalions, bringing the three rearmost ranks of each into the extended line, leaving a gap between each half-battalion and a much larger one in the centre. Behind this centre gap he was setting up his little cannon. His regiments stood in the order in which they had emerged from the Pass; first Lauder's Fusiliers, the Balfour's and Ramsay's Regiments, Kenmure's Foot, Mackay's own Scots Brigade, and, on the extreme right, Hasting's Horse. It was a formidable army, not a doubt of that, near enough five thousand men to the clans' less than two, disciplined, excellently armed.

Claverhouse thrust his glass into his pocket, and galloping along the front of his army, issued brisk orders, now in English, now in the Gaelic. He did not need to explain the necessity to extend his own line lest Mackay, with his vastly superior numbers, wrapped himself about the flanks of the clans. He did not need to explain anything; as with the little troop of horse which had followed him in Galloway and had stuck by him ever since, so with the chiefs, the volunteers, the clansmen, the Irish, his bare word was enough. He was acting, as he had done ever since had defied the Convention, entirely on his own responsibility, inexperienced as he was in battle; and all his professional skill, all his initiative, were being brought into play. The issue of the fight depended on his men; it was for him to ensure that they fought at the best possible advantage.

Because his enemy's line was so much longer than his own, he was obliged to leave huge gaps between the clans; he knew it was dangerous, but he could not help it, because on no account must he be overlapped on the flanks. Because of the Highlanders' terror of cannon, even such trifling cannon, he must place his tiny body of horse in the direct line of the gun-fire, there in the large space in the centre of his line. And there was something else he must do, the most important task of all: he must prevent the eager clans from charging until he gave the word.

As he galloped up and down, he saw signs of impatience among them. They were unfastening their plaids, preparatory to casting them aside as was their habit in battle; their naked broadswords were gripped in their hands, and many a horny thumb tried the edges which had been sharpened during the night. Bare feet shifted restlessly, itching to be off in a wild charge; targes, nail-studded, and with a wicked steel spike in the centre, were clasped before naked breasts; eyes, fierce as a hawk's, were fastened greedily on that mass of uniformed men down there. Their bards were inspiring them by rehearsing aloud the heroic deeds of their ancestors, and promising them the 'fame of the song'; the pipers were stalking up and down, firing the blood with their pibrochs; voices vied with one another in shouting out clan slogans.

"Patience, my friends, patience!" he cried at them. "We must wait till the sun goes down. We cannot attack while it shines in our faces."

"Ach, it is two hours till sunset, my lord," exclaimed Glengarry, as the galloping figure went past. "You'll never hold them whatever."

But he was resolved to do so. Backwards and forwards he galloped along the line, his voice now commanding, now appealing; the slight figure in buff-coat and corselet, with the greying locks and the eyes looking enormous in a face thinned by privation and mental stress, seemed to be every where, the personality vivid as a flame. The Macdonalds were the most impatient of any; Keppoch was not with them, for his was among the clans pledged to come in to the muster on Monday, but his kinsfolk had not forgotten Claverhouse's challenge to them all at Auchindoune, and they were on fire to be the first into the fight. He had given them their ancient place of honour on the right wing, and there, sitting his horse at the head of them, he made an impromptu speech.

"You are come hither this day to fight, and that in the best of causes. There is no proportion betwixt loyalty and treason, nor should there be any betwixt good subjects and traitors. Think upon the wrongs of your King and country!

The fate of each depends on you. Let us, by this action, redeem the credit of our nation, laid low by treachery. Think upon your noble forebears, who gave their blood in this same cause! Think upon those who, upon the hill of Lude yonder, stood with Montrose when he raised the Standard of King Charles! I ask of you nothing but what he asked; if you seek in vain for me when the fight is over, search where the dead lie thickest, for I will conquer this day or I will die! The master of your foe is he who thought to bribe Highland gentlemen into betraying their lawful Sovereign. Give him your answer; give it with the bright steel in your hands!"

"In the name of the Trinity, let us fall on!" yelled old Glencoe, tears of rage streaming down his withered cheeks.

"Not yet! Not yet!" shouted Claverhouse, wrestling with the fierce spirit he was at the same time deliberately provoking. "Wait for the word, brave sons of Somerled. Your foe is as nervous as you are restless; his spirit sinks with the delay, while yours increases. Was it not here that Lochiel slew the last wolf in Scotland? – here, upon this very spot. Yonder ravens a beast more cruel than any wolf; wait one hour more and we have him by the throat!"

Something other than Gaelic voices answered him then. There was a loud report, a puff of smoke, and a ball from one of Mackay's little cannon, pitched too low, tore up the turf and heather on the slope beneath. Claverhouse noticed instantly the look of alarm upon the clansmen's faces. If they were afraid of cavalry, they were utterly unnerved by these infernal machines to which they had no reply. His own answer was to laugh, loudly and joyously.

"They waste powder and ball," he cried. "They'll never get their aim from down there. And wait you till we capture these 'Sandy-stoups'; what fine brogues they'll make us! Come, let them hear the guns of the Highlands, more terrible than their pitiful cannon. Your slogans, clansmen! Those are your guns."

Instantly the booming of the artillery was drowned in a thunder of voices from the tartan host, one deafening, sustained roar of defiance; it was answered by the scarlet-clad ranks of the enemy, their voices echoing feebly from crag to crag.

"They are doomed!" Lochiel's voice shouted. "That dying fall was ominous of death."

As he uttered the last word, the sun dropped suddenly behind the hills, leaving behind it a dull red glow like a fire. Claverhouse, who had been watching it, willing it to sink, turned again to his army, and so sat for an instant, his hat in his hand, the sunset light behind him.

"The sun has left the hill," he cried. "Now let every clan fall upon its opposing regiment, and in the name of God and King James, gentlemen, charge!"

Then he was off and away, galloping breakneck down the hill in front of them all. The last glimpse they had of him before the gun-smoke hid him from their sight, was his figure half-turned in saddle, and his arm waving them on.

(iv)

In the very moment of the charge, Jock Johnson's horse broke a girth; the saddle slipped sideways, and Jock found himself lying on the ground, in danger of being trampled to death by his comrades who, in close-order, were trotting behind the unfurled Standard. Among them, riderless, trotted Jock's mount.

He was a heavy man now, and for a few seconds he was dazed by the fall; he stood there, cursing feebly, his mind blank with a feeling of helplessness. He was a horse-soldier, and he had no horse, and General Grahame needed every man of his little troop today; they were the only real soldiers in his army. And then as he stood there, alone, and not yet recovering his wits sufficiently as to act, he saw a sight he was never to forget; he saw the charge of the clansmen.

Jock had never ceased to regard the Highlanders as savages, undisciplined, heathen barbarians. It had astonished and dismayed him that General Grahame actually should contemplate giving battle to Mackay when he himself had only such pitiful material at his command. Jock had watched the clansmen during the past few hours, fidgeting to be off and away in no sort of formation, throwing off their plaids that they might fight half-naked, even their chiefs going barefoot into battle; he had listened in disgust to them bellowing in their outlandish language, to the horrible scream of the pipes and the silly speechifying of the bards. It was a farce of an army, and Mackay's regulars would wipe it out in half an hour; he had sweated blood when he had thought of General Grahame having to rely upon such men; but it was not a farce of an army which was charging now.

The clansmen were loping down the hill, slowly at first, in silence, a rolling blue-green wave of tartan, subjected all the way to murderous volleys from the enemy below them, but not one man replying by a shot. His smugness pricked, Jock realised that by some miracle these barbarians were maintaining a discipline akin to that which had kept Captain Grahame's troop of horse sitting motionless in saddle at Drumclog; he had heard the order given to the clans today that they were not to fire until they were at point-blank range, and they were obeying. Disregarding the dead and wounded who dropped among them, they swept on in silence, the pace quickening; then their muskets spoke once; clan-slogans merged into one indistinguishable roar of voices; and the blue-green wave hurled itself upon the scarlet line, extinguishing it as water puts out a fire. Jock had one bizarre vision of a broadsword cutting through three bodies at one stroke, before he came to his senses and began to run, impeded by his boots, yelling he knew not what, into the gun-smoke and the struggling, cursing heart of the fight.

As he found a riderless horse and leapt on to it, he was already aware of victory; it could not have been more than ten minutes since the charge of the clans, yet that great army of regulars was beaten. Everywhere he looked he saw fleeing figures; one whole regiment was fighting to escape by the Pass, which was already blocked by baggage-horses, another was in full flight along the road to Blair; the swollen Garry was choked with dead and wounded; the trumpets were frantically playing the *Retreat*. But Jock had lost interest in the battle; his mind was full of the man who had created this victorious little army out of nothing, who had instilled discipline into savages, who had achieved the impossible, and who had last been seen riding into the gun-smoke, cheering on his men.

Johnson broke into a cold sweat of relief as, galloping out of the fog around the now abandoned cannon, he saw the figure of his commander ahead of him, his sword out, his hair streaming behind him like a banner; a spurt of musket-fire picked out for an instant the laurel leaves he had stuck into his hat. He seemed to have got separated from his troop again; to the horror of Johnson, he was dashing straight upon a body of the enemy Horse which had been left standing as grass is left between the teeth of a rake. But it too was retiring, or trying to retire; firing raggedly, it was pressing back upon the foot-soldiers, carrying them with it in the wildest confusion. A trumpet sounded near at hand, sharp and brazen with victory; exultant to have found his comrades at last, Johnson yelled to his commander:

"We are here with you, sir! Are we to pursue?"

There was no answer. The distance between himself and that lone figure was lessening; perhaps General Grahame was waiting for his troop to come up with him, for it seemed to Johnson that his pace slackened. Or perhaps his horse is wounded, thought Jock, remembering that other horse, the sorrel which had bolted from the field of Drumclog; it was a horse which nearly prevented me from taking part in the Battle of Killiecrankie, he thought, feeling light-headed with relief and with enormous pride.

"Here's a fresh mount, sir," cried Jock, overtaking his commander at last and at the same instant leaping from the saddle and making a grab at the other's bridle. "I'll make shift to chase the blasties on my ain twa feet."

He lifted his smoke-blackened face to grin at his hero; he heard the thunder of hoof-beats galloping past in pursuit of the fleeing Mackay. Then, without a word or groan, General Grahame fell limply from his saddle and into Jack Johnson's arms.

(v)

For awhile he did not seem able to make Jock hear what he was asking so frantically. There was a great confusion in his senses, and perhaps in his efforts to fight off faintness he was not able to speak loud enough. He was conscious of pain when he moved; it was centred, he thought, in his left side just below the breastplate, but it sent tentacles all over his body, seeming to feel its way along nerve after nerve. It did not matter; nothing mattered except –

"Jock – Jock – can you not hear me?"

"Ay, sir, but you maun bide quiet."

"Jock" – he was desperate with impatience – "tell me, man, how goes the day?"

"Well for the King," came a choked voice, "but I am sorry for your lordship."

The old realism and the old humour stirred in him. 'I am sorry for your lordship'; Jock, to whom he was never anything but 'General Grahame,' was trying to tell him with due solemnity that he was dying; and if that were so, who would lead the clans, who would carry on the struggle? Desperately he searched for names – Lochiel, Colonel Cannon, Dunfermline – No, he must not die just yet. But if he must –

"It is the less matter for me," he said clearly, "seeing that the day goes well for my master."

The pain came again, cold, knife-like, deadly, and his senses left him.

When he came to himself, the confusion was gone from his mind; he realised that someone had stripped him of his armour, and that he was wrapped in a plaid. He thought that he must have been moved from the place where he had fallen; for here there was not the same sickening stink of blood; he could wee a whin-bush above him, full of little yellow flowers like stars, and the heather was springy and soft to his limbs beneath the plaid. It was not yet fully dark; he could see the hills he had grown to love, grey shapes against the pearly sky; he wanted to lie quiet and watch them, lifting his eyes to those mountains from which came strength. But he must not think of rest; he was still on active service.

There was a torch flaring somewhere in his immediate neighbourhood, and in the red light of it he saw faces hovering around him, faces of anxious friends. There was his brother David, almost unrecognisable because of the bloody gash upon his cheek; young Robin, his nephew, white-faced, large-eyed, sitting back on his heels and still holding the sword which he had used for the first time this day. Good Mr Edwards, the chaplain, was on his knees, praying silently; close to him in the heather, supporting him, was poor Jock, his face blotched with tears. But there was someone else for whom Claverhouse was looking; he murmured a name, and in response to it there bent over him the noble countenance of Lochiel.

"Give me the news quickly, Lochiel. There is not much time." (Why had he said that? He could not die just yet; there was so much to do.)

A gabble of voices broke out before Lochiel could reply. They were going to carry his lordship to Blair; they had sent for a wise woman who lived hereabouts and who was famed for her treatment of wounds; his lordship must lie very still meanwhile, for he had lost much blood, but his wounds were not mortal; they assured him of that. He was not really listening; he was looking at Lochiel; their eyes spoke to one another, and he knew at last why the old Chief had been so solemn and strange in manner when first they had met at Holyrood House, and again at Auchindoune, and yet again this morning when he had begged my Lord Dundee not to engage in battle personally. He had begged without hope, for he had the 'two-sights' and long ago he had had a vision of death.

But Lochiel was a soldier, and it was as a soldier that he spoke now. Briefly he told of the downward charge of his people, of a decisive victory in ten minutes, of the utter rout of Mackay and his regulars, of the number slain, of the great spoil which had fallen into the hands of the victors. Claverhouse lay listening with his eyes closed, an enormous pride in his heart, hearing as a background to the old man's voice the pipes playing a coronach for the dead, the groans of the wounded, a distant confused shouting which told of fugitives still struggling in the narrow Pass, the voices of the bards giving the 'fame of the song' to new heroes; and all the while he was gathering the remains of his strength for a last duty.

"Amerlieclose," he muttered, when Lochiel had finished his brief report. "Is Amerlieclose here?"

There was a movement in the group, and then the face of the scholar, drawn and pale, was looking down on him.

"Where is the Standard?" asked Claverhouse, suddenly sharp, suddenly the disciplinarian again. "Is it safe lodged?"

"I gave it into the hands of another when I heard that your lordship – "

"The duty of a standard-bearer is never to let the colours pass from his hands until they are safe lodged after action. Remember that." Then he smiled. "I need you, Jamie. Have you your tablets and ink-horn with you? Any paper will do; the back of that fine epic of yours perhaps. You must write a letter; I cannot write myself."

Again the buzz of voices. His lordship positively must not fatigue himself; any letters could wait till they carried him to Blair. He brushed the voices aside; it was dreadful to feel irritable when he was dying, but the time was so short and the duty so urgent. Queer it was, too, not to be able even to write a letter, he who had written on a drum-head night after night throughout his campaign; now he had strength sufficient only to dictate this last letter of all, to the master he served and the friend he loved.

" 'Sir,

It has pleased God to give your forces a great victory over the rebels, in which three-fourths of them have fallen under the weight of our swords. I might say much of the action, if I had not the honour to command in it; but of five thousand, which was the best computation I could make of the rebels, it is certain that there cannot have escaped above twelve hundred men. We have not lost full out nine hundred.' "

Nearly half his little army. His mind groped after those nine hundred lying somewhere out there in the darkness. But what was it they said in the Highlands? – 'It is an ill thing to grieve immoderately for those who have earned the fame of the song.' Had he himself earned it?... He must not let his thoughts stray like this; his strength was ebbing rapidly, and it was a race between duty and death.

" 'This absolute victory has made us masters of the field, and of the enemy's baggage, which I am giving to the soldiers, who, both officers and common men, Highlands and Lowlands, and Irish, behaved themselves with equal gallantry to whatever I saw in the hottest battles fought abroad by disciplined armies; and this Mackay's old soldiers felt on this occasion –' "

"Water!" he gasped, as the pain in his left side stabbed viciously at him, and faintness threatened him once more.

He glanced at the doleful faces as a cup was put to his lips, and before he drank he tried to hearten them by murmuring in Gaelic the toast to the King: '*Deoch slainte Righ*!' The water revived him a little, and he hurried on with his dictating; he must impress upon King James the necessity to follow up this victory; it could win him the kingdom; if only the stupid, tactless Melfort were not his Majesty's adviser...well, that was not his business now.

"'I cannot now, Sir, be more particular' (can you hear me, Jamie? Come closer, then; I cannot speak loud) – 'but take leave to assure your Majesty the kingdom is generally disposed to your service, and impatiently awaits your coming; and this success will bring in the rest of the nobility and gentry, I having all their assurances of it, except the notorious rebels.' (Atholl would undoubtedly come over now, and even Queensberry might go so far as to send some money; he smiled wryly to himself, seeming to hear the frantic whispering down there in the South, the turning of coats, the eating of words.) 'Therefore, Sir, for God's sake assist us, thought it be with such another detachment of your Irish forces as you sent us before, especially of horse and dragoons, and you will crown our beginnings with a complete success and yourself with an entire possession of your ancient hereditary kingdom of Scotland.' (There was more to say, much more, but –) 'My wounds forbid me to enlarge to your Majesty at this time, though they tell me they are not mortal. However, Sir, I beseech your Majesty to believe, whether I live or die, I am entirely yours –"

He tried to lift a hand for the pen that he might sign the letter, but he found that he had no longer the strength even for this. Only speech and sight remained to him, and the first was going fast.

"You must – write – my name, Jamie. Write – 'Dundee'. Is it done?"

He could not catch the answer. Hearing had gone too. But a paper was placed in his line of vision, and in the red glow of the torch he saw his title, spelled in a way he never spelled it, and written in a hand not his own, the title which soon would belong by right, though not in fact, to an ailing little baby, christened James after the great Montrose.

Then, as his glance wandered to the hills again, he saw that something occupied the sky above those dark grey shapes: the evening star. It was as clear as duty, bright as love; and it was the last thing he saw before he died.

Epilogue

King William the Third stood at a window of his Closet in Whitehall, looking down upon the river and waiting until it was time to receive in private audience one of the Secretaries of State for Scotland, Sir John Dalrymple of Stair.

But he was not thinking about Scotland; he had enough upon his hands without having to concern himself with that unimportant little country. There was the French struggle, which was dragging on and on, and there was Ireland; he would have to send a very large army thither, and because he did not trust any of the English regiments which once had served under King James, he was determined to raise twenty-six new ones. Parliament was being difficult about voting him the money for them; it infuriated him to realise that he, the Protestant Deliverer, was finding parliaments as obstreperous as the Stuart kings had found them.

To refresh his mind he began to think about his personal affairs. He was in negotiation with the Earl of Nottingham for the purchase of my lord's fine house in Kensington, for William was determined that he was not going to spend another winter in Whitehall. Apart from its dampness, which plagued his asthma, he detested the place; it was England in miniature, all that was worst in the land he had coveted and conquered. The common street running through it was full of gaping mechanicks and sweaty housewives, come to stare at him, and the Park was as bad. This rabble actually expected to see him eat his dinner. The warren-like buildings seemed to be permeated with a past which was both alien and hostile, art treasures collected by Charles I, clocks beloved of Charles II, ship-models made for James II, portraits of kings and queens, of princes and princesses, whose painted eyes seemed to regard him as an intruder.

At Kensington he would be himself, King William the Third, not so much by the Grace of God as by his own superb statesmanship; and there he would have the kind of palace to which he was accustomed, he would lay out his gardens with geometrical flowerbeds and orderly regiments of trees like so many soldiers, and he would furnish his rooms in the Dutch style, with cleanly tiles and well-scrubbed floors and twinkling brasses. The fact that his Ministers of State would be obliged to traverse the miry, footpad haunted road from London to wait upon him, was an added inducement to his removal to Kensington, for he was perfectly aware that a large proportion of those Ministers were beginning to intrigue against him as they had intrigued against the uncle and father-in-law whom he had supplanted.

There was a scratch upon the door, and on his permission to enter, the Gentleman-in-Waiting ushered in Sir John Dalrymple, Master of Stair.

William noticed at once that Sir John's slightly porcine face was troubled, and that his usually jovial air was absent. He frowned. Dalrymple was the one Scotsman he found congenial; he admired the cold realism, the legal mind, the detestation of sentiment, and he appreciated the fact that Sir John spared his master the tedium of dealing with Scottish affairs, himself dealing with the blustering letters of Duke Hamilton, the verbose dispatches of Mackay. But it seemed that today, his Majesty was going to be teased with the petty troubles and unrest of that barbarous little kingdom.

"I was obliged to request this audience with your Majesty," began Sir John, after he had kissed hands, "because the very gravest news is come from the North." He cleared his throat, and added abruptly: "The rebels have utterly defeated Mackay at a place called Killiecrankie."

For a moment William stared at him in a bewilderment that was almost ludicrous.

"I do not understand what you say, Sir John. Are you asking me to believe that the rebels (by which I presume you mean the Highland tribes, for I know of no other of any consequence) have defeated General Mackay in pitched battle? It is absurd. Mackay has been sent many more reinforcements than I could spare; he has veteran troops under him; he – it is absurd," repeated William, tapping his hand upon the table.

"I am as astonished as your Majesty", said Stair, drawing some papers from under his arm, "yet I fear it is a fact. I have dispatches from Mackay sent by an express, and likewise letters from Duke Hamilton and from divers Lords of the Council. There can be no doubt whatever that Mackay, with an army of five thousand men, was routed by my Lord Dundee and a parcel of Highland savages; Duke Hamilton's letter contains a report that Mackay himself was slain, but happily this is contradicted by a dispatch from the General writ from Stirling, whither, it seems, he fled from the battle."

"Dundee," murmured William, his hand suddenly clenching itself as it lay upon the table.

Stair waited respectfully for him to continue, but as he remained silent, the Secretary asked briskly:

"Have I your Majesty's leave to read to you such portions of these letters and dispatches as contain the salient facts? I have marked what most concerns us, and will not trouble your Majesty with trifles."

William nodded curtly and sat down at the table, motioning the Secretary to do the same. There was silence for a few moments while Stair glanced through his papers, rejected an hysterical petition from the General Assembly of the Kirk asking for a day of public humiliation to be appointed, and debating whether the disaster was due to the sins of the people, or of the Army, or of the Estates of the Realm; and selected a letter from the Duke of Hamilton.

" 'Several inferior officers and soldiers,' " he read aloud, " 'that are come to Edinburgh this evening give us an account that, after a sharp engagement, Dundee being much the stronger, General Mackay was quite defeated; and I have yet heard of no officer of quality that is come off but Lieutenant Colonel Lauder, who gives the same account of their being wholly routed; but the confusion here is such that the particulars are hard to be got – ' "

"What does he mean," interrupted William testily, " 'Dundee being much the stronger'?"

"I fear it is but Duke Hamilton's way of excusing Mackay's defeat, Sir. The man's in a panic, no doubt of that, 'Now Dundee will be master of all this side Forth, where there are so great numbers of the disaffected to join him. We have got no notice of his motions since the battle, but we fear all Perthshire and Angus will be in arms for him presently. I think the other side of Tay is lost, and Fife is in a very ill tune. Just now there came in the alarm that a French fleet was sailed into the Forth, but the Lord be praised, it is a mistake, and they are but Dutch herring-busses.' "

He paused to shoot a humorous glance at William, but the thin lips did not smile.

" 'My humble opinion is, that his Majesty must first beat Dundee, and secure this kingdom, ere he attempt any other thing. If he makes not haste to assist us, we shall not be able to defend this side Forth, and if Dundee carries Stirling, he will have all Scotland. In this confusion and disorder we are in, I intend to adjourn the Estates, for it is not safe – ' and so on, Sir. I would heed his Grace's fears the less were it not that more sober gentlemen write in the same strain."

William rose abruptly and began to pace the room, his hands clasped behind him, his head downbent, the folds of his periwig concealing his expression. The Secretary dutifully rose with him, and for a few minutes there was silence.

"I can ill spare more troops for Scotland at this juncture," said the Dutchman at last. He raised a face flushed with anger. "And it is abominable that I should be constrained to do so, after the many reinforcements I have sent Mackay."

"Yet your Majesty sees the necessity for it? Consider, Sir, that so complete a victory may cause the disaffected here in England to – "

"I see the necessity for it," interrupted William curtly. He returned to his chair and sat down, forgetting to give Stair the signal to reseat himself. "The dispatch from Mackay, if you please."

"It is writ from Stirling," said the Secretary, taking another paper from the pile, "which the General reached, it seems, the day after the engagement, bringing the news of his own defeat. He can scarce have drawn rein since he fled from the field of action. After describing the ground on which the engagement was fought (and from this it is plain that Dundee had the choosing of it), he continues: 'By a *quart de conversion* I got me a ground fair enough to receive the enemy, but not to attack him; so thus we stood and looked upon one another for the space of at least two hours, the Highlanders out of irresolution, Dundee outflanking me that he might have a sure line of retreat at his back.' "

Again he glanced at William, and this time he found the cold eyes resting upon him; they were full of contempt, and he knew what the king must be thinking; a soldier from his youth, he must realise what nonsense it all was. Perhaps, like Stair himself, he was seeing in imagination a breathless, dishevelled, bewildered and indignant Mackay arranging wineglasses on a table in Stirling Castle to explain his clever *quart de conversion* to the Governor, saying over and over again how careful and thorough he had been, trying to convince himself that none of it was his fault.

" 'I was resolved to stand it out,' " Stair continued reading, " 'though in great impatience to see the enemy come to a resolution either of attacking or retiring, in which he had more choice than I; and to provoke him, I ordered the firing of my little field-pieces, which proved of small value, and indeed several blew up after the second discharge.' (He goes on to explain at great length what was amiss with these guns, but I need not trouble your Majesty with that.) 'My troops of horse I hid out of sight of the enemy, not daring to expose them to his Horse, which was composed all of gentlemen, and reformed officers, and such as had deserted of his regiment in England; which was the reason why I placed my Horse behind the guns, till all the fire was over on both sides.' "

"It seems a pity," said William tartly, "that he did not hide his Foot as well. From his dispatches before this engagement, I remember he was at pains to impress on us that Dundee's volunteer Horse numbered not more than forty – but pray continue, Sir John."

" 'When the enemy at length came down, I called out my said two troops with intent to have them take Dundee and his cavaliers in flanks from right and left, which certainly would have been of such effect, had they had the resolution to obey this order, that in all appearance the enemy would soon have run for it. But instead, they reversed upon the Lord Kenmure's right wing, which caused the first breach, so near as I could remark in the confusion. And indeed, sir, there was no regiment or troop with me but behaved like the vilest cowards in nature, except Hasting's and my Lord Leven's. They stood not to receive the Highlanders' charge, but threw down their arms and ran for it, whereby I have lost the Standard, and all my baggage, tents and equipment, besides a vast number of men slain and captured.' The rest of the letter, Sir," concluded Stair, "is concerned a with an appeal for reinforcements."

It was not William's habit, as the Secretary was thankfully aware, to indulge in useless recriminations. He was angry, and he had ample cause for it; he would deal with Mackay later, but at the moment he would concentrate all his energies on picking up the broken pieces of his power in Scotland. But even as Stair reached for a quill to take down instructions, there was a quick step in the ante-room, a scratch on the door, and the Gentleman-in-Waiting was making his apologies for the intrusion.

"There is an express come from Scotland, Sir, and it was told the messenger at Sir John's lodging that he was with your Majesty. So he has brought it hither, it being, he says, of great moment."

Without speaking, William motioned the Secretary to take the sealed packet, and waited, with expressionless face, while Sir John broke the wax and unfolded the paper. But Sir John was silent so long, his head bent over his reading, that at last the King said impatiently:

"Well, sir, what news now?"

The wary, intelligent eyes were raised, and William was astonished at the undisguised malice in them.

"Good news, Sir," said the Secretary softly." This express is another from Duke Hamilton. After telling us that he has got word that Mackay is come safe to Stirling, he continues: 'This morning we got news to comfort us a little; for I see letters to my Lord Murray, from sure hands, that Dundee was killed in the action, and there is one likewise from Mackay which relates how, much about the middle of his line, Dundee and his Horse wheeling to the right, came upon the battalion of his regiment, by whose fire Dundee was slain at the first onset.' "

He laid the letter down, and his smile was broad and gay.

"It is somewhat surprising, Sir, I must confess, that Mackay should have omitted such news in his first dispatch. I can scarce believe he deemed it unimportant – "

He broke off in surprise as his master rose with such abruptness that he knocked some papers off the table. Sir John bent dutifully to pick them up, glancing in puzzlement at the figure of King William who stood in the window again, his back turned to the room.

"Duke Hamilton, Sir," continued the Secretary after a moment, "still impresses upon us the necessity for strong reinforcements to be sent into Scotland. Shall I – "

Without turning, William interrupted. He said with his cold prescience:

"Armies are needless now. The war is over with the life of Dundee."

Jane Lane

A Call of Trumpets

Civil war rages in England, rendering it a minefield of corruption and conflict. Town and country are besieged. Through the complex interlocking of England's turmoil with that of a king, Jane Lane brings to life some amazing characters in the court of Charles I. This is the story of Charles' adored wife, whose indiscretions prove disastrous, and of the King's nephew, Rupert, a rash, arrogant soldier whose actions lead to tragedy and his uncle's final downfall.

Conies in the Hay

1586 was the year of an unbearably hot summer when treachery came to the fore. In this scintillating drama of betrayals, Jane Lane sketches the master of espionage, Francis Walsingham, in the bright, lurid colours of the deceit for which he was renowned. Anthony Babington and his fellow conspirators are also brought to life in this vivid, tense novel, which tells of how they were duped by Walsingham into betraying the ill-fated Mary, Queen of Scots, only to be hounded to their own awful destruction.

Jane Lane

His Fight Is Ours

His Fight Is Ours follows the traumatic trials of MacIain, a Highland Chieftain of the clan Donald, as he leads his people in the second Jacobite rising on behalf of James Stuart, the Old Pretender. The battle to restore the King to his rightful throne is portrayed here in this absorbing historical escapade, which highlights all the beauty and romance of Highland life. Jane Lane presents a dazzling, picaresque story of the problems facing MacIain as leader of a proud, ancient race, and his struggles against injustice and the violent infamy of oppression.

A Summer Storm

Conflict and destiny abound as King Richard II, a chivalrous, romantic and idealist monarch, courts his beloved Anne of Bohemia. In the background, the swirling rage of the Peasants' Revolt of 1381 threatens to topple London as the tides of farmers, labourers and charismatic rebel hearts flood the city. This tense, powerful historical romance leads the reader from bubbling discord to doomed love all at the turn of a page.

Jane Lane

Thunder on St Paul's Day

London is gripped by mass hysteria as Titus Oates uncovers the Popish Plot, and a gentle English family gets caught up in the terrors of trial and accusation when Oates points the finger of blame. The villainous Oates adds fuel to the fire of an angry mob with his sham plot, leaving innocents to face a bullying judge and an intimidated jury. Only one small boy may save the family in this moving tale of courage pitted against treachery.

A Wind Through the Heather

A Wind Through the Heather is a poignant, tragic story based on the Highland Clearances where thousands of farmers were driven from their homes by tyrannical and greedy landowners. Introducing the Macleods, Jane Lane recreates the shameful past suffered by an innocent family who lived to cross the Atlantic and find a new home. This wistful, historical novel focuses on the atrocities so many bravely faced and reveals how adversities were overcome.

Printed in Great Britain
by Amazon

45593091R00210